Samuel Davidson, Anne Jane Davidson

The Autobiography and Diary of Samuel Davidson

With a Selection of Letters from English and German Divines...

Samuel Davidson, Anne Jane Davidson

The Autobiography and Diary of Samuel Davidson
With a Selection of Letters from English and German Divines...

ISBN/EAN: 9783744716680

Printed in Europe, USA, Canada, Australia, Japan

Cover: Foto ©Raphael Reischuk / pixelio.de

More available books at **www.hansebooks.com**

AUTOBIOGRAPHY AND DIARY

of

SAMUEL DAVIDSON

I am yours ever sincerely

Samuel Davidson

THE
AUTOBIOGRAPHY AND DIARY

OF

SAMUEL DAVIDSON

D.D., LL.D.

*WITH A SELECTION OF LETTERS FROM ENGLISH AND
GERMAN DIVINES, AND AN ACCOUNT OF THE
DAVIDSON CONTROVERSY OF 1857 BY
J. ALLANSON PICTON, M.A.*

EDITED BY

HIS DAUGHTER

WITH A PORTRAIT

EDINBURGH
T. & T. CLARK, 38 GEORGE STREET
1899

PRINTED BY MORRISON AND GIBB LIMITED

FOR

T. & T. CLARK, EDINBURGH.

LONDON : SIMPKIN, MARSHALL, HAMILTON, KENT, AND CO. LIMITED.
NEW YORK : CHARLES SCRIBNER'S SONS.
TORONTO : FLEMING H. REVELL COMPANY.

EDITOR'S PREFACE

THESE reminiscences and reflections were undertaken, as my father himself states, at the suggestion of my mother, but only after her death—and were intended as a tribute to her memory.

In selecting parts of the MS. for publication, I have therefore felt bound to include portions of those anniversary memorial-notices which my father never omitted till the failure of sight and strength took from him the power of writing, but which, owing to their sacred and intimate character, I should not otherwise have published. Those friends who knew my father well, will recognise how truly they represent his feelings.

The same friends will, I think, feel how inadequately these records of my father's thoughts and opinions portray that gentleness which was so marked a trait in his personal intercourse. The fact that they were written at various times between his sixty-seventh and his eighty-ninth year, as also their diary-form, will account for some looseness of style and repetition.

The narrative of that part of his career in which his loyalty to truth had to endure the severest test, was intrusted by him to other hands. To him that story was a "prophecy," and, like other prophecies, "not of any private interpretation." His attitude in memory of it was one of serene detachment, and, though he spoke plainly on that as on most other things, and considered that he had been treated very unjustly, he shrank from recording the story himself. But the account was written in his life-time, and submitted to him while his memory still retained its vigour. So far as the statement of facts is concerned, he entirely approved it. For the view taken, and the feelings expressed, the writer of it alone is responsible.

It was my father's desire to make a strong protest against persecution for so-called heresy, and to emphasise his conviction of the innocence of intellectual error, where the conduct is good.

The rectitude, sweetness, and simplicity of his own character can be most fully estimated by those who knew him best.

ANNE JANE DAVIDSON.

HAMPSTEAD, *April* 1899.

TABLE OF CONTENTS

PORTRAIT . *Facing Title-Page*

EDITOR'S PREFACE *p. v*

TABLE OF CONTENTS . *p. vii*

CHAPTER I

IN MEMORIAM . . *p. 3*

CHAPTER II

EARLY LIFE AND EDUCATION—Time and Occasion of Writing — Birth, **1806-1833.** Parentage, and Early School-days—James Darragh—Captain O'Hagan— **Age 1-27.** Entrance into Belfast Institution—Under-Master in Schools at London-derry and Liverpool—Divinity Studies at Belfast—Logic, Theology, and Hebrew . . . . *pp. 7-12*

CHAPTER III

ENTRANCE ON ACTIVE EMPLOYMENT—Called to a Chair of Biblical Criticism **1833-1842.** in Belfast—Licensed to Preach—Marriage—Degree of LL.D. from Aberdeen **Age 27-36.** — *Lectures on Biblical Criticism*—Presbyterianism—Dr. T. D. Hincks— Rev. William Brown of Tobermore — Rev. A. Montgomery — *Sacred Hermeneutics* compiled and published . . . . *pp. 13-19*

Letter from Professor C. E. Stowe.

CHAPTER IV

ENTRANCE UPON THE PROFESSORSHIP OF HEBREW AND BIBLICAL CRITI- **1843-1848.** CISM IN LANCASHIRE INDEPENDENT COLLEGE—First Visit to Germany— **Age 37-42.** Neander—Bleek, Tholuck—Translated Gieseler's *Ecclesiastical History*— Congregational Lecture . . . . . *pp. 21-25*

Letters from Gieseler, Hare, Thirlwall.

CHAPTER V

1848-1856. *Introduction to the New Testament* in 3 vols.—Made D.D. of Halle—Visit of
Age 42-50. Tholuck—The Education Question—New Edition of *Biblical Criticism*—
Family Bereavements—Second Visit to Germany—Hupfeld and Tholuck—
Wrote the second volume of Horne's *Introduction* . . *pp.* 26-34

CHAPTER VI

1856-1857. DETAILED NARRATIVE of the Proceedings of the Lancashire College Com-
Mr. Pic- mittee, terminating in Dr. Davidson's Resignation, by J. ALLANSON
ton's Nar- PICTON, M.A., J.P. . . . . . . *pp.* 35-70
rative.

APPENDIX.—Addresses of Students—*Letters from Students, Bunsen, and
Knobel* . . . . *pp.* 70-77

CHAPTER VII

1858-1865. KINDNESS OF FRIENDS—Liberal Sympathy of the Laity—Sir James Watts—
Age 52-59. Residence at Bank House, Hatherlow—Takes Pupils as Boarders—Writes
Introduction to the Old Testament—Kamphausen—Ewald—Removal to
London—Bishop Colenso—Visit of Ewald—Friends in London—Sect-
arianism—Church of the Future . . . . *pp.* 78-90

Letters from Kamphausen, Ewald, W. J. Conybeare.

CHAPTER VIII

1866-1872. Dr. CHALMERS—Sects in Scotland—Death of Hupfeld—Translation of Fuerst's
Age 60-66. *Hebrew Lexicon*—Dr. Pusey's Attacks—A Rejected Preface—New Edition
of *Introduction to New Testament*—Articles in the *Theological Review*
—The Unitarians—Poland—An Established Church—Mr. Heard—
Learning in the Ranks of Dissent—H. B. Wilson—B. Jowett—*The West-
minster Review* . . . . . . *pp.* 91-103

Letters from B. F. Westcott, Canon Cureton, Lunemann.

CHAPTER IX

1872-1879. FAMILY SORROWS—Death of Youngest Son—Illness of Mrs. Davidson—Her
Age 66-73. Death—Journey with his Daughter—Revision of Authorised Version Old
Testament—Sojourn in Rome—Professors there—Tischendorf—The Sorrows
and Bereavements of Life—Loneliness—Naples—Milan—Antonio Ceriani
—Visit to Switzerland—Ragatz—Article and Work on the *Canon*—De-
velopment of Religious Opinion—Visits to Homburg—The Engadine—
Florence—Death of Dr. Willis—Winter in Rome . . *pp.* 104-122

Letters from Tischendorf, Matthew Arnold.

CONTENTS

CHAPTER X

EUROPEAN TRAVEL.—Bavarian Tyrol—Passion Play at Oberammergau—Huss at **1880-1882.** Constance—Ullmann's Change of View—The Revised New Testament—New **Age 74-76.** Edition of *New Testament Introduction*—John Wesley's Latitudinarianism —The Basis of Revealed Religion—Visit to Contrexéville—*Doctrine of the Last Things*—Poem in German by De Wette—Bunsen and Cureton— Political Views—Gladstone—Ireland and Home Rule   .   *pp.* 123–136

CHAPTER XI

REMINISCENCES—The Peace Society—Morning Readings in the Old Testament **1882-1884.** Hebrew and the New Testament Peshito Version—*Meditations of Marcus* **Age 76-78.** *Aurelius* — Bishop Lightfoot's view of the Fathers as Witnesses to Christian Doctrine—The Pauline and the Johannine Teachings—Visit to Ireland ; to his Birthplace, Kellswater, near Ballymena—Many and Sad Changes   .   .   .   .   *pp.* 137–147

CHAPTER XII

BIBLE READINGS—Isaiah and St. John—Deaths of Alexander Stewart and John **1885-1886.** Walker of Bowdon—Professor Pfleiderer of Berlin—Death of Dr. M. **Age 80.** Kalisch—His Character and Works—Letters in *Inquirer* on the Revised New Testament—Professor Schrader—The Book of Daniel—The *Synoptics* in the Syriac—General Election of 1885—The Annexation of Burmah— *New Testament Introduction* revised—Job, Ecclesiastes, Song, Proverbs— Bombardment of Alexandria—Wants for England's Welfare .   *pp.* 148–159

CHAPTER XIII

TRANSLATION OF JOB XXXVI.—Readings in Minor Prophets : Hosea, Zechariah, **1886.** Malachi, Jonah, Micah, Nahum, Habakkuk—Translation of Hab. iii.— **Age 80.** Zephaniah, Haggai—The *Acts* in the Peshito—Joel, Amos, Obadiah— *Romans* in the Peshito   .   .   .   .   .   *pp.* 160–175

CHAPTER XIV

REMINISCENCES—England's Robberies, Mandalay—Meeting in Hyde Park **1887.** against the Tory Coercion Bill for Ireland—The Queen's Jubilee—Death **Age 81.** of Professor Pott of Halle—Magee, Bishop of Peterborough, at Contrexé- ville—Miracles—True Evidence for Christianity Internal—1 and 2 *Timothy* and *Titus* in the Peshito — The Psalms — Some by David — None Messianic—Commentaries—Perowne—Psalm xlv. 7—Jennings and Lowe —Kay   .   .   .   .   *pp.* 176–188

CHAPTER XV

**1888.
Age 82.**   BIBLE READINGS CONTINUED—*Philemon* and *Hebrews* in the Peshito—*James*—
1 and 2 *Peter*—Bishop Colenso's Life—Bishop Butler's Sermon on Balaam—
The Two Traditions regarding Balaam—Numbers xxii.—Colenso's Hymn-
Book—Prayers Addressed to Christ—2 Cor. xii. 8—The Ten Commandments
—Colenso as a Critic—1 *John* in the Peshito—The Worship of Christ—
Gladstone and Disraeli, their Ecclesiastical Appointments—Death of Isaac
Nelson, M.P.—The *Apocalypse* in the Peshito—Pan-Anglican and Pan-
Presbyterian Synods — Darwinism — Development in Religion — Death of
Rev. H. B. Wilson—Works of Henry Taylor, Rector of Crawley—Con-
ference of Anglican Bishops—1 and 2 Samuel—*Robert Elsmere*—Lord
Shaftesbury's Memoirs   .   .   .   .   .   *pp.* 189-212

Letter from Professor Jowett.

CHAPTER XVI

**1889.
Age 83.**   PERSONAL AND HOME REFLECTIONS—H. B. Wilson's Theory of a National
Church—Mr. Call on Daniel—*St. Matthew* in the Peshito—Mr. Rodwell
—Archdeacon Hare's *Victory of Faith*—The Temperance Bible—The Re-
vised Old Testament—Isa. liii.—Chillingworth—Death of Professor Godwin
—Cyrus in Isa. xlv.—Cuneiform Inscriptions—English Wars and Annexa-
tions—Death of Dr. W. Wright—Various Readings—1 and 2 Kings—
The Texas Independent Pulpit—Harper's Editorials—Semler—The Con-
quest of Canaan—Gilgal—The Passover   .   .   .   *pp.* 213-240

CHAPTER XVII

**1889-1890.
Age 83, 84.**   ANECDOTES OF GERMAN SCHOLARS — Fackelzugs — Athanasius — Life of
Frederick Robertson—Ben Mordecai—Readings in Ezekiel—R. Browning's
Death—His Poetry—Book of Esther—Difficult Passages—Death of Dr.
Döllinger—Of Dr. Littledale — Readings in Ruth—Report of Church
Congress—Herbert Spencer—Deaths of Dr. Leonhard Schmitz, of Mr.
Call—The Universalists—Canon Liddon's Death—Pfleiderer on Develop-
ment .   .   .   .   *pp.* 241-263

CHAPTER XVIII

**1891.
Age 85.**   ILLNESS AND FEEBLENESS—The name *Christian*—Dean Stanley—The Koran—
Rendering of Mic. v. 1—Death of J. D. Morell—Second Reading of Minor
Prophets—Haggai—Zechariah—Malachi—Amos—Death of Dr. Sadler—
School Board Scheme—Objections .   .   .   .   *pp.* 264-273

CHAPTER XIX

OLD AGE; Hopes of Everlasting Happiness—Death of William Bickham— **1892.** Remarks upon the Book of Daniel—Bible Dictionaries—Kitto—Smith— **Age 86.** Notes on Eccles. xii. 9-14—Isa. xix. 18—Kuenen and Wellhausen—Late Dating of Psalms—Delitzsch on Isaiah—The Plural *Elohim*—The Assembly's Catechism—The Teaching of his Boyhood—Gradual Liberation of Thought—Documents in Pentateuch—Lord Bolingbroke the Deist— Plagues of Egypt . . . . . . *pp.* 274-290

CHAPTER XX

KANT ON PERPETUAL PEACE—Watts and Doddridge—Butler's Analogy— **1892—** Messianic Hopes—Honesty in Doctrinal Profession—*Pirke Aboth*—Various **contd.** Renderings of Prov. xxvi. 10—The Holy Spirit—Portraits around Me— **Age 86.** German Acquaintances—Baptism—A Hudibrastic Poem—Hobbes—Eternal Punishment—Abraham Calov—Christian Socialism—Ezra's Revision— Gen. xxxii. 24-29 . . . . . . *pp.* 291-309

CHAPTER XXI

FINAL VIEWS—Heresy Trials—The Prophets—Their Grandest Theme—Put **1893-1894.** on the Civil List by Mr. Gladstone—Job xix. 25-27—Ps. xxii. 17—Is **Age 87, 88.** Christianity Played Out?—The State of London—Rhythm of English Bible—The Home Rule Bill—Death of Jowett—English Civilising Processes Unjust and Cruel—Wholesale Murder of Matabele—The Innocence of Error—The Sands of Life are Running Out—The Religion of Jesus a Safe Anchor . . . . *pp.* 310-324

Editorial Note.

CHAPTER XXII

CONFESSION OF FAITH—Supplement . *pp.* 325-345 **Death, April 1, 1898. Age 91.**

CHAPTER XXIII

REMINISCENCES BY FRIENDS—Dr. Simon—Dr. Gloag—W. Urwick *pp.* 346-361

LIST OF WORKS . *pp.* 363, 364

INDEXES—
    I. Names of Persons and Places *pp.* 365-370
    II. Texts referred to . . *pp.* 371, 373

[The following Mottoes are inscribed on the first leaf of the Autobiography.—ED.]

> " O felix hominum genus,
>   Si vestros animos amor,
>   Quo cœlum regitur, regat."—BOETHIUS.

" Miratus saepe fui, quod homines, qui se christianam religionem profiteri jactant, hoc est, amorem, gaudium, pacem, continentiam, et erga omnes fidem : plus quam iniquo animo certarent, et acerbissimum in invicem odium quotidie exercerent, ita ut facilius ex his quam illis fides uniuscujusque noscatur."—SPINOZA.

" There is indeed no reason to be assigned in general why men should be any more displeased with one another for being of different opinions than for their being of different sizes, or for having a different personal appearance. And were it not that experience convinces us of the matter of fact, it would be hard to believe that men's passions could carry them to that degree of animosity against each other on account of opinions barely speculative, which we find practised in all countries and almost all ages."—CLAYTON'S *Essay on Spirit*.

" Keep thyself simple, good, pure, serious, free from affectation, a friend of justice." . . .—MARC. AURELIUS.

AUTOBIOGRAPHY AND DIARY

OF

SAMUEL DAVIDSON

CHAPTER I

In Memoriam

THIS day, December the 15th, 1872, has been the saddest of all the days of my life on earth, for early in the morning of it (8.50 a.m.) my beloved wife was taken from me, to leave a blank in the heart that cannot be filled up. It is now thirty-six years since we were joined together; and I have had all the satisfaction arising from cordial congenial sympathy. I found her everything that I expected, and much more. She took me for her husband when I was poor. We began our earthly life together with an income of considerably less than a hundred pounds per annum. But she had faith enough in me, as I had in her, to think that we might get on together. In all my plans and purposes she took a deep interest. I undertook nothing without her counsel and approval. Possessed of a good judgment as well as a warm heart, she encouraged, restrained, guided, and helped me. I left the management of all financial matters to her, and I found her very judicious, and liberal to the extent of her power. She husbanded our resources, and made them as efficient as possible.

But it was in her uprightness and scrupulous conscientiousness that I felt the most unbounded confidence. Here she was beyond all praise. In the deep trials through which I passed when the hue and cry of heresy was raised against me, and I was made the subject of persevering vituperation, I was encouraged by her to stand fast, and to say or do nothing contrary to my convictions. Yet the contumely I was exposed to, and the turning out of her and her children upon the world without house or home, sent many a bitter pang through her heart, which I did not know of till years after, through a serious bodily ailment that seemed to have originated in mental anxiety. With her affection and fidelity to principle, she united a thoughtfulness unfavourable to heartfelt cheerfulness. But indeed her bodily health, especially the weak state of her lungs, prevented the feeling of joyousness. How could she be happy in her mind when, in addition to the severe bodily sufferings she passed through, the loss of so many dear children rent the heart? Three sons were summoned away by death ere they had time to enter upon the business of life. When the last of these was taken from us just a year ago, she felt that her own time was not far off, and frequently said that she should not live through the next winter. Neither did she. The departure of that son was soon followed by her own. Her faith in God and immortality was strong. It was also undemonstrative. Seldom did she speak even to me of her religious belief. I know, however, that it had expanded: that she had got away from the narrowest dogmas in which she had been educated, especially the Calvinistic doctrines of election and reprobation, as well as of a particular atonement. Her piety was evidenced by her life, not by her professions.

Her loss affects me in a way that none other could do. But I must not repine at the inevitable, or question the divine wisdom. She is gone from suffering to happiness, gone to rejoin those beloved children whose company she was permitted to enjoy but for a little. That blessed immortality she has attained to is now the rest and balm of her soul. Why then should I complain in the spirit of selfishness of the irreparable loss I have sustained? Is she not fit to be received into the immediate fruition of God's presence after the toilsome life she has led? Her scourgings have been sufficient: the reward of grace must begin in the Lord's own merciful time.

I cannot express the various distracting thoughts that are now passing through my mind, as I sit solitary to-night in the house of death, and feel my earthly stay withdrawn. I can only say with the Psalmist, " I was dumb, I opened not my mouth, because *Thou* didst it." Perhaps her spirit hovers about me as I write, and is not ignorant of my state. Perhaps I shall be helped by it in ways I dream not of, to persevere in well-doing unto the end, pursuing the onward course she trod while on earth. Let me be patient, therefore, humble, prayerful, ever looking unto Jesus, the Author and Finisher of faith. The Preacher saith, " Vanity of vanities, all is vanity." The world as such was vanity to her, for she experienced largely its hollow insufficiency to satisfy the soul's longings; but she made it yield something better than vanity by doing good work in it, and setting a worthy example of disinterested action. How I long to be at rest with her from the perturbations of earthly passions and the motions of sin within me! I believe in my inmost heart that we are separated only for a while; and that I shall rejoin her and the children whom the Lord gave us, in a higher state of being. Blessed spirit of my beloved wife, thou art in that state now! Enjoy thy repose. God will help me to act as thou wouldst have me. With His strength and the example thou hast left to me as a legacy, I mean to go on, endeavouring to realise more vividly the nearness of the eternal world. Weak though I be, I may yet feel strong because I have faith in the unchanging love of God.

I fear I shall not meet the King of terrors with half the calmness that my dear wife did. She had no fear of His approach. Her calmness in contemplating and speaking of His coming was wonderful. Whence did this arise but from the depth of her faith? Oh that I had as much! Brave companion of my earthly pilgrimage, thou wilt ever be fresh in my memory; thine image will not fade while I am in the world; but each returning year, and especially each returning December, will stamp thee anew on my heart, till I haste away hence to the mansions where thou art, and recognise thee with a delight never to be interrupted.

Note.—The late Dr. W. B. Kirkpatrick of Dublin was my mother's brother, and a sister was married to Rev. J. G. Murphy of Belfast, also deceased.—Ed.

CHAPTER II

January 1*st*, 1873.—On this the saddest of all New Year's days to me, I commence my autobiography. It was the often-expressed wish of my dear wife that I should commit to paper some particulars about myself which might perhaps interest various friends. But I was always reluctant to do so, deferring the matter from time to time, as other duties seemed to be more pressing. After she was taken from me, her wishes were recollected with a fresh distinctness; and their disregard or non-fulfilment could not be thought of. I now blame myself for wilful neglect, because it would have given her some gratification to read what might have been written, and to pass a friendly criticism upon it; advising, suggesting, correcting, according to the sound judgment which was so helpful to me in past days. These autobiographic sketches will lose much through lack of her counsel. But I trust to a higher guidance in what I may say or omit. My purpose is to state facts and impressions, impartially and charitably. My enemies I freely forgive, as I hope to be forgiven myself; my friends I thank most warmly for their help and sympathy. Countless benefits conferred by honest and sincere-minded men, even in an evil-judging, evil-speaking generation, demand gratitude.

I was born at Kellswater, near Ballymena, in the county of Antrim, Ireland, in the year 1806, probably in September. The month and day, however, are somewhat uncertain, for the family Bible bears two dates of birth different both in year and month, but I believe 1806 to be correct. Registers were then kept irregularly by people in country districts. My father's name was Abraham Davidson, my mother's, Margaret-Mewha. Both were of Scottish descent; I understood that my forefathers had come from the West of Scotland not long before, and have an impression that my grandfather did so. My father was of a somewhat speculative turn of mind, having little steady perseverance or proper control of himself at all times. My mother was a pious, simple-minded, straightforward woman, of an affectionate disposition, industrious and persevering. The emotional side of my nature comes from her; and to her example I owe the better part of my character.

One of my earliest recollections is the first going to school at six years of age, and my childish pride in soon rising to the head of the little class; for I could read before I went, having been taught to spell at home. The humble schoolhouse, about a mile distant, was the gathering-place of the children belonging to the surrounding district. It was furnished in a style of rustic simplicity, and consisted of a single room. The fire was in the middle of the floor, a hole in the roof letting out the smoke, though more escaped by the door, which was usually open. Rude benches were ranged round part of the walls; another side being furnished with a couple of tables, at which those learning writing and arithmetic sat. The fire was supplied by what each boy or girl carried under the arm in the morning, namely, two "turf"; which were thrown down in a heap on entering. The master was asked periodically to the houses of the parents for dinner or tea, so that his expenses were small. I remember some deep snows which broke up the school for days: the roads being impassable. Fresh air and hearts untouched with care gave a healthful aspect to those days. The summer sun was then warmer, the days longer, the people more innocent than now; fancy colouring past events with her own brightness!

The school was fortunate in having a teacher well qualified for his work. His name was James Darragh. He was an enthusiast in his humble profession; a man without guile, simple and sincere, who took delight in his pupils, and was very anxious about their progress. Having a passion for elocution, he even went into Ballymena to take lessons from Mr. Blakely, a pupil of Sheridan Knowles. When strangers happened to visit the school, James Darragh's pride was to make one of his best readers give a specimen of his or her powers. Milton's *Paradise Lost* was often selected, or a piece in Scott's *Elocutionist*. On Saturday, which was a half holiday, the Assembly's Shorter Catechism was learnt and repeated. The parents of almost all the pupils were Presbyterians; the master himself a Reformed Presbyterian. I shall never forget the manifestations of his guileless character, his innocent jokes, his affection for his pupils. He was even known to shed tears when a favourite boy or girl left the school.

Peace be to the *manes* of this country schoolmaster! Poor in substance, he was rich in faith and good works, spending his allotted time on earth in the exercise of his limited abilities, and benefiting the rising race by example and precept as far as he could. I cannot tell what I owe to his teaching; one thing I know, that in goodness of heart and modesty of deportment I have never met his superior. He occupied a humble sphere most worthily; entering into his work with an energy that inspired his rustic scholars with unbounded confidence in his attainments. I continued with him for years as a day-scholar, till he taught me all he knew. Long after I left his

little school, I could not but think of the man as one of
God's unsophisticated children, whose aspirations were unusual for a man in his circumstances. His seminary was
all the world to him; and little did he care for things
temporal, as long as he had the opportunity of training the
young to speak, read, and think.

After leaving him, I was sent to Ballymena to a school
over which Mr. Blakely presided, a man who excelled in
elocution and little else. He had, however, teachers
acquainted with mathematics and classics. On his retirement, a Dublin scholar succeeded him, a man of a different
stamp, Mr. O'Hagan, a good classical scholar, whose chief
aim was to prepare young men for entrance into Trinity
College, Dublin. But although his classical knowledge was
considerable, his habits were irregular. Fits of drinking
came upon him at times; and his example was by no
means salutary. I continued too long with him, reading
the same Latin and Greek books over and over again. I
am now of opinion that the walks I had each day to and
from school, six Irish miles there and back, were a great
strain on the health of a growing youth. But I took them
cheerfully and contentedly, feeling no harm. Breakfasting
before nine o'clock, I got no dinner till my return after
4 p.m. With my satchel on my back, I trudged along the
same road, over bogs and hillocks, often preparing the
lessons for the next day on my way home in the after-
noons. I must have been eager for knowledge, because I
recollect watching for the sun's rise in the summer mornings, that I might get out of bed and study. I did not
sleep so well or soundly as boys generally do, else I would
have lain till the rest of the family had risen. The young
require more sleep than the old.

By O'Hagan's advice I made more than one attempt
to get a sizar's place at Trinity College; but I was too
young and too timid to succeed, especially as there were

a great many candidates for a very few places. It was therefore resolved that I should repair as a student to the Royal Belfast Academical Institution, with a view to the ministry of the Presbyterian Church. Having passed an entrance examination before the Presbytery, I proceeded to Belfast, and enrolled my name in the classes of Greek, Latin, Logic, and Belles Lettres. This was in the year 1824; the session beginning with November and terminating with the end of April in the following year. I was then eighteen years of age. At the college entrance examination, conducted by Professor W. Bruce, I was awarded the first place in Greek and Latin. In like manner, at the close of the session, the students' votes assigned me the first prize in the Greek and Latin classes. In the session of 1825–1826 I passed through the mental philosophy and mathematical classes. The study of French was also attended with much benefit.

My college course was now interrupted by going to Londonderry to be under-master in a school over which Mr. James Creighton presided. Here I was associated with W. Murphy O'Hanlon, afterwards Congregational minister at Burnley and other places, a man of superior taste and culture, who met with unkind treatment in the denomination to which he had the misfortune to belong.

From Londonderry I went to Liverpool to serve as under-master in a school which the Rev. Dr. Stewart had just transferred to a Mr. Rowland. Here I remained too long, and did not reap the material benefit I might have received; for I was not well treated either by Rowland or his successor.

Returning to Belfast in 1829, I attended the Natural Philosophy class; and at the close of the session, when there was an examination in the departments already passed, and a general certificate was given by the professors, equivalent to M.A. in the Scottish Universities, I got the silver medal in classics. I also received a premium in logic, which I studied again during the same session. The next two sessions were devoted to theology and Hebrew. In the latter class I always obtained the first prize.

CHAPTER III

Entrance on Active Employment

My college education having been completed on the first
of May 1832, the Ballymena Presbytery "licensed" me to
preach in November 1833. Being required to subscribe
the Westminster Confession of Faith, I did so with exceptions; but my mind was in traditional fetters at the time,
and I hardly realised the serious responsibility of declaring
assent and consent to an extensive system of metaphysical
theology.

The next two years were spent in preaching here and
there as opportunities offered or invitations came. Having
declined a settlement as pastor over a country flock in
County Down, on the ground of insufficient income, a new
prospect opened before me by the College Examination
Committee reporting that they had maturely considered
the propriety of appointing a Professor of Biblical Criticism
to lecture to the students under the care of the Church,
then called "the General Synod of Ulster," recommending
the latter to establish such a professorship forthwith; and
to appoint me as "every way fitted to discharge the important duties of that office." It was accordingly moved
and unanimously agreed to, that "this Church having long
felt the necessity of a Professorship of Biblical Criticism
for the benefit of its students, and such an appointment
appearing to be especially required by the state of society
and literature at the present time, do appoint Samuel
Davidson Professor of Biblical Criticism in connection with

this Church, to commence his labours on the 10th November (1835); that all students of divinity shall be required to attend Mr. Davidson's lectures during two complete sessions, each paying a fee of two guineas to the professor; and that the class, when formed, be placed under the care of the Divinity Professorship Committee; that the College Education Committee arrange with Samuel Davidson the amount of salary and the time and place of lecturing; and that it be remitted to the Government Committee to take steps to procure an endowment for this chair."

Having been appointed to a public office, I began to devote myself to the diligent discharge of its duties. The records of the General Synod at the close of the sessions 1835–1836 and 1836–1837 express satisfaction with the mode in which the duties were performed. I continued in the office from 1835 till 1842, a period very eventful in my life.   On the 21st September 1836 I married Anne Jane Kirkpatrick, of Belfast, whose affection and continuous counsels in all my proceedings brightened my path.   I could not have found a more congenial help-mate—one more true-hearted and trustworthy at all times and under every condition.   The providence of God led me to such a choice.   We were both poor enough; but we comforted ourselves with the hope of a better future, and were content.

Marischal College, Aberdeen, waiving its rule of con-ferring a higher degree on none but an M.A., made me an LL.D. on the 10th May 1838; even before I had written such a work as is usually required to justify the honour. Soon after, I published *Lectures on Biblical Criticism*, exhib-iting a systematic view of that science; Edinburgh: Clark, 1839.   The volume was favourably received by the public, owing in part to a long and discriminating critique in the *Edinburgh Review* for October 1840, written by the Rev. Dr. Hincks, the celebrated Oriental scholar.   Soon after its appearance, the Professorship of Hebrew in Glasgow College became vacant, and I offered myself as a candidate. I received flattering testimonials not only from such as knew me best in Ireland, but from two eminent English scholars, Drs. Pye Smith and E. Henderson. In this matter I was unsuccessful; the choice of the electors (the college professors themselves) having fallen upon a minister of the Church of Scotland at Maybole, who belonged to the " Moderate " party, and was elected mainly on that account; not unanimously, however, for my friends Professors Thomson and Nichol, with others, were in the minority.

In the first year of my married life, all my income was derived from the students' fees, which amounted to less than a hundred pounds. During the remainder of my stay in Belfast I had a salary of £100 in addition to these fees, that is, about £160 altogether. The procurement of a Government endowment, spoken of when I was chosen to office, was never prosecuted with earnestness; nor was any leaning shown towards it, when applied for, at Dublin Castle. Meantime my studies continued unabated; and my lectures were attended by inquiring students. But reading and reflection gradually convinced me that the Presbyterian system of Church government is not found in or favoured by the New Testament; that it is not a *jure divino* system, as all candidates for the ministry were required to say and believe. I had also become disposed in my own mind to the " Voluntary principle in religion," and thought I discovered in the New Testament the outline of the independence of Churches held by the Congregational body in England. In fact, I had become all but, if not altogether, a Congregationalist. Hence my mind was uneasy. I had not, indeed, to lecture on Church polity or the Voluntary principle; but I was connected with a Church, some tenets of which I did not hold.

Fortunately, as it then appeared to me, some friend in England had spoken of me to a Congregational minister in Liverpool, member of the committee of a new college which was being established at Manchester. In consequence of this casual allusion, my name was brought before the committee; and an invitation was sent to me that I should become one of the professors there. This I accepted, because it fell in with my altered views of Presbyterian Church government, and of ecclesiastical establishments. In the autumn of 1842 I removed to England, but had to wait in Liverpool till the new college was ready for opening in the spring of the following year.

Though the General Assembly of the Presbyterian Church passed a resolution of regret at the severance of our connection, and I had a few warm friends in that body, I believe that the great majority were wholly indifferent about my removal, because it relieved them from payment of my salary (£100 per annum), which, though small, was irregularly given; and because they did not wish to have among them anyone who claimed independence of thought. A stereotyped belief in doctrine and government pervaded the whole atmosphere. Besides, the Arians and Trinitarians were so far separated in Belfast and the North of Ireland generally that it was dangerous for one, however orthodox, to associate with persons stigmatised as heretics. I disliked this exclusive spirit among professing Christians, especially as the Rev. Dr. T. D. Hincks, Professor of Hebrew, was one of my best friends. Arian though he was, I have seldom known a truer Christian, or one that reflected more clearly the Master's spirit. After years of unseemly disputings, of noisy argumentations and bitter feelings, the General Synod of Ulster had repelled from its midst all who would not subscribe the Westminster Confession of Faith without qualification, that is, all Arians, Socinians, and Arminians.

This separation left its hurtful mark on the spirit and conduct of the dominant majority; especially on the leaders of the orthodox party. It was lamentable to witness the *animus* displayed: the *odium theologicum* in its worst form. A schism, brought about by appeals to passion, prejudice, ignorance, and tradition, could promote neither truth nor religion. Majorities are oftener wrong than right; and the tyranny of them works mischief in Church and State. Calm and thoughtful men, overpowered by their decisions, retire in silence to mourn over human nature. As usual, orthodoxy prevailed by numbers. But all assemblies are unfavourable to the fair statement of a question; rather are they an arena for popular demagogues, or persons gifted with ready utterance, in which victory over opponents is the main object. The parties should have remained together, and the terms of subscription been gradually relaxed. For years after, the spirit, especially of the orthodox leader, who was the chief instrument of the division, seemed alien to the gospel of peace. I had too many opportunities of seeing the manifestations of selfish tyranny and ambition in the great ecclesiastical demagogue, not to turn from the spectacle with a feeling of disgust.

Yet in this brief period of work among the Presbyterians, I associated with some whom I could speak to freely and without reserve. The Rev. W. Brown, M.A., of Tobermore, was my warm-hearted confidant; a man eager in the pursuit of knowledge, tolerant, charitable, a foe to all oppression, a friend to humanity. He came to Belfast to study and attend the collegiate classes there, though he had been pastor of a congregation for years; he learnt German, bought German books, read the most advanced in theological speculation, foresaw the influence of Strauss's *Leben Jesu*, and watched the results of new theories. More than once I visited him at his retired country seat in the

2

county of Derry, where he ministered to a plain people and lived in their affections. A man of purity and godliness was William Brown. An advocate of free thought and speech amid those who were opposed to such freedom, he followed the even tenour of his way, and welcomed light wherever he could see it. Though of a searching disposition, he was devout withal.

Another kind and valuable friend was the Rev. A. Montgomery, who had a mind susceptible of high culture. But the pressure of outward circumstances hindered his mental development. The pastor of a poor congregation near Belfast, he felt the invasion of worldly cares, and could not free himself from it. Had he been in a position favourable to the cultivation of his powers, he would have exerted much influence for good. In many ways he was helpful to me, and promoted my success. As life advanced, the world did not frown upon his fortunes the less; but he followed the right path of duty and was useful.

Two little sons soon brightened the domestic hearth, the eldest of whom was exceedingly winning and intelligent; the second, of a less delicate organisation and more stirring. Alas! the earthly life of both was doomed to be short, though their future was then coloured with the warm tints of hope.

After the publication of my first book, I began a sequel to it which cost far more reading and thought, and for which I was obliged to visit Trinity College, Dublin, that I might work in the library. The resources of Belfast were of little use in the preparation of the *Sacred Hermeneutics Developed and Applied*, etc. etc. For three years I laboured incessantly upon it with an ever-increasing knowledge of the difficulties connected with the great subject. The volume was put to press in 1842 (Clark, Edinburgh), and appeared in the spring of next year about the time when the new Independent College at Manchester was inaugurated. Sufficiently orthodox, the book was well received by the public.

Ten years afterwards, Dr. Davidson received the following testimony :—

FROM PROFESSOR C. E. STOWE

"*1st December* 1852.

"In my lectures on Hermeneutics this term, I have for the first time read your admirable treatise on that subject. I cannot refrain from expressing to you the very high gratification which it has afforded me. I blame myself that I had never read it before. You have taken just the right course between *rationalism* on the one hand, and *irrationalism* on the other. Professor Stuart was altogether too rationalistic, and so, in my opinion, is Professor Robinson ; and there must be a different style of exegesis from theirs, and I am very glad you have led the way in introducing some of the old element into the new. . . . Your *Introduction to the New Testament* I became acquainted with some time ago, and esteem it very highly. It is too voluminous and expensive for our students. If you could by any means compress it to the size of Guericke's, it would go well in the United States. Excuse my freedom ; but I intend from this time to recommend your writings to all my pupils, and the more accessible they can be made, the better. . . . I suppose you have read *Uncle Tom's Cabin*, and I am proud to tell you that *the Mrs. Stowe* is *my Mrs. Stowe*,—the mother of my seven children,—and we both would be very glad to welcome you to our cabin here in Andover, if you can make us a visit."

CHAPTER IV

AT THE LANCASHIRE INDEPENDENT COLLEGE

HAVING spent all but a year in Liverpool prior to settling at Manchester, I began my career in the college auspiciously; though the situation of the building and the dwelling-house assigned to me promised little comfort or health to the family. A large structure placed in the midst of an undrained bog showed little practical wisdom in the originators. The climate of Manchester, cold and wet as it is, was not mitigated to the inmates of a house on which the rays of the sun seldom fell. No wonder that it told with fatal power upon the health of children doomed to live in it.

During the summer vacation of 1844 my wife and I, with two young friends, went to Germany for the first time, and visited a number of its cities. I was anxious to see some at least of the distinguished scholars with whose works I was familiar. At Berlin, Professor Zumpt was exceedingly obliging. Encke, whom I saw at a scientific and literary meeting to which I was introduced by Zumpt, professed his readiness to conduct me over the Royal Observatory; and Neander asked me to his house, where my wife and I had tea. The Professor's sister took charge of her; Neander entertained me with his talk in the library. But he did not excel in conversation. His library presented an odd spectacle: it was a chaos of books. The classroom in the University was his congenial home, where he poured forth stores of knowledge, without any notes before him, to about two hundred students, all enthusiastically attached to their teacher. In the same room I listened to Schelling lecturing on philosophy to a much larger audience. Neander had been ill shortly before, and had just resumed his work. How glad I should have been to witness the warm reception he met with when he presented himself in his old classroom again; and when one of the students, standing on a bench, shouted, " Long live our illustrious Professor Dr. Neander," with waving hands, amid the echoing voices of the rest: the master being so deeply affected that he could utter not a word. His eyes moistened, and after a pause he took up the thread of his former lecture. I heard him discourse at different hours, both on the New Testament and Church History. I also became acquainted with Bleek of Bonn, with whom a friendly intercourse was maintained by letter up to his death; with Hupfeld, my dear and valued friend; with Roediger and Tholuck. I visited Bretschneider at Gotha, and found his room enveloped in tobacco smoke. He was a kindly old man, a learned theologian, a good preacher. I was specially attracted to Halle, the seat of Prussia's leading theological University, where Gesenius had laboured and died; where Tholuck still exercised a salutary influence, and Julius Müller was lecturing on Dogmatik with applause. The trip to the land of learning stimulated and encouraged me greatly. Conversing freely with men of repute, I learned a great deal from them; while they received me cordially as a young professor. To my great regret, Gesenius was gone. I visited his simple grave more than once, and I lamented his premature removal. That of Semler I was never able to find; nor could any of the professors tell in what part of the *Gottesacker* it is.

During the next years my work was hard. I taught Hebrew, besides lecturing on Biblical Literature and

Ecclesiastical History. One of these is sufficient to engross the time of a tutor, be his talents what they may. Believing the Church History of Gieseler to be an admirable compendium for the use of students, I translated the first portions of the work for T. & T. Clark of Edinburgh, forming two volumes, which were issued in the years 1846, 1848. The chief value of this history lies in the notes, which are mostly extracts from the original sources. The prefatory notice of the first volume indicates my opinion of the entire work. But the task of translating became irksome, and I undertook no more. The following are extracts from two letters of Professor Gieseler :—

(Translated from the German.)

" GÖTTINGEN, 1848.

"I feel highly flattered by your intention of translating my Church History into English, and thus making it known in an evangelical country of so much weight and importance. Notwithstanding the Puseyite attempt to separate England from the German Evangelical Church, and to incline it towards Rome, I am convinced that the adherence of the English people to the fundamental principles of the Reformation is too strong to permit such an attempt to be successful. And inasmuch as the history of the Church affords the strongest guarantee against a relapse into papacy, it would be matter of great rejoicing to me if my book, through your kind means, should help in some measure to confirm such adherence to the pure principles of the Reformation.

"It would be very desirable for German theological literature if we had a work on recent English Church History (beginning, perhaps, in 1795, the year of the founding of the great Missionary Society) from the pen of an Englishman—a work setting forth not only the history of the Episcopal Church, but also that of the various Dissenting Bodies, with their inner developments, their relation to one another and to the State, their influence on the people and their literature. We have, it is true, many good works treating of isolated parties : on the most recent aspect of the Scottish Church question for instance, and on Puseyism ; but so far we have no comprehensive work by an Englishman, who would naturally be better acquainted with the conditions than a foreigner could be. Should you be disposed to undertake such a work, but should feel some hesitation in speakly freely on all the circumstances in your own name, I would gladly see to the publishing of it, both in English and in a German translation. I have already edited an anonymous work of this kind by a Dutch theologian on the latest developments of the Church in Holland, and shall perhaps soon be in a position to do the same for a similar work on the French Church by a French theologian. The *honorarium* which German booksellers are accustomed to pay is certainly not large; but in this matter, too, I would do my best for your interest. On the other hand, your work, printed here, would be cheaper than if it had come out in England, and since the recent convention between Prussia and England, it could easily be transmitted to England.

"I and my colleague Lücke look with great interest for your work on the Ecclesiastical Polity of the New Testament.

"In Puseyism, in my opinion, there is an outbreak of morbid matter which has long been accumulating in the Episcopal Church, in consequence of which the Evangelical reaction will, it is to be hoped, be the more vigorous; and if that Church gradually abandons her political character, in accordance with the irresistible impulse of the times, she may then awake to new life. To me it seems strange to see Mr. Pusey at the head of this erroneous system. I knew him well more than twenty years ago in Bonn, where he resided for a considerable time in order to study Oriental languages, and I had no presentiment then that he might one day become the head of such a sect."

In 1847 I was invited to deliver the Congregational Lecture in London, which was published immediately after, in January 1848. I had studied this question pretty well before I left Belfast, arriving at the general conclusion enunciated in the book. When the volume was reprinted some years later, and I wished to rewrite it, I was not allowed. It was repeated *verbatim* contrary to my wish. I would have changed it to a great extent: having convinced myself that Church government is a matter of expediency, and that it may be shaped by the spiritual consciousness of the Church, agreeably to the circumstances and exigencies of the period. The apostolic age presents no definite constitution existing in all congregations; and even if it did, it may have been conveniently altered after the time of the apostles, as it was in fact; the popular and democratic character having passed into the episcopal or aristocratic in the second century. Congregationalism had its roots in the nature of the Churches which were founded directly or indirectly by the Apostle Paul; though the crude, incipient state of a new religion can hardly be taken as a model for all future time. I fear that I should have incurred odium by adapting the book to my better ideas; for all the ministers of the Body with whom I came in contact, with one notable exception, believed in *the divine right* of Congregational Independency; though they did not conform to the New Testament plan in some respects, as I carefully pointed out in the Lecture. In fact, they had not studied the subject; but were Independents because circumstances had ordered their lot and determined their outer life to that system. Holding vaguely by the apostolic pattern, they were unwilling to shape their churches to it altogether; especially in cases which might be detrimental to their status, influence, or incomes. *One church* in a city or town, as was the custom in the earliest times of Christianity, they did not like. Did it not savour of episcopacy? Was it not impracticable? they said. The work contains some correct interpretations of Scripture passages, and served, perhaps, a useful purpose when it appeared; though Pope's maxim is the right one, " Whate'er is best administer'd is best." I remember, upon saying to Neander that some people held the binding nature of the earliest Church government, his decided assertion that he did not believe that view.

CHAPTER V

MUCH of my leisure was now spent in preparing an *Introduction to the New Testament* on an extended scale, containing a discussion of the principal topics included in that term, as thorough as I was capable of. The first volume of the work appeared in the year 1848,[1] the second in 1849,[2] the third in 1851. After the publication of the first, the Theological Faculty of the University of Halle conferred upon me the honorary degree of " Doctor of Theology," the highest they could give ; and, therefore, the

---

[1] In 1848, in acknowledging the present of a copy of Dr. Davidson's *Introduction to the New Testament*, Archdeacon Hare writes :—" I am thankful that the English student of divinity should have a better work than Horne's utterly uncritical compilation"; and again : " Feeling how impossible it is for us to ignore the questions now agitated in German theology, and how pernicious it must needs be if the negative portion of that theology comes upon us without preparation, I rejoice to see a competent scholar engaged in preparing us for the time when we shall be under the necessity of discussing them."—ED.

[2] In 1849, Dr. Connop Thirlwall, Bishop of St. David's, writes :— " Your excellent work must be ranked very high among the most valuable additions that have ever been made to this department of our literature. And I may add that I believe it to be the only one which sufficiently meets the requirements of our day in this branch of theology. I have everywhere found marks of that patience, candour, and judgment which are so peculiarly requisite in dealing with the vast mass of opinions and conjectures which has been accumulated on the comparatively scanty body of evidence remaining to illustrate the origin and character of our canonical Scriptures. I anticipate at least equal pleasure and instruction from the continuation of the work, and most heartily hope that you may enjoy health and leisure to prosecute your labours to a close."—ED.

second volume is dedicated to that body. I have always looked upon this as the greatest honour ever conferred upon me, not only because of the University from which it proceeded, but because of its rarity among Englishmen. At that time, Dr. Samuel Lee of Cambridge was the only Englishman so titled. I cannot tell the exact number that constituted the Theological Faculty then; but I know that Hupfeld and Tholuck recommended the degree, none objecting, else it would have been negatived. The conduct of Halle University in conferring degrees is very different from that of some other German colleges, since it requires unanimity in the members composing the Faculty. In my case the rationalists, who were the majority, made no objection, though the aged Wegscheider was one of them. Since that time, the only other Englishman counted worthy of the distinction was Dr. Cureton, the eminent Syriac scholar; also by Hupfeld's recommendation. Here is part of a note addressed to me by Tholuck immediately after :—

" HALLE, 7th December 1848.

" I have sincere pleasure in greeting you as *Doctor of Halle*, and in thus seeing the fulfilment of a wish that I have long cherished. May God preserve you long to Christian science, and make you the means of blessing and prosperity to the Church. . . ."

The worthy Professor Tholuck had paid me a visit at Manchester in the year 1847. But he spent a very few days only at the college, weak and ailing as usual, his sight much impaired, but having a good deal of his wonted elasticity, and that passion for walking which he found it necessary to indulge during the greater part of his life. Delicate, as he always was, the feeblest-bodied member of the Theological Faculty in Halle, he survived the strongest. He expressed surprise at seeing the imposing Building erected by a Dissenting Body, thinking that an Established

Church only could have afforded it. We walked in the neighbourhood, and talked on such topics as "ob Schrift ob Geist," a phrase which I was often repeating from the well-known pamphlet of Wislicenus, once pastor of a church in Halle, who was deposed from his office because of his prominence among the "Lichtfreunde," having undergone persecution at the hands of Guericke and the Saxon Consistorium, as well as the Prussian Government. The life of this worthy man was a troubled one. His free opinions made him obnoxious to the powers then in the ascendant; poverty came upon him and his large family; he emigrated to America, and found at last a congenial home at Zurich, where he ended his days in peace. A touching incident is related of him. His eldest son, six years old, seeing his father's face pale and sad, once asked him why he appeared melancholy. The father stooped, put his hand on the head of the boy, kissed him and said, "Ich kann nicht lügen." Had he lied for God, his lot had been different. All honour to the memory of the man!

Tholuck's opinion was that we must have both *Schrift* and *Geist*, but he did not define their relative places. Like most Germans, the Professor was an early riser. After four o'clock in the morning he was heard singing hymns to himself in his bedroom, and was employed in writing for his *Literarischer Anzeiger*. Few German scholars have shown greater aptitude for writing good commentaries on the New Testament; but none of his expositions has permanent vitality, except those on *the Sermon on the Mount* and the *Epistle to the Romans*. His orthodoxy was much modified in later years; he accepted most of the critical conclusions established by the great Hebrew scholars in the Old Testament books, without adopting the views of the Tübingen school in the New. I always thought he was unfair in his criticism on Baur, against whom his humour and sarcasm were often pointless. In some things he was very tenacious; as in a note to his commentary on the Epistle to the Romans, ix. 5, where I showed him that the reading θεός, instead of ὅς, in 1 Tim. iii. 16, was wrong, notwithstanding the proof of the former to which he appealed in the pamphlet of Dr. Henderson on the text. But he would not change the note, and it remains as at first. His labours had a good effect on the students. Pious, benevolent, humble, his example and teaching were most valuable. He left Manchester for Scotland, and I saw him no more in this country. The English style of living did not agree with his constitution. I remark, in conclusion, that his orthodoxy differed from the Scotch and English type. But he was always reserved in the expression of his opinions, except to a few. His theology was rather of the *Vermittelungs* sort, stopping short of the conclusions at which a sounder criticism than his had arrived.

During my abode in Manchester I took considerable interest in the question of education. An association, which took the name of "The Lancashire Public School Association," having been formed, I became a member of the committee, and attended its meetings regularly, taking part in the lectures, papers, and discussions. The scheme advocated a system of secular education established by the State, and was the precursor of the School Board system. It was simpler, however, and had less of the element of compromise in it. The Church of England and the religious bodies generally set themselves against it as godless. We published a small volume, entitled *National Education not necessarily Governmental, Sectarian, or Irreligious*, London, 1850, which contains a paper of mine. The system set forth was an excellent one, and would, in my opinion, have contributed greatly to the spread of education. The very agitation of it did good. Yet the Congregational body looked upon it with disfavour, calling it irreligious; and those who were actively engaged in recommending it were suspected. My honest attachment to it made me somewhat unpopular among my co-religionists, who prudently stood aloof, because of the *secular* character belonging to the plan. We had able men on our side, Richard Cobden and W. J. Fox among others; and though we failed in getting Parliament to pass our Bill, many were induced to think about the question and consider its practicability.

My lectures on Biblical Criticism being out of print, it seemed desirable either to revise them for another edition, or to write a new work on the same subject. I did the latter, publishing it in 1852—*A Treatise on Biblical Criticism, Exhibiting a Systematic View of that Subject*, in two volumes, the first devoted to the Old Testament, the second to the New. The method followed in this work still seems to me the best. I considered it at the time one of my chief performances, and a good part seems to me to be of permanent value. New materials and the advancing state of our knowledge would necessarily modify, enlarge, and correct various chapters. If it were revised by a competent hand, it might still occupy the place it was meant to fill in the literature of the subject. The two volumes were afterwards issued in one.

These ten years were marked by my first family bereavement—the death of my first-born in June 1849, to whom allusion is made in the preface to the second volume of my Introduction to the New Testament. Well does Scripture speak of the bitter sorrow for one's first-born as specially severe. The death was a sad blow to his parents, chiefly to me, who saw in him early prognostications of future eminence. His remarkable precocity was the precursor of an early departure to another sphere, as is commonly the case.

In the year 1854 my wife went with her four children

(three sons and a daughter) to Halle, to live there for several months, chiefly to have a better climate in the spring and summer, but also on account of the facilities for social intercourse, and for learning German, which that university town afforded. Unfortunately, her health was not much benefited, chiefly because of the unexpected difficulties encountered in getting suitable house accommodation. Professors Tholuck and Hupfeld were exceedingly kind; Mrs. Tholuck and Miss Hupfeld the same. I joined my wife for a time, and need hardly say that I was warmly welcomed by both professors, but I was obliged to return when the classes met again. My wife's letters from this German abode are full of details showing the uncommon helpfulness and generosity of these two professors and their families. The time we spent together in Halle was a pleasant one, for several of the professors were very friendly—not merely the two already mentioned, but also Roediger, Herzog, and Erdmann. Herzog had just commenced his *Real-Encyklopädie*, and was invited to Erlangen. The memory of happy evenings spent with Hupfeld and the rest can never be effaced. In the cool of the evening the gardens attached to the houses were a pleasant retreat, where coffee and wine filled up the intervals of conversation.

I had just resolved to return home by Göttingen, to see Gieseler and Lücke, when news of the former's death reached Halle. My translation of his Church History had already brought me into epistolary connection with Gieseler; and I had also corresponded with Lücke, who kindly sent me the second edition of his book on the Apocalypse, in which he noticed my Introduction to the New Testament. The letters of both were written in the brotherly tone which all scholars should adopt, and showed a lively interest in the theological progress of the English. I regret that I never saw either. Lücke died the year after Gieseler, leaving Georgia Augusta shorn of her professorial strength. The loss of these eminent men could not be repaired. Returning by Heidelberg, I made the personal acquaintance of Baron Bunsen, who had taken up his abode in the beautiful villa "Charlottenberg," across the Neckar, and was working might and main upon his *Bibelwerk*, assisted by several scholars. He was a genial man and a noble-minded Christian. The last note he wrote on leaving London had been addressed to me, and I desired greatly to see his face. It was the first time and the last I did so. Though he laboured energetically at his task, he was not permitted to finish it. Death cut it short. How I missed his presence in London when I came to live there!

The Hebrew Text of the Old Testament, revised from critical sources, being an attempt to present a purer and more correct text than the received one of Van der Hooght; by the aid of the best existing materials, with the principal various readings found in MSS., ancient versions, Jewish books and writers, parallels, quotations, etc. etc., London, 1855, was my next work—one suggested by Hamilton's *Codex Criticus.* The necessity of applying existing materials to the correction of the text, after the collations of Kennicott, De Rossi, and others, is apparent to every scholar. The volume was intended to be the first of a series of books in which the Hebrew text should be critically emended more and more effectually. I knew that Roediger purposed such a work, for he told me of it, and I was glad to hear of his design, for none was more competent to execute it. But his procrastinating habits stood in the way, and nothing was done.

After all, materials of importance for correcting the present Hebrew text are not available. We seek for them in vain. The Masoretic text has established itself, and cannot be displaced even where it is obviously corrupt, except by some of the ancient versions, or oftener by conjecture. Yet there must have been considerable variations among the MSS. at an early period. In the first and second centuries of the Christian era, the various readings of Hebrew codices had so multiplied as to alarm the Jewish doctors. Nor did time abate this fear, till some scholars, anxious about their sacred books, resolved to remedy the evil by a bold stroke. Collecting all the copies they could, and selecting a small number of the best, they destroyed the rest, making a revised recension out of the remainder. In some such way the text afterwards called the Masoretic originated. Emerging from the ruins of many varying copies, it soon got sole possession of the field. As the means of correcting it were wanting, it was multiplied in the state in which it was made. In any case, it was not a *critical* text. Probably it was made in haste, without the application of sound principles, or a desire to do thoroughly what less superstitious scholars would not have shrunk from. As to the variations of the Masora itself, they are too insignificant to be worth the labour of collection, and are quite insufficient to restore the Hebrew to its original state.

In the spring of the year 1856 I was honoured by a visit from Professor Hupfeld, who wished to see something of English life and manners. I showed him all the attention I could, and he was much gratified by what he witnessed in this foreign land. In our conversations and walks many topics were touched upon. A story which he heard in the shop of a London bookseller amused him greatly. A clergyman who entered and was looking at some books on the counter, had the *Die Quellen der Genesis* put into his hands as a recent production. He asked if it were orthodox, a question that embarrassed the bookseller. But the *Die Quellen* arrested the clerical eyes, and he anticipated an answer by saying, " Oh, I see it is heterodox. ' *Sources* of Genesis '—there is but one source, the Holy Spirit." This incident excited the professor's

3

humorous propensity, and led to inferences about the literary status of some clergymen far from favourable. Leaving me, he proceeded to the Lake district. I never met with a more honourable or upright individual than this genuine friend—a man who united the simplicity of a child with the most profound learning. The pupil and successor of Gesenius was one of God's nobility, from whom I learned much—much to stimulate healthy thought.[1]

My second son died on the 27th April, aged seventeen years. He had just entered on business in Manchester, and exhibited great manliness, with much refinement of feeling. His untimely departure smote me sorely, and I grieved long for his loss. But another trial was close at hand, not indeed of the same kind or character, but unexpected and rough.

In May 1856 there appeared, as the second volume of a new edition of Horne's *Introduction to the Scriptures*, " *The Text of the Old Testament Considered, with a Treatise on Sacred Interpretation, and a Brief Introduction to the Old Testament Books and the Apocrypha.* London." This work was fraught with momentous consequences to myself and family, since it led to our being turned out of house and home, with a name tainted and maligned. It is not my purpose, however, to give a history of the proceedings taken against me. I shall only say here that my enemies succeeded in blasting my name and blighting my prospect of public usefulness among Congregationalists. I have little doubt that many of them thought they were serving God. These I cannot blame. The decision between them and me I leave to others. The whole matter is the one part of my brief history on earth which I wish to be fully narrated as a lesson of warning and instruction.[2]

---

[1] A strongly expressed wish on the part of Prof. Hupfeld's daughters prevents quotation from his characteristic and charming letters.—ED.

[2] It will be observed that these words were written not long after 1872. It was in his last years, after 1890, that Dr. Davidson expressed a wish for the narrative by Mr. Picton which follows.—ED.

CHAPTER VI

THE COLLEGE CRISIS

By J. ALLANSON PICTON

DR. DAVIDSON always regarded the great struggle through which he passed in 1856–57 as the most important crisis of his career. It was his wish that the story should be told by one of his old students, who had in a manner passed through that crisis with him; and there need not be any concealment of the fact that his choice fell upon the present writer.

It is now more than forty years since the controversy of which I am to speak. Opinion has not stood still in the meanwhile; and we must be careful how we judge either actions or words so long gone by precisely as we should at the present day. This caution must be applied impartially. The composite character of the Pentateuch and the late origin of most of its constituent parts are now facts so familiar that they are ordinarily discussed in popular magazines, and are acknowledged in many orthodox pulpits. But we must not allow this to prejudice our judgment on the fears awakened in England and Scotland by any suggestion of such ideas forty years ago. On the other hand, we are not to assume that the Dr. Davidson of 1857 already held the opinions published by the Dr. Davidson of, say, 1887. What his opinions had become at the latter date is of no concern whatever to us in considering the controversy of the former year. The question which the authorities of the Lancashire Independent

College had to decide was not whether a consistent rationalist might retain a post as tutor in an evangelical seminary, but a very different one, as will presently be apparent.

In 1856 Dr. Davidson had already attained such a position among Biblical scholars, that his name was sure to be one of the first to occur to any enterprising firm of publishers as likely to command the confidence of students in Great Britain.   He was exceptionally honoured in Germany, where English scholarship was in general but lightly esteemed.   Indeed Lücke, no mean authority, had recommended the translation of his *Introduction to the New Testament* into German.   Under these circumstances, when Messrs. Longman, in 1854, contemplated the issue of a new and revised edition of that venerable work, Horne's *Introduction to the Sacred Scriptures*, they naturally wrote to Dr. Davidson for his advice.   Mr. Horne, who had lived to see his work pass through nine editions, was no longer strong enough to undertake the whole labour of revision. Dr. Davidson readily communicated to the publishers his ideas of what was required.   Messrs. Longman then wrote, inviting him to undertake the revision of vol. ii., dealing with the Old Testament, and of vol. iv., dealing with the New.   Dr. Davidson, however, declined this proposal.   He considered that the progress made in Biblical Criticism since the original publication of the book, or perhaps, to put it more accurately, the increased literary and scholarly intercourse between England and Germany, made it impossible to keep up any longer in this country a little water-tight compartment, as it were, of effete criticism guaranteed against the floods of better-informed opinion that had broken loose elsewhere.

The next thing was that the publishers requested Dr. Davidson entirely to rewrite the two volumes.   He was unwilling, however, to undertake vol. iv., because he had but recently given to the world his latest ideas on the

New Testament in his *Introduction*.   But he consented to
rewrite vol. ii., treating of the origin and authorship of the
books of the Old Testament.   At the same time, he mentioned Dr. Tregelles as a scholar fitted to undertake the
fourth volume.   The recommendation was accepted by the
publishers.   But it should be noted that the arrangement
with Dr. Davidson to rewrite the second volume was completed before Dr. Tregelles had been engaged, or indeed
communicated with.   To show the unreserved freedom
demanded by Dr. Davidson and accorded by Messrs. Longman, it may be as well to quote the words of a letter written
by the former to the latter on 17th February 1854.   After
stipulating that his name should appear on the title-page,
and that it should be known that he, and no one else, was
responsible for the part he undertook, he proceeded—

"I must also state that I shall, if engaged in the work,
not retain any of Mr. Horne's matter, but rewrite the whole,
just as if I were writing a new book on my own account.
I shall probably retain no sentence of his, but start entirely
on new ground—such ground as the subjects have been
brought to, not only here, but especially in other countries."

Amongst the "other countries" here mentioned, Germany was no doubt most prominent in the thoughts of
the writer.   While in our country any doubt as to the
authorship of the ancient books traditionally ascribed to
Moses, or Joshua, or David, or Daniel, or other Hebrew
worthies had been hitherto for the most part confined to
opponents of Christianity; in Germany, on the other hand,
from the beginning of the century theological students at
various Universities had been accustomed to hear revered
professors discussing with fearless candour the reasons for
suspecting a more complex origin of the books in question.[1]   The highly cultured, large hearted, and genial

---

[1] The anecdote of Hupfeld in a London bookseller's shop, p. 33
ante, will illustrate what is said here.

Bunsen probably did more than any college tutors to create in English society an interest in German critical research. When he retired from his brilliant career among us, the names of Schleiermacher, Strauss and Baur, De Wette and Ewald, were beginning to be familiar in the mouths of many Englishmen who had never read them. But to how very slight a degree the cultivated or half-cultivated classes in Great Britain had awakened to the dawn of a more scientific treatment of Old Testament questions is shown, amongst other signs of the times, by the treatment of such subjects in the eighth edition of the *Encyclopædia Britannica*. That work, of course, endeavours in each edition to adapt itself to the average intelligence of fairly educated Englishmen. Now the article on the Pentateuch, issued in 1859, while admitting that some misguided scholars doubted the Mosaic authorship, appears to assume that the chief reason alleged for any such doubt is the fact that the Pentateuch speaks of Moses in the third person, and sometimes in terms of respectful eulogy. At a time when such notions satisfied the editor of the *Encyclopædia Britannica*, it must be acknowledged that a professor in an evangelical college who undertook to rewrite the second volume of Horne's *Introduction* in the light of the most recent conclusions of competent scholars, " not only here, but especially in other countries," showed a very remarkable courage.

What passed through his mind in writing the book he has not told us. He must have known, as he candidly worked out the reasons which made belief in the Mosaic authorship of the whole Pentateuch impossible, that his conclusions would very much astonish some reverend members of the College Committee. But the knowledge of such a probability could not justify him to his own conscience in suppressing or disguising his impressions of truth. He had a duty to the Church and the world as well as to the college. And so far as his knowledge and experience went, there was no reason whatever to apprehend that his duty to the best interests of the college could interfere in any way with his duty as a witness for truth. He was, of course, bound by a trust-deed and "schedule of doctrine." It was not to be expected that practical Manchester men would leave future generations to the guidance of the Word and the Spirit. No; the money had been raised amongst them on the understanding that, so far as this college would enable them, they should have the privilege of binding their opinions on all who should come after them. There is no dispute about that. The amazing arrogance of such a claim perhaps should not concern us here. But the time will surely come when it will be recognised to be as impious and as mad as would have been a trust-deed in the days of Copernicus to bind the professors of a college for ever to the teaching of the Ptolemaic system of the universe.

But let that pass. It is not disputed here that both in law and honour Dr. Davidson was bound to teach according to the trust-deed in his classes, or that in honour, if not in law, he was bound to abstain from substantially controverting as an author the doctrines enshrined in that deed. But on such points he could have no anxiety in prosecuting his work, because he had no intention of doing anything of the kind. The first article of the college declares—

"That the Holy Scriptures of the Old and New Testaments contain the only revealed will of God, and are therefore the sole and exclusive authority in the Christian Church."

There is not another word in the deed that can be stretched to imply any belief one way or another as to the human authorship of any book from Genesis to Revelation. There follows, of course, the "schedule of doctrines" which, while centuries and schools of thought revolve, every professor and every student of that college is bound to infer from the Bible so long as the world endures. And those doctrines are what are called " evangelical." But the Dr. Davidson of 1854–56 had no difficulty on this score, because he held them himself. How simply, how fervently, how devoutly he held them was evident in all his teaching, his preaching, and his devotions. The present writer may not be regarded as an authority on this point. But he can refer to fellow-students who remained afterwards, as they were then, believers in and preachers of the simplest possible gospel, and who prized Dr. Davidson's moral and spiritual influence more even than his scholarship.[1] It was the common talk of the college, that the tutor who had most learning was also the simplest and most devout in prayer and preaching. Congregations who had the benefit of his occasional ministrations were almost inclined to feel disappointed that they could understand him so easily. Except for a few hints at the commencement of his discourse about the correct rendering of the text, they seemed to be listening to a practical Quaker address.

So much explanation of Dr. Davidson's religious position at the time seemed necessary in order to prevent mistake as to his motives in writing the book on which he was engaged. He had then no misgivings as to the chief doctrines ordinarily accepted as constituting the Christian revelation. But he saw that many traditional opinions as to the origin, authorship, and character of the

---

[1] The addresses presented in June and July 1857 from students, present and past, and which will be given at the end of this chapter, confirm what is said above. The majority of the names appended are those of men who have since ended, or are still continuing, faithful work, highly appreciated by worshippers of fervent evangelical sentiments. But personal recollection enables me to recall still more emphatic testimony given in conversation by men who had no desire in life, but—in Wesley's words—"to administer bliss and salvation in Jesus' name."

books bound up in the Old Testament were no longer
tenable; and he considered that he would be doing a
service to religion in Great Britain by helping to acquaint
English people with the sounder views already prevalent
in Germany. Still, he must have foreseen that, amongst
the little world of the college constituents, any doubt
thrown upon the Mosaic authorship of the Pentateuch
would seem like sacrilege; and his quiet persistent application to the work for two years during the intervals of
his college duties must have been an effort of silent
heroism. However, he may very well have derived encouragement from the fact, that while proofs were constantly interchanged between Mr. Horne, Dr. Tregelles,
and himself, no hint was given that either of his colleagues
had any apprehension that his work would create alarm.
As both these gentlemen might well be taken to represent
the more conservative section of evangelical Christians, Dr.
Davidson might fairly take their silence as a token that he
need have no fear of disturbing the churches in whose
interest the college was maintained.

The volume was issued from the press in October 1856,
and was well received by all English readers who were
anxious to bring their Biblical studies into the light of
knowledge. But on the 24th of November there was a
memorable meeting of the College Committee. The Rev.
David Everard Ford, then minister of Richmond Chapel,
Broughton, informed his colleagues, with much manifestation of emotion, that he had received numerous letters
expressing great alarm at the religious opinions set forth
by Dr. Davidson in the new volume of Horne's *Introduction.*
Mr. Ford was an estimable and active minister. He was
a man of fine presence and of a very great voice. But
his warmest admirers would never have thought of setting
him up as an authority on Hebrew scholarship. His
simplicity of mind is well indicated by an anecdote told

by himself in the hearing of the present writer. He had formerly been pastor of a congregation at Lymington, where he had occasionally been brought into contact with Lord Palmerston. On one occasion that popular statesman had encouraged Mr. Ford to speak freely upon the religious life of Protestant Dissenters and their various denominations. After a while he said: "Well, Mr. Ford, it always seems to me that the Christian religion is the best, and it quite satisfies me." Now Mr. Ford thought that this was an amazing instance of the gross spiritual darkness in which the most illustrious men may dwell. He had not the faintest perception, that his lordship was, after his manner, poking fun at sectarian divisions that he could not understand. Mr. Ford imagined him to think that the Christian religion, the Independent, the Baptist, and the Methodist, were so many separate denominations. It is not difficult to sympathise with the alarm that such simplicity might feel, when told by various correspondents that the committee of which he was a member was maintaining an apostate and an infidel in the chair of Biblical Criticism.

The reason for the correspondence mentioned by Mr. Ford may now be explained. Within a few days after the appearance of Dr. Davidson's volume, Dr. Tregelles sent a letter to the *Record* newspaper, amongst others, complaining that his reputation was likely to suffer through the appearance of his name together with that of Dr. Davidson as responsible for the new edition of Horne's *Introduction*.

"In writing on the subject of Holy Scripture," he said, "I trust that I have ever sought to uphold its plenary authority as inspired by the Holy Ghost; and thus it has been with sorrow as well as surprise, that I have observed that Dr. Davidson has used this work as the occasion for avowing and bringing into notice many sentiments and theories with regard to Scripture which his former works would not have intimated that he held, and his adoption of which was wholly unknown to Mr. Horne and myself."

From this is would appear that Dr. Tregelles had not read the proof-sheets regularly forwarded to him by the publishers while the volume was passing through the press. Perhaps he was not bound to read them, but at anyrate the omission should have been stated when he informed the public that he had known nothing of Dr. Davidson's modification of opinion until the book was published. The letter attracted a good deal of attention from religious newspapers, and also from theological and literary journals of a higher class. The fire ran swiftly amongst the dry tinder of zeal without knowledge, and hence the agitation of Mr. Ford's correspondents.

The alleged causes for alarm may be conveniently summarised here. The prime reason, though not always avowed, was Dr. Davidson's surrender of the Mosaic authorship of the Pentateuch, and his acceptance of the theory of its evolution in the course of centuries by a process of growth, selection, and combination. At the same time, it should be borne in mind that he allowed more surviving relics of Mosaic origin than are sanctioned now by the editors and annotators of "the Polychrome Bible."

He had also discussed freely the probable date and authorship of other parts of the Old Testament, and had to a very limited extent surrendered traditional views concerning them. While still maintaining the Davidic authorship of a few of the Psalms, he ascribed far the greater number of them to later dates. It may here be noted, however, that never, even in his later days, when his opinions had become very much developed, did he approve of the fanatical iconoclasm which allows the Hebrews no national literature whatever before the Exile. As to such books as Proverbs, Ecclesiastes, Esther, Job, Solomon's Song, and Daniel, his views were substantially the same as those now generally held by intelligent orthodoxy: that in their existing form they all belong to later periods of Hebrew literature than those to which they were traditionally assigned. In treating of the Prophets, he regarded them rather as preachers of political and social morality than as soothsayers. And perhaps one of the most notable instances of the conservatism of his book was his refusal to surrender the "evangelical" prophet Isaiah to the chorizontes who would saw him asunder.

In view of the comparative freedom with which such points of Biblical criticism as the above are now discussed in popular magazines, commonly seen on the tables of religious households, it is difficult for a generation then unborn to realise how opinions of so moderate a character could excite the alarm of good people. But at that period any dissent from received traditions as to the date and authorship of Bible books was supposed to imply all other heresies. Accordingly, the correspondents of Mr. Ford readily accepted the judgment of religious newspapers that Dr. Davidson's language on various points of theology justified grave uneasiness. He was supposed to cast doubt on the doctrines of the Trinity, the Incarnation, the Fall, original sin, the depravity of man, the atonement, and justification by faith. It would be out of place here to enter upon any examination of the phraseology that was complained of. It must suffice to quote the words of Dr. Davidson himself in the pamphlet issued by him in 1857, under the title *Facts, Statements, and Explanations, etc.*:—

"On all essential and vital matters—those constituting the evangelical system—the truths most surely believed among genuine Christians—the volume contains unmistakable utterances of belief. Nothing in it will, in my opinion, be found to infringe on the completeness and sufficiency of Holy Scripture as an unerring rule of faith and practice, man's original depravity, regeneration by the Holy Spirit, justification by faith, the atonement made by the Divine Redeemer for the sins of the world, and the application of it in redemption. Assuredly there was no intention to contravene any of these and *other necessarily-related doctrines*, whatever may have been hastily inferred from isolated and loose expressions. I do not think, however, that the phraseology employed by others in enunciating and explaining them has always been happy or appropriate, for it has given rise to objections from adversaries. This remark applies especially to the older divines, who often presented the peculiarities of Calvinism in a repulsive aspect. But the moderns have done much to obviate such misapprehension, by presenting the truth of the gospel in a reasonable manner. Perhaps I may not agree with them in *every* particular ; but that does not prevent me from avowing my cordial attachment to the doctrines commonly termed *evangelical*. I have looked at them too long and often to be disturbed or troubled with the slightest doubt about their truth. They are an impregnable rock, on which I hope to stand for ever myself, and whose safety to immortal souls I trust I shall ever commend to others. Christ, in all His excellency and offices as the Prophet, Priest, and King of His people—the only and all-sufficient Mediator—is the precious corner-stone of the believer. May He ever be mine!"

On the nature of his personal beliefs, which no one could know by intuition except Dr. Davidson himself, it would be superfluous and impertinent to quote other testimony. But that there was nothing in his ordinary college lectures, or in his preaching, inconsistent with such a declaration is abundantly evident from the testimony of students and hearers referred to above.

We may now return to Mr. Ford and his correspondents. The committee of the College were already too well aware that the book was exciting great searchings of heart among their constituents. For the *Record* newspaper and its kindred amongst various Denominations had been brimming over with invective during the previous month, and Mr. Ford found a very responsive audience. When he sat down, the matter was taken up by a very different man. The Rev. John Kelly of the Crescent Chapel, Liverpool, was one of the ablest men in the lamentable list of perverted intellects prostrated before the idols of the sanctuary. His keen, handsome face, which somehow reminded one of the great Napoleon, was not matched with a voice fitted for oratory. That voice was like Cromwell's, "sharp and untuneable"; but it had great penetrative power, and the most comatose of hearers found slumber hopeless within its reach. He was a man of much cultivation within his range as a theologian; and if he had not quite committed to memory Calvin's *Institutes*, he was ready on the instant to correct any misquotation of any part of them. His strong, eager mind was logical in the sense of caring much more about correct syllogisms than about sound induction of premisses. Though very unlike Cardinal Newman in his ideas of religion, he started from the same point—an assumption that there must, as a matter of course, be some infallible authority available for men in their aspirations after the truth concerning God, the soul, sin, and salvation. Newman found that authority in the Church, and for him the Church spoke through the Pope.[1] Mr. Kelly found that authority in the Bible, and for him the Bible spoke through Calvin's *Institutes*. Calvin in his commentaries on Scripture is often very free. But there Mr. Kelly did not follow him. There was a thoroughness about Mr. Kelly which in its way was delightful. On a small scale he was a reproduction of John Knox. When he devoted his strong, clear intellect to the discussion of some mundane topic on a neutral platform, it was a joy to hear him. If Providence had differently arranged his circumstances, he might have been an uncommonly effective debater in Parliament.

It was an ill omen for the committee and for the college when such a man took in hand the complaints of Mr. Ford's correspondents. He produced and moved a resolution, which ran as follows :—

---

[1] Of course he believed the infallibility of councils. But still the decrees of councils needed interpretation, and this was the business of the infallible Pope.

"That this committee having had its attention directed to certain general charges brought against the views set forth by Dr. Davidson, one of the professors of this institution, in the second volume of the last edition of Horne's *Introduction* just published, and of which Dr. Davidson is the author, as unsound, feels it due to Dr. Davidson, as well as to the interests of the college, to ascertain the truth of these allegations; and with this view appoints a sub-committee to examine the book in question, and to report to a subsequent meeting of this committee.

"That the following gentlemen be the sub-committee:— Rev. Dr. Halley, Revs. P. Thomson, W. R. Thorburn, R. M. Davies, and James Gwyther."

Of this list it may be said that the first was a man of considerable learning, and the last was one of the best of men. The other three were fair average specimens of active and useful ministers, but with no special fitness for the critical task imposed upon them.

Reporters were not admitted to the meetings of the committee, and what Mr. Kelly said is not recorded, nor is it handed down, like the discourses in the Acts of the Apostles, by hearsay. But he carried conviction to his hearers, and the judicial committee was appointed. There is no doubt that they took great pains with their work, or that they were all animated both by respect and regard for Dr. Davidson, and by a sincere desire to come to a right conclusion. They took nearly three months to complete their report, and in the meantime Dr. Davidson continued his work at the college.

If the secrets of all hearts could be revealed, it would probably be found that no savagery or malice has succeeded in working as much misery among men as the fatal and foolish craving to stereotype religious belief. Heretics have been the most unfortunate of criminals. For, putting aside the tribe of Simon Magus, who make a trade of sensationalism, honest heretics have usually been sensitive, their consciences tender, their piety fervent, and their love to mankind an absorbing passion. To many amongst them one of the cruellest penalties on their inability to believe according to the fashion of their age, has been their exclusion from the one field of work in which they felt themselves specially fitted to serve their generation by the will of God. The temptation to pious lies in the interest of truth has been overwhelming, and the heroism that resisted it has been accounted only obstinacy and self-will. Most of them have been entitled to the blessing pronounced on poverty, for they have rarely possessed much of this world's wealth. But that blessing has been embittered at the period of the trial by anxiety for the sustenance and comfort of those dependent upon them. While Bunyan calmly proceeded with the cottage service, which he knew would be interrupted by his arrest, only the Searcher of Hearts could tell the anxiety that racked his loving heart when he thought of his blind daughter. But the noble army of martyrs is not confined to those who have suffered under kings and magistrates. The gradual emancipation of religion from superstition has had its thousands of nameless heroes, who have seen deprivation of office and consequent destitution slowly drawing nearer day by day, and who to every appeal of fear and love could only answer, " God help me, I can do no other."

There is a chill, worldly wisdom which says, " Serve them right : que diable faisaient ils dans cette galère ? " If men will persist in a false position, they must take the consequences. A man who regards the Mosaic account of the Creation and the Deluge as mythical, has no right to be the minister of a congregation who all stake their soul's salvation on the prosaic and literal accuracy of those narratives. Such criticism is plausible, but not conclusive. We are not dealing with the case of men who evade by explaining away the doctrinal conditions on which they hold office. It has often been urged as an advantage of legally established Churches that, by the assistance of judges, they enable their clergy to do this with impunity. Whether that advantage be a spiritual gain or not is a question, the answer to which must depend on our ideas of duty, and on the sensitiveness of conscience. But this is not the sort of case before us now. Voluntary congregations always profess that within the limits of their trust-deeds they are sincerely anxious for more light and knowledge. Amongst the points not usually, if ever at all, included in "schedules of doctrine" is the definition of inspiration, or any statement as to the date and authorship of the various books of the Bible. In this respect, as we have already seen, the trust-deed of the Lancashire Independent College is like those of most chapels. Therefore, from the legal point of view, the professors of the former, and ministers and teachers of the latter, should be perfectly free to accept and to teach all conclusions of modern criticism consistent with a belief "that the Holy Scriptures of the Old and New Testaments contain the only revealed will of God, and are therefore the sole and exclusive authority in the Christian Church." But it has been precisely in the exercise of this freedom permitted by their legal position, that hundreds of good and pious men have had to suffer persecution.

Again, though it is true that claimants of liberty of prophesying in unestablished Churches have usually been subject to a schedule of doctrine more narrowly guarded than the Anglican Articles, yet no one has contended that the schedule was infallible, and the professed admirers and followers of Pastor Robinson, who believed that "the Lord had more light and truth to break forth out of His Holy Word," might surely be expected to give a generous interpretation to an imperfect human document. It is bad enough that while declaring the Scriptures to be the "sole and exclusive authority in the Church," the followers of

4

Pastor Robinson should stultify themselves by setting up another standard, formed neither by apostles nor prophets, but by modern lawyers. If possible, however, it is still worse that they should supplement such clumsy canons by inarticulate suspicions and fears of that spiritual freedom and devotion to truth at any cost which they claim for their spiritual progenitors and themselves.

It was precisely this spiritual cowardice that was perhaps the most repulsive characteristic of the proceedings against Dr. Davidson. When the College Committee met on 16th February 1857 to receive the report, they were presented with a document that occupied more than two hours in reading. It was in some respects creditable to the intelligence and consistency of the gentlemen responsible for it. There was evidently no disposition on their part to substitute faith in Moses for faith in Christ. They wisely refrained from attempting to bind a great Hebrew scholar more closely than the trust-deed allowed on points of Biblical criticism. But it was clear that the generally liberal tone naturally engendered by freedom of criticism had caused the sub-committee much uneasiness. The same kind of goodness, however, which led Barnabas to champion the cause of that suspicious character, the recently converted Saul of Tarsus, almost compelled the sub-committee to come to the conclusion that so good a Christian as Dr. Davidson must mean well, however startling his words might occasionally seem. An official abstract of their judgment, printed for the information of the college constituency, gave in a single paragraph the general conclusion. It ran as follows :—

" After noticing the extent of the work, comprising eleven hundred closely printed pages, the vast variety of subjects which it embraces, the peculiar character of some of these, and the great difficulties which must have arisen from these sources, the report adduced and animadverted strongly upon many passages, which taken by themselves seemed to indicate very unsatisfactory views on some important doctrines of the gospel: such as on the Trinity, human depravity, the sacrifice of Christ, justification by faith, etc.,[1] as well as upon the inspiration of Holy Scripture. Other statements, however, found in different parts of the volume, as well as the explanations given orally by Dr. Davidson, fully satisfy the sub-committee that he holds all these vital truths, and regards Holy Scripture as inspired,—an unerring authority in morality and religion, and infallible in every other important matter."

Here, surely, the inquisition might have ended, and the happy relations hitherto existing between the Professor of Biblical Criticism and his devoted students might have been confirmed. But the curse of such inquisitions is that their real motive is not any definite issue between the terms of a legal contract and an alleged shortcoming in its fulfilment: it is rather the suspicious temper of ignorance which nothing but a victim can appease. Mr. Kirkus, in his clever satirical story of *Frederic Rivers*, tells how all attempts to secure a definite statement of a liberal preacher's crimes could get no further than the allegation of "a something and a want." To a certain extent the same thing was experienced in the Davidson controversy. The sub-committee had reported that he held "all these vital truths," including even "etc."; but still, as it turned out, the minds of Mr. Ford's correspondents were haunted by "a something and a want."

The extent of their acumen and the justification of their suspicions by Dr. Davidson's later career will be discussed presently. Meanwhile, let us proceed with the

---

[1] This "etc." is noteworthy. What a dim perspective of unmentioned heresies it opens up! How well calculated it was to aggravate the fears of Mr. Ford's correspondents and of the constituency! And how characteristic of a "voluntary" and untrained tribunal! Imagine judges of an ecclesiastical court delivering judgment in this slipshod style! Does this prove the value of a legal establishment of religion? Scarcely. But it certainly proves the value of a judicial temper, and of careful accuracy of statement where important issues are involved.

narrative. The weak point of the report was that it failed to deal firmly and bravely with the vague suspicions which it declared to be substantially groundless. It pronounced an acquittal, but very weakly threw on the accused the onus of justifying the pronouncement of the tribunal. It did so in the following distracted utterance:—

"Our unanimous recommendation is that the committee of the Lancashire Independent College earnestly request Dr. Davidson to prepare, as speedily as may be consistent with due care in its revision, such an explanation of parts of his book which are deemed objectionable, as may remove misunderstanding, which his own language may have occasioned, conciliate opposition which his own haste may have provoked, make concession where concession may be justly due; and thus take the most effectual means of vindicating himself from unjust and malevolent aspersions."

Even at the distance of nearly half a century it is difficult to speak with patience of this feeble and fumbling attempt at an unworthy compromise. As already admitted, the men who drew it up were well-intentioned and good men. But so also were the Scribes and Pharisees, who, nevertheless, were the objects of the most tremendous invective ever uttered by the incarnation of truth, purity, and love. If we go to the Gospels rather than to the Jewish Apocalypse for an interpretation of that strange and fearful phrase, "the wrath of the Lamb," we shall find that the one vice of humanity, which even divine patience could not endure, was the moral cowardice of religious men.[1] The first martyr, Stephen, showed in regard to this the same susceptibility as his Master. For when his survey of religious evolution, as he knew it, had brought into a focus all the timid sophistries, the mean cavillings, the temple and altar fetichism which forbade the eternal dawn to spread one hair's-breadth beyond their walled garden of privileged luxurious pietism, he could bear it no longer,

[1] Compare Gal. ii. 14.

but was overborne by the storm of sacred passion that swept him to his doom.[1]

It is a grievous error to suppose that we are always guiltless when we are conscious of no sin. The amiable Pharisees, whose "unanimous recommendation" we have quoted, had in their minds, as on their lips, nothing but "Peace, peace!" Yet they were guilty of a very odious form of moral cowardice in throwing upon one unjustly accused the justification of their acquittal. They were guilty of presumption in requesting a scholar, whose enormous superiority in knowledge they owned, and whose religion they pronounced to be sound, to accommodate his way of expressing his knowledge and religion to their standard. They imputed "haste" to a man who had been meditating his subject during a quarter of a century, and had taken two years to expound it. What was the sort of "concession" they had in mind? Concession to whom? Presumably to Mr. Ford's correspondents. But in making such a suggestion they betrayed a paltry fear for the bag their treasurer carried, when at the moment they had no duty toward heaven or earth but to give a just decision on the points submitted. And their last words accentuated their fault. For they admitted "unjust and malevolent aspersions" to have been cast at a good man. Yet, instead of vindicating him themselves, they asked him to undertake the duty—meaning, of course, that he should prove that there was really no difference between his beliefs and those of the Rev. David Everard Ford.

"Tantum religio potuit suadere malorum."

In order to carry out the recommendation of the sub-committee, Dr. Halley proposed the following resolution :—

"That while this committee expresses its continued confidence in the general soundness of Dr. Davidson's theological views, its appreciation of the value of his services

[1] Acts vii. 51 *et seq.*

to the college, and its regard for him personally, it is still of opinion that explanations of several parts of his recent work are due to the constituency of the college, on account of the incautious language he has there employed; and therefore earnestly requests him to afford such explanations as speedily as may be consistent with due care in its revision, and in a spirit as kind and conciliatory as the exigency of the case may require, and a due regard to his own position may allow."

The Rev. John Kelly seconded this resolution, and the present writer has so much respect for the memory of that most able man that he heartily wishes he had not. In view of the part Mr. Kelly afterwards took in the inquisition, it is difficult to conceive what he meant by it. However insulting some of its terms may now appear, it was intended at the time as a vote of confidence. To any one, whatever his opinions may be, who now reads the then " recent work," the imputation of " incautious language " must appear as ridiculous as a similar criticism on *Coke upon Littleton*. The dry judicial cautiousness with which almost every suggestion of a conclusion is balanced by an admission that another is quite possible almost provokes impatience. But the reference in the resolution to the constituents of the college explains the phrase. It was an expedient platitude, amiably intended at once to gratify Mr. Ford's correspondents, and to open a way for the retention of Dr. Davidson's irreplaceable services. The recommendation of a "kind and conciliating" spirit is only comparable to an exhortation from inquisitors to a victim on the rack not to use bad language. Still, the resolution amounted to a vote of confidence, and it was seconded by the Rev. John Kelly.

Judging at this distance of time after the event, we may think that Dr. Davidson would have been well advised to decline the course suggested to him. But it must be remembered that there was a great deal more

than his own personal feeling to be considered. Somewhat
in the spirit of Socrates, he regarded himself as an advanced guard on an important post of duty. He felt
himself to represent the interests of the very limited
freedom of inquiry possible in "free Churches." His position was peculiar. He was sincerely and firmly attached
to the evangelical theology prescribed by the college
trust. In some respects he was more conservative
than many Congregational ministers of that time.[1] He
was therefore well fitted by his general religious sym-
pathies and beliefs to work with the Independent denomination. On the other hand, the college trust, like the
articles of the Anglican Church, left men perfectly free to
frame their own ideas of inspiration, so long as they would
allow the authority of the Bible to be supreme and conclusive on questions of religion and morality. Now Dr.
Davidson, with good reason, believed himself capable of
making good use of this liberty to communicate "more
light and truth" concerning the Bible to the ministers of
a new generation. This was not a post to be held or
relinquished simply according to his own feelings. He
was bound to it by a duty far higher than any consideration of his own comfort. He therefore held on, and
undertook to prepare the "explanations" asked.

But in a fortnight afterwards, that is, on 2nd March

---

[1] *E.g.*, commenting on 1 Pet. ii. 8, Dr. Davidson wrote (p. 292):
"There is an intimate connection between the ideas of appointment to
destruction *as* disobedient and appointment to destruction as *the
punishment* of disobedience. In ordaining men to the punishment of
disobedience, God ordains them to disobedience. What *He* does *He*
wills to do. We need not perplex ourselves with the consistency of all this
with human responsibility. The apostle asserts both. So do we. Both
must be true. Why such morbid shrinking from what Paul unhesitat-
ingly declared?" Very few of the younger Independents at that time
would have been as "dour" in their Calvinism as this. Even the
Rev. John Kelly rather shrank from putting the "decretum horribile'
so clearly as this,—at least if the writer may trust his memory of
conversations with him.

1857, another committee meeting was held, at which there were symptoms of a very different tone of feeling. The particular purpose for which this meeting was summoned was a consideration of the best mode of communicating to college constituents and to the public the results of previous deliberations. It was resolved that an abridgment of the sub-committee's report should be printed and circulated. Such a document had already been prepared. But on its being presented to the committee, some dissatisfaction was expressed by those whom we might charitably call the weaker brethren, were it not that prominent amongst them was the strongest man on the committee, the Rev. John Kelly. It must be allowed that this was unfortunate, because so far had Mr. Kelly been from disapproval of the longer recension of the report, that he had himself, as we noted, seconded a resolution endorsing its conclusions. The resolution was in effect a vote of confidence, coupled with a request that the subject of that vote would justify it. The shorter recension of the report certainly did not strengthen the halting expressions of confidence in the longer. Nevertheless, Mr. Kelly was now dissatisfied, and moved an amendment reversing the resolution he had seconded a fortnight before, and expressing want of confidence. It is useless trying to understand how a generally honourable man could do this thing. That he thought he was doing God service appears certain. But if we believe the Gospels, that is no justification.

The committee, however, were not as a body so agile in tergiversation as Mr. Kelly, and therefore, with a keen eye to the balance of feeling, such as would have made him a good strategist in Parliament, he deferred taking a vote on his amendment, and proceeded to suggest others of a more detailed nature, all calculated to make the abridged report less favourable to Dr. Davidson. In this shape it was passed, and with a patience which seems to us now heroic, the persecuted professor set to work on his *Explanations*.

That under such circumstances, and amidst the laborious work of the college, the desired document should have been printed and circulated in May 1857, is a noteworthy instance of Dr. Davidson's endurance and industry.   It was a pamphlet entitled *Facts, Statements, and Explanations*, and extending to 124 large 8vo pages.   Its main scope was to show that the views of the origin and inspiration of the Old Testament contained in the impugned volume were not new, and that their truth was substantially upheld by ancient and modern authorities generally respected by evangelical sects.   A secondary purpose was to explain and defend the *obiter dicta* which were said to be "unsound" on various points of theology.   The first authority quoted was Mr. Horne himself.   The quotations need not be here reproduced.   Logically interpreted, they certainly limited inspiration to the communication of "religious knowledge"; and strictly construed, they implied that even in regard to this there was no assurance of absolute infallibility.[1]   If this was orthodoxy in Mr. Horne, why should it be heresy in Dr. Davidson?

[1] *E.g.*, vol. i. p. 528, Mr. Horne had argued that differences of style and variations in detail, where the same events are related by different authors, show that "the sacred penmen were permitted to write as their several tempers, understandings, and habits of life directed." "Nor were they inspired in every fact which they related, or in every precept which they delivered." "But whenever, and as far as divine assistance was necessary, it was always afforded; so that every such inspired writing is free from error; that is, material error." This, of course, excludes infallibility. But Dr. Davidson overlooked a fact familiar in religious literature and conversation. Prisoners of creeds find liberal sentiment a luxury provided that it is to have no definite application. It is like the sovereign intrusted to the daughters of the Vicar of Wakefield on the express understanding that it should never be practically employed. Thus, I remember very well that the late Dr. Allon, when chairman of the Congregational Union, was applauded by bold spirits for observing, in the course of his address, that there was no need to suppose the writers of the Bible to have been infallible in geology, or

After contrasting Tregelles with Horne, and referring with not unnatural warmth to the action of the former and his communications to Church papers, Dr. Davidson appealed to the Fathers of the Church, and quoted from Justin Martyr, Origen, Chrysostom, and Augustine, passages inconsistent with a belief in complete Biblical infallibility. He then passed to Luther, Calvin, Erasmus, Grotius, Lowth, Baxter, Howe, and many more recent theologians of acknowledged authority. He had no difficulty in quoting even from Dr. Candlish and Thomas Scott words which virtually admitted the possibility of error in the writings of inspired men. But he was probably himself aware that all this was beside the real issue. Because Dr. Candlish and his kind could be trusted not to apply their admissions inconveniently, while Dr. Davidson and his kind could not.

Yet he did not neglect the latter aspect of the case. In the course of the pamphlet he showed conclusively that all his doctrinal remarks which had alarmed Mr. Ford's correspondents, were well within the evangelical schedule. Both as regards Original Sin, and the Trinity, and the Incarnation, and the Atonement, he urged with transparent earnestness that his endeavour had been only to free such doctrines from the narrow and incongruous and non-scriptural forms into which great mysteries had been with little reverence compressed. The words in which he reiterated the sincerity of his own belief in the substantial verity of such doctrines can hardly be read even at this distance of time without sympathetic emotion.

The effect of this pamphlet upon public opinion, as well as upon the College Committee, was perhaps not quite what Dr. Davidson intended or desired. So far was it from proving an Eirenicon, that it aggravated differences

zoology, or in any other branch of science. But they applauded far more eagerly when he immediately added : " The first error, however, has yet to be discovered."

of opinion. It quickened the sympathy of his friends;
but it intensified the hostility of his opponents. On one
point, however, there was general agreement if not entire
unanimity. The *British Banner*, conspicuous for its adverse
zeal in this controversy, said on 28th May 1857 :—

> "It is due to Dr. Davidson that we at once avow our
> conviction that, so far as personal questions between himself
> on the one hand, and Mr. Horne and Dr. Tregelles on the
> other hand are concerned, his defence is more than sufficient ;
> his honour is fully vindicated."

This, however, was a question requiring only common
sense and right feeling for its decision. The larger issues
of the controversy required something more. They needed
that exceptional sort of moral courage which gives free
play to common sense and right feeling, even when these
may threaten the idols of the sanctuary. It must not be
supposed that the line of division among those concerned
in this dispute coincided exactly with lines of separation
in theological opinion. Among Dr. Davidson's defenders
on the immediate issues before the committee were some
who were as conservative as Mr. Kelly in their opposition
to what they called "German Neology." But having the
courage to treat the question as determinable solely by
the college trust - deed, and the degree of confidence
inspired by Dr. Davidson's known religious character, they
were resolved to stand by him and leave the future to
take care of itself. While those who, like the Pharisees
of old, allowed their fearful doubt "whereunto this would
grow" to warp their judgment of the immediate issue,
were determined that neither facts, statements, nor applications should have any influence with them.

The committee met again on 1st June 1857. On
28th and 29th May there had appeared in the *Banner*
and *British Standard*, two papers then widely read among
Nonconformists, articles which amounted to an imperative

and impassioned demand for the professor's displacement.
There was little surprise, therefore, when Mr. Kelly repro-
duced his motion of want of confidence, and still less that
Mr. Ford should be eager to second it.   The deliverance
of his correspondents from their fears was now at hand.
The words of the motion were as follows :—

"That, deeming it only fair and reasonable before coming
to a final decision on the recent volume published by Dr.
Davidson in connection with the last edition of Horne's
Introduction, to afford him the opportunity of giving such
explanations as he may think necessary of the objectionable
passages in that work at variance with those views of divine
truth which he has again so strongly professed to maintain,
and having now carefully and candidly examined the explanations afforded in his published pamphlet, the committee
are constrained with deep regret to declare that, without
questioning the sincerity of his profession, these explanations are in their judgment far from satisfactory ; that,
while several material concessions have been made, and
misapprehensions removed from some points, yet in the
main the most formidable objections are rather passed over
than fairly met, and great doubt and uncertainty at least
left on matters of essential importance ; it is therefore their
painful duty to state that, on the ground of these grave
faults and the rashness which he still exhibits in dealing with
divine truth, their confidence in him as a professor in this
institution is greatly shaken, and that they view with serious
apprehension the effect of his teaching and influence on the
students committed to his care."

This resolution was surely very far from judicial in
its form.   It drew no distinct indictment.   It made no
articulate accusation.   It did not allege any doctrine in
the schedule of the trust-deed to be impugned by Dr.
Davidson.   It convicted him of no dereliction of duty.   It
even recognised "the sincerity of his profession."   The
"grave faults" condemned entirely lacked identification.
The only attempt to define them is in the words asserting
the opinion that, in the *Facts and Statements*, the most
formidable objections are rather passed over than fairly

met, and great doubt and uncertainty left on matters of essential importance. In fact, there was "a something and a want." A long discussion followed, and we are told that Dr. Davidson replied to some points that were raised, but there remains no record of what he said. The committee was so divided that no one could be quite sure what the issue would be were a vote to be taken at once. An expedient of a piece with the whole proceedings was then suggested and adopted. The committee was adjourned for nine days, and a deputation appointed to wait upon Dr. Davidson in the meantime, in order to represent to him "the strangely divided state of feeling in the committee."[1]

When the committee met again on 10th June there was, as might have been expected, nothing to report from Dr. Davidson. His final words to the deputation who had waited upon him were, "I believe no reply is best under the circumstances." For him, if the question had ever been a personal one in any degree, it had long ceased to be so. He stood now simply for reasonable liberty of teaching within the terms of the professorial contract, and for judicial equity in deciding any question affecting the tenure of a chair. It was not his duty, indeed it would have been a breach of duty, to relieve the moral cowardice of a possible and probable majority by resignation at that stage. Accordingly, the issue was left with them.

At this adjourned meeting the following gentlemen were present. It is well that their names should be recorded :—

Dr. Raffles (in the chair), Drs. Vaughan, Halley, and Davidson ; Revs. T. Atkin, G. B. Bubier, R. M. Davies, D. E. Ford, J. Gwyther, J. Kelly, G. B. Johnson, A. Newth, A. E. Pearce, N. K. Pugsley, W. Roaf, J. G. Rogers, P. Thomson, W. R. Thorburn ; Professor Hall ; Messrs. R. S.

---

[1] The words are so given by Mr. Joseph Thompson in his *Jubilee Memorial History of the College*, p. 137.

Ashton, R. Bevan, S. R. Carrington, G. Crux, J. Dracup,
T. Gasquoine, T. F. Hampton, J. Knott, Hugh Mason,
C. Potter, T. Southworth, James Sidebottom, J. Stitt, W.
Sunderland, James Thompson, Thomas Thompson, James
Watts, Geo. Wood, and Sir Elkanah Armitage.

The interview with Dr. Davidson was reported, and his
attitude was fully approved by all who could realise the
sacredness of self-respect; it will easily be understood that
weak waverers found in it an excuse for deciding against
him. At anyrate, Mr. Kelly saw that his hour was come,
and pressed his resolution, which was worded as above.
The supporters of Dr. Davidson wished to have the motion
ruled out of order on the ground that it had been withdrawn. But here they were undoubtedly wrong, for it
had neither been defeated nor definitively withdrawn, but
only postponed till a more favourable opportunity; and the
chairman rightly decided in favour of Mr. Kelly.

Thereupon a long and somewhat ambiguous amendment
was moved by the Rev. G. B. Bubier, then minister of Hope
Chapel, Salford, and seconded by Mr. R. S. Ashton :—

"That the committee, having given long and anxious
attention to the *Facts, Statements, and Explanations*, published by Dr. Davidson, relative to the second volume of the
last edition of Horne's *Introduction*, of which volume he is
the author, are of opinion, that while there are still many
matters on which the members of the committee reasonably
differ from Dr. Davidson, and from each other, the explanations, taken as a whole, are sufficient and satisfactory. And,
further, resting on Dr. Davidson's solemnly declared adherence to 'the doctrines commonly termed evangelical,' and
remembering the services to revealed religion which he has
rendered in the defence of the genuineness and authenticity
of the canonical Scriptures, and in the exposition of the
principles of criticism and interpretation, not only in his
formerly published works, but also to an unquestionably
large extent, and most valuably, in the volume to which the
special investigations of this committee have been directed;
and still more, having in view the general character and
results of Dr. Davidson's tutorial labours during fourteen

years' connection with the Lancashire College, as estimated both by themselves and the ministers who have enjoyed the benefit of those labours,—the committee feel constrained to declare that Dr. Davidson is judged by them to agree fundamentally and essentially with orthodox Congregational churches in his views of the authority, interpretation, uses, and doctrines of the Holy Scriptures,—that he has been in no respect unfaithful to the articles of the Christian faith set forth in the schedule appended to the trust-deed of the college, and that he continues to possess the confidence of the committee ;—and this declaration is made not out of mere personal regard which the committee may justly be supposed to entertain for one who has laboriously and faithfully discharged the duties of a responsible position in the institution so solicitously cared for by the churches herein represented, but on the clearness and force of the various evidence now before the committee ; yet, at the same time, with the distinct admission that there are members of the committee who, on various grounds, seriously dissent from particular opinions, or modes of stating opinions, occurring in Dr. Davidson's recent volume, and with the explicit acknowledgment that it is the hope and expectation of those agreeing in the present resolution, that Dr. Davidson's future teaching, both from the professorial chair and from the press, will justify, by its soundness and its evangelical spirit, the continued confidence now expressed, and will thus speedily sink the memory of the recent painful discussions in the depth of Christian affection for himself personally, and of respect for the learning, judgment, and responsible spirit by which all his efforts for Biblical science shall be distinguished."

Mr. Bubier was in many respects a remarkable man. Though not above the medium height, he had a very striking presence. The combination of large grey eyes with raven black hair is not common, and it was accompanied in him with a grace of feature and form that commanded interest at once. He had been for some years minister of a chapel at Cambridge—not then a very enviable position ; and he used to say that it was he who sent out Mr. Spurgeon, then a boy of sixteen, to preach his first sermon in a cottage. Mr. Bubier was a man of considerable cultivation, with that sort of appreciation of literature which is quite distinct from and higher than interest in subjects. From the first start of the *Nonconformist* newspaper until his death, he managed its literary department, and usually wrote all reviews and notices himself. He succeeded in giving that paper a reputation for criticism which extended far beyond the circle of Mr. Miall's supporters. His work was much facilitated by the friendships he had made at Cambridge, where his attractive appearance and brilliant conversation conquered the narrow prejudices natural to our old Universities. He was one of the most fearless of men. He used to say that "an Independent minister who fears is the most wretched creature on earth." His opinions, while liberal, were thoroughly evangelical. The late John Bright was once taken to hear him, and coming out murmured, "The atonement, always the atonement! Have they nothing else to say?"

Such a man was peculiarly fitted to defend an accused professor, whose only crime consisted in daring to use the limited freedom left to him, and to give a liberal interpretation to orthodoxy. For some time previous the columns of the *Nonconformist* had been adorned by brave and outspoken utterances from his pen, which notably distinguished that organ of "the Dissidence of Dissent" from all other dissenting papers, except only those of the Unitarians. It is worthy of remark, as illustrative of the unreality of the panic manufactured about Dr. Davidson, that his most outspoken defender on the committee was within a few years selected to be Principal of Spring Hill College, Birmingham, an institution based on precisely the same lines.

A second amendment was moved, and the chairman, who had ruled rightly in the previous case, now actually allowed two amendments to be before the committee at the same time. It is not worth while reproducing this second amendment, which was moved by the late Rev. R. M.

Davies of Oldham, and seconded by the Rev. T. Atkin. It suggested the clumsy compromise of a suspension of Dr. Davidson from his college duties, " so as to devote his undivided energies to the important work of making his volume to harmonise with itself and with those truths most surely believed among us."

At last a division was taken. Contrary to all order, the chairman put the second amendment before the first was disposed of. Ten voted for it, and twenty against, leaving four who did not vote. Presumably, the chairman and Dr. Davidson's colleague, Dr. Vaughan, were two of the latter. The first amendment was then put with a precisely similar result. Finally, Mr. Kelly's was put, when the whole committee voted, including the chairman and Dr. Vaughan. The numbers were eighteen for the motion and sixteen against it. It was thus carried by the vote of the chairman, who had never been known to vote before unless the balance was equal, and by that of Dr. Davidson's own colleague, who ought not to have voted at all.

This resolution, so carried, was of course forwarded to Dr. Davidson, doubtless in the expectation that it would be met by an instant resignation. But the trials of the committee were not yet over. For instead of sending in his resignation, Dr. Davidson wrote the following letter :—

" GENTLEMEN,—I have received a resolution passed by you at your meeting of the 10th June. It does not state the grounds on which it is based, being couched in vague terms of indefinite import, affirming nothing positive on which your judgment therein recorded is founded, but leaving the most unjust and injurious conclusions to be drawn respecting me.

" I therefore require in writing the precise grounds on which the clauses of the resolution are based, believing that those who profess to be actuated by justice, truth, and fairness will not refuse to state explicitly the reasons which have led them to their conclusion.

" SAMUEL DAVIDSON.

" *25th June* 1857."

5

This was read at an adjourned meeting of the committee on 25th June. Thereupon Mr. R. S. Ashton moved, and Mr. James Sidebottom seconded, a very proper resolution :—

"That this committee states the objectionable passages which are not satisfactorily explained, and the essential points on which doubt and uncertainty are still left."[1]

Whether any reason was given against the adoption of this resolution is not recorded. But it is recorded that the Rev. John Kelly moved as an amendment, "That a communication having been received from Dr. Davidson 'requiring in writing the precise grounds on which the clauses of the resolution' passed concerning him at the last meeting 'are based,' this committee respectfully declines complying with his demand, as unnecessary." Of course the amendment was carried. At the same meeting a second letter was read, which speaks for itself :—

"I have been informed that one of the committee made an assertion in my absence, to the effect that my influence over the students was such as to make them reluctant to take a text from the Old Testament for the basis of a sermon ; and, also, that my teaching generally has been of an injurious character for some time past. As I believe that such statements are incorrect, and that they must have had a prejudicial effect on the mind of the committee, I request you, in justice to me, to examine fully into their truth. The evidence is at hand, for the students are still in the house. The most searching investigation will be to me the most satisfactory.   SAMUEL DAVIDSON.

"25th June 1857."

There can be no doubt that the "assertion" made in Dr. Davidson's absence was peculiarly well calculated to win votes. And seeing that there were only two votes to spare, it is quite likely that the "assertion" settled the matter. Most assemblies of gentlemen would have con-

[1] So given by Mr. Joseph Thompson in his Jubilee Memorial of the College. But this motion is not recorded in the College Report for 1857 ; and I have not had access to the original minutes.

sidered the request a very reasonable one. And it is satisfactory to know that Mr. R. S. Ashton was supported by the Rev. R. M. Davies of Oldham in moving that the letter be considered. But, immovable as Calvin in the case of Servetus, the Rev. John Kelly would not hear of it, and carried a plausible but shabby amendment to the effect—

" That this committee cannot go into the consideration of any speeches delivered by gentlemen in the course of discussion at a previous meeting."

Dr. Davidson now felt that his duty was at an end. There was much more humour than malice in his nature, notwithstanding his innocent bitterness of language at times. Malice might have impelled him to force on the committee the humiliation of dismissing him. But the humour of the situation, tragic humour though it was for him, was now overflowing, and it satisfied him. Convicted of dangerous tendencies as a Hebraist by men of whom not one in four knew א from ח, and of heresy by men who would not or could not point out the errors they condemned, he tendered his resignation, which was accepted.

It is of course a matter of history that after the severance of his connection with the Lancashire College, Dr. Davidson's critical opinions rapidly advanced in the direction of pure rationalism, though his religious feeling retained to the last its devout simplicity. And perhaps there are those who consider his intellectual development to constitute a retrospective justification for the action of the College Committee. But surely this is a very dangerous position to assume. It is bad enough that teachers of truth should be subjected to procrustean standards compacted by elderly theologians and case-hardened lawyers ; but if, in addition to this, they are to be at the mercy of individual bigotry, or nervous fear, or prophetic speculation, the post of professor in a theological college would be too humiliating for anyone but a Vicar of Bray.

The whole story is only one out of innumerable illustrations of the futility of tests to stereotype doctrine. Such tests may divert the current of living opinion away from effete institutions; but they are utterly powerless over the evolution of thought, and they demoralise all but the most honourable and upright among the seekers of truth. These are precisely those whom churches and colleges and schools can least afford to lose, and they are the only victims of theological trust-deeds.

There is a kind of conscience which is capable of combining a large degree of suppleness with effusive sensitiveness to the social ethics surrounding it. Such a conscience it was which enabled the late Cardinal Manning, in the latter years of his incumbency at Chichester, to maintain publicly the validity of Anglican rites, while privately he was lamenting their invalidity. The same kind of conscience enables no inconsiderable number of preachers and teachers to have two sets of opinions, official and conversational. Such men are honest and truthful in all ordinary affairs. They would suffer any loss rather than be fairly chargeable with meanness according to the standard of the society to which they belong. But gripped as they are between formulas belonging to a departed age and the strong needs of the present, their moral nature becomes strained and contorted, so that, without compunction, they play a double part. Such people are never incommoded by theological trust-deeds. But they give a worldly, conventional tone to churches and colleges, which operates like dry rot, and when the fatal moment comes, collapse ensues. The men who are lost to churches and colleges by means of schedules of doctrine are those whose veracity of thought and speech might be the most potent means for evolving the future out of the past. The men who keep their posts are by no means exclusively those whose ideas or influence are honestly limited to the doctrinal schedule. There are, of course, a certain number of this latter class, well-meaning men of feeble mind and moral timidity, who sit crouching in their " garden walled around," unconscious that a great landslip is carrying both them and their garden and all their surroundings into entirely new relations with the world. But the majority of those who keep their posts under theological trusts are such as have a fatal gift of making the worse appear the better reason when questions of conscience and creed arise. That churches and colleges should prefer the moral influence of these men to that of the upright and straightforward, who cannot warp their consciences for convenience, is one of those characteristics of the time which will puzzle future generations as much as the moral value once attached to the Holy Inquisition puzzles us now.

But it was not in vain that Dr. Davidson passed through the crisis we have sketched. The inevitable reaction followed. There was hardly an organ of devout learning in Great Britain, Europe, or America which did not lament and condemn the infatuated blindness of the Lancashire College Committee. Dr. Vaughan, who had given his ill-judged and uncalled-for vote against his colleague, soon felt his position intolerable, and resigned his post. The new appointments, made in the interests of a sacred conservatism, did not keep out the rising tide of liberalism. Imperceptibly the teaching of the lecture-rooms came into practical accord with the volume which had deprived the college of its greatest scholar and most inspiring tutor.[1] And if Dr. Davidson himself afterwards

---

[1] Professor A. S. Wilkins, writing to Dr. Davidson in 1895, says : " I forward by this post a copy of an article on an address, which may interest you, as indicating what changes have come about here. The address itself had little value, except perhaps in its adaptation to its audience. Any interest that it may have is simply due to the fact that it was made by the chairman of the committee of the Lancashire Independent College, and that it was received with almost unanimous

went much further, that was only because he was before his time.

"Before his time." Yes; because of his singular union of simple devoutness with unreserved freedom of thought. We do not forget that he owed much to German scholars, and that even in Great Britain and America his latest opinions are common ground to liberal theologians. But what differentiated him was the marked survival throughout all his intellectual pilgrimage of meek reverence and simple devotion, such as made the prayers of his old age like those of a worshipping child. Those to whom the universe is a temple, or rather the Living God Himself, find no paradox in such a combination. But paradox or not, it points the way to the religion of the coming age.

APPENDIX TO CHAPTER VI

The following addresses and letters of former students are here added as illustrative of what has been said of the religious influence of Dr. Davidson's teaching on the young. The letters of Chevalier Bunsen and Professor Knobel, on the other hand, are given as showing the feeling excited amongst prominent representatives of scholarship and literature :—

ADDRESS FROM OLD STUDENTS OF THE COLLEGE

"To the Rev. SAMUEL DAVIDSON, D.D., LL.D., late Professor of Biblical Literature in the Lancashire Independent College.

"REVEREND AND DEAR SIR,—Having formerly attended as students your lectures in the Lancashire Independent College, we feel called upon by the circumstances which have led to your withdrawal from your professorship, respectfully to express our gratitude for your efficiency and kindness as our tutor, our high esteem for your erudition as an author,

assent. May I take this opportunity of saying how warmly every reference to your name was received at the jubilee of the college a year or two ago? There were many who felt how great a debt was due to your courageous truth-seeking."

our admiration for your love of truth, and our sympathy with you in present troubles.

"You, sir, would be the last to require others to coincide in all points with your views, as expressed either in your lectures or in your works; but while occasionally differing from you, we must give utterance to our conviction that the tendency of your teaching was, not to shake, but to establish our faith in the divine authority of Holy Scripture, and in the essential Doctrines of the Gospel. For while you were willing that we should know all difficulties connected with the revelation of God, you were ever ready to guide our inquiries after truth, aiming to induce in us not only habits of honest independent thought, but also—what you maintained to be absolutely necessary to this—a serious recognition of our need of divine enlightenment. Your reverence for the Word of God tended to preserve us at once from rash speculations, and from embracing opinions merely because generally held. Whatever success, therefore, may attend us as servants of Christ, we shall feel it to be largely owing to your care and ability in teaching us the principles of a sound Biblical interpretation. We believe that your attachment to divine truth is unchanged; and deeply regret that you have been so greatly misunderstood by some, and so uncharitably treated by others. You will, however, we hope, accept the accompanying testimonial as a token that having had the best opportunities of knowing you, and having ourselves experienced the character and tendency of your instructions, we still cherish towards you the warmest feelings of gratitude, sympathy, and esteem.

"We subscribe ourselves, with great respect, your former pupils—

"STEPHEN HOOPER.	WILLIAM URWICK, M.A.
SAMUEL SHAW.	EDWARD W. JOHNS.
ABSALOM CLARK.	GEORGE F. H. SYKES, B.A.
THOMAS NICHOLAS.	DAVID W. SIMON.
JOHN STROYAN.	THOMAS J. HARRISON.
JOHN HODGSON.	JAMES W. BENSON.
WILLIAM PARKES.	ALEXANDER STEWART.
NICHOLAS HURRY.	JAMES CAMERON, B.A.
ROBERT W. M'ALL.	GEORGE ROBBINS.
SIMEON DYSON.	ROBERT BRUCE, M.A.
GEORGE W. CLAPHAM.	J. ALLANSON PICTON, M.A.
RICHARD G. SOPER, B.A.	JOHN FIRTH.
ROBERT W. SELBIE, B.A.	EDWARD L. ADAMS.
EDWARD STRAKER.	JOSIAH HANKINSON.
WILLIAM KIRKUS, LL.B.	JOSEPH HALEY.
ABRAHAM STROYAN.	RICHARD SALKELD."

"13th July 1857."

ADDRESS FROM STUDENTS IN THE COLLEGE

" To the Rev. SAMUEL DAVIDSON, D.D., LL.D., Professor of
Biblical Criticism, Lancashire Independent College.

"DEAR SIR,—We, the undersigned, students of the
Lancashire Independent College, fearing that the painful
circumstances in which you have been placed, as regards
your position in the college, may lead to your seeing it right
to take a step which will deprive us of your oversight,
cannot allow ourselves to think of the possibility of this
without expressing our appreciation of your character and
attainments, and our gratitude for the valuable services you
have rendered this institution, as well as our deep conviction
of the loss the college will sustain by your removal,—a loss
which those of us who remain, in returning next session, will
in your absence especially feel.

"The zeal with which you have devoted yourself to our
interests, your readiness to aid us in all that concerns the
studies in which we are here engaged, have secured the
grateful esteem of all.   And we would also give expression
to the consciousness of the good we believe we have derived
from your personal influence in our midst.

"Of our strong sympathy with you in your present trial
no assurance need be given.

"We trust this small testimonial will be regarded as a
manifestation of our gratitude for the past, and fervent hope
that, wherever your lot be cast, you will, still sustained by
the presence and approbation of God, enjoy many years of
great usefulness and happiness.   And our hope is that our
future lives may be the best proof of the good we have
derived from your instructions, and of the place your name
will ever have in our hearts.

"We are, yours respectfully,

"JOHN HARKER.	W. F. GRIFFITHS, M.A.
RICHARD ENGLAND LONG.	WILLIAM C. PRESTON.
JOHN H. GWYTHER, B.A.	FRANCIS CLARKE.
GEORGE C. SMITH, M.A.	C. HAWORTH.
R. G. HARTLEY, M.A.	HENRY KENDALL.
THOMAS LAWSON.	E. K. EVANS.
THOMAS GASQUOINE, B.A.	GEORGE ALLAN COLTART.
THOMAS H. JACKSON.	JOHN T. BARKER, B.A.
WILLIAM SYKES.	WILLIAM BURROWS, B.A.

"*24th June* 1857."

FROM REV. ROBERT W. M'ALL

"LEICESTER, 3rd February 1857.

" If I use undue freedom in writing to you on a subject in which I feel deeply interested, you will allow the sincerity of my motive to become my apology. For many weeks past I have *wished* to convey to you the assurance of an esteem which, when I had the privilege of being numbered among your students, did not, I fear, receive its just and adequate expression. I can truly say that esteem, always genuine, has been deepened on every remembrance of my college days ; and my appreciation of your great services to the cause of truth corresponds with that, of which, I doubt not, almost numberless testimonies have recently been borne to you. I cannot refrain from writing the statement of my anxiety in respect to the house in which I studied—that those who seek in it preparation for the great Christian work may not be deprived of the invaluable aid you are so truly able and willing to give them. I do trust you will not suffer any influence arising out of the marked tendency in certain religious circles to place all excellence in the adoption of certain modes of phraseology, to induce your withdrawal from a position in which, if the united testimony of those who received your instructions (men, moreover, of most diversified tendencies intellectually and otherwise) can afford evidence, you have been incalculably useful. *We*, who were with you, have become, in subsequent studies and efforts, more and more sensible of a *real debt* to you. Be not surprised, then, at our anxiety that those who follow us in the college should have the same wise and faithful direction.

" The day *must* come to a close in which it shall be deemed the part of fidelity and Christlikeness, to rise up and draw inferences as to a thousand not necessarily involved subjects, from a difference of estimate on some one point— candidly avowed ; that difference, moreover, being from a standard arbitrarily set up. I need not assure you that great numbers regard the mode in which you have been assailed as simply one among fifty developments of this false rule of action. When Dr. Halley was in Leicester I expressed to him my wish that, in case of more definite proceedings, *we*, your former students, might be permitted to unite in a testimony of our unlimited confidence and affectionate regard. I trust the matter has been so far adjusted as to render this course unnecessary,—or I should, most gladly, have moved in it—or co-operated with others, more qualified than I am to guide it."

FROM REV. THOMAS J. HARRISON

"*17th June* 1857.

"I have often had it in my mind to write to you expressing my sympathy with you in the circumstances in which of late you have been placed. But as I had not enjoyed the privilege of intercourse with you since I left college, I feared you might consider such a proceeding on my part intrusive and unwarrantable. But now that I am addressing you with a different object in view, allow me to assure you very heartily and sincerely of my fixed and continued respect and affection towards you, and of the grief and indignation with which I have seen you subjected to the treatment you have now for so long a time endured. I trust and pray God, my dear sir, that you may be enabled to derive good from these seeming ills ; and yet more, that the cause of truth— that cause that you have so much at heart, and which you have ever instructed others to value far beyond their own personal and temporal success—may be advanced even by these very circumstances which seem at present only most ominously to threaten to retard its progress."

FROM MR. J. ALLANSON PICTON

"CHEETHAM HILL, *8th July*.

"I enclose you a copy of the address which we are to have the honour of presenting to you, if all be well, on Monday next (13th), at three o'clock, together with the names of those who are signing it, thirty-two in number. And in order that you may be aware of everything, I had better inform you that our modest testimonial is in the shape of a silver standish, with a gold pen and holder,— emblematic, we trust, of the benefits which we are yet to derive from you in the future,—with the following inscription : 'Presented to the Revd. Samuel Davidson, D.D., LL.D., as a token of gratitude, sympathy, and esteem, by a number of his former students, on the occasion of his retirement from the chair of Biblical Literature in the Lancashire Independent College.'

"' Εὔφρων πόνος εὖ τελέσασι.'

"In suggesting the above quotation from Æschylus, I thought that the word πόνος, with its depth of meaning, would be peculiarly appropriate at the present time, and might refer not merely to your fourteen years of admirable devotion to the duties of your position, but to the troubles through which God has lately called you to pass. I need not say that the enclosed address fails to express the strength of my own feelings about recent events ; and the same would be said by many whose names are there. But if that address is true, never was there a more monstrous proceeding than the late action of the College Committee. This, I think, must be felt by all on reading it, for it quietly gives the lie to the substance of the charges which have been made against you, and will prove to the world that, whatever people may say who know nothing on earth about it, having no means of judging, you have impressed the great body of your students with feelings of the deepest affection and gratitude for those very benefits which an unreasoning generation says you are so far from conferring, as to be the source of their opposite evils. I have said 'the great body'—for to the thirty-two you must add nine or ten who are incapacitated by distance or very peculiar reasons from taking part with us, before you count the minority who are not acting with us."

FROM BUNSEN

"*14th November* 1857.

"The tyranny of ignorance and bigotry in this country in everything touching religious prejudices is most deplorable. It *must* absolutely be broken down, and it is my firm resolution, with the help of God, to do my part in that holy work to the best of my power, as long as I live, out of grateful love to this country as well as out of love of truth. I live in the faith that if we show that our apparent destruction is restoration, reconstruction of God's own truth, such as has a response in every serious Christian heart, and that we want *more* religion, not less, *we shall be heard*. That is all which I want, for truth works its own way. 'Remoto errore, nuda veritas remanet'; for *there is* truth at the bottom of Christianity as well as of God's creation in the Universe. I have prepared works of an infinitely greater importance as bearing upon the foundations of Christianity, and the whole History of Prophecy and of the Old Testament in general. And now let me renew my thanks for your kind letter. I had long wished to know you personally, and if possible to have you as reviewer of my researches."

From Bunsen

"Heidelberg, 13*th May* 1857.

"You would have received many months since an acknowledgment of your kind and instructive letter. But the book sent to Bleek (to whom I wrote immediately) never seemed to arrive ; then Bleek kept it a long time for the grand article that is to appear on it in the *Studien und Kritiken* ; when finally he sent it to me, I was in the midst of preparing vol. ii. of my *Gott i. d. G.* for the press. At last I have had some leisure days to study that great *Thesaurus*, and my first business is to wish you joy for such a moderate and noble evidence to sacred truth as it contains. I regret exceedingly that the name of *Tregelles* should stand foremost in the crowd of your assailants ; but certainly you could expect nothing less than a furious attack. The fanaticism of ignorance and indifference is worse than that of party spirit in its acute form. . . . Taylor informed me last month of the end of those incredible but serious proceedings against you, which I regret more on account of those who attacked you, or showed themselves indisposed towards you, than on yours. The least one can do is to bear evidence to truth ; and still nothing more is generally required in our time !

.   .   .   .

"My method as to the fanatics is rather different from yours : it is *aggressive*, not *apologetic*. I tell them that their views of inspiration are as unspiritual and unevangelical, yes unchristian, as they are ignorant and presumptuous. They shall hear that still more strongly in my *Great Bible-work*, in seven volumes, each of one thousand pages. . . .

"I have endeavoured to reduce everywhere the critical as well as the theological questions to intelligible common sense, and there I have found your work has set a very laudable example. As to Ewald's conjectures, I cannot accept one in a hundred ; of Hitzig's I think, not one at all. Thenius is also fearfully temerarius ; De Wette and Gesenius are the most prudent. But we have learned something since De Wette. How superannuated Eichhorn is on most points !

"Of course I print the Bible in paragraphs, and the poetical parts in *verses*, namely, in hemistichs. As to the poetical and prophetical works, the shortcomings in *all* authorised versions are more the produce of want of knowledge; but in the historical books it generally is want of honesty; and there the English translators have *a heavy score* against them."

From Professor A. Knobel

(Translated from the German.)

"GIESSEN, 27*th October* 1861.

"The *Esssays and Reviews* I have not read, but have of course seen what the German papers say of them. I rejoice greatly that there is so powerful a movement in England in the direction of a freer theology, and especially towards a freer inquiry into the Bible. It will, I have no doubt, lead to the best results, though the process may be slow and gradual: opposition to the truth will cease in the end. I wish you many readers for your *Introduction to the Old Testament*—readers eager for knowledge, determined to listen only to the voice of truth, and ready to reject error, however dear it may have become. Let us pay no heed to the hostile attacks of the men of darkness. In this respect, indeed, things may be worse in England than in Germany, where the people are more enlightened."

CHAPTER VII

My regret at leaving the Independent College was much lessened by the unhealthy situation of the place, particularly of the house I lived in, where the young children suffered and sickened. I believe that the death of my two eldest was chiefly caused by the tank under the floor above which they slept: a thing that was not discovered till it had done mischief. My youngest child, born there, evinced a delicate constitution from the first.

The entire edition of Horne's *Introduction*, in four volumes, I sent to Professor Bleek of Bonn, who reviewed it at length in the *Studien und Kritiken*, in consequence of whose essay, and through my friend Hupfeld, it became known to German scholars that I was obliged to renounce my position. They wondered, of course, at the small deviations from orthodoxy which sufficed to hereticate a man in England.

Protestants have set up an infallible Book against an infallible Pope, ignoring the fact that infallibility is an attribute of Deity. The collection of writings commonly called *the Bible* is of various import,—a valuable guide to faith and conduct; precious to many a seeking soul; a never-failing source of comfort to the weary spirit,—but still subordinate to reason, which, as Bishop Butler says, "can and ought to judge not only of the meaning, but also of the *morality* and the evidence of revelation." The candle of the Lord within turns its light upon writings which are human as well as divine. A Bible medium between absolute authority and reason cannot be infallible; nor is it the object of true faith any more than Protestant theology is; that object is Christ, according to the New Testament. Let every Protestant choose between the religion of the heart and that of indolent submission, acknowledging all the while that truth pure and unalloyed is not within mortal apprehension; and that though much advantage and high satisfaction arise from such partial glimpses of it as are attainable here, we must await a higher state and the possession of nobler faculties before we can see it as it is in God. Varying and even contradictory opinions are enunciated by the sacred writers, conditioned as they were by the times and circumstances in which they lived. God speaks through holy men now as He spoke through the Bible authors; in other words, conscience, feeling, and faith are the purest source of their sentiments, but these coming through an imperfect medium are necessarily imperfect or even erroneous. While the limitations of man's nature remain, his ideas cannot be exempt from the possibility or probability of error. If the limitations were removed by miracle, man would lose the nature he has, and enter into a superhuman condition.

Holding such belief, I have no hesitation in asserting that the Bible must be taken for what it is, not for what it is forced to be—not as infallible, which it never claims to be, not as supernatural, not as the "word of God." It abounds in noble thoughts, pure and gracious sentiments, exalted ethical principles in commendation of a holy life, which will always endear it to earnest men, making it a guide and comforter. But the circumstances in which it came into existence are presumptive evidence against the uniform truth of its contents; and we are assuredly under no obligation to accept any of its statements which are not in harmony with reason or moral principle.

A goodly number of the laity in Manchester and Lancashire showed me great practical kindness at this time. Their ready sympathy did not linger. Sir James Watts took the lead, and others co-operated.[1] The laity, as is well known, are ever more charitable than ecclesiastics, more tolerant, less bitter in their hatreds to those who deviate from the beaten track of traditionalism. Perrin would not have condemned Servetus to death: Calvin brought about the extreme sentence. I expressed my gratitude to my friends as well as I could; and still cherish the memory of their generosity. Alas! many of them have gone into eternity.

After considerable anxiety as to my future in the world, I withdrew to Hatherlow in Cheshire, and undertook the education of a few pupils. Some of my friends in and around Manchester intrusted me with the training of their sons there; and I did my best to confirm their good opinion of my ability to do what they wished. I remained there till 1862, when my election as Scripture Examiner in the London University determined a removal to the metropolis. At Hatherlow I had the congenial companionship of the Rev. W. Urwick, M.A., my former pupil, who sympathised in my struggles for freedom throughout the weary controversy into which I had been dragged.

In 1862–63 appeared my *Introduction to the Old Testament, including the Apocrypha*, three volumes octavo; London. This extensive work arose out of the Horne volume and the controversy to which it gave rise. All the spare time I had at Hatherlow was devoted to the preparation of it. I resolved to put forth my best powers in its composition; and to enunciate freely whatever con-

---

[1] A public meeting was held at which much sympathy was expressed with Dr. Davidson in defending the right of free inquiry into the origins and history of the Bible. A subscription was also proposed, which resulted in the presentation of a sum of £1500 as a testimonial. The amount was afterwards doubled.

clusions I had come to, as far as the multifarious topics discussed seemed to require. It prepared the way for Bishop Colenso on the Pentateuch; and contributed to the advanced criticism of the Hebrew Scriptures. It met with approval in Germany. Professor Kamphausen reviewed it at length in the *Studien und Kritiken*, and Ewald in the *Göttingen Gelehrter Anzeiger*. Of course the book separated me still further from the Congregational body; but for that I cared little, since I was already excommunicated because of the Horne volume. I should like to revise it now: to correct, abridge, and improve it: but the opportunity does not occur. With various changes, important and unimportant, I think it one of my best books; and should wish it to be perpetuated in my name, because much of the matter has a permanent value. Later investigations modify some of its conclusions, especially in the part relating to the Pentateuch and Joshua; other portions must stand as they are. The careful reader will find that it contains the outcome of more independent thought than some incline to allow, since I differ not unfrequently from the German scholars to whom I am most indebted.[1]

Soon after my coming to London in the year 1862, Bishop Colenso had arrived from South Africa to lay his inquiries into the Pentateuch before the public. I found him an honest and bold student of the Old Testament. Little idea had he of the agitation which his book would arouse, or of the odium to be freely heaped upon his head. Having had a taste of such myself, I ventured to hint to him beforehand the opposition he would encounter. But he resolved to proceed. He had set himself manfully to learn the truth and proclaim it. After the publication of the first and second volumes, I encouraged him as well

---

[1] Dr. Davidson was able to carry out the wish here expressed, in 1894, when he published a new edition of this work.—ED.

6

as I could to proceed as he had begun. He did not seek help in his investigations, and I did not volunteer it. He used my book on the Old Testament, going much further than I had done in the path of negative criticism. Successive volumes showed increasing critical perception and marked ability on his part. The service he rendered to the cause of rational religion was great. Being a bishop, he had access to a wide circle of readers, and his influence was all the more extensive. Pleasant and profitable was our intercourse. The mode in which his brethren treated him seemed to me disgraceful. The bishops were specially culpable. If I am not mistaken, all of them issued protests more or less violent against what were called his heresies. He was virtually excommunicated by the English Church, as I had been by the Independents. Yet none of the clergy, from the highest to the lowest, was able to answer him. It is true that many replies were issued,—some large, some small,—but they were usually distinguished by ignorance of Hebrew, want of critical ability, and copious abuse; while, faithful to its old spirit against all who distinguished themselves by writings out of harmony with narrow evangelicalism, the *Record* newspaper readily lent itself to attacks upon the worthy bishop.

The Mosaic authorship of the Pentateuch cannot be proved. The five books are clearly later than the time of the leader; and the bishop has put the question in a strong light before the English public. Whatever the orthodox may say or write henceforward, criticism has disposed of the Pentateuch's Mosaic date. These Hebrew books were a growth, not the production of one time or one person. Any thinking layman can see this, more easily perhaps than a minister of religion educated in the tenets of orthodoxy; as is shown by Dr. Willis's book called *The Pentateuch and Book of Joshua, in Face of the Science and Moral Sense of our Age.* By a Physician;

London, 1875. It was fortunate for Bishop Colenso that he belonged to a Church protected by law. The Dissenting bodies can make short work in cases where one of their members is supposed to hold heretical sentiments. They turn him out of house and home with a brand upon his brow. As the offender cannot appeal to a civil court, he must succumb. The important advantage belongs to a State Church, that those who are attached to it may have recourse to a tribunal which dispenses justice, where neither passion nor prejudice predominates. Bigotry resorted to its usual game in withholding the bishop's income, but failed. The power of English law was too strong for it.

The year 1862, which was that of the London Exhibition, was marked by a visit from Professor Ewald, accompanied by his wife and daughter. This distinguished scholar remained with us for about six weeks, and appeared much pleased with his visit. Most of his days were spent in the British Museum among the MSS.; nor were his evenings in the house idle. He had sympathised with me in my troubles; and we conversed freely together on Old Testament topics. Though all his views were fixed at the time, he could bear with certain differences of opinion. His peculiarities were kept in the background; his simplicities and excellences came out during his brief stay in my house. Henceforward a friendship was cemented between us which terminated only with his life. He was a man of noble courage, conscientious, upright, truth-loving, a hater of superstition and tyranny. I cherish his memory and mourn his loss. Few worked with the same untiring energy; none with higher confidence in the final triumph of right over might.[1]

---

[1] Rev. Rowland Williams of Broadchalke Vicarage, Salisbury, writes: "Ewald I like very much personally. A sort of fervid simplicity and nobleness in his character are almost as remarkable as his vast learning."—ED.

In 1865 I went again to Germany. My wife and daughter had preceded me, and were first at Göttingen with the Ewalds. I joined them at the Hupfelds', where I had the pleasure of renewed intercourse with the successor of Gesenius, and spent many happy days in the university town to which I always felt attracted. When Hupfeld heard from my wife from what place she had just come, he exclaimed, with his usual pleasantry, "What! from Ewald to Hupfeld? That will be found remarkable." The two professors had written severely against one another on points of Hebrew scholarship in which they differed. At Leipzig we were entertained by my ardent friend Tischendorf; and at Berlin we enjoyed the society of Roediger, whose acquaintance I had made years before at Halle. The remembrance of an evening spent at his house with Lepsius, Weber, and Petermann can never pass from my mind. I breathed there, as I always did in the society of German scholars, an atmosphere of freedom unlike that from which I had been emancipated on leaving Manchester. I felt that learning cannot flourish under the management of a religious sect; least of all theology, because a dogmatic creed tends to stifle inquiry. The teacher of theology who expresses opinions differing from such as prevail in a denomination which can enforce its creed without legal check, is in danger; and he will assuredly suffer if dependent for position and maintenance on the body in question. The writer of *Church Comprehension: a Letter to the Right Hon. W. E. Gladstone, M.P.*, says with perfect truth: "It would seem that this large and important section of the Nonconformists (*i.e.* the Congregationalists) have not yet attained any better idea than the Wesleyans of what is due to religious liberty, or of the nature of religious liberty, or learnt to manifest any greater reliance upon the native power of religious truth, even though it should be left to witness for itself, without the 'patron-

age and control' either of the State or of a doctrinal
schedule.

"The same conviction is forced upon us by the known
practice of some of the Congregational colleges, perhaps
of most of them. These, it appears, have little sets of
articles,—not indeed thirty-nine in number, but equally
stringent ones,—in which the essentials of Christian faith
are embodied, and to which professors and students are
expected to adhere. The public is aware that such restrictions are not allowed to remain a dead letter. There
are cases which might be named, in recent times, both
in the north and in the south of England, in which
repressive measures are seen to have been very effectually
enforced; and it is no uncommon boast of both Congregationalists and Wesleyans, that *they* would soon know
how to deal with a Jowett or a Colenso, if one should
happen to make his appearance in their ranks—an unlikely
contingency, as matters stand!"

The years of my London life are likely to be the last;
and they have been the most favourable to mental culture.
During them I have been a free agent, though suffering
under the ban of social excommunication from the Congregationalists. But that is no loss. Others, with whom
my intercourse has been friendly and instructive, have
welcomed me. Liberal theologians of the Established
Church, such as Professor Jowett and H. B. Wilson; Unitarians like the late J. J. Tayler and Dr. Martineau;
Professor W. Wright, formerly of the British Museum; and
the Rev. Dr. Littledale, Dr. J. D. Morell, Dr. Leonhard
Schmitz, my true friends and former pupils Dr. Nicholas
and Rev. William Urwick, Rev. J. H. Godwin and others,
have shown much kindness. Nor can I refrain from mentioning my sympathising friend Mr. W. M. W. Call, an
honest and able scholar, who left the Church of England
when his opinions changed, and found a vehicle for the

large views, which philosophers and theologians may read with satisfaction, in the *Westminster Review*. But there is a solitariness in the position of him who really belongs to no outward Church or sect. Even large-minded individuals say, " He is not one of us; he is an eclectic and peculiar." An undefined suspicion hovers about him. He represents nobody but himself. The highway to outward success is to be a thoroughgoing Churchman or Dissenter. Stick to your party, and defend it at all times; for if you do so, worldly promotion is likely to follow; but some cannot be party men, and I am one of them. I cannot subscribe creeds or articles, parts of which I disbelieve; I cannot fight for small doctrinal peculiarities or crotchets; I cannot approve of the ecclesiastical machinery within which many are contented to live; I cannot but turn away from the shams of religious agitators; and must discountenance the questionable tactics which are too common among the representatives of sects.

The bane of this age, at least in Great Britain, seems to be sectarianism. And the only way of getting rid of it is to break up the sects. These hinder the progress of truth, and dwarf Christianity to their little standard. Instead of trying to purify Christianity, and bring it back to something like its first state, they cling to the creeds of after ages in which a portion of divine truth is embodied, while others are disfigured. I have small hope for the revival of vital religion in England—small hope for the advancement of spiritual truth—till existing Church organisations crumble to pieces, and something better appear in their place—something that rejects adventitious elements and retains a few cardinal principles. Why should we not revert to the simple ethical precepts of Jesus as the basis of thought and life? Richard Baxter proposed at one time the Apostles' Creed, the Lord's Prayer, and the Decalogue as the terms of Church communion; and when it was objected that this would be too lax a bond, since it would include even Papists and Socinians, he replied, " So much the better, and so much the fitter it is to be a matter of our concord."

Could not the sects merge into one another and lay aside their distinctive creeds? Could they not agree in two or three propositions, consigning the rest to individual judgment? I fear that this idea is far away out of their sight; if it be not realised, the advance of Christianity in the world will be small. A disunited house cannot withstand assaults from without, internal antagonisms depriving it of resisting power. I do not expect that the sects themselves will initiate such radical reforms as would lead directly to amalgamation. They will not even curtail their creeds. Wesleyans, Congregationalists, and Baptists, having dogmas as dearly cherished as those of the Established Church, though some of them cry out against subscription, stick to it all the same. Traditional views bind them strongly. The Church of England might well set the example of *actual* comprehension. But the temper of modern bishops and dignitaries is disinclined to it. All that any do is to *speak* in complimentary terms of evangelical Dissenters, not to *take action* in welcoming them to equality. The latter, again, are jealous of their little rights. In the meantime, the various Churches are in some respects impediments to real progress. Their forms of priestism obscure direct access to the Creator. My fond dream is of a better age—one of liberty and love, in which the theological rubbish, accumulated for centuries, will be cleared away. My dream is of a Church of the future, different from any now existing—broader, simpler, baptized with heavenly fire, having a large measure of the spirit that dwelt in the Divine Master without measure. It will bring together men of varying beliefs — men yearning after righteousness, and seeking the truth with pure hearts. The charity which hopes all things will throw her mantle around it, and the jarrings of theologians be heard no more; their envyings, hatreds, and jealousies nestling henceforward in the dwelling-places of demons.

Thus I disagree with Chalmers in his thinking it well that sectarianism should flourish and prevail for the good purpose of alarming the dignitaries of our land; nor can I see " the great direct service rendered to Christianity by the instrumentality of sectarians."

From Professor Adolf Kamphausen

(*Translated from the German.*)

"Bonn, 25*th June* 1862.

" I still hope to find the necessary leisure for a notice of your *Introduction* in the *Studien u. Kritiken.* If, contrary to my expectation, I should be prevented doing it myself from want of time, I shall get a friend and colleague to write the notice. I should prefer to do it myself, however ; and I shall certainly ask several friends to notice your work in other German periodicals, so that it will become known to us not alone through the medium of the *Studien u. Kritiken.* We work for a common cause, and the boldness with which you have sought to open up a way, in spite of all the fanatical uproar of the enemies of the truth, should serve as an example to us in Germany.

" That you have had to suffer for the good cause we know well; thank God you have not let yourself be embittered, but have with confident faith carried on your work for the truth,—a work which cannot fail in the end to be blessed by God. When you in England do not lose courage, much less should we Germans despair, however much we may be hereticated by those who are zealous for God without judgment."

From Professor Ewald

"Göttingen, 11*th November* 1864.

" Pray pardon our delay in answering the friendly notes of yourself and your dear ones. Unfortunately I have not been very well for the last few weeks : a new thing for me, for till now I have always enjoyed the best of health, but now suddenly I find myself failing. The immediate cause of this failure, indeed, is one that ought to be matter for great rejoicing on my part; you have no doubt heard something of the deep and powerful ecclesiastical movement that has taken place principally in Hanover, but also throughout Germany, and of the lively interest that I have taken in it. God be praised, we have in these few years gained what is of the highest importance: our nation has fought for complete ecclesiastical freedom, and has gained it; at last, after three hundred years, the German Revolution will be fully accomplished; its opponents within and without will be silenced, and there will no longer be any obstacle to a better development of all that is Christian. Our science has been a powerful factor in this result; but not the smallest Christian truth has suffered by it, or will suffer; and the contrary of all that the enemies of Christianity desire will come about. My indisposition is a consequence of my active exertions in the last few years; but be it so, if it is only the body that suffers, and perhaps I may soon be fully restored to health, since no nobler part of me is affected—it is only for a short time that my lectures have been interrupted. Meantime the new edition of *Part IV.* of the *History* appeared last summer, and that of the second volume is now in the press. If only I still have the time for many other things!

"Pusey's *Daniel* is not yet to hand. As soon as it arrives it will be reviewed at length in the *Gött. Gelehrt. Anz.* I wrote a notice lately in that journal of Madden's most imperfect and misleading work on Jewish coins. I am greatly rejoiced that Dr. Rowland Williams has at last been fully acquitted. I have been following Colenso's case, too, very closely, and hope the Privy Council will protect him: possibly the decision has already been given. The misfortune is that I see no deeper beginning of anything that is really better in England—Stanley's departure from Oxford has probably only left more scope for the powers of evil. Even the acquittal of the Essayists and of Colenso (if it is confirmed) has been of little use on the whole. There is no desire for real knowledge, and no true apprehension of the deeper evil of the national life. If we in Germany were only as well off politically as the English, what a powerful influence for good we should now be able to exercise! But Prussia is always the bane of Germany, and the present king in Berlin is nothing but an English Charles I., only that he wants to enslave and subjugate not merely his own Prussians, but also all the rest of Germany."

From the Rev. W. J. Conybeare

"*19th December* 1866.

"I have read the parts of your work in which your views on inspiration are explained, and am surprised at the attacks which they have called forth, since you have said nothing stronger than was previously said by Dr. Pye Smith and Dr. Arnold; but it would seem as if the advocates of 'verbal inspiration,' in proportion as they feel the hopelessness of their untenable position, were increasing the violence of their defence. I think you have laid down the right principle, both positively and negatively, when you say (p. 373) of the scriptural writers (1st) that 'they *were* religious and moral teachers'; (2nd) that 'they were *not* teachers of geography, astronomy, botany, physiology, or history.'

"Moreover, I find that while you acknowledge the imperfect development of the Mosaic morality, you maintain the infallibility of the *New* Testament in all questions of religion and morals. This makes more inexcusable the misrepresentation of which you have been the subject."

CHAPTER VIII

I ONCE had the privilege and pleasure of meeting that eminent divine Dr. Chalmers, who was on his second preaching visit to Belfast, in the year 1842. He was decidedly the greatest preacher that Scotland has ever produced. His *Astronomical Discourses* and his *Sermon on the Death of the Princess Charlotte* are remarkably eloquent, showing even genius. Among other statements which he made to me, for he had heard that I was about to go to England, he said that I would get justice and fairplay in England for whatever I did or published. He little knew the persevering rancour of the *odium theologicum*, which is the same in all countries. I found him a man not only to be admired, but loved, for he was liberal and large-minded within the bounds of what is commonly called orthodoxy. His spirit, notwithstanding his creed, was the spirit of the gospel. After many years some friends of his justly thought that he would do honour to the Chair of Theology in the University of Glasgow; but the professors, who were the electors, committed the disgraceful error of rejecting him for a respectable nobody. I recollect that Sir James Graham of Netherby went all the way to Glasgow to vote against him. It recalled to me the fact that when I was a candidate for the Hebrew professorship in the same university in the year 1839, the same professors ranged themselves into two classes opposed to each other, the Moderates and

the Evangelicals.   As to Dr. Chalmers, it is to be regretted
that he was prevailed on to leave the Established Church,
and to form what is called the Free Church of Scotland.
He never changed the opinions which he enunciated in his
lectures on Establishment at the Hanover Square Rooms in
London.   In his views of Establishment he agreed with all
the professors I met in Germany except one.   The Independents brought Dr. Wardlaw up to London to answer
him in lectures; but the whole question is one of expediency, not of Scripture.

The Sects show the divisions and weakness of Christianity—not the inherent weakness of itself, but the
unwholesome hold it has upon its professors.   Is not
sectarianism a thing discouraged by the Apostle Paul?
Is it not a foe to love and union?   The picture which the
eloquent advocate of ecclesiastical endowments [1] draws of
the rivalry between an Established Church and the Dissenting sects in England, as an efficient instrument for pro-
moting Christianity, has its dark side, for the rivalry is a
disintegrating element stirring up bad passions and selfish
interests.   He admits that many sectarian academies in
England have failed, but calls them excellent institutions,
though they are the nurseries of a sectarianism which is
the bane and blight of religion.

The year 1866 witnessed the decease of my steadfast
friend Hupfeld.   In 1865 I left him sound in body and
mind, performing all the duties of his office with freshness
and vigour.   The summer heat, so trying to me in Halle,
appeared to have little effect upon him : he was ever ready
to take a long walk in the midst of it.   I wrote a brief
notice of him in the *Athenæum* (volume January to June
1866, p. 635).   This same year I translated for Baron
Tauchnitz Fuerst's *Hebrew and Chaldee Lexicon to the Old*

---

[1] See *On the Use and Abuse of Literary and Ecclesiastical Endowments*, by Dr. Chalmers, *Works*, vol. xvii. part i.

Testament. My desire was to improve and correct the book, making such additions and alterations as it seemed to require. As both author and publisher disapproved of this, I had to restrict myself to the mere rendering of German into English. I could not even prefix a preface. But I wrote one separately, and in it took occasion to refer to a pamphlet against Hupfeld by Dr. Kay; as also to Dr. Pusey, who had alluded to me, without the least provocation, in his *Irenicon*, styling me a " Dissenting teacher," by way of reproach, I suppose, and also attacking me in the introduction to his work on Daniel. The preface showed that the knowledge of Hebrew possessed by the regius professor of that language at Oxford was far from accurate or profound—a fact attested by his former teacher, Ewald. I know well that the celebrated Göttingen professor had a poor opinion of Pusey's Hebraistic attainments; and who that reads his book on Daniel could have any other? I think it no reproach to be a " Dissenting teacher." As such, I am contented to be where Baxter, Lardner, Jones, Taylor, Doddridge, Priestley, Watts, Pye Smith were—men who did more for truth and religion than the regius professor of Hebrew with all his Tractarian associates. It is no reproach to refuse subscription to the articles of an Established Church when one does not believe them. Rather is it questionable policy in a clergyman to explain away or pervert the plain sense of ancient creeds —the sense which the framers intended. If some could assent and consent to the forms of orthodoxy, as the modern clergy do with a sigh or a smile, their lot would be different. To subscribe in either way is repugnant to conscience. The interests of morality suffer from the least disobedience to the authority of this faculty. Far be it from me to judge the average clerical conscience. It is enough that I try to keep my own conformable to its proper office.

And here I may be allowed to say, that the object of the articles which are to be subscribed by every clergyman is neither peace, nor a remedy for errors which occasion disturbance and frustrate the end of social religion. The purpose of those who drew up and imposed them was to secure uniformity of belief in matters of religion. All creeds should be liberal, and ambiguity in the words is a disadvantage. A poor office is assigned to them when they are considered only " as means of answering the ends of religious society "; or, " as it were, a partition wall; not intended for war, so much as to keep all things *quiet*."[1]   A printed creed, whatever be its length, is better than an unprinted one, because the latter must be shifting, and may therefore be, and often is, an instrument of persecution.   Who does not know that the " commonly understood creed " of a religious body is vague enough for the use of bigots to annoy obnoxious or independent thinkers? There is a practical freedom within the Anglican Church which exists in none of the Sects, except the Unitarian.

In 1868 there appeared, in two volumes, *An Introduction to the New Testament, Critical, Exegetical, and Theological,* which was meant to take the place of the treatise on the same subject formerly issued, and now exhausted. This I considered my best work at the time.   Corresponding in some degree to the three-volume *Introduction to the Old Testament,* it is written with greater freedom from traditionalism, and effectually supersedes the old one.   I had got much light in the interval, had studied the subject anew, had read all sides, and given due attention to the investigations of Baur as well as those of his followers.   I was able to think and write without the feeling of restraint, unimpeded by the dense atmosphere of sectarianism.   It would have been impossible to issue such a work within the circle of Congregational Independency, where traditional

<hr>

[1] See Hey's *Lectures on Divinity,* pp. 4, 83.

doctrines prevail, and the infallibility of the Bible is commonly believed in.   No teacher in one of the Dissenting orthodox academies who questioned the traditional origin of the Gospels or Epistles would be tolerated for a day.   The Bible is *the Word of God*, and woe to the man who says it is not.   Even in Manchester I could not stereotype my beliefs; far less could I do so when I had left the place. Well does Mr. Lynch, the noble-hearted, persecuted preacher, say: "Let anyone who has watched society, and listened to the utterances of men and Churches, ask himself whether it is not true that what passes for orthodoxy is a mask upon the face of truth, which men mistake for the face itself.   And sometimes institutes for theological instruction are only mask manufactories." [1]

The quarterly organ of the Independents attacked the book in an article written by a Presbyterian minister, and other Dissenters decried it as heretical.   But the *Theological* and *Westminster Reviews* did justice to its merits in lengthened and discriminating notices.   The same may be said of M. Carriere's review in the *Revue de Theologie*, vol. vi. 5te. livraison; Strasbourg 1868, p. 319, etc.   After various attacks, I wrote, by way of supplement, an article in the *Theological Review* for July 1870, referring to the Fourth Gospel alone, and disposing of the testimonies of Irenæus, Polycarp, and others.   The arguments relied upon by traditionalists are there met and refuted.

From that time I worshipped no more among orthodox Dissenters, but repaired quietly to the Unitarians, and sometimes to the Church of England, taking my place among the unnoticed there, enjoying many of the prayers and the devotional part of the services without attaching importance to the sermons.   One is compelled to listen to such platitudes, and to hear such distortions of Scripture, as are sufficient to keep him away from churches and

[1] *Group of Six Sermons*, p. 64.

chapels altogether. The pulpit is behind the age, having ceased to be the teacher of the people.

I was now treated more decidedly as a heretic by Congregationalists, as far as they could do so. I was excommunicated from the body directly and effectually. The excommunication, indeed, existed before, to all intents and purposes; it was consummated now. Formerly I had bidden farewell to Lancashire College; I was now completely alienated from Sects. The words of Toland with respect to his time (1702) have not lost all applicability to the present: "Such is the deplorable condition of our age, that a man dares not openly and directly own what he thinks of divine matters, though it be never so true and beneficial, if it but very slightly differs from what is received by any party, or that is established by law; but he is either forced to keep perpetual silence, or to propose his sentiments to the world, by way of paradox, under a borrowed or fictitious name. To mention the least part of the inconveniences they expose themselves to, who have the courage to act more above-board, is too melancholy a theme, and visible enough to be lamented by all that are truly generous and virtuous."

On the 5th July 1869 I wrote a letter in the *Daily News* about prosecution for heresy in the Church of England, where I expressed views which I can never abandon. The epistle excited some attention, and was commented on by the *Pall Mall Gazette*, *Saturday Review*, and *Scotsman*, as well as the *Daily News* itself.

I believe that theological learning cannot arise or be nurtured in any Church but one that is established. Voluntary Churches cannot take much part in the search for truth, or the honest declaration of it. The voice of the multitude will soon drown the voice of the teacher who adduces new views or new aspects of old ones, as long as he is dependent for daily sustenance on such as are more ignorant than himself. And as doubt is known to be dangerous,— doubt of beliefs inherited or instilled by education, — the temptation of falling into different beliefs, a temptation that might possibly prove too strong amid honest inquiry, is turned aside. Voluntary Churches probably produce better preachers. They stimulate the desire for public speaking as well as the love of praise and of public applause. But they do not produce better *teachers* or *thinkers*. On the contrary, the superficial orator succeeds best among them. The passion for popularity is fed; and there is great danger of pure motives being tainted with worldliness. It is true that the same thing happens in Established Churches; but the facilities and temptations towards it are fewer. I am persuaded that an Established Church alone provides for learning and progress within its pale. Adequate leisure and independence are usually absent from Nonconformist circles. Where the Church of England is weak seems to be in the presence of that *vis inertiae* which prevents internal reforms.

It is often asserted, as for example in Mr. Heard's plausible book entitled *National Christianity, or Cæsarism and Clericalism*, that the Christianity taught in a State Church is much more corrupt than that which is propounded in Voluntary ones. The one is said to be tainted with sacerdotalism and slavery; the other is freer and purer. America is adduced as an example of this; the Congregational and Baptist denominations of England attest the same thing. I admit that priestly assumption, ghostly pretensions and power are readily nurtured in a large organisation like the Episcopal Church of England. But are the Voluntary Churches in America more efficient conveyancers of an unworldly religion than the Anglican Church? Is the Christianity taught in Dissenting pulpits and exemplified in the life of Dissenters better than that which the Establishment holds forth? Are the ministers

7

of Voluntary Churches freer or more independent of undue control than Episcopalians? Are they able to propound with greater fidelity the cardinal doctrines of the New Testament, or to press home the lessons of self-sacrifice and truth with more plainness? An impartial witness will surely admit a superiority in the nature, spirituality, and simplicity of the religion taught in Episcopal pulpits to that which is ordinarily found among Dissenting sects; while he contrasts the liberty of the one with the bondage of the other; finding the known maxim exemplified that it is easier to obey one master than many. State Churches have their priestism; but is it confined to them? Is not sacerdotalism founded in human nature, and developed as readily in the overseer of a Voluntary congregation as it is in others? The one man who harangues an assembly of professing Christians, and sways their passions from week to week, may be a priest in heart and soul as much as any State-paid clergyman. He may exhibit as much spiritual lordship. All that can be conceded is, that a monarchical system develops sacerdotalism more readily than little republics.

I fear that Voluntary religious associations, held together by a rope of sand and developing a narrow isolation, are not fit to cope with the great problems of theological science at the present time. They neither rear men of learning, nor do they encourage them in their midst. Had Butler continued among the Presbyterians in England, he would not have written the *Analogy*. It is only within an Establishment that a great work in defence of some doctrine commonly received in Christendom is produced. It is only when there is an asylum for learned leisure that an Ecclesiastical Polity like Hooker's is built up. The Usshers, Barrows, Stillingfleets, Clarkes, and Waterlands do not arise out of the soil of Voluntary Christian societies. In the ranks of Dissent, learning is withered by neglect, or starves. On the whole, the advantages are on the side of ecclesiastical endowment, which does not necessarily involve bondage or restrict individual freedom.

There may, of course, be much that is injurious to spiritual religion within an Established Church, but abuses are not of its essence. Were the Anglican communion thoroughly reformed, its revenues redistributed, its ranks equalised, its creeds shortened so as to comprehend more and give less occasion to the formation of distinct parties within it by cutting off all ground for disbelieving what has been solemnly subscribed, it would be a purer and stronger body. A national Church should be as comprehensive as possible; and to be such, a very short creed is necessary. But it is the fate of long-established corporations to become corrupt, resisting salutary changes till destruction takes the place of reform. The Church of England, to ensure stability, should be a teaching body—an instructor of the nation in the principles of morality and the conduct of life, rather than the enforcer or expounder of dogmatic propositions. Meanwhile it is the only religious body in the land which has any perceptible effect upon the thought of the age. A few within it contribute to the advancement of rational beliefs. If, indeed, they help or go along with the current of freedom, they are heretical; but there is an amount of practical freedom which allows them to speak, though their prospects of preferment may be blighted by it. The orthodoxy which dominates almost all Dissenting denominations, and the absence of culture, are the causes of their impotence in the domain of thought. Ignorance, prejudice, traditional fetters, contentedness with the prevalent and popular, keep them in the rest they chose at first.

The *average clerk*, be he in or out of the Establishment, is neither a very enlightened nor a thinking man. He is stereotyped, satisfied to move on in his daily routine, equally indisposed and unable to prosecute inquiry to its

utmost, imbued with little learning, encircled in an
atmosphere of professional etiquette, respectable and proper
in his general deportment, with a fair appreciation of lucre.
He sets a good example to all around. But he is seldom
ahead of the age in culture; or even abreast of it. He
has certain views to uphold, and looks with prejudiced eye
upon science as it runs counter to them. He takes his broad
stand upon *the Word of God*, without a due perception of
what it is. A sense of danger keeps him from innovations
in theology. On his side is antiquity, the venerable past,
illustrious divines; why should he cherish the thought of
examining afresh, or questioning the truth of what he has
solemnly professed? Why run the risk of tarnishing his
fair name for the sake of unpopular beliefs? There is
a widespread suspicion among men of business and of
science that ministers of religion are not perfectly candid.
And if the former were better acquainted with the conditions of the Bible problem, they would *know* that many
in the clerical profession are not candid. It is impossible
for an ordinarily instructed man to maintain the infallibility
of the Bible as a whole, or its supernatural origin. Yet
ministers ostensibly treat it as such, or speak from it and
of it as if it had that character. Though the idea may
suggest itself that it is not what their usual teaching
implies, they suppress the rising notion and follow modes
of declamation which fall in with their perfunctory habit.

In 1869 the Rev. H. B. Wilson, one of the writers in
the once famous volume called *Essays and Reviews*,—the
editor, indeed, of that volume,—addressed a note to me
asking that I should contribute to a second volume or
series of such essays. Professor Jowett and he had consulted together, and proposed to issue another work. The
subject suggested to me was *The Revision of the English
Old Testament*. For various reasons none of the former
contributors was prepared to make a second venture except

the two just mentioned. Six or eight were thought of,
avoiding *seven* because of the sarcasm levelled against the
first series, "Septem contra Christum," which had an
effect upon the ignorant. I set about my task forthwith,
and discharged it according to my ability. Delays intervened. Mr. Wilson was laid aside by illness before he
had written much of his essay. Professor Jowett was
occupied with Plato, and waited till he should finish his
translation. When he had done, he pleaded ill-health, and
could not work. Thus unforeseen hindrances prevented
the accomplishment of the project about which the pro-
moters had been sanguine at first. Seeing that all hope
of the volume was gone, I published my essay separately
at the end of the year 1873.

In 1871 I was requested to undertake the section
of the *Westminister Review* headed "Philosophy and
Theology," under the general head of Contemporary
Literature. The Rev. H. B. Wilson could not continue
the work, having been suddenly seized with illness. Hoping
that he might soon be able to resume, I agreed to write,
though the task was irksome. I took part in all the
numbers of 1872 and the first three of 1873, but ceased
to write with the July number of the latter year.

FROM REV. B. F. WESTCOTT, D.D.

"*18th February* 1861.

"I hasten to offer you my hearty thanks for your present,
which I shall value most highly as coming from one whose
early work in Biblical criticism first formed and directed my
studies in sacred literature. You lay me under a still
greater obligation by your flattering notice of my name
among the names of men whom I have long learned to
reverence. In many points I still cling to beliefs which
you, perhaps, would think had exploded ; but at least I can
sincerely respect every form of reverent scholarship. Truth
and the earnest search for truth are the most noble ends at
which we can aim ; and if the noblest, then by no means, as

many would tell us, the easiest. There is on all sides need for patience and forbearance, which those rarely show who have not themselves suffered. I am very glad that you meditate a larger work upon the Old Testament. In this field—though I speak here with very partial knowledge—there is indeed much yet to be done.

"I venture to send you a copy of my book on the Gospels. You may have it already, but I wished to acknowledge in some way my earliest debt. Some of my critics tell me that I am painfully 'irreverent.' You will, I think, acquit me of such a charge."

From Canon Cureton

"*5th August* 1862.

"I was delighted to hear of your appointment to the examinership. . . . I did not know that you were an applicant. . . . I have had your new volume some time, and have read a great part. It did me good to see how candidly you speak out the truth, fearless that the truth can be otherwise than good. You are now in a position to speak without shocking the prejudices of the ignorant, who believe they know not why, and yet only half believe, because they are afraid of having their faith shaken if they venture upon calm, simple, intellectual inquiry, and call in history, philosophy, and criticism to their aid. What a state is this when men are afraid to use the noblest faculties which God has given them in searching 'whether these things be so.'

"Anthropomorphism is the prevailing error which clouds the minds of religionists of the present day, and with a clouded mind how can the heart be divinely pure?"

From Professor Lünemann

(Translated from the German.)

"Göttingen, *20th July* 1868.

"I should have answered your friendly note of 8th May long ago, but waited till I could say that I had received the valuable gift it promised me. This is now to hand, and I can no longer put off the expression of my most hearfelt, sincerest thanks for the kind attention you have shown me. I began at once to read, with the greatest interest, and very soon preceived that thoroughness, solidity, independence, and freedom of judgment were striking features of the work, as also wealth of new evidence and the opening up of new points of view. Your *Introduction to the Study of the New Testament* has thus rapidly become one of my most cherished and valued possessions, and I shall take special pleasure in noticing it not only in a possible new edition of De Wette's *Introduction to the New Testament*, but also wherever an opportunity occurs. The comparatively small attention given to English theological literature by German scholars, which you deplore, is due not to a want of appreciation of the good that is in English books, but mainly to the difficulty in obtaining them. The high prices that English booksellers are in the habit of asking for their publications are generally prohibitive to German scholars, whose means for the most part are very limited ; hence they are obliged to content themselves with the use of those *few* books which are purchased by the libraries of the Universities.

" I should be glad to send you, in return, the *third* edition, which appeared in 1867, of my two Commentaries on the Epistles to the Hebrews and to the Thessalonians, as well as the *seventh* edition, which I published in the same year, of Winer's *Grammar of the New Testament*; but do not know whether you may not already have them. If this should not be the case, you would greatly oblige me by accepting these books from me, and by sending me a line to let me know. In the meantime, I take the liberty of enclosing one of my photographs. If you would be good enough to send me yours in return, you would do me a *very* great pleasure. You would by this means enable me to form an external idea of the personality I have learned to estimate so highly. *Your* likeness will be sure of an honoured place in my album."

CHAPTER IX

IN 1871 the health of my youngest son awakened apprehensions on the part of his parents. Through the kind aid of Professor Tischendorf, the way had been opened up for his entrance into a publishing firm in Leipzig; but he became so weak that a removal to Hastings was tried to effect his restoration. The change did not benefit him, and he got gradually worse, notwithstanding all the means which were employed to arrest the progress of disease. Consumption developed itself rapidly, and he sank on the 4th December. I sat up with him several nights before his death, and witnessed his last moments. He never enjoyed good health, but was always delicate. Silent, thoughtful, studious, he loved books, and had few companions besides. He was unfit to battle with the world. Retiring and contemplative, he was over-sensitive. It was well that he should be removed from the evil to come, and taken to a higher abode, where no frail body drags the spirit down, or hinders progress in the divine life. His mother bent over the dead and pondered, conscious that she herself would not survive the following winter. Even before his decease she had made preparations for her own, putting aside parting tokens for each of the children to keep her in their memories. Thus my third son was taken and but one left. Death entered my home often. Had I not cherished the hope of a blessed immortality and believed in the salvation of all, had I not had strong faith in the fatherly love of God, I should have sorrowed in darkness.

Towards the close of the summer of 1872 I paid a short visit to Leipzig in order to leave my surviving son at the Conservatorium. I was received as cordially as before by Professor Tischendorf, with whom I spent several happy hours. Our interviews were confidential. He accompanied me to the railway station on leaving, giving me the salutation on the cheek which Germans accord to intimate friends alone. I left him full of hope and vigour, preparing the Prolegomena to his final edition of the Greek Testament. We arranged for an English translation of the text, which his own printers undertook to publish. Little did I think that I should see him no more in the flesh.

My return home was a sad one, because I found my dear wife in a precarious state. New symptoms had appeared. In addition to her chronic bronchitis, gout had attacked the head. She continued to suffer greatly, becoming weaker and weaker, till speech failed and death intervened. We conveyed all that was mortal of her to the cemetery in Manchester, where the bodies of my three sons moulder into dust.

7th July 1873.—Had a restless, sleepless night. My mind would not allow the body repose. After tossing about, I got up a few minutes before 4 o'clock a.m. and proceeded to work. Wrote a short review of Lord Stratford's book, *Why am I a Christian*, for the *Athenæum* before breakfast.

8th July.—I trust this day will be a little brighter to me than yesterday. I greatly need a few gleams of light to illumine my path ; for since the 15th of December last, a dark shadow has been upon me, and solitary musings have given little peace to the troubled spirit. I cannot bid thee farewell, thou dear departed one. Thou art in my thoughts by day and by night—present, visible. But this is a poor satisfaction at the best. The true satisfaction is to come. Then shall we see one another again, and our cup of joy be full. Meanwhile let me not be idle or faint-hearted. I am sad but not forsaken. God is my strength and my salvation. Many tears have I shed over her who is gone from me; I must shed fewer, and try to realise her immense gain. To die is gain to the Christian—to her. I must now shed a tear over my lamented friend Tischendorf, and write a few lines in commemoration of his labours and worth. How many true-hearted and illustrious friends have I lost; how few comparatively are left. But I shall follow them, and rest, as they now do, in the kingdom of heaven above.

When my little book on the revision of the English Old Testament was in press, in the autumn of 1873, I was induced to seek relief from melancholy, and rest of mind, in a sojourn abroad. Accordingly I set out, with my daughter, son, and sister-in-law, in October for Italy, by way of Strasburg and Munich. In the former place I had the satisfaction of seeing Nöldeke, but did not find Reuss at home. At Munich I had an interesting conversation with Dr. von Döllinger, who said that he was acquainted with some of my books. He knew also the treatment I had received at Manchester. On many points our views coincided; our aspirations in more. I took my leave of the learned and upright professor with regret, believing him to be in an ecclesiastical position logically untenable. The Roman Catholic religion forbids freedom of individual opinion, so that whoever exercises the right of private judgment is so far disloyal to its authority. A *via-media* between Catholicism and Protestantism is impossible. The professor judged the pope rightly; but he himself was bound in the fetters of traditional dogmas.

His acquaintance with English books and religious affairs abroad, I found to be remarkable.

The sojourn in Italy included a three months' stay in Rome, in which time I saw the greater part of its treasures—treasures of art beyond price, and remains of antiquity unequalled in interest elsewhere. I was introduced to Pio Nono, received much attention from Roman ecclesiastics, from Monsignor Stonor, Father Lambert, and Dr. Grant of the Scotch College. Professor Lignana of the Sapienza, being a layman, was more confidential. He is an ardent lover of liberty, and a foe to ecclesiastical assumption. In like manner Professor Amari, the Arabic scholar, was courteous and obliging. As to Dr. Smith, Professor of Dogmatic Theology at the Propaganda, the best theologian I met at Rome, he received me as a fellow-countryman, and was ever ready to help me to the utmost of his power. I must confess disappointment with the state of learning among the ecclesiastics, who knew very little of what Biblical criticism had done within the last thirty years. Some of my experiences and impressions are recorded in a letter to the *Athenæum*, which excited considerable interest, especially in Germany; so that Professor de Lagarde of Göttingen wrote to me for a copy of it, nearly ten years after its publication (1882).—See *Athenæum*, 1st volume for 1874. The treatment I met with at the Vatican Library was not very unlike that which Tischendorf and others before him had experienced on different occasions. His collation of Codex B was stopped before he had done, though he worked at it with a quickness of which none other was capable. His merit in bringing about a facsimile edition of it under the superintendence of Vercellone was turned aside, and he was calumniated in the *Civiltà cattolica*. The jealousy of some who are always about the library is embarrassing to strangers. Long ago, Professor Hug, who had examined the MS. in Paris, whither it had been transferred by Napoleon, was not allowed to see it again after it was returned to Rome. The Leipzig scholar suffered much from the envy and falsehood of those who meddled with the subject in which he was *facile princeps*; so that he was obliged to defend himself against them on various occasions; as in the *Responsa ad calumnias Romanas*, and in the Prolegomena to the seventh edition of his Greek Testament. Men who excel their contemporaries are always exposed to the insinuations and false assertions of inferiors. Alas that human nature should exhibit such meanness!

Roma, 15*th December* 1873.—I cannot forget this day. Though far away from London, surrounded by strange people, in a city full of historic memories, I feel as a solitary wanderer, a sojourner on earth, bereaved of her who was my bosom friend and counsellor. Little did I dream of being here, when my irreparable loss occurred this day last year: the future was a blank, dark and dreary, into which I hardly ventured to look, for I was stricken by the severest blow; but I have endeavoured to follow since then the feeble light I have, and have come to winter here for the sake of my dear daughter's health. When I look back on the past year, I am conscious that I have done but little compared with what I might have done. I had not the energy or the heart of former times. But I have at least performed the half of the task whose results I mean to consecrate to her memory, viz. the new translation of the Greek Testament from Tischendorf's text. It is a solemn but pleasing thought that she knows what I am doing, and sympathises in my honest efforts to rise higher in the pursuit of goodness.

In the midst of this ancient city, where the noble apostle of the Gentiles lived for two years, and a Church existed to which he addressed one of his characteristic epistles, I hope that my time will not be spent altogether unprofitably. As to the Roman people, and especially the Roman ecclesiastics, I can have no real communion with them. They have fallen from the faith of the great apostle; and there is not a church in the city which has the faith of the congregation of saints to whom Paul wrote. I know that the Church which existed here in his day was mainly Jewish-Christian, and therefore St. Peter is the head who is exalted above the other apostles; but Pauline, not Petrine Christianity, has been embodied in the creeds of Western Christendom. In Rome the Scriptures are not properly or profoundly studied; the ecclesiastics are bound in the fetters of tradition, and have no proper insight into the genius of the New Testament, or the history of the Christianity of the second and third centuries. They are familiar with the legends of saints, with reputed miracles and vain impostures, not with the early records that give an insight into the state of the Church after it had begun to make an inspired canon by way of counteracting heresies, especially Gnostic ones.

The increase of my knowledge during the past year has hardly added to my happiness, for the great loss I have sustained has left a dark shadow across my path that cannot be removed. The shadow will remain, I suppose, till the light of eternity dispels it. And that light cannot be far distant. Age creeps on with its feeble step and tottering gait, its failing memory and distaste for things innocent or harmless in themselves. If my bodily strength decays day by day, my prayer is that my inward strength may be renewed, that I may be more and more changed into the image of Christ and made meet for the inheritance of the saints. I know that I shall see my beloved partner again, and rejoice with her in our heavenly Father's love, but it is sad to pass even a short time on earth without her bodily presence; for she had entwined herself with my very existence. Yet I must not be unduly cast down.

She is better, infinitely better, where she now is. I am not yet prepared for reunion. Perhaps there is something more for me to do upon earth. Then let me try with all diligence to do it.

How mysterious is life! How little we know of the divine purposes in the destinies of His creatures! What mistakes do we make even in our short journey through the world! Our blunders are innumerable. When I think of myself alone, my relations to others, my deeds, my purposes, it seems that I have been groping my way, ignorant of the future, not learning from the past as I ought. Why should I have suffered the loss of so many promising children, and at length the loss of her who was dearest? Why should I have outlived young sons just entering upon life, who might have done better work here below than I can do? These questions are perplexing. I cannot solve them, but wait for their solution in that blessed world whither children and wife are gone before me.

Leaving Rome, I visited Naples and its neighbourhood, ascended Vesuvius to the Observatory, explored Herculaneum and Pompeii, passed a week in Capri, and stood on the shore of Lake Avernus. The poet who is chiefly in the visitor's mind at Naples is Virgil, and his tomb is shown there. Pozzuoli reminds one of St. Paul, who landed at the place on his way to the metropolis. Passing through Bacoli, the village where Nero planned the murder of his mother, we took luncheon on the flat roof of a house near Capo Miseno, the burial-place of Æneas's trumpeter. Reaching Milan with its splendid cathedral, I hastened to Dr. Antonio Ceriani, the learned head of the Ambrosian Library, who was expecting my visit, and who showed me the most valuable books and MSS. with obliging readiness. A priest of simple habits, he delights in the work he has to do, and far exceeds his prescribed duties in editing hitherto unknown productions and making important contributions to literature. To the Old Testament Peshito he has given great attention, and no living scholar is so competent to edit the text of it critically. Ever ready to facilitate the work of scholars, his knowledge is freely communicated to inquiring students. When he frequented the reading-room of the British Museum years ago, for a considerable time, and collated Syriac MSS., I often sat beside him, and wondered at the rapidity with which he copied. It is well that the Ambrosian Library is under such a man.

Returning home after seven months' absence, I settled down to my usual employment, resumed the task of translating Tischendorf's Greek text, and prosecuted it without interruption till it was accomplished. The volume was published in May 1875, and was well received. The preface explains the circumstances in which it originated and the motives which urged me to proceed even after my friend's death. I thought it due to his memory to do what I had promised.[1]

During the last half of the year of 1874 two of my friends departed, Roediger and Tischendorf. Acquaintance with the former was made at my first visit to Halle in 1844. Well do I remember his pleasantly-situated dwelling outside one of the gates, the evening spent with various friends there, and the barred gate kicked open by Professor Pott, who escorted me to my hotel in the market-place. Roediger was a kind-hearted, simple man, full of learning. I paid a brief tribute to his memory in the *Athenæum*, vol. July to December 1874, p. 19. With Tischendorf I was on most intimate terms. *He* died prematurely, before his work was done, apparently, having laboured beyond his

---

[1] A new edition, thoroughly revised and considerably improved, was prepared in the early part of the year 1876, and published in May.—ED.

strength. My notice of him appeared in the *Athenæum*, vol. July to December 1874, p. 830.

The summer of 1875 tempted me away again to the Continent. We went to Schwalbach, and thence to Schlangenbad in Nassau, where a few weeks were spent. Journeying to Heidelberg, I looked once more at Charlottenberg, the delightful abode of Bunsen, with whom I had an interview years before. Lucerne and its charming lake, the Rigi, Amsteg, Göschenen, Andermatt, the Oberalp, Reichenau, Chur, Thusis, the Via Mala, Ragatz, were explored. At the last place we spent several weeks, making excursions round about, climbing mountains, and enjoying to the full the fine scenery. On the annual pilgrimage day we went to Einsiedeln, witnessing the throng of worshippers, and inspecting the ancient monastery, thinking of Zwingli as parish priest there, and lamenting over the superstition which had settled down on a place where the great Swiss Reformer once preached. The little island of Ufnau in the Lake of Zürich, opposite Rapperschwyl, to which Ulrich von Hutten fled at last, and where he died, was looked upon with a feeling of sadness. After remaining several days in Zürich, I hurried home, for the purpose of writing the article "Canon" for the new edition of the *Encyclopædia Britannica*, at the time promised, leaving my daughter and sister-in-law to explore other places. The difficulty of compressing all that is essential in the large subject into a small space was felt, but I did what I could. Yet the article was marred and abridged, naturally against my wishes. I had recourse, therefore, to separate publication.[1]

January 1877.—Another year has passed. . . .

As I look back, I feel that I have made many mistakes,

---

[1] The essay, revised and enlarged, was issued in a small volume at the beginning of the year 1877. A third edition, amended and enlarged, appeared in 1878.—ED.

and that my ignorance is still great. Who can fathom
the mysteries of Providence and life? Yet I always tried
to grow in knowledge and to supplement former beliefs.
In the light of opinions which appeared more correct, I
abandoned others. I have not scrupled to learn from
sceptics; neither have I rejected orthodox teaching.
Knowledge has been welcome from every source—from
the unbelieving Strauss and the believing Hengstenberg
—from John Calvin and John Toland. If I was not able
to stereotype my theological sentiments at an early period,—
if they shifted and enlarged,—I could not help it without
resisting the authority of conscience. The reproach of
changing is surely unfair. Where is the thinker who has
not done so? It is Satan who says he has "a mind not
to be changed by place or time." Milton, though always
an Arian, seems to have imbibed a metaphysical pantheism, and even a materialism, at a comparatively late
period. He left the Presbyterians and associated with
Independents, especially with the liberal thinkers among
them. A mind like his, stamped with strong individuality,
could not be stationary. What is more, the views of Paul
himself developed and changed. Calvinistic theology adhered to me long. It was instilled by early training, and
recommended by the public offices I was put into. I
cannot deny, however, that it has its root in the dogmatic
views of Paul; yet *that* is not conclusive for its absolute
truth. The apostle took Judaic views into the new religion,
and applied them to the eternal destinies of men. As the
progenitors of the Hebrew race were divinely chosen, and a
covenant concluded with the race in and through them, a
fact necessarily involving the rejection of other peoples, so
Paul represents God as electing some from eternity and
leaving others to perish. The Divine Being prepares some
for honour, some for dishonour (Ep. to Rom. ix. 20–22).
When I see that this doctrine is opposed to the great

8

truths enunciated in John iii. 17, v. 22; James i. 17, there is no special difficulty in refusing to accept it. Though Pauline, it is contrary to the attributes of Deity, even to His justice. When John Hales of Eton bade good-night to Calvin at the Synod of Dort, probably he did not think he turned his back on St. Paul at the same time. The conduct of Calvinists has been sometimes better than their creed. The latter is narrow, opposed to reason, derogatory to the character of God. Hence I could not rest in it. Making religion too much a thing of dogma, and putting it in the understanding instead of the emotions, the mind becomes hardened. The Bible must be judged by another standard than that which orthodoxy applies. Far be it from me to think that I have attained to correct ideas on all religious matters, that I have arrived at just conclusions in philosophy and theology; but I have faith in the unchanging love of God, and am persuaded that there will be perpetual advancement in all that constitutes the happiness of a creature bearing the divine image. The immortal spark in man will have endless development; it is the fountain which God fills with Himself.

Having consulted Dr. Quain at different times, I resolved to follow his counsel and go to Homburg to drink the waters there. He told me that I should return a new man; and he was not far from the truth. Accordingly, accompanied by my daughter, I repaired in 1877 to that much-frequented place, and passed through the prescribed course of waters. The benefit derived from the drinking and the pure air was immediate and considerable.

Situated on a spur of the Taunus hills, the place is an outlet to the Frankfurters. And as it is within a tolerably easy distance from London, many English resort to it in the season. I received an impression, which still remains, that the waters have gradually lost some of their power, and are not so efficacious as they were in the days of the gaming-tables.

The year 1878 saw us both again at Homburg, where we stayed from the 14th June till the 5th July, and resolved to pass on to the Engadine. Arrived at Basel, I sought out Professor Kautzsch, with whom I had some correspondence previously respecting an English translation of Gesenius's Hebrew Grammar, which he had edited and improved. No London publisher, however, would undertake the work. The professor lived in the house which Hagenbach occupied for forty-one years; and one room of it was full of MSS. belonging to the University, many of which relate to the time of the Reformation. Among them are letters written by Ulrich von Hutten which Strauss did not consult when he wrote the life of that bold and persecuted scholar. I visited the Museum in which is the University Library, saw De Wette's marble bust, with his portrait, in a room where are upwards of one hundred portraits of professors and other learned men connected with the University. The Münster, with its two imposing towers, is a fine Gothic church of red sandstone, capable of holding five thousand persons. De Wette did not often preach there, but usually in the Elisabethen Kirche, when his discourses on faith and other subjects, though expressed in perspicuous language, must have had too much thought in them to be appreciated. The most popular preacher in the city was Orelli, pastor of another church.

The cloisters adjoining the Münster are interesting. In them are to be seen the grave-stones which cover the bodies of Erasmus, Buxtorf, Wetstein, Œcolampadius, and others. I was afterwards sorry at not having visited the *Gottesacker* to see De Wette's grave. Time did not allow me to call upon Professor Overbeck, the editor of De

Wette's *Commentary on the Acts*, an acute and able critic, who touches with a masterly hand whatever subject he treats of.

We next sojourned at Ragatz, where I sought out Martin Haug's grave, surrounded by those of the unknown, with no marble monument like that of Schelling in the same churchyard. From Chur we went over the Albula Pass to Samaden on the 27th July, but found the village without interest to the traveller. The weather was cold and the walks unsheltered. Having stopped too long in the place, we went to Pontresina, beautifully situated and full of visitors. But though the sun was hot in the day-time, the nights were exceedingly cold, producing much discomfort to the sensitive. The walks about the place, especially that to St Moritz across the woods, form an agreeable outlet to such as cannot climb mountains or glaciers.

From the Engadine we descended to Lake Como over the Maloja Pass, and arrived at Cadenabbia, where my daughter's illness detained us for a time. Leaving Cadenabbia, we journeyed to Varese, remained there in quiet for a short period, and got to Florence by Milan and Bologna on the 16th of October. Here places and churches were revisited, including a second ascent to Fiesole, a visit to the Certosa, and to Torre del Gallo, the watch-tower of the illustrious Galileo. In Florence I was startled by the news of Dr. Willis's death. My dear old friend, who bade me an affectionate farewell when I left London, has gone to his reward with the fragrant reputation of a just, generous, honest, truthful, and conscientious man, whose love of knowledge was strong to the last. Often did we walk together and took sweet counsel in common. I venerate his memory. I had no warmer or more generous friend in London. I call to mind his last visit to 61 Warwick Gardens, Kensington, and his expressed pre-

sentiment at the door that I should see his face no more.
For years he attended my wife, supplied her with medicines,
sat and talked pleasantly, and ever cheered the household
with his conversation. I had been wont to see him and
his bright daughters in the old house at Barnes, with its
large garden behind, where we interchanged ideas on
subjects of common interest. His knowledge of the Bible
was unusual for a layman, his acquaintance with Spinoza's
works extensive; he read, translated, and wrote books,
showing thinking-power of a high order. Sympathetic,
unselfish, beneficent, his ideas and life were pure. Very
highly did I esteem and love him. Having procured a
copy of Servetus's very scarce *Christianismi Restitutio*, his
desire was to reprint it; and he wrote a prospectus, to
which our names were attached, soliciting subscribers.
The project failed to elicit support. This prospectus is
a fair specimen of the doctor's literary learning, and will
repay perusal.

On the 4th December my daughter and I arrived at
Rome, and remained there till the 26th February 1879.
The chief places were revisited and new ones examined.
One of the most interesting to us was the Auditorium of
Maecenas, on the Esquiline, in which it is highly probable
that Horace read some of his poems to a select audience.
I pictured to myself Virgil and other literary friends seated
there listening to the recitations of friends. Dr. Smith
was as kind as he had been before; I visited him in his
cell in the Trastevere, and in the Propaganda. In like
manner, Monsignor Stonor afforded ready help. As to
the Protestants in the eternal city, mostly English and
American, I found them divided much as in their native
countries. Parties belonging to the Church of England
have their separate buildings; Baptists, Wesleyans, Presbyterians, American Congregationalists, have their little con-
venticles, where small congregations assemble. The

Waldensian and Free Italian Churches are also separate. Verily Protestantism is a weak thing in the headquarters of Romanism. Instead of union, it presents dissension. The sectarian spirit thrives, and religion is dwarfed.

To me the two most interesting spots in the imperial city are the room or hall in which St. Paul stood before Nero, on the Palatine; and the rostrum in the Forum, where Cicero pronounced some of his orations. Both are easily identified. In the one, I tried to select the very standing place of the great apostle in presence of the Cæsar to whom he had appealed; in the other, I was pretty sure that I was within a few inches at least of the spot on which the feet of the illustrious orator rested. Alas! memory failed to recall even a sentence of the *pro lege Manilia* there spoken.

Wandering over the gardens of Sallust on the Quirinal, I could not but muse upon the moral reflections prefixed to the history of Catiline, proceeding from a man who had enriched himself by rapine when governor of Numidia. In the language of Gibbon, " he usefully practised the vices which he has so eloquently censured."

I seized the opportunity presented by the 17th February of sending a short paragraph to a London newspaper respecting the burning of Giordano Bruno in the *campo di fiore*. The restless Italian, whom the Inquisition got hold of at last, was sacrificed to Dominican hatred. But there is a *Nemesis*. A monument in honour of the martyr has been set up in the place where he was consigned to the flames, while the Dominicans have been dispossessed of their convent and library in the city. The very room in which Galileo was forced to kneel and recant is no longer in the power of the persecuting order. I had the opportunity of seeing it, with its place of torture, once hidden, whose existence was denied by the Dominicans.

Free thinkers have not had an easy life. Servetus

was burnt at Geneva, chiefly through Calvin's hatred of his opinions; Toland's *Christianity not Mysterious* was burnt by order of the Irish House of Commons, the author escaping seizure by leaving the country; John Biddle died in a noisome prison; and the body of Huss was consumed at the stake. The zeal of the cleric usually outruns that of the magistrate against heresy; and Gibbon may well observe with sorrow, that the three writers of the last age before his, by whom the rights of conscience were so nobly defended, Bayle, Leibnitz, and Locke, were all laymen and philosophers. The theory of toleration may be preached: it is still violated in practice, nourished as it is by the fanaticism of ignorance or the bitterness of orthodoxy.

I had the privilege of hearing Father Mullooly explain again the ornaments, figures, frescoes, and details of the very ancient Church S. Clemente, where he had unearthed two temples below the upper. With great politeness and kindness the prior acceded to my request that he should himself point out all that was to be seen, and on a private day. This he readily did in the presence of four or five whom I had taken the liberty of inviting to accompany myself and daughter. The Irish Dominican did honour to his country, and was deservedly esteemed by all who made his acquaintance. Not long after my return to London, an account of his death appeared in the papers.

Another conspicuous act of kindness was done by Dr. Smith in interpreting the interior of the Catacombs of St. Calixtus. No better expositor of these old subterranean cavities than he could have been had. A few of us followed his patient and minute exposition for hours, and listened to his discoursings. It has not happened to many to enjoy such a treat. During this residence in the imperial city I gave considerable attention to the state of religion there, especially the various manifestations of Protestantism, about which I wrote a few letters addressed to the *London Echo*.

Leaving Rome for Naples, where we inspected the great Museum, we went to Pompeii, and spent a whole day in wandering through the streets and houses of the deserted city. Thence to Capri, where we stayed nearly a fortnight, and returned to Naples. Revisiting Baiæ, Avernus, and Capo Miseno, we went to Salerno and Amalfi, once places of importance, now poor and decayed. I did not meet old Moses in the streets of Salerno, though he was once a noted scholar among his brethren there. Returning through Rome to Florence on the 9th April, we continued in the latter place till the 30th May, and got to Marienbad at the beginning of June. We returned home by Dresden, chiefly from a desire of seeing the Gallery, though the Saxon Switzerland was also an attraction.

Thankful to the Almighty for our preservation after so long an absence from home, for we had left Kensington on the 26th April of the preceding year, my daughter and I rested again on the 28th August 1879. We had been mercifully protected in all our wanderings round this world of care. She had passed through a severe illness and recovered. I felt better in body if not in mind, and had grown weary of iddleness. My life had been almost a blank as far as literature was concerned, though I had access to the best libraries in Italy—except the Vatican, which I never visited again after the refusal of a Jesuit father there to allow me to handle the Vatican MS. on my first visit to Rome. The Minerva Library is open to all without hindrance, because it belongs to the Italian Government.

From Professor Tischendorf

(Translated from the German.)

"LEIPZIG, 11*th* *November* 1869.

"Why am I so long in answering your last welcome letter? For this reason: that I had to sit down and write off at once an answer to the Roman impertinences—a terrible hindrance to a professor already over head and ears in lectures and publications. It has reached to three and a half sheets. A great length, no doubt; but I thought it well to give a proper answer to such stupid, shameless audacity. In ten days or so I shall send you a copy. I am anxious to hear what you will say to it.

"You were on the point of writing an article for the *Athenæum*, on edition 8, Critica major. This pleases me greatly. Respecting the principles which I have followed, and which differ essentially from those of the seventh edition (which meet with severe censure even in England), you will find a clear intimation, to say the least, in the Preface, pp. vii and viii. I have followed Bentley and Lachmann much more closely, but have the exceptional advantage of an incomparably richer apparatus. The application of the principles affects just that part—the Gospels—where the inner criticism, especially where the parallels are concerned, must necessarily be taken into account. I could have wished to give you a fuller account of the many mistakes in Tregelles; but for the present purpose you will have found enough yourself.

.   .   .   .

"I am much interested in Lightfoot's publication of the Clementine Epistles of the Cod. Alex., and regret that he has not sent me a copy. He has certainly made good use of me. I should be glad if you would be so kind as to send me a copy through Williams & Norgate."

From Professor Tischendorf

(Translated from the German.)

"LEIPZIG, 8*th* *May* 1870.

. . . "You have given me a great pleasure by your notice of the *Nov. Test.*, ed. 8, Critica major, and of the *Responsa*. Friend Tauchnitz sent me the article at once, and I read it with great satisfaction. I know that you have written it in *accordance with your own conviction*, hence I must value it the more highly. It is probably the most arduous work of my life, and has cost me the most time, but I myself believe it to be epoch-making in the domain of New Testament textual criticism. I rejoice from my whole heart that you, so able a scholar in this department, should have made my view and my hope your own, and have put it before the great English public with such candour and confidence. You have written with equal judgment and knowledge. That hostile readers will find something to carp at, we cannot doubt; and without noble friends like yourself, how could I work on cheerfully in the face of so much opposition? Having such magnanimous and true friends, however, I can continue my work with pleasure. I am now at the *Catholic Epistles*. As far as the beginning of 1 Peter is already printed. By the end of May I hope to be ready with a new part of twenty sheets (Acts i. 1–1 John iii. 20), that it may be published in the beginning of June. By November I hope to be ready with another part of the same size, and by Easter of 1871 with the conclusion of the text. The Prolegomena, of about twenty-four sheets, will come out, please God, before the end of 1871."

FROM MATTHEW ARNOLD

"*31st October* 1876.

"When I saw your book advertised I marked it for purchase, but I shall be extremely glad to have it as a present from yourself. Your work in the region of Biblical criticism has been unique of its kind in England, and of the greatest value: I am, therefore, deeply gratified by your praise. My task, so far as Biblical criticism is concerned, has been rather that of a populariser than anything else ; for such work to do good, it will always be necessary that more solid and complete work upon the same subject should be behind it. I will certainly suggest to the editor of the *Contemporary Review* to call attention to your volume when it appears : the critic should, I think, be a specialist, which I am not.

"If you have time, I wish you would look at a suggested origin for Matt. xvi. 18, in an article of mine in the forthcoming number of the *Contemporary Review*. The article is my farewell to theology."

CHAPTER X

EUROPEAN TRAVEL

15th December 1879.—To-day is the seventh anniversary of my dear wife's departure, and I cannot but give expression to some of the thoughts which have filled my mind since the month began—the melancholy month that first cast a dark shadow over the path of my life on earth. Oh, how little and empty does this world appear when those we loved most are taken from us! How unsatisfying are the best enjoyments it affords! I feel this deeply every day, and can only cast myself upon the mercy of God, with the sure belief that He orders all things for the good of His creatures, though they walk for a time in darkness, seeking rest to their weary souls without finding it. It is this rest in God that I am daily longing after and thirsting for. May God, my Heavenly Father, give it to me!

I look to God, my help and hope, my rock and my salvation. May He be my guide and comforter ever more! He has supported me amid the severe trials through which I have passed, and will support me to the end. If He has taken away her that I loved most, He has lifted her higher, releasing her from suffering and filling her with joy. Hence I cannot entertain a rebellious thought against His dispensation. But I go about sad and thoughtful in this dreary world, with no bosom companion into whose soul I can pour my best feelings, thinking ever of her with whom I took counsel in times of sorrow and of joy. My wish and prayer is, that I may

imitate her example so far as that example was moulded
and fashioned after the perfect pattern of Christ Jesus.
While on earth she loved and looked to Him; it is my
desire to do the same. The year 1879 is near its close.
What will the next year bring forth? Whatever befalls
me, I know that I am under the moral government of a
merciful God.

On the last day of May 1880,[1] my daughter and I
left London for Marienbad, arriving there on the 3rd of
June. The usual course of water-drinking was finished
by the end of the month, and on the 1st of July we visited
Eger, with its small museum in the Burgermeister's house,
and the dismal room in which Wallenstein was murdered.
The Schloss with its chapel, and the banqueting-room in
which the General's guards were cruelly murdered before
he was himself attacked, were inspected with no pleasant
feelings; for who can think of the treacherous slaughter
without detestation? The Scotch and Irish dragoons
who were the perpetrators disgraced their countries; as
multitudes have done since by hiring themselves to the
unchristian business of war.

Passing through Munich, we arrived at Partenkirchen,
and rested in that beautifully situated village of the
Bavarian Tyrol, making excursions to the Eibsee and
Badersee, Mittenwald, and the Barmsee. These are
beautiful spots. We had a mind to stop at the quiet
hotel beside the Badersee, and remain in the secluded
nook for a week; but it was full. Bound for Oberammergau, we arrived at the village on the 10th of July,
and witnessed the *Passion-play* next day. This dramatic
exhibition was solemn and impressive to us both. At times
it was very pathetic, so that some of the spectators wept.
The peasants went through their parts with the ability of

[1] In September of this year Dr. Davidson took up his abode at
14 Belsize Crescent, Hampstead. —ED.

practised actors, especially the representatives of Christ, Peter, and Judas. Whatever brings the closing scenes of Jesus' life on earth with vivid reality before the eyes must impress the spectator, raising his thoughts to the loving Father who sent His Son to be the life of the world. The feelings of him who could look upon the *Passion-play* without emotion have little tenderness. Horace rightly says :—

> " What we hear
> With weaker passion will affect the heart,
> Than when the faithful eye beholds the part."

Leaving Partenkirchen on the 13th, we journeyed through scenery of surpassing loveliness to Lermoos, thence to Nassereit over the Fern Pass ; to Imst, Landeck, and Bludenz.

The journey between the last two villages is long and wearisome, but the scenery of the Vorarlberg is grand. Having got to Constance, we saw the spot where Huss was burnt, which is well marked, as it deserves to be. I thought it significant that the street through which one goes to see the simple monument is named Paradise Street, and was glad to observe another called after the Reformer. The memory of the martyr dwells in the city where he suffered. The railway from Constance to Carlsruhe passes through the finest scenery of the Black Forest, and Triberg was viewed with longing desire to stay there. From Carlsruhe we travelled onward through Heidelberg, Darmstadt, Köln, Vliessingen, and Queenboro', arriving in London on the 25th July 1880. Carlsruhe had lost Ullmann, who did not shine as prelate. He should have remained at Heidelberg, where he had long lectured and written. Circumstances have a wonderful effect upon opinions, and the professor furnishes a good example of it. The editions of his treatise *On the Sinlessness of Jesus*, from the fourth onward, published while he was at Heidelberg, explained the narrative of

the Temptation as Neander does; that is, that the thing
was merely internal, but clothed with an historico-symbolic
dress.   This was changed for the worse in an edition
issued after his Carlsruhe experiences (the 7th).   I talked
with Tholuck about the alteration, both of us disapproving
of it; for I need hardly say that my friend was too
enlightened to explain the narrative in the old orthodox
fashion.   During the few years of Ullmann's residence at
Halle he appeared as the strenuous advocate of professorial
freedom, in opposition to Hengstenberg's denunciations of
Wegscheider and Gesenius.   Governments are more liberal
than individual theologians or committees in their dealings
towards professors; and though despots commit arbitrary
acts,—as did Frederick William the Third, who, to his eternal
disgrace, deposed De Wette from his professorship at
Berlin for a cause which bespoke right feeling on the part
of him who wrote the letter to Sand's mother,—yet they
are less cruel than corporations with their want of a
conscience.   Wolf the philosopher was honourably re-
instated in office at Halle by Frederick the Second; the
authorities of King's College, London, deprived the Rev.
F. D. Maurice of his lectureship for denying the doctrine
of everlasting punishment.

Darmstadt reminded me of Strauss, who lived there for
years, patronised by the Princess Alice.   This noble lady
read his books without aversion to their views; and under
her auspices he delivered the lectures on *Voltaire* that
make an excellent volume.

On the appearance of the Revised New Testament in
1881, I reviewed it in the *Athenæum*, but could not get
space or freedom enough there to descant upon the
translation of Matt. vi. 13.   I therefore wrote in the
Echo, first briefly; and afterwards at some length, by desire
of the editor.   The old version needs another revision, the
present not being entirely satisfactory.   There were too

many about it, and orthodox opinion prevailed. How could it be otherwise, with a bishop at the head of the company, supported by dignitaries and deans?

The year 1881 was spent in much anxiety as well as in study: the one in consequence of the illness of my daughter, the other from preparing a second edition of the *Introduction to the New Testament*. The latter had occupied most of the years 1879, 1880, and was continued till the volumes were put to press. Looking upon this as my best work, and desirous to improve it as much as I could, I tried to bring it near my ideal, and make it superior to any existing one on the subject. Hence the first was almost rewritten. Permanent value, I fondly think, belongs to the book, so that it may not perhaps be superseded in the English language for a long time. Of course it has been assailed by the orthodox; but that is of little account. The only question is, are the results correct? It is easy to denounce, but harder to refute. Dean Milman was pleased to say that my *Old Testament Introduction* is an honest book; I believe that the present one is not less so. Neither of them is the expression of a stagnant Protestantism which struggles to remain where it is. The organs of religious sects are alive to my latitudinarianism, and use strong language against it. But the earnest latitudinarianism which excludes indifference deserves praise rather than censure, however narrow-minded zealots may decry it. It is attached to the persons of illustrious divines in the Church of England, and belongs to not a few in secret. The name, indeed, has a bad odour, and names weigh with the ignorant. They are useful stones to pelt opponents with.

John Wesley expressed latitudinarian opinions. He would not deny that Mr. Firmin (an Arian) was a pious man, "although his notions of the Trinity were quite erroneous." Of Marcus Antoninus he makes no doubt "but this is one of those ' many,'" who " shall come from the east and the west and sit down with Abraham, Isaac, and Jacob," while " the children of the kingdom," nominal Christians, are " shut out." He conceives that no man living has a right to sentence all the heathen and Mohammedan world to damnation. " It is far better," in his opinion, " to leave them to Him that made them," and who is " the Father of the spirits of all flesh," " who is the God of the heathen as well as the Christian, and who hateth nothing that He hath made." He also quotes with approbation an author who says, " what the heathen call reason, Solomon wisdom, St. Paul grace, St. John love, Luther faith, Fenelon virtue, is all one and the same thing: the light of Christ shining in different degrees under different dispensations." Elsewhere Wesley writes: " I believe the merciful God regards *the lives and tempers of men* more than their ideas. I believe He *respects the goodness of the heart* rather than the clearness of the head." How different the tone of these expressions from the dictum of the Westminster divines to which all orthodox Presbyterians subscribe: " much less can men not professing the Christian religion be saved in any other way whatsoever, be they ever so diligent to frame their lives according to the light of nature and the law of that religion they do profess." These divines run against the apostolic assertion in the Epistle to the Romans (ii. 14, 15). They also contradict Baxter's just and charitable statement that the heathen have power to repent and believe. It is wrong to blacken human nature, even for the purpose of exalting the Bible; and Hooker is right in saying, " God's very Commandments in some kind, as, namely, his precepts comprehended in the law of nature, may otherwise be known than only by Scripture, and that to do them, howsoever we know them, must needs be acceptable in His sight"; though this disagrees

with the articles of the Anglican Church and with the
Westminster Confession of Faith. But it is common to
depart from Articles to which one has subscribed, when the
intellect gets beyond the trammels within which it put
itself at first. In such cases, the outgrowth may be
praised ; not the state of the conscience.

Instead of vilifying human nature, saying that it is
" utterly indisposed, disabled, and made opposite to all good
and wholly inclined to all evil,"—whoever finds not within
him something that attaches itself to the moral law demand-
ing the exercise of the will, has departed from his better self
and from the receptivity of what would restore him to the
natural perfection of his being. That something, by whatever name it is called,—reason, conscience, the moral sense,
—is the foundation on which revealed religion rests. Natural
religion should not be impugned, else revelation, which is
the main part of it, embodying its abstract principles in
perspicuity and efficiency, unavoidably suffers. To injure
the basis is to injure the structure. Though human
nature has an inherent tendency to corruption, it has still
the power of choosing between good and evil, and is capable
of compliance with the moral law.

A comparative estimate of the internal and external
revelations involves the question at issue between deists and
the defenders of Christianity. The former in past times
discredited revealed religion, subordinating it unduly to
the internal truth inscribed on the human mind, and argu-
ing that it is not certain because it depends on written
tradition. In this way the necessity for Revelation was
minimised or done away. The advocates of revealed
religion depreciated man's ability to repent and worship God
acceptably. They decried reason and vilified human nature.
In thus exaggerating internal or external truth, parties must
disagree. The evidence of natural religion is universal,
and therefore stronger than that of Christianity. Natural

9

religion is sufficient for man's salvation if he could follow it purely. But his state is such that he seldom does so. The hindrances are so great as to put the desired end almost out of reach. Hence an external Revelation was needful — a clearer and more efficacious publication of natural religion. The practical inadequacy of the one led to the introduction of the other. The state of the heathen world shows the desirability of an economy of Grace, that mankind may be prevented from sinking into a barbarism which obliterates all evidence of the divine image within. The blessings brought by an uncorrupted Christianity are incalculable by the side of the inner light shining dimly in a sinful world. Christianity reveals the will of God more clearly, presenting additional motives to the pursuance of a good life, influences which do not infringe the law of nature, the rule of right within, but only lay man under new obligations to attend to that law honestly. So far from depressing or superseding the authoritative principle of conscience which God has implanted, external Revelation imparts to it light and force, bringing out its native tendency into broader view, and facilitating its exercise in harmony with that tendency.

What is Latitudinarianism? It is the catholic spirit which Christ Himself enjoined and exemplified. It is the religion of tolerance and love, not of dogma and damnation. It is the religion which asserts, with Chillingworth, that "God will be satisfied if we receive *any degree of light* which makes us leave the works of Darkness and walk as children of the Light." It is the religion which echoes the sentiments of Jeremy Taylor and Cudworth, the former of whom affirms: "a holy life will make our belief holy, if we consult not humanity and its imperfections in the choice of our religion, but search for truth without designs save only of acquiring heaven, and then be as careful to preserve charity as we were to get a point of faith; I am much persuaded we shall find out more truths by this means ;

or, however, which is the main of all, we shall be secured though we miss them"; and the latter: " if we did but heartily comply with Christ's commandments, and purge our hearts from all gross and sensual affections, we should not then look about for truth wholly without ourselves, and enslave ourselves to the dictates of this and that teacher, and hang upon the lips of men ; but we should find the great eternal God inwardly teaching our souls, and continually instructing us more and more in the mysteries of His will." Religion is a spiritual operation in the human soul, an internal revelation. It is the tuning of the divine instrument whose notes speak of the Eternal.

But it is not the religion of Puritan exclusiveness, limiting salvation to those who hold what is called " sound doctrine," and anathematising by word and deed the advocates of rational opinions. It is not the religion which hugs a long creed, and shelters unchristian conduct beneath it. It is not the religion that puts authority above reason, the Bible above conscience, an external rule above the law written in the heart. It is not the religion that has ready names wherewith to bespatter non-traditionalists, calling them latitudinarians, rationalists, sceptics, free - thinkers, infidels, deists. It is not the religion of men who desire to have God to themselves, hating and persecuting one another for God's sake. It is not the religion which makes God require what man is by nature unable to do. The spirit of love, *that alone is religion*, carrying with it belief in the universality of the divine love, in the innocency of intellectual error, and accounting badness of heart the greatest heresy. Not till Christianity be fully recognised as a *divine* life, apart from its corruptions by interpreters, disputers, and defenders, will it be accepted by rational inquirers as eminently adapted to promote the happiness of man.

The second edition of the *Introduction to the New Testament* was published in January 1882. At the end of

June in the same year, I set out for Contrexéville in the Vosges, accompanied by my daughter, having heard and read of its wonderful springs, whose efficacy in curing certain disorders is well known in France. At Amiens we stayed to see its great cathedral; but hastened from Paris to our place of destination. More than seven weeks were spent in Contrexéville, during which drinking of the waters was kept up regularly in the early mornings. Returning by Dover, we went to St. Leonard's, and after remaining there for a time, I came back to London at the close of September, leaving my daughter behind. In the month of October was published *The Doctrine of Last Things contained in the New Testament, compared with the Notions of the Jews and the Statements of Church Creeds.* Small as this book is, it cost much thought, especially "the concluding observations." It may be that eschatology is the last subject on which I shall be allowed to write, for my years exceed threescore and ten. The close of life is best given to meditation upon God—His wondrous ways and wondrous mercy in the mission of His Son. Above all, it should be a season of lively faith, hope, and love centred in Christ, the image of the Invisible. Away from the jarrings of theologians, heedless of the shafts of bigotry,[1] which play their part in the world's arena outside God's Church, one should dwell with religion that eschews bitterness, breathes love to God and man, sanctifies the heart and life, tarries with the lowly. Oh that I had more of its presence and peace!

The following poetical effusion, written by De Wette

---

[1] Professor Hassencamp thought: *procul a theologis, procul a fulmine.* Hume says of Cromwell, "he found that very little policy was requisite to foment quarrels among theologians." Not till the professors of Christianity show its sanctifying power upon their tempers and lives will they demonstrate its heavenly origin. The stumbling-blocks of priestly additions and superstitions will not be rolled away till its *true essence* comes into prominence.

only four months before his decease (1849 A.D.), and found among his manuscripts, is so applicable to *my* situation and feelings that I cannot forbear transcribing it:—

> "Nicht weit ist's mehr zum Ziele hin,
> Mit Wehmuth blick' ich auf mein Leben.
> Was nehm' ich mit mir als Gewinn?
> Wie eitel war mein Thun und Streben!
>
> Mit Wahrheitsdurst, rastlosem Fleiss
> Hab' ich der Forschung Werk getrieben:
> Wie wenig ist's nun, was ich weiss,
> Wie viel ist dunkel mir geblieben!
>
> Den Samen hab' ich ausgesaet:
> Doch wo ist nun die reife Ernte?
> Wie selten das man recht versteht,
> Und recht benutzet, was man lernte!
>
> Ich fiel in eine wirre Zeit:
> Die Glaubens-Eintracht war vernichtet:
> Ich mischte mich mit in den Streit,
> Umsonst, ich hab' ihn nicht geschlichtet.
>
> Für Freiheit und Gerechtigkeit
> Ward und wird noch der Kampf gestritten—
> Mir Herzens-Angelegenheit,
> Gern hätt' ich mehr dafür gelitten.
>
> Noch ist errungen nicht der Sieg,
> Die Waffe klirrt, Parteien toben:
> Wenn auch einmal das Gute stieg,
> Stets ist das Schlechte wieder oben.
>
> Für Lieb' und Freundschaft schlug mein Herz
> Zum Schönen, Edlen hingezogen:
> Ich hatte Freude, mehr noch Schmerz:
> Des Glückes Traum hat mir gelogen.
>
> Und dennoch, mein Gewinn ist gross!
> Gerettet hab' ich mir den *Glauben*;
> Ich rang von Wahn und Trug ihn los,
> Der Zweifel kann mir ihn nicht rauben.
>
> Des Glaubens holde Schwester steht
> Die *Hoffnung*, freudig mir zur Seite:
> Sie weissagt, was kein Aug' erspäht,
> Den Sieg, die Ruhe nach dem Streite.

> Was alle Weisheit dieser Zeit,
> Was List, Gewalt nicht kann erringen,
> Der *Glaube* wird Gerechtigkeit,
> Freiheit und Glück und Frieden bringen.
>
> Was Glaub' erkennt für alle Zeit,
> Was Hoffnung schaut als künft'ge Blüthe,
> Das lebt der *Lieb'* in Wirklichkeit
> Im edlen menschlichen Gemüthe.
>
> Im Alter ist erloschen nicht,
> Nur reiner glüht ihr heilig Feuer:
> Und mit der schönen Seele flicht
> Den Bund sie inniger und treuer.
>
> Sie liebt, was in sich rein und schön,
> Sie liebt in Freude wie in Trauer,
> Sie liebt, was nicht kann untergeh'n :
> D'rum kennt sie nicht des Todes Schauer."

The two men whom I have most missed in London are Baron Bunsen and the Rev. Dr. Cureton, both scholars of large sympathy and noble tendencies, though widely different in the character of their studies. To me their loss is incalculably great. Reflective and tolerant, possessing extensive learning and high attainments, they adorned the spheres in which they moved, and left a blank in the metropolis which has not been filled. In all questions, moral or religious, their influence was in favour of liberty. Though disagreeing with various opinions entertained by both, I esteemed them no less on that account ; and I do not think they felt any dislike to me because I held views which they rejected. They were honest seekers after truth : what greater praise can be given them?

27th November 1882.—I do not often meddle in political affairs, though I cannot but form definite opinions respecting them as they pass in review before the public eye. Sympathising in the policy of the party called *Liberals*, but regretting that their reforms do not go far or fast enough, I am not blind to their mistakes. The Liberals are better in opposition than in office. When in power, they proceed too much on Conservative lines. They are strongly infected with Whiggism—a thing that should have been left behind long ago. Little radical change will come forth from a Cabinet in which the principles of the old Whigs make themselves felt. Mr. Gladstone, the greatest statesman of the time, has carried measures of general utility, and might have carried more. But he is not thoroughgoing. No great reforms will be got from any other than a Radical ministry—no considerable reduction of the public expenditure, no cutting down of the army; no curbing of the military spirit. The active promotion of peace abroad as well as at home ; the lessening of intemperance, an evil which hangs heavily upon the nation ; the abolition of the House of Lords, and rigid economy in all departments of the State from the highest to the lowest, especially the former, are reserved for a future ministry composed of Radical members. Mr. Gladstone deserves the thanks of Englishmen for many things which he has done to promote the people's welfare. He has left the stamp of his comprehensive mind upon the legislation of Queen Victoria's reign. But he has made some grievous mistakes. A stringent Coercion Bill for Ireland passed this year is a disgrace to his ministry. What Ireland wants is not Coercion Acts, of which she has had enough, but fair and full justice, a thing she has never had under English rule. She wants self-government. The land should belong to the people, and not to a few landlords, who are absentees, spending the money paid by the poor tenants, in England or the Continent. The way in which much of the property in Ireland was acquired by the English will not bear examination. Thus in the severe protectorate of Cromwell—severe and cruel towards the conquered country—five millions of acres were divided partly among the adventurers who had advanced money to the Parliament, and partly among the English soldiers who had arrears due to them. Well might Hume say, that "examples of a more sudden and violent change of property are scarcely to be found in any history." The history of Ireland is a blot upon English government that can never be effaced; and a retribution will assuredly overtake the perpetrators of wrong, if not in themselves, in their descendants or representatives.

With these sentiments, I cannot but look favourably upon the Home Rulers in the House of Commons, whose patriotism puts to shame the ignoble conduct of the so-called Liberal members whom the North of Ireland sends to Parliament.

It is grievous to see the facility with which our rulers, Liberal and Conservative, go to war for the sake of enlarging an empire too extensive already; or oftener, for the sake of gain. They do not shrink from aggressive war. The Egyptian campaign, undertaken without just cause in this year, must be condemned by every true disciple of Christ. But it was popular, as *every* war seems to be: to me a manifest symptom of national degeneracy; for the Bible says that "*righteousness* exalteth a nation." A standing army will ruin a nation sooner or later.

CHAPTER XI

SORROWFUL RETROSPECT

15th December 1882.—Little did I think when my dear wife left me ten years ago that I should be continued so long after her. Yet so it is, and the sad anniversary of her death has come round again with melancholy recollections. The dull, dark day without adds to the gloom within. I am still a lonely old man, without a bosom friend to whom I might pour out my feelings of pleasure or of sadness. Alas for the departed joys that never can return! Sorrowful memories are the usual inheritance of the bereaved. But mourning time does not last for ever: that of reunion is nigh.

Though not idle, I have not been able to do much work in the past year. The preparation of my little volume on eschatology for the press occupied me much. As it is about the *last things*, it brought vividly to my mind the future world and the reunion of friends. I can never think that broken heart-ties will remain so for ever; and I therefore cherish, with deeper and deeper conviction of its truth, the idea that the love once existing between the departed one and myself will be renewed in a pure, intensified, and imperishable form in the spiritual world.

So my dear spouse has had the wondrous progression of ten years in happiness and knowledge! That space may seem insignificant to an inhabitant of the eternal mansions in our Father's house, but to a poor denizen of the earth like myself it is considerable. Does she expect me soon to join her? Oh, how I long to know what are her feelings towards me and the loved ones who are still here; what are her relations to the three sons in the same abodes! But speculation on such themes should not be entertained; it is idle and unavailing. Let me only have more faith and a livelier hope—more preparedness for the realms of light. Should I be spared to see another anniversary, let me be found with greater love to God and man. I am conscious of having done little good in the past year; and with my small abilities as well as opportunities, I *can* do little, strive as I may; but I pray that I may not go back, or become less meet for the inheritance of the saints above. In the meantime, I have still the consolation of retaining with me my daughter, who will, I trust, be restored to perfect health in due time. I thank and praise God for blessings still enjoyed, however much I mourn the loss of her who left me solitary indeed.

30th December.—I have been thinking much of late on the evidences of Christianity, and believe that the internal are the stronger. I should rest this religion on its adaptation to the wants of human nature and its own intrinsic excellence. It is capable of reforming, renewing, and elevating man, presenting such motives as lead by natural consequence to right conduct. Above all, it shows the example of a Perfect Man, a sinless Being, to follow and imitate whom is true life. He that came into the world to save the ignorant and erring from sin, exemplified in His person the perfection of goodness, that they might be lifted up to the same standard. The external evidences are. less valid. Prophecy and miracles are now discredited, and he who bases religion upon them acts unwisely in regard to opponents in making it more vulnerable. The credibility of the narrative given of events is not confirmed by the concurrent evidence of contemporary witnesses. It is reported, indeed, that the events took place before the eyes of an intelligent nation, but a generation passed before the alleged facts could be tested by a learned public. Christianity bears its own self-evidence, appealing to and going hand in hand with the part of human nature which has the clearest stamp of a divine origin; as a moral and spiritual religion it is adapted to every nation and time; but historic considerations and traditional expositions often weaken its native strength. Let it be received as a moral religion, and its evidence is impregnable.

1st January 1883.—The new year has dawned gloomily. May I be better and wiser in it than I was in 1882. The past twelve months were not without their anxieties and fears, their troubles and disquietudes, but blessings far outweighed these light afflictions. I look toward the future with hope; and whatever may happen, I know that my Heavenly Father does not leave any of His creatures to sink into darkness, but brings them forth at last into the full light of day. Though clouds obscure their vision here, the moral Governor of the world will make all things manifest in the future, and universal peace pervade His limitless domain.

I arrived at the conclusion long ago, that though War is consonant with the Jewish Scriptures, it is opposed to the spirit of the New Testament, and to the teaching of Jesus in particular. During my Manchester abode I was asked by the Peace Society to deliver a Lecture on the subject in London. But the sentiments expressed in it did not please some in the religious body with which I was connected; and a speech of mine at one of the Society's annual meetings gave great offence to the editors of the religious press which represented the Independents at that time. As my views about war have not changed, I thought the old Lecture might be useful if printed, and it appeared accordingly in the *Homilist* for February 1883. Parts of it have been revised and altered; the substance is unchanged. The wars of our country in the Crimea against Russia, and in Egypt against the Egyptians, were unjust and antichristian. Yet they were approved and applauded by the ministers of religion generally. How often are the precepts of Christ ignored by those who are called His disciples !

In the month of June my daughter and I paid another visit to Marienbad, drinking the waters as before, and conforming to medical directions. On the way to it we saw Nuremberg, and spent an entire day in inspecting the chief places of interest belonging to the quaint old town—its museum, where there is an excellent portrait of Schopenhauer ; its churches ; and its fort or palace, from which there is an extensive and fine view of the surrounding country. On our return, we went from Rotterdam to the Hague, where the two most notable things are the Royal Picture Gallery and the bronze statue of Spinoza. The latter is not in a good place, but it is opposite the house in which he lived. The philosopher's grave was pointed out in the Nieuve Kerk, or " new church," under the pulpit, where there is nothing to distinguish it, so that no stranger would think of the spot as that in which his body was laid. The memory of the great thinker does not seem to be reverenced at the Hague, else his tomb would have some suitable inscription.

During the year I began a course of regular reading every morning in the Old Testament. For this purpose I chose Genesis, carefully perusing ten verses of the original text ; and am now, in the middle of December, in the Book of Numbers. This practice leads to familiarity with the Hebrew. In the same way, I have perused a portion of the *Meditations of Marcus Aurelius* every morning. The Greek of the emperor is not always easy. There is a studied brevity in these memoirs which contributes to their obscurity. Written as they were during the brief intervals of a campaign, and for the satisfaction of the emperor himself, they were not revised or corrected. The younger Casaubon might well say "the work is not only the most excellent, but the most obscure of all the remains of antiquity." But I have had good helps, chief among them the edition of the learned Gataker, whose notes show an extent of reading which would be pronounced uncommon even in the present day. I have also by my side Jeremy Collier's translation, or rather paraphrase, with the later and better one of Graves. Both are very free. After I get through the twelve books of the original, I intend to revise the whole by means of George Long's translation, which is said to be the best.

1st January 1884.—The first thought that rises in the mind at the beginning of a new year is thankfulness to God for His sparing mercy. " Bless the Lord, O my soul, and forget not all His benefits." . . . May no unforeseen calamity fall upon me or mine during the present year! May we be guarded and guided by our Heavenly Father, living godly, righteous, and sober lives, to the glory of His name!

26th February.—I finished to-day the reading of *Marcus Aurelius's Meditations*, and cannot but admire the purity and nobility of the sentiments expressed. Yet how inferior are they to the Sermon on the Mount! The emperor has only one allusion to the Christians, showing his total ignorance of their principles, and speaking of their obstinacy, that is, their adherence to the new religion amid persecution and the horrors of the cruel death which they had to undergo.

The reader is apt to grow weary of the repetitions in these Meditations, and the careless way in which the sentences are constructed. The text is undoubtedly corrupt in many places, and can only be corrected by conjecture, in which Gataker indulges often enough. Having procured

Long's translation, I found it faithful and excellent. It is as literal as it can be in giving the sense of the original, and the notes are always pertinent. It is matter of regret that the emperor did not revise the *Meditations*. But we should recollect the circumstances in which they were committed to writing. The author was in a strange land, carrying on war against supposed enemies, and warfare is not conducive to quiet reflection.

On the 8th May, in the *Christian Register* of Boston, the following appeared :—

" The Bishop of Durham, who is considered by many of his brethren in the Church of England the most learned of her sons, writes as follows in his Commentary on the Epistles of St. Paul to the Colossians and Philemon : 'The Church needed a long education before she was fitted to be the expositor of the true apostolic doctrine. A conflict of more than two centuries with Gnostics, Ebionites, Sabellians, Arians, supplied the necessary discipline. The true successors of the apostles, in this respect, are not the Fathers of the second century, but the Fathers of the third and fourth centuries.'"

This statement seems to me entirely incorrect. I am unable to believe that the fathers of the fourth century were better representatives of apostolic doctrine than those of the second. Neither, indeed, can the latter, men like Tertullian, Justin Martyr, and Irenæus, be accepted as correct expositors of the original doctrine, since their sentiments were taken out of the New Testament writings without proper discernment of the discordant views or relative value of those writings. The fourth century forsook the apostolic teaching for a metaphysical system with a controversial aim—anti-Gnostic, anti-Arian, anti-Sabellian. The process to which the primitive teaching was subjected abolished its original simplicity, when men put Scripture statements and their inferences from them on the same footing, ignoring all the while the dogmatic differences of the New Testament authors. As soon as we get beyond the middle of the second century, we see how imperfectly the fathers apprehended the sacred writers, while they pursued the idea of a catholic doctrine and a Catholic Church, the one introducing superstitions alien to the spirit of the apostles, the other burdening Christianity with a worldly organisation. Thus the Ebionite or original aspect of Christ's Person retired behind the advanced Logos doctrine of the Fourth Gospel, and the latter itself was outstripped amid the straining to suppress heresy. The creed of the fourth century cannot be taken as a fair outcome of the teaching peculiar to the first—not merely because the latter did not present one uniform type, but because the influences under which that creed was formed were adverse to the conservation of the ethical element. Uncritical times deteriorated the common belief, and hardened it with the crust of baseless traditions. The Nicene Creed marks no good advance upon the so-called Apostles'; and the latter itself, with its apparent simplicity, deviates from the teaching of the first century—notably from that of the original apostles. Let one compare the extended creeds of the fourth and following century with the doctrine of Christ Himself, and he will see how the latter recedes from view, more importance being attached to the Pauline, which is even set above the Johannine. If there be one apostolic doctrine, it is Jewish Christianity; and that was not the faith of the fourth-century fathers, having been supplanted by Paulinism. The first phase of Christianity passed away. Imperfectly reflecting the essence and aim of Christ's ethical teaching, it seemed unsuited to the Gentile world. The teaching of Paul, who broke away from Judaism, though he could not entirely disengage himself from it, took hold of the minds of men as if it satisfied their spiritual wants, though its leading principle readily tends to lessen the value of good works. It is true that the creed of the fourth and fifth centuries has fastened itself upon the Christian world, but its propositions and distinctions have done little to make that world resemble the Master's spirit. Anti-heretical definitions of His Person occupy the room of moral precepts.

Let it not be thought that I am opposed to the doctrine of development, which is only that of progress in the human race,—the doctrine of man's increasing elevation in the scale of being. Like other sciences, theology is progressive. What I object to is the assumption that the fathers of later centuries developed the doctrine of the first rightly, and are therefore its true exponents. On the contrary, they misapprehended what they appealed to. The Churches, they say, had the rule of faith which was delivered by the apostles who received it from Christ; and it was handed down through their successors, the bishops,— a hypothesis resting on a foundation of sand. What is the rule of faith in question? It is embodied in the early Symbols, such as that of the Roman Church, appearing in a less compact form in Tertullian and Irenæus. But it disagrees in some particulars with the views of the original apostles, and adds to them, besides, what is not in the New Testament at all, namely, belief in the resurrection of the *flesh*. The Valentinians were more correct in asserting " the resurrection from the dead." When we read in Irenæus strong expressions about the tradition of the apostles being one and the same, having been delivered to all the Churches and religiously preserved by them in its integrity, it is easy to see that the good bishop's imagination supplants his judgment. Zeal against heretics drives him to the assumption of an opposing bulwark summarily constructed and extravagantly vaunted.

Tertullian's judgment is no better. He speaks of one Church founded by the apostles, whence all come, and into which they resolve themselves. Unity, fraternity, identity of doctrine, mark the Churches. The African father is as vehement as the Gallican against heresy, and his assertions about having the one apostolic faith are still more rash. With him, as with Irenæus, the Roman Church has the greatest authority, because of its being founded (so it was supposed) by Peter and Paul.

The substance of the creed which has dominated Christendom originated in the latter half of the second century, and was subsequently enlarged. Its framers must be judged by the rules of evidence, not by the mere age to which they belonged, or by the sanctity of their lives. A century intervened between them and the apostles, during which tradition had free scope. Even to John, the other apostles must have appeared in hazy retrospect during his latest years. The fathers of the second century built upon the Synoptists, St. Paul, and oral tradition, having materials both genuine and unhistorical; but they built without much discernment, and dealt with things in the mass, hastily throwing doctrines back into the time and authorship of the apostles. Their task was a difficult one, and it was accomplished not wholly without success; but the result needs rectification at the present day. Above all, what really belongs to the Judæo-Christian teaching of the primitive apostles should be separated from the Pauline or semi-Pauline, and this again from the so-called Johannine of the Fourth Gospel.

The education which the Church went through in the first two centuries, so far from being salutary, was in many respects injurious. The raising of dogma above ethics, of creed above conduct, of theological propositions above life, cannot be commended. The third and fourth centuries departed still further from the pure precepts of Christ Himself; and if the modern Church is to be regenerated, she must revert to the teaching of Him who spake as never man spake.

10

I attach importance to these remarks because there is a strong tendency among those who call themselves evangelical to rely upon the fourth-century creeds as the best exponents of New Testament doctrine. And the orthodox Dr. Lightfoot is looked up to in his own Church as the champion of the truth. Yet in his encounter with the author of *Supernatural Religion*, he merely picked a few holes in his arguments, without overthrowing the main positions.

15th July—15th August.—After an absence of eleven years from Ireland, I paid a short visit to my native place, Kellswater, where a sister still lives, but in the enjoyment of poor health. I looked forward to the visit without any pleasurable anticipations, well knowing the changes I should witness, the strange faces about to meet me, a new generation, the absence of such charms as youthful feeling once threw around the humble dwellings, and simple people where I once strayed all unconscious of the future. The lowly schoolhouse I first frequented is demolished, the roads are altered; the holy well which I passed daily, drinking of its pure water, the sobered inhabitants of the cottages, the absence of dance and song, no violin player, the footsteps of poverty—all these pressed upon the spirit. A few old men recognised me. Some of my playmates were in the poorhouse at Ballymena, dragging out the residue of their days. The contrast between the old picture recalled by a glowing imagination, and the prosaic objects around, was sombre indeed. Where were the cheerful voices of the women at their spinning-wheels singing the songs of Burns? Where were the weavers whose looms rattled with the sound of the shuttle? It is true that the town of Ballymena has increased fourfold, and that its business has multiplied in proportion; but unknown dealers occupy the places of the old ones, the Celtic population has decreased, and with it the people's vivacity. I was told that the young men and strong generally go to America, to seek what they cannot find at home. The country, alas, is still rent with party divisions. Catholicism and Protestantism clash bitterly with one another. Races are antagonistic. Presbyterians are as much opposed to Roman Catholics as ever, having reached little breadth of view or of charity. And their preachers repeat the old Calvinistic dogmas, the people liking to hear them. How hard it is to cast off the shell with which the surroundings of youth and manhood encrust the mind, closing it up against advancing light. As I strayed amid scenes once so bright to the lightsome heart, I could not avoid repeating to myself the words of the poet—

> " Thou minds me o' departed joys,
> Departed—never to return !"

CHAPTER XII

15th December 1884.—Another anniversary of the day on which my dear wife left me desolate. . . . Spared as I have been through another year, I lift up my heart in gratitude to God, whose mercies cannot be numbered; and praise Him who rules over all, and appoints us our times. I am unable to say that I have done much work in the past year, though I have not been idle. I have carried on the reading of the Hebrew Scriptures, and passed through the Pentateuch as well as the books of Joshua and Judges. Leaving the historical parts, I am now in Isaiah. Along with the Hebrew, I have read a portion of the Syriac Testament every day. After going through the first two Gospels, I turned to the portions printed in Nestle's *Syriac Grammar*; but purpose to leave some pieces there unread, and return to the Scriptures, which give me most pleasure. I have also revised, corrected, and improved parts of my *Introduction to the New Testament,*—a work which has, I hope, some permanent value, though its sale is slow.

The children that have been taken away years ago are safe in the arms of divine love; and about *them* their earthly father can have none other feeling than that of satisfaction. Are they and their mother together, if heaven be a place! Do they know my thoughts about them! Ye blessed ones, ye left me in deep distress and passed into a state of pure enjoyment! And thou beatified spirit with whom in the body I took sweet counsel, dost thou know where and how I am now: a solitary old man lingering on earth amid a people whose religion is so unlike that of Jesus! Yet the Lord reigns on high, and His purposes are purposes of love. May my faith in Him grow and strengthen till it becomes fruition! I commit myself to His guidance, and know I am safe. Amen.

1st January 1885.—Blessed be God for the light of a new day and a new year! Blessed be our Heavenly Father, who preserved and sustained me through the past year! His goodness and sparing mercy are unceasing. May I live in a manner more conformable to His will throughout the present year, should I be on earth till the close of it. Strength gradually fails, but God is my strength and shield at all times.

2nd April.—Finished to-day the reading of *Isaiah*. After going regularly through the Pentateuch, Joshua, and Judges, taking a small portion every morning, I turned to Isaiah and perused it in the same manner. The prophetic utterances in the second part of the book are sublime and far-reaching, expressing the hopes and aspirations of an inspired prophet at the time of the exile in Babylon. Difficulties of language and construction occur in different places; but with the masterly commentary of Gesenius and that of Ewald, the sense is tolerably plain. It is elevating to converse with the old Hebrew prophets, and to catch their spirit.

Yesterday I also finished the perusal of *John's Gospel* in the old Syriac version, having read a few verses every morning. It is interesting to peruse this early translation of the New Testament, but it adds little to the interpretation of the original Greek. If we had the Syriac text as it was at first, considerable light would be thrown upon the Greek.

Melancholy news arrived this morning, announcing the death of my old pupil and valued friend Alexander Stewart, whose unvarying kindness, generosity, and hospitality must be ever remembered. He was a truly good man, sincere, upright, without guile. What a loss! Alas, one not to be repaired. My ever-to-be-deplored friend John Walker of Bowdon and my true companion Alexander Stewart leave a blank in my heart that will not be filled in this world. But they live and are happy—taken from the evils and uncertainties of an earthly existence to the felicities of eternity. The memory of the just is blessed. Farewell, amiable friends; we shall see one another again.

7th May.—Have parted with Professor Pfleiderer of Berlin, whose acquaintance I made during his sojourn of five weeks in London. We talked over together at different times the greater number of the difficulties inherent in the New Testament books. I think I see both his strength and his weakness. He has moved away considerably from Baur and Zeller. But he holds fast the *substantial results* gained by the Tübingen school; and is able to make important inquiries into the Pauline Epistles, bringing forth fresh views. His judgment is good. Though speculative, he is not rash. The author of the *Paulinismus* is an able scholar and an agreeable man.

17th August.—Went with my daughter to Contrexéville. The time there is fully spent in drinking the waters before breakfast, in walking about, sleeping, and eating. Nothing can be done in the way of study. Have resumed to-day my regular reading in the Hebrew Bible and the Syriac New Testament. Blessed be God for His continued goodness to me and mine.

27th August.—I have just lost my old and much valued friend Dr. M. Kalisch, a fine Hebrew scholar not surpassed by any in Great Britain, and who would have occupied a very high place even in Germany had he chosen to live in his native country. What is of more value than scholarship, he was upright, conscientious, open-minded: an Israelite in whom was no guile. It was curious to watch the progress of his Hebrew studies in the Old Testament, from his commentary on Exodus, which was in some degree tentative, to that on Leviticus, where he appears to have thoroughly imbibed and carried out the views of Graf and Wellhausen. His two monographs on Balaam and Jonah are excellent specimens of commentary; while his last volume, *Path and Goal*, proves him to have been an able and sound rationalist. The death of such a scholar is a severe loss, chiefly to me, who enjoyed his friendship and shared many of his views. Such as he cannot but be vividly and mournfully remembered while life lasts. Alas, my dearest friends are leaving me! Indeed, the greater number are gone before my departure. But there is the glorious hope of reunion in an exalted state, where bodies of flesh and blood clog the immortal spirit no more.

19th September.—Have written two short letters on the Revised Old Testament in the *Inquirer* of the 12th and 19th instant. I have no desire or inclination to give a long critique upon the work, pointing out its excellences and defects. It is not so good as it should have been when one takes into account the years spent upon it and the number of persons employed. A good many marginal readings should be in the text, and the textual ones abolished. One cannot help thinking that the text usually represents the opinion of an orthodox majority, the margin that of a scholarly minority. Taking it as a whole, it seems inferior to De Wette's German version. I adhere to my former view that a work of this nature should be done by a Royal Commission; not by a Committee, the creation of Convocation. One thing about it will arrest the attention of scholars, namely, the retention or occurrence of renderings which the Hebrew cannot bear.   And there might surely have been insight enough to see the incorrectness of "*the earth* shall be full of the knowledge of the Lord," etc. (Isa. xi. 9), which should obviously be "*the land* shall be full," etc., and the blunder that retains *Michal* in the text of 2 Sam. xxi. 8, instead of *Merab*.   It is also in my opinion unjustifiable to keep *sprinkle* in the text of Isa. lii. 15, since the verb so rendered can only mean to leap for joy, exult, rejoice, in the passage.

22nd September.—Professor Schrader of Berlin spent the evening with me; a scholar of European reputation whose Oriental studies and researches are of high value. I regret that he did not pursue the department he entered upon at first at Zürich, and in which he would doubtless have excelled; for his edition of De Wette's *Introduction to the Old Testament* embodies much valuable criticism of the Hebrew Scriptures. Having laid aside all that, he is now engrossed with his Babylonian and Assyrian studies.   I asked him about the Hittites, but he said there is yet no key to their language; and also about Darius the Mede in Daniel, who, as he justly remarked, is excluded from authentic history, there being no place for him. Schrader is a plain, simple, unsophisticated scholar, genial, kindly, not without humour, capable of true, disinterested friendship.   It is a pleasure to know such a distinguished Orientalist.

8th November.—Finished to day the reading of *Daniel*, to which book I turned after the daily perusal of *Jeremiah* was completed.   The change from Isaiah to Jeremiah is great.   The style of the latter is wordy, and has much repetition.   Compression and energy are wanting.   The text, too, is in a very imperfect and corrupt state.   But the high moral tone of the prophet, notwithstanding his melancholy, is manifest throughout.   The Book of

Daniel is unmistakably of late origin, and deficient in the characteristics of true Hebrew prophetism. History is clothed in a prophetic dress. The diction is degenerate; and the writer, not being at home in Hebrew, slides at times into Chaldee. To understand the book, it is necessary to be acquainted with the history of the Maccabean times, with the insane attacks of Antiochus Epiphanes upon the Jewish people and their religion. In Daniel the idea of Messiah's superhuman Person appears for the first time. Before, he had been described as an exalted King and Conqueror who should reign in Jerusalem over the Jewish people restored and at peace; the Gentiles having been converted and incorporated with the chosen race; or subdued and destroyed, according to other prophets.

19th November.—Finished to-day the reading of the Gospels according to *John*, *Matthew*, *Mark* in the old Syriac version. A portion was read each morning, along with an equal portion of the Hebrew Bible. The Peshito is not of much use either in the verbal criticism or the interpretation of the New Testament. It deviates but little from the common text. One cannot help thinking, with Griesbach, that this version underwent some revision at an early period, so that old readings disappeared in many cases, and those of later MSS. were substituted. The extent to which this revision was made is greatly exaggerated by Dr. Hort, so much so that his conjectures must be rejected.

14th December.—The general election is over, and the Liberals have not got a majority sufficiently large to carry on an effective administration. I do not wonder at the revulsion which has left them as they are. During their five years of office they did little good and much harm. Their invasion of Egypt was wicked and unchristian. But Christian principle seems to be disregarded by both the political parties that now strive for office. Government by party is bad government. Measures should be judged and voted upon for their goodness or otherwise: not by the effects which would follow to party. The clinging to office, the lust of power, ambition, selfishness, are too manifest among our politicians, whether Conservative or Liberal. The empire suffers while politicians squabble. Retrenchment and reform are unheard of. Nothing of national importance or benefit will be done till a Radical Government comes into power. At present the Whigs are as great obstructives to real reform as the Tories. They thwarted Pitt long ago in his wise designs regarding Ireland; they are doing the same now in trying to check Mr. Gladstone in his constructive plans about it. They are the advocates of tradition, reluctant to advance where progress is imperatively needed.

Surely every true Christian will read with sorrow and indignation the proclamation respecting Burmah issued by the present Governor-General of India. This annexation of another territory to the English Empire is simply an act of robbery, unjust and antichristian, which adds to the burden of national sins, and will surely bring retribution. England, a professedly Christian country, seizes upon property belonging to another, and the majority of the inhabitants applaud. If such be the effect of commerce, and the greed of gain which it fosters, our commerce is rotten at the core. One cannot but think of Tyre, and the denunciations of her by Isaiah.

8th February 1886.—During the past two years I have been revising the second edition of my *Introduction to the New Testament*, going through it very carefully, correcting minor errors, expunging passages, sentences, and clauses, adding new matter, making the sense clearer, and introducing as much improvement as I could within the old space. Hence the text has been considerably amended.

With one exception no essential change has been made.
The book is now nearer the state in which I should like it
to be. I have not grudged the time spent in such minute
inspection, hoping that the improvements may appear in a
new edition, probably after my decease; for it is my strong
desire that they should not be lost to the public, as the
work may be referred to, occasionally at least, by scholars
who succeed me. The value of these early Christian
Writings is incalculable. They are the believer's charter,
his guide, his spring of comfort, his support in adversity,
his faithful companion in a sinful world. To put them in
their proper times and places while showing their phases
of thought: to bring out their lessons; to separate the
transient from the permanent, the historical from the unhistorical: to extract the pure teaching and wonderful acts
of Jesus from successive incrustations and perversions, is a
task not unworthy of high endeavour on the part of him
who looks and longs for a blessed future. In my own
case, these Sacred Records have soothed the sorrow of many
an hour, and lightened burdens not a few. In the multitude of my thoughts within me, they have dispelled clouds
of doubt and darkness.

19th February.—Finished this morning the reading of
Job in Hebrew. I do not think that the strophe-division
of it by Koester was in many instances intended by the
original writers. In some it may have been. The number
three was evidently meant to divide the work into regular
parts. The Received Version is not good. Neither is the
Revised one satisfactory. Both miss the true sense in many
cases. The speeches of Elihu are the most difficult portion
of the work. I have endeavoured to translate the thirty-
sixth chapter, because it seemed the hardest to understand,
and I cannot agree with any of the versions I know. The
thought of translating all Elihu's words came into my
mind; but where could I find a medium for the print-

ing of it?   It is evident that Elihu is another writer than
the author of the rest; although the later writer has not
contributed to the solution of a problem, which cannot be
solved except in the light of the New Testament.

12th March. — Have just finished the reading of
Ecclesiastes, a work which has many difficult passages and
words.   There is little doubt that the date is late: not
much, if at all, before the year 300 B.C.   I also believe
that it was written by a bachelor, as is pretty clear from
ch. iv. 8–12.   He speculated freely, his moods being pessi-
mist, epicurean, sceptical, without belief in a future state.
The appendix, ch. xii. 9–14, was added by the men of the
Great Synagogue, which saved the work from being excluded
from the canon.   It is not easy to perceive any proper
arrangement or order; and the strophes, though their
existence is apparent, cannot be always separated.

14th March.—This morning I finished the reading of
Luke's Gospel in the Syriac, and am still convinced that
the Peshito version is not a good authority for original
readings of the text.   For example, in the concluding
chapter it has these additions, " and of an honeycomb "
(ver. 42), which the Curetonian Syriac lacks; " and carried
up into heaven " (ver. 51); " and they worshipped him "
(ver. 52); " and blessing" (ver. 53).   It is remarkable,
however, that the oldest and best MSS., ℵ, A, B, C, have
also these later insertions of the 51st and 52nd verses.
In the same way, the version has the 40th verse with
almost all uncial MSS. except D; but against the Curetonian Syriac.   Tischendorf has rightly rejected the verse,
and his note has been copied in part by Westcott and
Hort.   The so-called Western readings are often right, in
opposition to the Vatican and Sinaitic MSS.   The 12th
verse is an example of the same kind.

24th March.—Finished the *Song of Solomon* this
morning.   The composition is in my judgment a love-song

written by an Israelite of the northern kingdom some time after the reign of the luxurious monarch whose name it bears. The fidelity of a woman's pure love for one man amid great temptations is described and enforced. Most of the difficulties inherent in the interpretation of the poem arise from an incorrect separation of the speakers. I cannot think that the divisions in Bunsen's *Bibelwerk* are judicious or probable.

13*th June.*—Finished the reading of *Proverbs* to-day. It is plain that the book is an aggregate, made up of different parts which were written or collected at different times. How strange that Moses Stuart should place the first division, that is, ch. i. 7–ix., in Solomon's time, if it is so much later than ch. x.–xxii. 16, which may be correctly referred to that monarch's reign, and in part to his authorship. As to the text of the work, much help towards its restoration may be got from the LXX. Not a few corrupt passages occur which are difficult of interpretation as they now stand. In these, Bunsen's *Bibelwerk* affords but small satisfaction. The Received Version often needs rectification, and the Revised Version should itself be revised. It is curious to see how ch. xvi. 4 is turned aside from its true sense by some interpreters, who in their anxiety to get away from apparent predestinarianism, and rightly rejecting the received translation, render, " Jehovah has made everything for its purpose"; whereas the pronoun should be His (purpose). Everything fulfils God's purpose; so also has He made the wicked for the day of misfortune. The wicked themselves work out the divine designs. Hitzig's tampering with the word rendered *purpose*, by taking away the suffix from it and making it " *a purpose*," is unnecessary; the Septuagint rendering is no justification of such treatment.

Left home in June for Contrexéville, and returned on the 11th August after a weary, unpleasant journey from

Gerardmer, to which place my daughter and I went for the first time, after spending four weeks at Contrexéville, and going through the usual course of water-drinking. Gerardmer is a pleasant change from Contrexéville. It is beautifully situated, surrounded by wooded hills, with a fine lake and an altitude of two thousand feet above the sea. In fact it is a miniature Switzerland. I escaped the turmoil and tumult of the political election, with its cry of Home Rule for Ireland on the one side, and Tory opposition to Mr. Gladstone's new measure on the other. For some years past I have been an advocate of Home Rule, believing it to be a measure of justice and right. A country which has been cruelly governed for centuries should be treated fairly at last. But England is not yet prepared to act righteously towards the conquered kingdom. The annexation of territory, aggressive wars, prompt yielding to the passion for acquisition abroad, boasting of England's greatness, show how little influence Christianity exerts upon the conduct of men in power. It makes little difference what party rules. Whigs and Tories in office differ little from each other. An orthodox Churchman on either side can sanction and justify by a Jesuitical quibble a wicked deed like the bombardment of Alexandria, and the consequent sending of troops to slaughter unoffending Egyptians defending their country. And such antichristian work goes on. Burmah has been seized; and who raised his voice against the robbery? Did the so-called religious newspapers? Considering such doings as these, I can only grieve for the future of England, for they are prognostics of its downfall. Under the providence of God, crimes cannot be perpetrated with impunity. Empires committing deeds contrary to the commandments of Him who rules over all, decay and perish. I blame those who call themselves Liberals, more than others, because they often speak of acting on principle and ameliorating the condition of the poor; whereas they do not set themselves resolutely to the work of retrenchment and reform when they are in power. What comfort could one have in this life were he without the hope of a blessed immortality? "The Lord reigneth, let the people tremble," but, "The Lord reigneth, let the earth rejoice."

Wanted at present, a statesman at the head of our national affairs who will follow neither Whig nor Tory traditions except so far as they agree with the eternal principles of justice and the spirit of Christ's teaching, who will be guided in all his measures by the golden rule, " Do unto others as ye would that others should do to you," avoiding offensive war, abolishing a standing army, reducing the taxation of the people as low as is consistent with social progress, putting the land in the possession of those who cultivate it, instead of allowing a few to possess thousands of acres for their pleasure or aggrandisement, so that the people, crowded in our cities, lack what should be rightfully theirs. Wanted, the disappearance of huge landlords and of prelates living in palaces. Wanted, a Republic in which the people may govern themselves wisely without the burden of monarchy and its costly surroundings. Shall England ever attain to these desirable ends, or has she reached her acme and begun to decline? The example of the Roman Empire damps the hope of the Englishman who loves his country.

CHAPTER XIII

I HAVE often desired to write a commentary on some part of the Old Testament—the Book of Job, Isaiah, Genesis, Daniel.

My mind runs most upon a commentary on Job, because there is none in English which is altogether successful. We have Hirzel's in German, which is excellent, and may be put beside Gesenius's masterly work on Isaiah. Dillmann's re-editing of it cannot be praised; nor is Ewald at all satisfactory. I do not like Delitzsch's; and Schlottmann's is a juvenile production. My friend Mr. Rodwell has made a fair attempt at translating the poem, but has he not departed too often from the Received English Version?

The following specimen of a new translation was presented to the readers of the *Christian Reformer* (July 1886):—

"It is well-known that the speeches of Elihu, in the Book of Job, embracing chapters xxxii.-xxxvii., have many peculiar expressions, differing so much from the rest of the work as to betray a later date and authorship. The Received Version is not fortunate in rendering them into English; neither can the Revised form of it be pronounced satisfactory. In my daily readings of the Hebrew Bible, the thought of making as correct a translation of some hard part of Job as I could do occurred to me; and having fixed upon the thirty-sixth chapter, the conclusion of which is surrounded with great difficulties, I offer the following version as a contribution to the interpretation of this most interesting book. It probably differs from the translations published

by English scholars within the last few years; how far
I cannot say, as they were not consulted. The strophes,
which are not so regular as Koester has marked them, are
distinguished by spaces:—

"JOB XXXVI

And Elihu spake still further.
Wait for me a little and I will shew thee,
  for there are still words respecting God.
I will lift up my knowledge far hence,
  and to my Maker do justice.
For truly my words are not falsehood;
One perfect in knowledge is with thee.

Behold, God is mighty and despises not,
Mighty in strength of understanding.
He does not allow the wicked to live;
And the right of the sufferers He grants.
He withdraws not His eyes from the righteous;
But with kings upon the throne
He makes them sit for ever; and they are exalted.
And if they are bound in fetters,
  caught in bands of affliction,
Then He declares to them their doing
  And their transgressions, that they conducted themselves
    proudly,
  and opens their ear to correction,
  and says that they should turn from iniquity.
If they hear and submit,
  they finish their days in prosperity,
  and their years in pleasure.
But if they do not hear,
  they rush upon the dart (of death)
  and expire without knowledge.

But the profane in heart lay up wrath;
They do not cry when He binds them.
Their soul dies in youth;
Their life is among the unclean.
He delivers the afflicted through their affliction,
  and opens through distress their ear.
Yea, He has also impelled thee out of distress,
  into the wide place where is no straitness;
And the quiet of thy table He has filled with fatness.
Yet thou art full of the judgment of the wicked;

11

Judgment and justice hold together
Only let not anger lead thee astray to chastisement ;
And let not the large ransom turn thee aside.
  Shall thy wealth array itself (for thee), oh ! not in distress ;
Neither shall all the resources of strength (do so).

Long not for the night,
When peoples in their place are taken away.
Take heed, turn not to vanity ;
For this thou hast chosen rather than affliction.

Behold God exalts Himself in His strength ;
Who is a teacher like Him?
Who has enjoined upon Him His way ;
And who has said thou didst iniquity?
Remember that thou exalt His doing,
  of which men have repeatedly sung ;
All mortals view it with pleasure,
Men contemplate it from afar.

Behold God is exalted
And we do not know (Him) ;
And the number of His years is unsearchable.
For He draws up drops of water,
  that purifies the rain into His vapour,
With which the skies flow down,
  and distil upon many men,
Can one understand the spreadings of clouds,
The thunder-crashes of His tent?

Behold, He spreads over Himself His light,
  and covers Himself with the roots of the sea.
For by them He judges peoples,
Gives food in abundance.
  He covers both hands with light,
And commands it on him that meets it.
His thunder announces Him,
Him even the cattle when He goes up . . ."

20th August.—Finished to-day the reading of *Hosea*, whose prophecies are attended with many difficulties of interpretation. The style is abrupt, and changes of construction are frequent. The time in which he prophesied is incorrectly given at the beginning. The first four things are copied from Isa. i. 1 ; and it is pretty certain that the concluding clause was written by Hosea himself. He lived under Jeroboam II. Strange it is that some should take the narratives in chaps. i., iii. literally. They are assuredly allegorical, as the names of the prophet's children show. Hosea predicts that Ephraim should be carried away captive to Assyria and Egypt (viii. 13, ix. 3–6). But he says again, there will be no Egyptian captivity (xi. 5). It would seem from this contradiction that the prophet wavered in his idea of the places of Israel's near captivity; and was less uncertain in his expectation of Assyria's than of Egypt's conquest of the kingdom. If both powers threatened Ephraim, the carrying away to Egypt might be in the prophet's mind at one time; at another, the deportation to Assyria. Of one thing he was certain, namely, the extinction of the kingdom to which he belonged. The balance turned at last against Egypt, so that he could affirm " He shall not return into the land of Egypt." Among the difficult passages, I shall only refer to a few.

Ch. v. 2.   " And the apostates are deep in corruption, yet I am a chastisement to them all."

„ vii. 16.   " they return to no-god," that is, idols.

„ ix. 8.   " Ephraim is a spy against my God ; as for the prophet," etc.

„ x. 10.   " when I chastise them for their two transgressions."

„ x. 12.   " sow to yourselves for righteousness, reap according to your piety," etc.

„ xii. 4.   In the last part of this verse the pronominal suffixes are suddenly changed : " at Bethel he will find *him*, and there he will speak with *us*." Jacob and his people are interchanged. Were it not for the vowel points, *us* might be read in both cases, as the meaning is the same.

Ch. xiii. 2 is obscure : I mean the last part of the verse, which is, " to them they speak. The sacrificers of men kiss calves." The rational conduct for men is to kiss men, not calves. Here the process is reversed : they sacrifice men and kiss calves at Bethel. The sarcasm is severe and cutting.

I cannot but think that Ewald is wrong in his exposition of the words.

In ch. xiii. 9, where the common translation can hardly be justified, and some have needlessly resorted to a change in the text, I translate, "He has destroyed thee, O Israel, for in me, in thy help" (thou hast not trusted). The sentence is left unfinished. Bunsen's *Bibelwerk* presents a strangely incorrect translation, "that thou art against me, against thy help"; and Hitzig concurs. The prefix בְּ never means *against*, though Gesenius says it does. It denotes the *direction* of an action *upon* a person; and it is the word with which it is coupled that indicates the nature of the action, hostile or otherwise. Ch. xiv. 3, "and adopt goodness," literally "*take to* goodness."

8th September.—Finished the reading of *Zachariah*. The prophet's predictions are contained in the first eight chapters, and lack originality. He depends too much on earlier prophets. His symbolism is not always clear. In Kuenen's opinion it is noteworthy that he is the only one of these post-Exile prophets that expects the restoration of the Davidic dynasty. But this rests on the improbable view that "the branch," or rather "shoot," represents a successor in the line of David, not the Messiah. The rest of the book (ch. ix.–xiv.) proceeds from earlier writers; ix.–xi. from one that lived in the eighth century, soon after the death of Jeroboam II.; xii.–xiv. from a writer in the time of Manasseh. But some critics, such as Vatke, are indisposed to the division of ix.–xiv., and refer the date of this portion either to the time of Artaxerxes Longimanus, or to the Maccabean period, with Geiger, Böttcher, and Stade. The symbolism of the third and fourth chapters is not easy to understand. "The branch" is Messiah, but was it the prophet's idea that Zerubbabel should be he? Not so, for the appearance of Messiah is spoken of as future (iii. 5). The high priest Joshua symbolises the nation, and is also definitely separated from Messiah. It is too late for scholars of the old conservative type to maintain the integrity of the work as if it proceeded from one author. Mede, Kidder, Whiston, Hammond, and Newcome had a better perception of Zachariah's utterances than some of their successors in the same Church.

13th September.—Finished to-day the reading of *Malachi*. This word I consider a proper name, not an appellative; nor can I approve of the Septuagint rendering *angel*, or suppose that some prophet is concealed under the term.

Like Zachariah and Haggai, Malachi leans upon the older prophets, and has little originality or genuine inspiration. He was a contemporary of Nehemiah, to whom there is an express reference in ch. i. 8, and of Obadiah. Tithes, offerings, and sacrifices—in short, the Levitical spirit —are prominent in the almost prosaic dialogues that convey his reproofs. It is a peculiar feature that Elijah the prophet is said to appear before the great judgment day, calling the people to repentance. Messianic hopes are not attached to a person; and it is superfluous to state that the "sun of righteousness" is only a poetical expression for the beginning of a new and brighter state. The passage ii. 15 has always perplexed interpreters; and I cannot avoid thinking that Ewald and Bunsen have missed its true sense. I propose the following: "And did not one do so, and yet the spirit remained with him?" But what did the one? "He was seeking a godly seed." The excuse of Abraham's example is put into the mouth of the people, and the reply follows. This translation is not new. It is in De Wette's German version; and was perhaps sanctioned by Gesenius, whose friendship the Basel professor enjoyed, and whose authority he usually followed in Hebrew questions, though he had an independent judgment of his own.

18th September.—Finished to-day the book of *Jonah*, which is generally allowed to be of late date, though it

should not be brought down to the third century, as it is
by Vatke, or to the Maccabean time, with Hitzig. The
prayer preceded the other parts, and was adapted to the
case of Jonah. The book is not properly a prophetic
one, and should be excluded from the prophetic roll, being
simply didactic. The author uses Jonah the prophet who
lived in the time of Jeroboam II. as the vehicle of his
religious ideas, meaning to show the all-embracing mercy
of God, in opposition to the exclusiveness of his countrymen.

Instead of Jehovah's care being confined to the Jews,
the writer describes it as extending to the heathen. He had
a more liberal belief than the majority of his co-religionists,
and wrote with the purpose of counteracting or correcting
their proud self-consciousness, which looked down upon
the Gentiles with contempt or pity, as if they were beyond
the pale of divine protection. Nineveh, which had been
destroyed before the book was written, is a type of the
heathen world; the fate of Jonah in being swallowed by
a great fish and vomited alive, a symbol of repentance and
deliverance. I do not agree with Kalisch in supposing
that the delineation of Jonah's personality is either good
or consistent. Why is *a prophet* described as fleeing from
the presence of God, as if the latter were only in Palestine? Why is he represented as peevish, fretful, angry,
because the Ninevites were spared? The picture of the
prophet lacks verisimilitude, exaggerating the notions supposed to be entertained by such as had the prophetic gift.

It is well that the framers of the canon included the
book in their collection, for it teaches a valuable lesson,
namely, the wide scope of the divine mercy, which has regard
to Gentiles as well as Jews, sparing repentant sinners, and
children not yet responsible for their actions. It inculcates
tolerance, so that the angry prophet is deservedly rebuked.

29th September.—Finished to-day the reading of *Micah*,

a prophet contemporary with Hosea and Isaiah, but a little earlier than the latter, and inferior to him in poetic vigour. He is fond of playing on words, has abrupt transitions, ungrammatical forms, and is obscure in parts, especially in ch. ii. 12, 13, a passage which should not be considered an interpolation, as it is by Ewald. The method of dialogue in the sixth and seventh chapters resembles that of the post-Exile prophets. The morality of Micah is pure, and his religious teaching of an exalted nature. Critics have unnecessarily assumed various interpolations, in which respect Stade is the chief defaulter, Vatke being not far behind. The only probable one is in ch. iv. 10, " Thou shalt go to Babylon," which may still be defended on the ground of authenticity, for Babylon was the metropolis of a province of the Assyrian Empire. But it is more likely that the time of the Babylonian captivity is referred to. There is an important difference between Isaiah and Micah. The former believes that Jerusalem should not be destroyed by the Assyrians; Micah expects the catastrophe to happen immediately from the same enemy (iii. 12). Both expect the continued existence of the Assyrian kingdom, Micah making the reign of Messiah contemporary with it (v. 5, 6).

4th October.—Finished *Nahum*, a prophet inferior to none in graphic power and sublimity. The time at which he wrote is variously estimated, but is inferred with probability from the allusion in the third chapter (verses 8 and following) to the destruction of Thebes, which was effected by Asurbanipal, the son of Asarhaddon, in his second Egyptian expedition against Urdamani Tirhakas's successor; and as Tirhakas died 664 B.C., Nahum belongs to the time when the overthrow of Thebes was fresh in the memory, and the Medes, with whom the Chaldeans united under Cyaxares and Nabopolassar, threatened Nineveh with a renewed and more formidable attack. The prophetic description does not, however, refer to this as past, but is based on the attack upon Nineveh by Phraortes, which was unsuccessful, as is evident from ch. i. 8. This is probably dated 627 B.C.; and if twenty-eight years intervened between the two sieges, as has been inferred from Ctesias, the second, which was of some duration, did not take place till about 597 B.C. The exact date of Nahum's prophecy is uncertain. The prophet predicts the same fate to the city of Nineveh which befell the capital of Upper Egypt. The very few Assyrian words and Aramæisms are easily explained without supposing that Nahum abode in Assyria.

10th October.—Finished *Habakkuk*, whose prophecies are written in a highly poetical style, full of freshness, force, and beauty, so that they may be put on a par with those of the best prophets. The enemies described are the Chaldeans, new and dangerous adversaries. But the continuance of the Jewish state is still assumed, and the safety of Jerusalem a thing hoped for (ii. 3–iii. 13). Though the prophet was contemporary with Jeremiah, it is impossible to fix his time exactly. He should be put before the first invasion of the Chaldeans, and in the reign of Jehoiakim, not after it, with Vatke. Schrader adopts the year 604 as the date of his oracles, which cannot be far from the truth. The third chapter, containing the highest lyrical ode which Hebrew poetry has produced, is so difficult in parts that the text has been pronounced corrupt. This is an expedient of interpretation which should be resorted to very seldom. It is best to take it here as it is, and explain it as well as we can. I present the following version of the piece :—

> "O Lord, I heard the fame of Thee, I was afraid.
> O Lord, revive Thy work in the course of the years,
> In the course of the years make it known ;
> *But* in wrath remember mercy.

God comes from Teman, and the Holy One from Mount Paran.
    Selah.
His majesty covers the heavens, and His splendour fills the earth ;
And there a brightness as of pure light, rays at his side,
And that is but the veiling of His might.
Before Him goes pestilence,
And a burning plague follows His feet.
He stands and measures the earth, looks and makes the nations
    tremble,
And the everlasting mountains burst asunder, the perpetual hills
    sink,
His paths of old.
I see the tents of Cushan under affliction ;
The curtains of the land of Midian tremble.
Is the Lord incensed against the rivers, or is Thine anger against
    the streams,
Or is Thy wrath against the sea ?
That Thou dost ride upon Thy horses, Thy chariots of safety,
Thy bow is entirely uncovered, curses are the rods of the word.
    Selah.
With streams Thou didst split the land.
The mountains see Thee, they writhe, a flood of waters passes
    over,
The deep utters his voice, lifts up his hands on high.
Sun, moon stand still in their dwelling,
At the light of Thine arrows which shoot along,
At the lightning glance of Thy glittering spear.
In indignation Thou marchest through the earth,
In anger Thou crushest the nations.
Thou goest out for the salvation of Thy people, for the salvation
    of Thine anointed.
Thou woundest the head from the house of the wicked (Babylon),
Baring the foundation even to the neck. Selah.
Thou borest through with his own arrows the head of his
    princes,
Who rush on to scatter me,
Their exultation was as if to devour the helpless in secret.
Thou didst tread the sea with Thy horses,
The foaming of many waters.
I heard and my body trembled ;
My lips quivered at the voice,
Rottenness comes into my bones,
And I tremble under me,
That I should quietly wait for the day of distress
For his coming up against the people to press upon them.
For the fig-tree does not bloom,
And there is no produce in the vines.

The fruit of the olive disappoints,
And the fields yield no food.
The flock fails from the fold,
And there are no oxen in the stalls.
And yet I will exult in the Lord,
Rejoice in the God of my salvation.
The Lord God is my strength,
And He makes my feet like those of hinds,
And causes me to walk upon my heights.

To the chief musician, with my stringed instruments."

15*th October.*—Finished *Zephaniah*, a prophet who probably lived in the early years of Josiah's reign. His chief theme is "the day of the Lord," a time of vengeance and destruction to the enemies of Israel, of justice to Jehovah's people. Yet he hopes for the improvement of the latter. As he indulges in general statements, it is impossible to say what enemies he had in his mind, whether the Chaldeans or the Scythians. Perhaps he thought of none in particular. As a writer, Zephaniah occupies an inferior position. He has used preceding prophets, but not slavishly, and his style is prosaic. Since he expected the destruction of Nineveh (ii. 13), he probably wrote about 633 B.C., during the first siege of Nineveh by Phraortes the Mede.

18*th October.*—Two articles published in the *Christian Register* of 19th and 26th August were suggested by the prevailing current of orthodoxy which has invaded this country for some time. Since they were written, one quarterly review has died, and I hope that others may soon share the same fate. They will do so when the moneyed patrons become weary of propping them up. I learn from a letter of Professor Holtzmann's, the second edition of whose *Einleitung in das Neue Testament* I have just received from the author, that the current in Germany is much the same as in England. Of course he regrets it, but hopes for a reaction. Unfortunately, disciples of the

Tübingen school are not unaffected by the tide, and are paring away parts and principles of the school; generally, I believe, to the detriment of truth. This softening, mediating process is exemplified in the recent writings of Hilgenfeld and Pfleiderer. Still it is noteworthy that the orthodoxy of Germany is not so stiff or crass as that of Great Britain. The lives of Christ by Weiss and Beyschlag show that concessions must be made to the free spirit which is not yet extinct in Germany.

19th October.—Finished *Haggai,* a prophet whose time is stated by himself with minute specification of years and months. His oracles assume the form of four short addresses to Zerubbabel and Joshua. Perhaps these are but abstracts of longer discourses. The prophet's book lacks originality and poetic elevation. The diction is flat and prosaic. He wrote in the declining period of prophecy, when the lofty aspirations of those belonging to the Exile period, and their ideal hopes regarding the glorious future, had vanished. The time was unfavourable to the origin of poems of a high order, though even in the fifth century B.C. some excellent oracles appeared. We must therefore suppose that Haggai was unable to write in a superior style; but his moral earnestness and deep concern on behalf of the national worship are prominent.

23rd October.—The reading of the *Acts of the Apostles* in Syriac completed to-day. As in other parts, the text of the Acts differs little from the Received one. It has not the common reading in ch. viii. 39, though Schaaf's edition inserts the verse. And xxviii. 37 is absent from the text in the editions of Widmanstad and the Bible Society (superintended by Lee), though the latter puts it in a note. Gutbir was the means of introducing it into the text of Schaaf's edition. The omission agrees with A, ℵ, B, E, but not with the Harclean Syriac or the Vulgate. Old as it is, the version contributes little either to the formation of a correct text or to the interpretation of the Acts.

27th October.—I completed the reading of *Joel* this day, having found in the book various obscure passages and uncertain allusions. The diversity of opinion respecting the time of the prophet is great and perplexing. When one sees Bunsen's date, between 945 and 940 B.C., and that of Merx, 445 B.C., he feels that he is almost free to put the prophecies in any intermediate period. After much deliberation and the careful perusal of Vatke's summary, it appears to me that the advocates of a post-Exile date, such as Hilgenfeld and Vatke,—as well as Kuenen, who fixes on a time immediately before the Exile, —do not make their views either plausible or probable. No mention occurs of Judah's great enemies, the Assyrians, Syrians, Chaldeans, Persians. Phenicians, Egyptians, Philistines, and Edomites are the hostile powers. The language also is too good and pure to belong to a post-Exile period. The most probable date is an early one, the reign of Jehoash of Judah, about 870 B.C. I do not think that the ʹprophet can well be brought lower, though it is a common opinion now to make the post-Exile time accountable for many parts of the Old Testament.

A few passages deserve a brief note.

In ii. 8. Translate "they rush into the midst of naked swords, and are not wounded.
ii. 23. The last word of the verse I translate "at first," notwithstanding Hitzig's authority.
iv. 20. "But Judah shall abide," etc., not "shall dwell," or "shall be inhabited."

5th December.—The book of *Amos* finished in my daily readings. The shepherd-prophet, though belonging to Judah by birth, directs his prophecies chiefly to Israel, because he was aware of its abounding idolatries (whose centre was Bethel), its luxury and immorality. Jeroboam II.

was king; Uzziah his contemporary. The date of the prophecies given by Kuenen (800 B.C.) is too early. Though Amos clearly refers to the Assyrian captivity, he does not name the hostile power which should desolate the kingdom (v. 27, vii. 11, 17, ix. 14). It would seem that he went to Bethel, and was confronted there by Amaziah the priest, who accused him to Jeroboam, so that he was driven out of the kingdom. The prophecies were committed to writing some time after they were delivered, perhaps about 750 B.C., when he thought that Assyria was just about to subdue and ravage Israel. The prophet believed in the extinction of the kingdom; but not in that of Judah, which he does not spare any more than its northern neighbour. Notwithstanding the gloomy picture he draws, he had a hope that God would not abandon His people for ever. A better future awaited Israel; and the fallen tabernacle of Judah should be set up again. Though the prophet anticipated the extinction of the northern kingdom, he thought it would come sooner than it really did. Still, he speaks of a restoration of Israel in the ninth chapter; as if the captives should be brought back to their own land, unite with Judah, and form one kingdom under a Davidic dynasty. The vague hopes of the prophets respecting the happy future of their countrymen were not realised. They were ignorant of future events. The language is plain, homely, lively; and all is arranged in regular order. It has even rhythmic strophes, so that plan and skill are observable. In vi. 8, viii. 7 occurs the expression גְּאוֹן יַעֲקֹב, "pride of Jacob," which is also in Ps. xlvii. 5. It means in all cases "that which Jacob is proud of"—her palaces, temple, etc., the Holy Land generally. Gesenius understands by the phrase in viii. 7 God Himself, and Hitzig agrees; but this is incorrect, though it is somewhat strange to represent God swearing by the pride of Jacob rather than by Himself. It is hardly necessary to remark that Jerome's judgment of Amos's language, *imperitus sermone*, is incorrect for the most part, though Rosenmüller repeats it.

The four visions at the beginning of the seventh chapter are poetic fictions of an incongruous kind. A fire which consumes the great deep as well as the field, and the Lord standing on a wall with a plumb-line in His hand, are unsuitable images.

7th December.—To-day *Obadiah*, and with that prophecy the reading of the minor prophets, was finished. Short as is the oracle of Obadiah, it is perplexing in many ways. The prophet inveighs against Edom for its conduct to Jerusalem in distress. A comparison of vers. 1–7 with Jeremiah's oracle against the same enemy shows either that the one made use of the other, or that both took from the same source. I believe that Obadiah followed Jeremiah and used his prophecy. The fall of Jerusalem was past, as appears from vers. 12–14; and the early dates assigned by Caspari, Vaihinger, and others are untenable. So is Hitzig's opinion that the prophecy belongs to the time of Alexander the Great. The most probable date is soon after 588 B.C. It is true that the Chaldeans are not mentioned as the captors of Jerusalem, but that fact is not explained by Hitzig's assumption.

The language presents various difficulties, so that it can hardly be considered an improvement upon Jeremiah's. The sequence of verses is irregular, and repetitions frequent. Thus " in the day of calamity " occurs three times in the 13th verse, and " the mount of Esau " is used thrice. As to Sepharad in the 20th verse, it has not yet been satisfactorily identified with any known place, though cuneiform inscriptions have been adduced by Lassen in favour of Sardis, and by Schrader for Sepharvaim. The former opinion is the more probable. The prediction of Edom's destruction, like those of Jeremiah and Ezekiel, has not been fulfilled. Gesenius found its realisation in the time of the Maccabees and Jerusalem's second overthrow, but their extinction did not then take place; nor can any catastrophe corresponding to the prophetical expectations respecting these hereditary enemies of Israel be found in history.

28th December.—Finished to-day the *Epistle to the Romans* in the Peshito version. Here the translation is not so exact or good as in the Gospels, perhaps because the difficulty was greater. The 15th and 16th chapters belong to the epistle according to this version, in agreement with all ancient authorities; but the 24th verse of the latter chapter stands at the end, which favours the opinion that it was there from the commencement.

CHAPTER XIV

ENGLAND'S ROBBERIES

15th December 1886.—This dreary day has come round again with its sorrowful associations. Fourteen years ago my beloved wife left me. Thou blessed one! how fain would I behold thee now, just as thou art, and commune with thee in thy exalted state. . . . While I write in solitude, I recall thy presence and bodily form, thy grave countenance, thy wise counsels, thy strengthening hopes. . . . I cast my care upon Him who shields and protects His people, believing that she of whom I think so much is safe in the pavilion of His glory, increasing in all that constitutes true life, developing in spiritual perception, in expansive activity, nearing perfection, nearing God Himself.

I am not without my anxieties and fears at the present time. God alone knows how many haunt and distract my mind. They centre in my daughter. I trust, however, that she will be spared to me in answer to many prayers. May God watch over her now and ever. She is my stay and comfort. And now let me express my thanks to my Heavenly Father for His continued goodness to me through the past year; and my hope that He will guard and guide me and mine in the coming one, leading us nearer Himself and preparing us for the world of light.

1st January 1887.—Blessed be God who has preserved me so far, and continued to me a good measure of health, with the use of all my bodily and mental powers, so that

I am still able to think, study, work, and walk. The past year cannot show much good fruit of my labour, but I have not been idle. The revision of my *Introduction to the New Testament* has been my principal employment: that in which I have had most interest; and I believe that the book will be much improved when it appears in another edition, though its substance will still be the same. Could I accept, with Holtzmann and others, a much later date for the Epistle to the Hebrews,—that is, Domitian's reign,—an important change would arise; but I am unable to do so. The tendency to depart from the conclusions of the Tübingen school and from other prior ones may be carried too far; as it will probably be by the current now prevailing in Germany, where orthodoxy is in the ascendant. The desire to meet orthodoxy as much as possible may be praiseworthy, but is also hazardous to truth. The Vermittelungs-theologie is a mongrel thing.

Looking back at the past year, I feel humbled because I have done so little of what I ought to have done. If God spare me to the end of the present, I hope to do more and better. But who can tell what a day may bring forth? Let me cherish the hope of a blessed immortality more and more. Whatever happens, I am under a moral Governor, a Father just and merciful, who loves His children and wills not that they should perish.

6th January.—From day to day the newspapers are recording the advance of British troops towards the ruby mines from Mandalay, without a word of censure or protest against the unjust and antichristian march, which will issue in the seizure of a valuable property that does not belong to the English nation. The robbery is looked upon as an innocent or even laudable thing. How can England call herself a Christian nation while she robs other peoples of their territories and treasure? She may send forth her missionaries to preach the gospel to the

12

heathen, but they will do little good as long as these palpable acts of injustice are perpetrated. It is not remarkable that the political newspapers of the day are silent about national wrong-doings in the annexation of foreign countries, but it is strange that the Christian Churches and sects raise no loud and indignant protests against what is clearly forbidden by the New Testament. Here the Positivists are better men than the professing followers of Christ; for they speak often and plainly against the robberies of England. I fear that the Christianity of our country is more of a name than a reality. Statesmen of all parties are not guided by the precepts of Christ and His apostles, but squabble about place, power, and pelf.

12th April.—The reading of the Peshito version of the *Philippian Epistle* finished to-day. I had thought that it might contribute help to the true meaning of the very difficult passage in ii. 6–8, but was disappointed. The sense of ii. 13 is surely misapprehended when it is made, " For God Himself works in you whether to will or to do *that which you wish.*" It is true that εὐδοκίας has no pronoun before it; but it must refer to God's good pleasure, not that of the Philippians.

Yesterday I attended the great gathering in Hyde Park met to protest against the Tory Government Bill introduced into Parliament to destroy the liberties of the Irish people. A more iniquitous measure could hardly be brought forward. It is a disgrace to the audacious proposers and supporters of it. The ideas of civil and religious liberty held by many in England are not in advance of those entertained in the days of Elizabeth. Everything I see confirms me in the opinion that England has passed the zenith of her power and greatness, and is on the decline. Her conduct at home and abroad is out of harmony with the principles of the gospel which Christ preached.

Contrexéville, 22nd June.—Is it not disgraceful that the Jubilee year should be distinguished by a Coercion Bill for Ireland, the worst that has ever been passed to enslave a generous people who have been treated with injustice and cruelty ever since the union with England? But retribution will come. The oppressive yoke of a conquering nation will be cast off, and Ireland freed from the fetters of her victor. The world is still under a moral Governor; and a people assuming to be Christian who daily act in opposition to the divine commandment, "Thou shalt love thy neighbour as thyself," will be judged by their actions in the sight of God, who judges righteously.

Among kings and queens the present sovereign of Great Britain and Ireland stands out as a conspicuous example of virtuous conduct. Kings and queens are subject to great temptations. The best government is that of a republic. An intelligent people should be able to rule themselves.

During these fifty years of the Queen's reign, the nation has made great progress in the education of the masses as well as in commercial activity. Women have been elevated, owing, without doubt, to the influence indirectly exerted upon her sex by Victoria. But the rights of women are not yet up to the standard they are entitled to reach.

Contrexéville, July.—In this remote, obscure place, I have just seen in a newspaper a notice of the death of Professor Pott of Halle, the celebrated philologist, whose books, full of valuable but undigested matter, have been plundered by many inferior scholars. Well do I remember the pleasant evening in which he and myself were the guests of Professor Roediger in the year 1844, on the occasion of my first visit to the university town, so famous for its theological faculty, and with which I have so many pleasing but now melancholy associations. Accompanying me on my return to my hotel in the market-place, he encountered an obstacle in the way. We had been outside the gates, and the one we had to pass through was shut on our return. My friend shouted for the porter, but no porter appeared. However, he was equal to the occasion. Stepping back, he took a race forward and gave a violent kick against the gate, which, being of boards, flew open, and we marched triumphantly through without molestation. I have reverted in memory to the scene, and to the delightful evening in which I made the acquaintance of my valued friend Roediger, who presented me with his edition of Wellsted's *Travels in Arabia*, having a suitable inscription. This was not the only time when I had opportunities of seeing Roediger, and talking with him over many subjects. As a scientific and comprehensive Orientalist, he had no superior in Germany; yet he published little, was rather indolent, and did not receive the promotion he deserved till Justus Olshausen got him removed to Berlin. Even there, however, he occupied no prominent place suitable to his merits. In Berlin I spent a very pleasant evening with him in company with Lepsius, Petermann, and others.

During my stay at Contrexéville this year I met with Dr. Magee, Bishop of Peterborough, with whom I had frequent opportunities of conversing during our morning walks day by day. He is an eloquent speaker and preacher, an agreeable and shrewd man, a staunch Churchman, orthodox but not very narrow in that faith. He is not, however, a theologian, nor has he read many theological books. To scholarship he does not pretend. His notions of several writers belonging to the Church are far from correct. His measuring reed is a small one. The question of the Ignatian Epistles he pronounces to be settled by Lightfoot, without having read the big book of the latter. But I told him that all the great scholars of

Germany believed the epistles to be forgeries, and that I held the same opinion. Developed episcopacy did not appear so early; and none can make it probable that it originated close upon the time of the Apostle John, or had his sanction. As long as the Pastoral Epistles are rightly dated about 120 A.D., the Ignatian letters cannot be put earlier. Almost all Episcopalians are prejudiced in favour of the authenticity of Ignatius's Epistles; and it is useless to try to convince them of the contrary. They will not exercise the critical faculty impartially on that subject, as also on many others. Put a man into a high position in the Church, and you need not expect from him much independent judgment on theological topics. Content with the creeds of antiquity, he sees no reason for departing from them. Tradition saves the trouble of toilsome and conscientious examination. Dr. Magee, like his Episcopalian brethren, is a good traditionalist.

27th September. — Arrived at home this day from Hampshire, where my daughter and I spent the last six weeks. When we left Contrexéville, we travelled to Dijon and spent a few days there, thence to Sens, the capital of the ancient Senones, who took Rome under their leader Brennus. It is a pleasant town, has a fine cathedral, planned by the same architect as that of Canterbury, and was the residence of Thomas à Becket for four years. Having stayed there a fortnight, we got to Appleshaw in Hampshire on the 18th of August.

Blessed be God for our safe conduct and return.

3rd October.—A miracle is a violation or temporary suspension of the laws of nature; and what is needed to make departures from these laws credible is sufficiency of evidence, in whose absence there must be hesitation in believing that such a thing took place. The uniformity of nature's operations is so well established that there is great difficulty in setting it aside. There may, indeed, be other laws unknown to us at present with which miracles accord ; but we can only proceed on the basis of such evidence as the senses and reason are able to verify. The evidence for the Bible miracles seems to be insufficient. None of it comes from an eye-witness. The writers who state or describe their occurrence were later than they. As long as the evidence for their existence fails to sustain it, all inquiry into their use is needless.

Advocates of the miraculous element in the Gospels find a difficulty in discovering its design and use. They shift from side to side, not knowing the best position to take. " A miracle," says Dr. Mozley, " is the guarantee and voucher for revelation." Is not this view closely connected with the proposition that revelation is the communication of truth undiscoverable and unverifiable by human reason ? Dr. Balmain Bruce supposes that miracles are signs, symbols, visible parables. If such be their nature and significance, they were scarcely needed for ushering a revelation into the world ; or should they be thought necessary, they were inadequate factors. The hypothesis fritters away any important function, and abolishes an attesting character. It is said they only hint a lesson they do not expressly teach ; if so, they might as well have been withheld, since an incipient revelation must, to every-one who believes in it, need more than a thing that hints to strike and convince the mind.

The true evidence for Christianity is internal. What are called the external evidences, *i.e.* miracles and prophecy, are weak attestations of its nature. If the inherent ex-cellence and power of this new religion do not commend it as divine, nothing else is adequate. But Christianity is a word that needs definition, because it is loosely employed and has various senses. The teaching of Christ is not identical with the system developed by Paul out of Judaism and his own consciousness ; nor is the theology of the Fourth

Gospel identical with Paul's. The new religion appears in the ethical precepts and parabolic teaching of the Founder, not in the statements of any disciple; and the Sermon on the Mount presents its best embodiment. As for the creeds of the Churches, they are dominated by the mystical and metaphysical system of Paul, which is preferred to the Master's precepts. Granted that Jesus's ethical doctrine was in a measure ideal, a high ideal is necessary to serve as an incentive and a standard to imperfect humanity. If our nature were pure, the ideal might become real. But modern society is so thoroughly artificial as to neglect or despise the injunctions of the sinless Galilean, whose enthusiasm pointed to heaven through self - sacrificing love.

22nd November.—Finished this day the reading of the *First and Second Epistles to Timothy* in the Syriac version. The reading in 1 Tim. iii. 16 is not $\theta\epsilon\acute{o}\varsigma$, but favours either $\ddot{o}\varsigma$ or $\ddot{o}$, apparently the latter. In 2 Tim. iii. 16 the translation is, "for every Scripture which is written by the Spirit is useful," etc. The $\kappa\alpha\grave{\iota}$ of the original is neglected. Many examples of careless and erroneous renderings appear in the Syriac of these two epistles. Thus in 2 Tim. ii. 15, instead of "rightly dividing" we have "rightly preaching." In iv. 13 we have "the case of books which I left at Troas with Carpus, when you come bring, and the books, and especially the fascicule of volumes." Neither the criticism of the text nor its true interpretation is benefited by the Syriac in the case of these epistles.

26th November.—Finished the reading of the *Epistle to Titus*. Ch. ii. 13 is literally translated from the Greek, and is, like it, altogether favourable to the separation of the great God from "our Saviour Jesus Christ." Part of the subscription, namely, "was sent by Zenas and Apollo," which is in the editions of Schaaf and Lee, is absent from that of Greenfield.

The Psalm-book is one of the most difficult in the Hebrew Bible. As the inscriptions are of little value in determining authorship or age, the contents are all the evidence available for that purpose, and they are too uncertain to give clear help in most instances. I cannot agree with those who deny that David wrote any of the psalms, saying that the collection contains nothing prior to the eighth century B.C. The first book or division contains several psalms that may be assigned to the royal singer with some probability. And it is pretty certain that some were composed in the time of the Maccabees, such as lxxiv., cx., and others; though Gesenius wrote plausibly against this in the *Allgemeine Litteratur Zeitung* (No. 81, p. 643), followed by De Wette and Hupfeld. Hitzig, von Lengerke, and Olshausen go to an extreme position in bringing down a great number to a late time.

In relation to the Messianic character of these poems, in my opinion none is directed to the person of the Messiah either as king or sufferer. All that can be truly said is that such as describe Israel's future in happiness, prosperity, and peace under the Davidic dynasty, in an idealising form, may be considered in a certain sense Messianic. They portray the golden age of hope. By a false interpretation involving a double sense, a Messianic reference is given to psalms, which their authors never dreamt of. To suppose that David speaks of himself, and at the same time of the Messiah prophetically, is against hermeneutical rules. The hypothesis of a twofold sense, or *undertone* as it is sometimes called, cannot be applied without the most arbitrary procedure. Nor can quotations in the New Testament which refer passages in the Psalms to Christ, or to things that happened in the apostolic time, demonstrate the originality of the meaning so assigned to them.

Hitzig is too ingenious in fixing the authors and times

of the individual psalms, though he is probably right in assigning some to Jeremiah. Hupfeld, again, is too sceptical in regard to the same. The titles in the LXX. are conjectural.

Of German commentaries, the best is Hupfeld's. This scholar did well to abandon the new edition of De Wette on the Psalms which he had agreed to undertake, and of which I myself saw the first two printed sheets. He suddenly resolved to compose an independent work. It was hardly wise to occupy so much space with animadversions on Hengstenberg and Delitzsch, or to propose so often alterations of the text. He has not even spared Ewald; though the latter, too, was ready to depreciate his rival, calling him an "old sceptic" when glancing at his portrait in my house. Besides Hupfeld's, there are the commentaries of De Wette, Hitzig, Ewald, and Delitzsch, all indispensable to those who wish to examine the Psalms critically. De Wette's was an epoch-making book, first published in 1811. The version is excellent, and the brief notes good. The introduction, which treats of the nature of Hebrew poetry, is admirable. Even Ewald's *Allgemeines ueber die Hebräische Dichtung* does not supersede it. The fine taste and chaste style which characterised all De Wette's writings are conspicuous in this *Einleitung* to the Psalms. Hitzig is distinguished by the acuteness and ability with which he explains the Hebrew text, but his judgment cannot be commended. He is deficient in imagination, and in sympathy with the lyric odes of the Hebrews. Ewald's work on the Psalms is not his best, but it is still excellent. Four friends adapted certain features of the volume to English readers, adding a few good notes. But they did not give Ewald's version, so that the best part of the original work is absent.[1] The

[1] A complete reproduction of Ewald's book in English appeared afterwards.

incorrect version followed by the friends is that of the great Bible of 1540, because it is in the Book of Common Prayer for the Church of England. Delitzsch, though a fair Hebraist, is somewhat fanciful. His mind having a rabbinical cast, seeks after remote or theosophic ideas, so that he is an uncertain guide in interpretation. Kamphausen's commentary in Bunsen's *Bibelwerk* is the work of a good Hebrew scholar, with useful notes. Hupfeld's influence upon it is perceptible; but the author shows independence even in a book intended for the German people.

Of English commentaries, the chief are those of Perowne, Jennings and Lowe, and Kay. Perowne's is little more than a translation of Hupfeld's, whatever was thought heterodox being omitted; but the work derives all its value from the German original. It is deficient in critical mastery of the Hebrew language and exact scholarship. How poorly prepared the author is for expounding the Psalms appears from the erroneous assertion, " the Psalms to a large extent foreshadow Christ, because the writers of the Psalms are types of Christ." Typology in the Old Testament is now exploded among scholars. The Psalms are not prophetical; and the writers, including David himself, are neither wittingly nor unwittingly typical of Messiah. Thus the 16th Psalm is not, as this writer makes it, a conscious prediction on the part of David in proof of the resurrection of Christ (though Peter applies the words so in the Acts); nor is there, at the same time, " a primary and lower reference to David himself." Such interpretation is erroneous. Wherever the Dean deserts his master, there is reason for thinking him wrong. This is notably exemplified in the explanation of Ps. xlv. 7, where the rendering of two Hebrew words by " thy God's throne," that is, thy throne given and established by God, thy divine throne, being adverse to orthodoxy, must give way to the usual, " Thy throne, O God," etc. Hupfeld and other scholars support the former rendering by various examples, most of which are appropriate, and are also repeated by Perowne. But to destroy their force, he proceeds to say, " it is of importance to observe that in all these instances the noun with the suffix may be explained as being in apposition (not in construction) with the noun following: " my refuge which is strength "; " his garment which is linen," etc. (Ps. lxxxi. 7 ; Lev. vi. 3); but it would be absurd to say, " Thy throne which is God." The construction, therefore, is not identical. This language is misleading. The apposition in question is inadmissible. Thus in 2 Sam. xxii. 18, the supposed apposition gives " my enemies which are strength "; in Lev. xxvi. 42, " my covenant which is Jacob "; in the same book, vi. 3, " his linen garment which is linen "; Ezek. xviii. 7, " his pledge which is a debt." Hence the assumed apposition yields either an empty tautology or an absurdity. The examples of a suffix inserted between the construct state and its genitive cannot be disproved, though they are still disliked by some grammarians, as Müller, who tries to explain them by what he calls an " adverbial accusative." See *Outlines of Hebrew Syntax*, translated by Professor Robertson, p. 54.

The same unwise desertion of his master on behalf of orthodoxy is exemplified in the last verse of the 17th Psalm (which is not Davidic); the note in favour of the verse's reference to waking from the sleep of death, and therefore to a resurrection, is a feeble attempt to justify what is incorrect. The verse alludes to intimate communion with God in the morning after awaking from sleep.

In Ps. xvi. 10 the translation of the Hebrew word *chasid* by *beloved* is incorrect, as it never has that meaning. " Thy *pious* ones " is the right rendering, the adjective being plural.

The work by Jennings and Lowe is better than Perowne's, but is very unequal. These scholars should not quote Perowne, as they do, for statements which are Hupfeld's. Notwithstanding their undue attachment to the titles of Psalms, incorrect Messianic references, evidences of juvenile criticism, and rashness in differing from the masters of Hebrew, their work is the best that has yet appeared in the English language. The introductory remarks on the 51st Psalm are a fair specimen of the authors' ability; but the rendering of *l'baddeka* (ver. 4), "Thou only self-existent One," is impossible; as is "kiss ye the chosen one" in Ps. ii. 12, because of the following context; since the nominative to the verb *be angry* is the *chosen one*, not Jehovah. The only tenable translation is Jerome's, namely, *worship purely*.

Dr. Kay's work on the Psalms cannot be commended, though it comes from one who was chosen to write on Isaiah in the *Speaker's Commentary* [1]—from one, too, who was bold enough to attack a scholar like Hupfeld. In the preface to my translation of Fürst's *Hebrew Lexicon* I made a few remarks on his perfunctory pamphlet. Dr. Kay's work on the Psalms is a poor performance, as may be seen from his making David the author of all the psalms in the first book, and from his interpretation of the vengeful patriotism exhibited in the last verse of the 137th Psalm, "the rock (against which the children should be dashed) as either the firm word of God, or He on whom Zion was founded." His imperfect knowledge of Hebrew appears in pronouncing עֹשָׂיו *osayv*, plural (Ps. cxlix. 2), whereas it is singular.

[1] The article, however, was rejected.

CHAPTER XV

15th December 1887.—It has pleased the great Disposer of all to bring me to another anniversary day that recalls the memory of my irreparable loss. As in former years, I lament over the sins, faults, and shortcomings which mark the twelve months elapsed, and feel grateful to God, who has upheld and brought me thus far. I am now nearer to my eternal state, and believe that I am so much nearer to reunion with her who was my bosom companion for thirty-six years of a chequered character. I have often wondered whether my departed partner enjoys the intercourse in heaven of those whom she loved to associate with on earth. But there is no response to our longings in regard to the employments of the future world. We walk by faith, not by sight, in the present state of existence. It is sufficient for me to believe that she with whom I companied a few years below is now above, happy, near to God, filled with the purest enjoyment, beyond the reach of decay or death. I shall soon be with her again, but oh how changed will both be! Spirits disembodied, yet clothed upon! Meanwhile, blessed, thrice blessed, is the memory of her whose true life has begun, and is advancing, while mine drags along in a world of sin and sorrow.

29th December.—Finished this day the reading of the Epistles to *Philemon* and the *Hebrews* in the Syriac version. The title in Greenfield's edition is " The Epistle of Paul to the Hebrews," incorrectly. Paul's name is rightly omitted in the editions of Schaaf and Lee. There are some awkward renderings in the Epistle to the Hebrews, and some that are paraphrastic. The common Greek text is still followed. The end of the third and beginning of the fourth chapter are erroneously given in Greenfield, but the reading is partly corrected among the *variæ lectiones* at the end of the book. At ch. vi. 1 an interrogation begins, which is carried on to the end of the second verse: "Or do ye lay again another foundation, etc." In vii. 3 we read: "Neither whose father nor mother were written in the genealogies, etc."; and in the twelfth verse, rather loosely, we have: "but as a change was made in the priesthood, so also a change was made in the law." In x. 38 the translation is, "but the just shall live by my faith; and if it be cut off to him, etc." The words "by my faith" are supported by some ancient authorities, as well as by the Septuagint; but there is little doubt that the pronoun belongs to the adjective *just, i.e.* my just one. In xii. 1 we have: "also (let us loose off from us) the sin which is *always prepared* for us"—an incorrect rendering. The New Testament revisers have put in the margin of the verse, as an alternative rendering, "admired of many," which is absurd.

Sunday, 1*st January* 1888.—Blessed be God that I am spared to see the first day of another year, that I have the use of all my powers, and enjoy the necessaries of life, with many of its comforts. What is infinitely superior to these is the light of divine truth which shines upon my path, and is guiding me, I trust, to a higher state. May I be enabled to follow this light, living in nearer communion with God as the days pass over me, and trusting more profoundly in His infinite mercy!

16*th January.*—Finished the reading of *James's Epistle* in the Peshito version. It is better done than is the

Epistle to the Hebrews; but, like the latter, it is of very little use in correcting the original text, and contributes nothing to the right interpretation of the epistle. The title given to the letter in this version is "The Epistle of James the Apostle," which is incorrect, for the word *apostle* is not in the oldest MSS. The Elzevir edition of the Greek text (1633) has "The General Epistle of James the Apostle," as in the Harclean Syriac. Professor Lee should not have inserted the noun *apostle* in the edition of the Bible Society; but Greenfield does the same in the convenient edition he produced for the Bagsters.

18*th February*.—Finished to-day the reading of the two epistles of *Peter* in Syriac. The version of the second is worse than that of the first, and is disfigured by not a few blemishes. To take a single example, ch. ii. 12, 13, is awkwardly rendered. In Greenfield's edition the subscription is, "the second epistle of Peter, head of the apostles, is finished," whereas in Schaaf's and Lee's we have only "Peter the apostle." But the version of 2 Peter is that of the Philoxenian, not the Peshito.

21*st February*.—In reading the life of Bishop Colenso, I met with a reference to Bishop Butler's sermon on the character of Balaam. The discourse is undoubtedly marked by great ability; but the writer did not study the nature of the sources from which all our knowledge respecting Balaam must be drawn, and he has therefore failed to apprehend the seer's character. This remark is not meant to disparage his analytical power in delineating mental phenomena. Where Philo was puzzled over the constituent elements of a peculiar character, Butler may be excused if he also failed.

There are two traditions respecting Balaam, one unfavourable, the other the reverse. In Num. xxxi. 16 and Josh. xiii. 22 he appears as a heathen soothsayer, through whose evil counsels to the Midianite women the

Israelites were enticed into the impure worship of Baalpeor. In Num. xxii.–xxiv. he is a true prophet, who refuses under great pressure to speak aught but what he receives from the Lord.

The unfavourable notices are in the Elohist document; the opposite proceed from an unknown writer, whom critics have assigned to different times. Whoever the latter was, his power of prophetic description is great; his picture of Balaam's conduct and utterances graphic. The scenes are unhistorical, the statements put into the seer's mouth being the writer's own, who uses Balaam in the long past time of Moses as their vehicle. Whether the prophet was a real or mythical person is of no importance. A dim legend had gathered round a heathen sorcerer in Mesopotamia, which sufficed to the Jewish writer for a medium of his elevated utterances.

The object of this sublime piece (Num. xxii. 2–xxiv. 25) is to glorify Israel in her conquests over the peoples who stood in the way of her entrance into Canaan, as also to exalt her religious character and future prosperity, though the writer deals in exaggeration and idealises extravagantly, else he could not say—

> " He hath not beheld iniquity in Jacob,
> Neither hath he seen misery in Israel";

and again—

> " There is no enchantment in Jacob,
> Neither is there any divination in Israel";

yet the true prophetic spirit actuated him whose vision was wider and higher than that of his countrymen generally.

The section relating to the ass (Num. xxii. 22–35) is plainly an insertion by a later hand. It breaks the connection and introduces jarring elements into the character of Balaam. From what purpose it proceeded is difficult to say; perhaps with the object of mediating between the favourable and unfavourable traditions by throwing some dark traits over the bright colours of the later picture. The interpolator narrates the occurrence about the ass as an historical fact, with no indication of Balaam having a vision or dream.

In like manner, internal evidence shows that xxiv. 20–24 was not written by the author of the whole piece, but by one who lived as late as Hezekiah. He was not the Jehovist who seems to have inserted xxii. 22–35.

I incline to the opinion that the writer of the poetic section before us was the second Elohist—not Vatke's so-called second Elohist, whom he puts before the usual Elohist, but Hupfeld's junior Elohist. If so, he may have been contemporary with Elijah. It is improbable that he belonged to the reign of David, as Kalisch supposes. David is described in ideal language, which savours of a time tolerably remote from his own. There were prophets indeed at this period—Gad, Nathan, and others. Samuel had instituted schools of them. These prophets may have written annals, but the character of the ideas and style suits a more advanced period than that of the first kings. Such far-reaching visions show more reflectiveness than is consistent with an age of the forming and consolidation of a kingdom by perpetual wars.

It is worthy of note that the New Testament writers follow the older tradition, which makes Balaam an evil-minded sorcerer. In the Second Epistle of Peter and that of Jude, as also in the Revelation, he is a perverter of the pious.

24th February.—In the life of Colenso there is reference to a hymn-book which he compiled, and from which prayer addressed to Christ was excluded, the bishop contending that Paul's epistles present no example of such prayer. A passage (2 Cor. xii. 8) immediately occurred to me, in which the apostle says, " I besought the Lord thrice that it might depart from me," De Wette explaining the word "Lord" by Christ, and referring to the answer following for such interpretation. Does the answer justify the interpretation? I think not. "And he said unto me, My grace is sufficient for thee: for my strength is made perfect in weakness. Most gladly, therefore, will I rather glory in my infirmities, that the power of Christ may rest upon me." *My* grace does not necessarily refer to Christ's grace; and *my* power is not the right reading, but only "power" by itself. "Power is perfected in infirmity." The Revised Version, though reading the original without the *my*, needlessly, if not improperly, supplies the *my*. When we recollect that Paul looked upon Christ as the heavenly man, a being who was in the form of God, which is certainly different from consubstantiality and coeternity with God, it is improbable that he should in this one instance speak of himself as praying to Christ. He would have been inconsistent had he prayed to a created being.

Colenso's hymn-book, now before me, does not, however, carry out the idea that worship to the Son is omitted; for while some stanzas of the hymn "Hark! the herald angels sing," referring to the deity of Christ, are omitted from 156, yet 159 advocates worship to the Son, namely—

> "Hymns of praise then let us sing
> Unto Christ, our Heavenly King,
> Who endured the cross and grave,
> Sinners to redeem and save."

27th February.—Is there any good reason for holding the opinion, now pretty general among critics of the Old Testament, that Moses did not write the Decalogue, or "the ten words," in the 20th chapter of Exodus? My attention has been directed to this subject by a perusal of Colenso's life, where is again brought forward the singular opinion that the Deuteronomist not only wrote the copy of

the Decalogue in his own work, but also inserted the other
in Ex. xx. Whatever be thought of the two copies, one
thing is certain: that the Exodus one is older and more
original than that of Deuteronomy. It seems to me that
the additions and variations made in the Commandments
have led many to assume a later date than Moses's time.
At first their form was very brief, and can be separated
from editorial accretions without much difficulty, as
follows—

     I. I am Jehovah thy God.
    II. Thou shalt have no other Gods before Me.
   III. Thou shalt not take the name of Jehovah thy God for
        falsehood.
    IV. Remember the Sabbath day to keep it holy.
     V. Honour thy father and thy mother.
    VI. Thou shalt not kill.
   VII. Thou shalt not commit adultery.
  VIII. Thou shalt not steal.
    IX. Thou shalt not bear false witness.
     X. Thou shalt not covet.

This original form may have proceeded from Moses, who
was instructed in the learning of the Egyptians; and *The
Book of the Dead*, a very old Egyptian work, has some
prohibitions similar to those in the Decalogue.

The copy of the Decalogue in Ex. xx. is Jehovistic.
It is not original, but derived from an older and Mosaic
document, and furnished with additions. The Decalogue
did not remain in its enlarged state, for the Deuteronomist
retouched and altered it. Bishop Colenso has correctly
pointed out, in the sixth part of his work on the Pentateuch and Book of Joshua, the variations between the
Jehovistic and Deuteronomist copies.

As his inquiries advanced, his critical power became
stronger and clearer. But he made mistakes, some of
them showing that he had not reached the highest stage
of critical discernment or of acquaintance with the Hebrew
language. Thus the name Jehovah was of earlier intro-

duction than Samuel's time, into which he puts it, as is shown by the song of Deborah. His views about the Elohistic and Jehovistic Psalms need correction. None in the second book is Davidic. The three, li. lx. lxviii., for which he argues very confidently as of that date, are much later. It was especially rash to contend for the early date of the 68th, the most difficult of all the Psalms, in opposition to the correct view of Ewald, Hupfeld, and Hitzig.

28th February.—Finished to-day the *First Epistle of John* in the Peshito. There is a curious reading in the 3rd chapter, 1st verse, "That He has called us sons, *also made us.*" This is nearly the same as Tischendorf's text, "And we are so." In v. 7 the edition of Schaaf has the incorrect reading of the received text respecting the three heavenly witnesses, but the editions of Lee and Greenfield are correct.

When referring above to 2 Cor. xii. 8 as bearing upon prayer to Christ in the epistles of Paul, I should have glanced at some other passages which are often adduced in favour of the orthodox view. The verb translated "to call upon" ($\epsilon\pi\iota\kappa\alpha\lambda\epsilon\omega$) is said to mean *to adore* or *worship* in Rom. x. 12, 13; 1 Cor. i. 2. But this is incorrect. Calling upon the name of Christ, or calling upon Him as the Lord, is simply acknowledging Him as the Lord, confessing His name as that of the Lord. And He is Lord of all, because the theocracy of which He is the head is destined to embrace all. This interpretation is in harmony with the general teaching of the apostle, which conveys the idea that the Son of God, after putting off His body on the cross, returned to heaven, where He is enthroned at the right hand of God as "our Lord," the Lord of glory. The distinction between Christ and the Father, the supreme God and His Son, which Paul always makes, forbids us to believe that he thought *worship* should be paid to the latter. He was a monotheist. The lexicons to the New Testament, Robinson's and Grimm's, should be corrected in respect to the verb "call upon"; and even De Wette's note on Rom. x. 12, 13 is lacking in precision.

6th March.—It is curious to watch the ecclesiastical appointments made by Prime Ministers, but it is neither instructive nor edifying. Most right-minded men think that politicians are poor judges of spiritual men, or of those who are well fitted for the discharge of spiritual functions by culture, temper, talents, learning, and piety. The Church of England, however, has to submit to politicians and their methods of administering ecclesiastical affairs. I have noticed that the appointments of bishops and deans by Mr. Disraeli were usually good, and those of Mr. Gladstone inferior. The former was an excellent judge of men, the latter not.

I have also noticed that the men elevated by Mr. Gladstone do not respond to his political views even when these are in harmony with the principles of Christianity. The clergy of the Established Church who signed, a few days ago, an address to Gladstone in favour of Home Rule for Ireland did themselves honour. They spoke out on behalf of justice, liberty, and the gospel principle of doing to others as they should wish others to do to them. But where are the bishops appointed by Gladstone? They are dumb. Not one prelate signed the manifesto; and almost all heads of houses in the Universities, with deans, canons, and the occupants of rich livings, were silent. As far as they are concerned, the conquered island is to be treated with unmerited cruelty. The Irish are to them an inferior race, unfit for self-government, incapable of managing their own affairs. The body of the clergy approve of conduct which I do not hesitate to call unchristian. It is disgraceful on their part to look with indifference or content on fellow-Christians suffering under the iron heel of a despotic executive. Happily the conscience of the Nonconformist ministers of religion is right on this question.

7th March.—News of the death of an old and much esteemed friend, the Rev. Isaac Nelson, formerly M.P. for Mayo, has reached me to-day. I knew him as a fellow-student in Belfast College many years ago ; and though the currents of our lives ran in different channels, I was glad to see him from time to time. He was a genuine man,—honest, faithful, truthful,—an excellent classical and oriental scholar, a hater of shams, an enemy to cant and hypocrisy. After joining the Home Rule party, his congregation deserted him, and his brethren shunned him, shoving him into the background, though he might have ably filled any theological office they had it in their power to give. Dislike of one who was not slow to expose their hollow measures caused him to be passed over, and incompetent teachers to be lifted above his head into positions for which they were unfit. He never did full justice to himself, or showed all the abilities he possessed. Hallowed be the memory of Isaac Nelson, who with all his faults (and where is the man without them?) did good service in his day. The loss of a trusty friend is heavy, especially in an evil-speaking, evil-judging generation; but severed ties will be reunited in a happier state.

17th May—Finished to-day the reading of the *Syriac Apocalypse.* One peculiarity struck me in the translation. The beast with the seven heads and ten horns is usually called " the animal of the tooth." Why so? I am unable to understand the reason of this designation. Nothing corresponds to it in the original Greek.

12th July.—During the past and present week many clerical strangers have been in London, owing to two councils or synods having met by previous arrangement to discuss their affairs—the Pan-Anglican and the Pan-Presbyterian assemblies. These gatherings are imitations of the ancient councils, though they are but feeble copies; for the old assemblies, whose histories are contained in books describing the progress of the Christian Church, were vigorous in their doings. Much benefit either to religion or morality is not likely to result from them. The character of the talk, and of the papers read, is usually vague and superficial. Actors and speakers do not think of going to the root of the all-important subject they ought to consider: they do not attempt to reform, abridge, or alter their creeds and articles, though these are out of harmony with the thought of the age. By allowing them to remain as they are, hypocrisy and moral cowardice are encouraged. It is strange to see all the orthodox Churches who deify Christ after the example of the Nicene Creed maintaining doctrinal symbols varying from and largely inconsistent with His teaching. Alas that the simple doctrine of Christ should be shoved aside by the traditions of men!

These congresses and councils are useless, because they concern themselves with mint, anise, and cummin, neglecting weightier matters; because the bodies they represent are more desirous to promote their own interests than the cause of spiritual truth, thinking themselves the best Churches, and boasting of their doings. A large organisation nurtures a feeling of self-satisfied pride. I see no prospect of Christianity becoming a universal religion till it be less outwardly organised, and Christ's religion be preached as the one medicine to cure the world's corruption. Prevalent Christianity is too dogmatic, superstitious, and unpractical to bring about a deep-reaching purity of motive and conduct.

Specimens of the sayings and statements put forth by these bodies might be quoted in proof of the spirit that animates their proceedings. At one of the Pan-Presbyterian meetings a professor of theology, who attacked the chief scientific heresies of the day and disposed of the whole in a few sentences, reminded one of Simon Browne, the man without a soul, writing against Tindal, author of *Christianity as Old as the Creation.* Feeble antagonists butt against strong barriers, and suffer in the estimation of all except themselves. Another champion called popery " an unmitigated curse."

14*th July.*—It is a common but none the less true saying, that when thinking begins, orthodoxy ceases. Unfortunately, thinking never begins with the majority of mankind, who move all their lives in the rut along which their parents crept. Being born Churchmen or Dissenters, and inheriting the faith of their fathers, they do not question its truth. What has been good enough for father or mother is equally good for them. " Quieta non movere " is their principle—a principle often pernicious.

17*th July.*—The words of Conyers Middleton, author of *The Life of Cicero,* deserve to be quoted and adopted by every independent thinker, to whatever time he belongs :—

" If religion consists in what our modern apologists seem to place it, the depreciating moral duties and the depressing natural reason ; if the duty of it be, what their practice seems to intimate, to hate and persecute for a different way of thinking in points, where the best and wisest have never agreed ; then I declare myself an infidel, and to have no share of that religion. But if to live strictly and think freely, to practise what is moral, and to believe what is rational be consistent with the sincere profession of Christianity ; then I shall always acquit myself like one of its truest professors."

22*nd July.*—The Darwinian doctrine of evolution has been welcomed as an evidence of the advance which man has made in his progress towards high scientific truth ; and I can endorse the language in which it is commended by Oliver Wendell Holmes :—

" It removes the traditional curse from that helpless infant lying in its mother's arms. It lifts from the shoulders of man the responsibility for the fact of death. If it is true, woman can no longer be taunted with having brought down on herself the pangs which make her sex a martyrdom. If development upward is the general law of the race, if we have grown by natural evolution out of the cave-man and even less human forms of life, we have everything to hope from the future."

Some of the methods by which it is thought that Darwinism has been refuted are failures, as is that of Max Müller, who argues that language and thought being identical, man has that of which no trace can be found in the most developed animal, and therefore his genealogical descent from the latter is impossible. But that language is necessary to the existence of thought requires much more evidence in its support than Müller can furnish. The characteristic feature of Darwinism is man's development from an animal—an idea which certainly disagrees with the account of the human creation in the Book of Genesis. As the Biblical narrative is a philosophical myth,—the attempt of some mind or minds to explain the origin of the human race,—the new hypothesis may be set over against the old one.

I could adopt the notion of man's descent from some of the lower animal species, or even from a primeval germ,— call it protoplasm or what you will,—if it were at all probable that the supposed original was endued with a vital principle capable of endless development by a power of supreme intelligence. A first cause of this nature cannot be dispensed with by any true philosophy; and the words *force, energy*, etc., which some thinkers prefer, are inadequate substitutes for a higher term.

In my apprehension, an important link has yet to be found between any of the highest animals and man. A gap still exists; and though it may disappear in the course of ages, its present existence should lead the scientist himself to pause before he accepts the Darwinian hypothesis. It is wholly unlikely that any of the so-called irrational animals will ever reach such upward development as to conceive the idea of God as a moral Governor of the world. The evidence in favour of man having gradually emerged out of a low savage state, instead of having fallen from one of perfect innocence, is strong, and his evolution still continues; but when and how he received the divine spark (the $\pi\nu\epsilon\hat{\upsilon}\mu\alpha$) that enables him to commune with God is unknown. He was not born with veritable guilt upon him, but with a tendency which either promotes or hinders his moral progress, according to surrounding circumstances.

It is important that science and Scripture should be kept apart, for most attempts at reconciling them do violence to one or other. As far as the Bible touches upon scientific subjects, it expresses the opinions current at a certain period in one part of the world, which it is unreasonable to force into agreement with the established results of modern philosophy. If there be discord, truth lies with the facts which science has clearly reached, as appears in the case of geology.

25th July.—It is now more than thirty years since I left the Independent Academy at Manchester, and my life has had its vicissitudes since then. I have gained liberty of thought, speech, and action such as I could not have had by continuing under the restraints which I had begun to feel rather acutely in the year 1856. Truly I have never regretted obeying the suggestions of conscience and welcoming the increasing light that continued to stream upon my mind, dispelling the ignorance, darkness, and prejudices which had enslaved it so long. I am thankful to the Almighty that I tried, not without success, to keep a conscience, and was saved from hypocrisy.

27th July.—I am glad to think that most of those who call themselves orthodox have abandoned the belief on which missions to the heathen were established, namely, that all to whom the gospel of Christ is unknown cannot be saved. I remember the time when that belief prevailed, forming the keynote of missionary sermons, and delighting listeners who cherished the inward satisfaction that *they* were not as these reprobate sinners. The discarding of such a notion is cheering, since it is terrible to think that the great majority of the human race are condemned to everlasting misery by a God under whose providence they are without any opportunity of learning the facts of Christianity. A Being of infinite goodness is libelled by one who says that He creates millions upon millions of rational beings who cannot but be, all their lives, beyond the reach of salvation. Verily, reason is perverted by multitudes. That divine gift is debased when it is used to belittle both God and man.

31st July.—We are now in the development period of Christianity, though not in an advanced stage of it. As time proceeds, those who think at all must witness the abandonment of doctrines long believed and still embodied in ecclesiastical creeds—such doctrines as the old tenet of the total inspiration of Scripture, the Athanasian Trinity, the sameness of Christ with the Supreme God in substance and attributes, vicarious satisfaction for sin, and the magical influence, however veiled or mysterious, of the sacraments. It is hard for any cultivated mind to entertain the idea that these can ever regain the hold they once had upon professing Christians, or enter into the honest convictions of a well-educated man. The passing away of such beliefs should gratify all who desire to see the corruptions of Christianity vanish into the past.

14th August.—The Rev. H. B. Wilson has been released at last from the frail tenement in which his spirit was enclosed. I knew him well, and valued him highly. Within the Church of England he had few equals as regards sound, independent thinking and general culture. Honest, upright, candid, sincere, modest, large-minded, he was one whom to know is a privilege seldom enjoyed in a world like the present. It was owing to him that the *Essays and Reviews* appeared, and the meeting held to arrange the contents of the volume took place in the old vicarage of Great Staughton. The general editorship was assigned to him, so that he had to conduct the correspondence with publishers and others. Those who were present will remember how his pleading before the Privy Council produced a marked effect on the learned judges, for it showed remarkable ability. To use one of his own phrases, he was a *bonâ fide man* all over, deserving a high niche in the temple which the noble - minded asserters of liberty of conscience have been trying to build. I visited him years ago at Great Staughton, before his illness; soon after, he was struck down, remaining in a state of helplessness for nearly twenty years. My visits to him always left a sorely depressing effect on the mind. Farewell thou noble brother, but only for a time. We shall meet again.

15th August.—Not long ago Mr. Peter Taylor, formerly member of Parliament for Leicester, and a lineal descendant of the Rev. Henry Taylor, rector of Crawley, kindly presented me with the productions of his ancestor, the author's own copies, furnished with MS. notes in his own handwriting. Along with these was Mr. Taylor's copy of the *Essay on Spirit* attributed to Bishop Clayton, but said to have been written by one of his clergy. Mr. Taylor was an Arian, who held that the angel of the covenant spoken of in the Old Testament was Christ, and at the same time believed in the personality of the Holy Spirit. The volumes show extensive reading, as also a fair amount of acquaintance both with the Bible and the Fathers. Mr. Taylor examines the creeds of the Church and finds fault with them, thinking it enough to subscribe to the Scriptures alone. When I was a student, I became acquainted with the views of Mr. Taylor through Hill's *Lectures on Divinity*, which was used as a text-book by Chalmers as an able exposition of the Calvinistic system. At the same time I learned the opinions advanced in Clayton's essay, which cannot withstand, any more than Taylor's, the force of impartial criticism at the present day. Neither writer perceived Paul's exact doctrine of Christ's person; and both were unduly wedded to the words of Scripture, as was formerly usual with Arians and Socinians. Both Churchmen were out of harmony with the creeds of their Church, but do not seem to have contemplated secession from it. In their works an intelligent reader will find a good deal of sound reasoning against the Christology of the creeds, mixed up with much that is untenable. There are many true statements along with incorrect interpretations of Scripture. It is easy to detect errors in former writers, but we should leniently judge those who may have helped us to the truth which they failed to apprehend. Mr. Taylor, who lived more than a century ago, was a man in advance of his time, and I respect his memory. A divine who could approve of this language in the year 1777,

" you will agree, then, that in history, geography, astronomy, and philosophy the messengers of God were no better instructed than others, and therefore were not less liable to be misled by the errors and prejudices of the times in which they lived. They related facts like honest men, to the best of their knowledge and information; and recorded the divine lessons of their Master with the utmost fidelity; but pretended to no infallibility, but sometimes differed in their relations, and sometimes disagreed in their sentiments; all which proves only that they did not write in combination to deceive,"

puts to shame many clerical instructors in the present day. Teacher is not synonymous with thinker.

24th August.—I have just examined the contents of a pamphlet entitled *Conference of Bishops of the Anglican Communion, holden at Lambeth Palace in July* 1888, and asked myself is this the outcome of the episcopal deliberations of weeks? The document is dry and the language guarded, without a suggestion about a thorough revisal of the creeds. On the contrary, the letter of the conference declares that they (the bishops) are united under one Head in " holding the one faith defined in the creeds, maintained by the Primitive Church, and affirmed by the undisputed Œcumenical Councils." This amounts to the assertion of adherence to the traditional beliefs which were gradually evolved among the Christians of the second, third, and first half of the fourth century, till they culminated in the Nicene Council 325 A.D. The statement that such " is the one faith revealed in Holy Writ" must be called an unfounded assumption. Besides the Apostles' and Nicene Creeds, it is strange to find the Athanasian recommended in the following words: " We accept the hymn *Quicunque vult*, whether or not recited in the public worship of our churches, as resting upon certain warrant of Scripture, and as most useful, both at home and in our missions, in ascertaining and defining the fundamental mysteries of the Holy Trinity, and of the Incarnation of our blessed Lord, and thus guarding believers from lapsing into heresy." An ecclesiastical body using such language is beyond the reach of legitimate criticism or hope of healthful reform. Darkened by the blind veneration of antiquity, it retains an uncharitable document for recital or singing during public worship.

20th September.—This day I finished my daily reading of the *Books of Samuel.* These present the history of the Hebrew nation from the birth of Samuel till close upon the death of David. The compiler used two sources, the older beginning with 1 Sam. ix. 1–x. 16, etc., the younger with 1 Sam. i.–viii. These documents differ little in diction and style, but the character of their narratives varies, the younger having certain prophetic elements. The later writer seems to have been acquainted with the former, though his object was not to supplement merely. Differences and contradictions prove the use of distinct sources, and an attentive reader will soon observe them. One example of their employment appears in the manner of David's introduction to Saul: the younger source representing him as a youthful musician taken to court to drive away Saul's evil spirit (1 Sam. xvi.), while the older makes him acquainted with Saul for the first time after his defeat of Goliath (1 Sam. xvii. 55, etc.).

The two sources were put together by a writer who did little to harmonise them, though he showed some skill in interweaving their contents. A few appropriate insertions are due to him, such as that in 1 Sam. xx. 1, where the older source is resumed, after the insertion of xix. 9–24 from the younger, that knows nothing of David at Ramah. To connect the two, the words "fled from Naioth in Ramah and came and" were inserted. After xix. 8 the older source continued to say, "And David said before Jonathan," etc., as in xx. 1.

The age of the work as it now is coincides with that of the Books of Kings, since the final redactor was the author of the latter. As the two sources belonged to the eighth and seventh centuries B.C., and the Kings were written towards the end of the Babylonian captivity, the latter must be the date of the Samuel books. Exaggerations and legendary notices prove that the writers of the main sources lived a considerable time after the events described.

The conclusion, continuing the history of David till his death, was cut off by the writer of the Kings, who used it for his own work at the commencement of the Kings, after inserting the appendix to 2 Sam. xxi.–xxiv.

The text is not in a good state, and needs emendation with the help of the Septuagint and other versions, as also the parallels in the Chronicles, and conjecture. Thenius is too fond of altering it by the Greek translation, and Wellhausen also corrects too much. Even in the notes to Bunsen's *Bibelwerk* there is more emendation than is necessary.

The legendary account of David's encounter with Goliath may have an historical basis. A combat with some Philistine gave rise to the laudation of the conqueror, with an exaggeration of stature, strength, and armour. In 1 Sam. xvii. *David* slays the giant; in 2 Sam. xxi. 19, *Elhanan*. The latter, however, has been corrected by the parallel in 1 Chron. xx. 5, where it is said that Elhanan slew *the brother* of Goliath; a correction we cannot adopt, though it is approved by Winer and Thenius. To remove the discrepancy and retain the victory over Goliath for *David*, the Chronicle writer has " Elhanan the son of Jair slew Lahmi the brother of Goliath," etc. Though the text in Samuel is not free from corruption, it is better than its parallel in Chronicles, where *Bethlemite* is made a proper name.

Another passage which needs a few explanatory remarks is 2 Sam. xii. 31, "And he brought forth the people that were therein (Rabbah) and put them under saws, and under harrows of iron, and under axes of iron, and made them pass through the brick-kiln." The textual reading of בְּמַלְכֵּן should be retained, and its Masoretic substitute rejected. It is the same as Milcam, Milcom, Moloch, an idol of the Ammonites and Moabites, in whose arms human sacrifices were offered up. "He made them pass through Malcen," *i.e.* they were burnt in the huge image.

The passage has given rise to considerable discussion, because it affects the character of David so darkly, depicting him as a man who could punish enemies with a savage barbarity seldom practised before. Apologists have recourse to a different translation. Thus Chandler (*Critical History of the Life of David*, pp. 398, 399, Oxford edition) translates, " he puts them to the saw, to iron mines, and to iron axes, and transported them to the brick-kilns," *i.e.* put them to the most servile employments, which is incorrect. So is his rendering of the parallel in 1 Chron. xx. 2, " he divided them to the saw, to the mines and axes "; both supported by bad criticism.

In reference to the last charge which David gave to Solomon respecting Joab and Shimei, this biographer presumes to write, " if I understand anything of justice and equity, it was an order worthy of a good king, and fit to be given in the last moments of his life." Does this language suit the bloody charge delivered to Solomon —the charge to murder two noted persons? Is the feeling of vengeance a virtue in the mind of a dying man? The deathbed of Socrates presents a far different picture to this. Verily the heathen's conduct at the end of life was nobler than that of him who is called " the man after God's heart."

30*th September*.—I have read *Robert Elsmere*, a novel displaying much ability, and full of interest. The gifted authoress has got hold of various views entertained by the advanced theologians of the day, and uses them appropriately in her description of the hero of the book. The character of the unbelieving squire is overdrawn. He is both unnatural and unamiable. Newcome's is exaggerated and even grotesque. But that of Robert Elsmere is finely drawn, as is his wife's also. Some noble sentiments are put into the mouth of the former. It is not easy to see whether the description at the end of the third volume is founded on fact or merely ideal. It is shaded off in lines indistinct and unsatisfactory. The authoress rightly sets

14

forth the emotional part of our nature as the seat of religion, though the intellect may reject Church creeds and dogmas as well as Bible statements. A deeply religious man may be highly sceptical. As long, however, as he believes in God, taking Christ for his inspirer, his sinless example, the life of his soul, the divine man revealing the unseen Father, he is a true Christian. Such I have known, seeing in them the brightest types of genuine piety, and counting their companionship an honour.

17th October.—A copy of the *Church Times*, containing a report of the proceedings of the Church Congress at Manchester, has just come into my hands, from which I see that the old spirit is still there. The chairman is blamed for throwing a sop to "the whining of that episcopal Cerberus," Bishop Ryle, and Sir George W. Cox's paper was received with "a unanimous outburst of execration." Strong language this, which, if true, disgraces none but the reverend hearers. The preparation of such a paper as that of Sir George reflects honour on my esteemed friend, whose candour and courage are worthy of all praise. Nor is he the only clergyman who holds similar views. Many entertain the like, but are careful to hide them. All the more credit is due to Sir G. Cox for fearlessly proclaiming them in the face of a great clerical assembly—an assembly largely composed of unthinking religionists who could only cry "shame." Both they and the organs of the religious parties they belong to can only ignore or simply denounce what they call heresy. Contented they are to repeat ancient creeds. How are clerics averse to the study of independent sources!

5th December.—I have looked over the pages of the late Earl of Shaftesbury's biography. The earl was a well-meaning, earnest, conscientious, philanthropic man, but his conscience was not highly enlightened, and his spirit was narrow. He was intolerant, uncharitable, bigoted, ignorant in Biblical matters, prone to denounce opinions which differed from his own bibliolatry. His diary is interspersed with intemperate language against Romanism, Ritualism, and Neology, evincing a mind not unlike that of John and James when they wished to call fire from heaven to consume the Samaritans. The following quotations attest the truth of what I have said. Of a spirit contrary to that which pervades the teaching of Christ, I can find no better example:—

Colenso on the *Pentateuch*: "This puerile and ignorant attack on the sacred and unassailable Word of God."

Renan's *Life of Jesus*: "A book written for the most iniquitous purposes."

Seeley's *Ecce Homo*: "The most pestilential book ever vomited from the jaws of hell."

Pusey's "marvellous essay on Daniel, which he could not have composed but by the special grace of God." This borders on the blasphemous.

"How deeply evangelical is that Book of Proverbs! How plainly one may see and feel Christ speaking under the Old as under the New Testament."

Revised Version: "These fellows are enfeebling our doctrine, and it is quite in harmony to enfeeble the language in which it is expressed."

Gladstone: "His language and his acts, his private statements inconsistent with, and contradictory of, his public statements: all prove him to be governed by the greed of place and salary and power."

"When Gladstone runs down a steep place, his immense majority, like the pigs in Scripture, but hoping for a better issue, will go with him, roaring in grunts of exultation."

Alas that even good men should present religion in such a light!

FROM PROFESSOR JOWETT

"OXFORD, 30*th December* 1885.

". . . Liberal views in theology make greater progress than formerly, but in a sort of subterranean, and also negative manner. People do not say much about this publicly, and the change in their opinions is seen more by what they do not say than by what they do. Perhaps it is better that the movement should be slow: so many strange, ill-considered notions become attached to it. I never hear anyone preach about eternal punishment, or vicarious atonement, or verbal inspiration; and very few about miracles—even the Bishop of London tells us that the miracles of the Old Testament have no sufficient evidence.

" I should greatly like to see subscription to the Articles abolished in the Church of England. But Church reformers seem indisposed to touch that subject: either in the Church of England or in the Church of Scotland. I was glad to see that Dr. Martineau spoke of it as the first reform which was required.

" The remembrance of the old struggle in which you bore so distinguished a part makes me send you these reflections."

CHAPTER XVI

Hastings, 15th December 1888.—Another of these dismal anniversaries has come round, bringing with it more than the usual sorrows. When I try to recall the course of events with which my life has been connected since the last anniversary, there is little of importance to note. I have been diligent in the daily reading of the Hebrew Bible and the Syriac Testament, have endeavoured to see the latest critical material explanatory of the Greek Testament, and have entered in my Autobiography reflections on different topics. I have made small additions to and considerable improvements in the revised *Introduction to the New Testament*, which will make it far superior to the last edition. This work of revision and re-revision must go on while the amended copy remains in my hands. The greater part of the year has been saddened by the illness of my dear daughter, on whose account we are now at this seaside place. Though months of anxiety have passed, solicitude is not over, for I am still harassed with fears day and night, so that comfort is at a low ebb. At my age one cannot but suffer in health from continuous trouble. Next to the departed, of whose companionship I was deprived sixteen years ago, no loss could be greater than that of my only daughter, who has been all in all to me of earthly associates. . . . Blessed is the memory of the wife with whom I lived so congenially for thirty-six years. I have not rejoined her, since God has prolonged my days beyond the usual span, and all His arrangements are right. Amid the practical atheism of the age we must cherish belief in the Infinite One, who has condescended to reveal Himself, through Jesus Christ, as our Heavenly Father; and we must hold fast the hope of a blessed immortality. We must believe Him to be the moral Governor of the world, to whom we are accountable for the use of the powers we possess. We must still cling to the teaching and person of Jesus, who is our best practical guide. This I try to do, in humble reliance on divine help.

22nd December.—The Theological Faculty of Giessen has recently conferred the degree of Doctor of Theology upon Prince Bismarck.

The reason assigned for the action, has been to express the gratitude of the faculty to Prince Bismarck for removing Professor Harnack, once a Giessen professor, to Berlin. Better that he should have been allowed to continue at Marburg. The idea of a military despot having to do with the selection of theological professors in the Universities is sufficiently absurd. Surely the Minister of Public Instruction is the recognised director of scholastic affairs; mere politicians are poor judges of what is best to promote the literary success of a University. The Faculty of Giessen has been lowered in the estimation of the great seats of theological learning in Germany by its action in the matter of degrees.

7th January 1889.—I see that Mr. Kennard, in his funeral sermon for the Rev. H. B. Wilson, has brought into prominence a principle enunciated and explained by the latter in the essay entitled *The National Church*—the so-called ideological mode of interpreting Scripture and the creeds, according to which different values are set upon them: the unlearned adhering to the letter, the learned extracting the spirit; the former taking the history as history, the latter concerned only with the ideas embodied. These put the spirit above the letter, or rather they abandon the letter and resort to the spirit. In this way the gulf which separates the learned and unlearned members of the National Church is bridged over, and both may unite in one comprehensive ecclesiastical organisation, worshipping together in peace. I reject this mode of dealing with Scripture and of subscribing creeds, because it permits, and even encourages, the rejection of the one sense which the original writers intended to convey—the frittering of it away in spiritual applications or thin emblems. The only honest course is for all, simple and thoughtful, to accept Scripture and the creeds in the sense which the writers themselves meant to express, and to adopt no unnatural methods of escaping from the literal through the spiritual. If Paul sometimes allegorised the Hebrew records in Rabbinical fashion, that is no rule for us. And he did not exalt occasional adaptations of the old history into a principle. The expedient resembles the expository idealising of Philo and Origen. Mr. Wilson has said all that could be advanced in favour of a method of interpretation which would make a National Church national in fact, but he felt at times the slipperiness of the ground ; for he told me that if he were called upon to subscribe the formularies again, he would hesitate or refuse. My lamented friend was subtle, ingenious, and learned, but his clear-headedness compelled him to suspect the soundness of the ideological process, in the application of which purity of conscience is liable to suffer. There is no proper place for it in the school of ethics. It has all the appearance of a device to get rid of Scripture statements and dogmatic creeds repugnant to reason.

17th January.—My esteemed friend Mr. Call, whose fine scholarship and extensive reading have often assisted me in coming to a decision on difficult questions, for his judgment is usually sound, writes that he has lately read the Book of Daniel three times over in the original, with Hitzig, von Lengerke, Ewald, and my own critical exposition by his side. It also appears that he has come across the lucubrations of Dr. Tregelles, whose English translation of Gesenius's *Lexicon* always tends to raise the anger of scholars because of remarks interposed to correct the great Hebraist's heresies. In all cases of Old Testament interpretation, in critical and grammatical questions, it need not be said that Gesenius is right and his corrector wrong.

The position of the Book of Daniel among others of the Old Testament has been settled for years past, so that every attempt to put it earlier than the Maccabean times is nugatory. Pusey's volume, impregnated with his usual spirit, only shows incapacity for interpreting the Hebrew Scriptures impartially. Where Hengstenberg failed, *he* could not succeed.

While referring to the British translation of Gesenius's *Lexicon*, I may speak of the American one made by Dr. Robinson, which is much superior, the production of a good and careful scholar. Even he, however, occasionally ventures to correct Gesenius when the latter is right, especially in passages where the authority of the New Testament seems to require another interpretation than that which the original warrants. Many have yet to learn that this authority is not paramount, and cannot set aside the true sense of the Hebrew. In regard to names of places, he has made some useful additions to Gesenius's explanation, and has sometimes pointed out the correct locality, instead of that given in the lexicon; but in lexical and grammatical points he interferes erroneously. An example occurs under the word *Elohim* (p. 55), where Robinson differs from the Halle professor. I am far from upholding the infallibility of the lexicographer, whose treatment of several words might be improved, but I protest against any other than a master setting himself up to contradict, whether he be Lee, Fuerst, or Robinson—a master such as Ewald, Hupfeld, or Hitzig. None else is competent. The present idol of the orthodox in regard to the Hebrew language and its interpretation is the venerable Delitzsch; but he moves away a considerable distance from their standpoint, and has too much Rabbinic "Spitzfindigkeit" to be a judicious or sound scholar. Hupfeld's estimate of him is not far from the truth (see *Die heutige theosophische oder mythologische Theologie und Schrifterklärung*, pp. 16, 17).

18*th January*.—Finished to-day the reading of *Matthew* in the Peshito, for the second time. The Curetonian is of more use in restoring the original text, but is unfortunately incomplete. In Matt. xi. 5, instead of "the poor have the gospel preached to them," the Curetonian has "the poor are sustained," which is favoured by Clement and Origen, and is probably correct, because it is nearly unprecedented to make *persons* the nominative to εὐαγγελίζομαι in the passive. Luke's reading is the same as the common one, being taken from Matthew's.

29*th January*.—During my Hastings sojourn there were two residents in the place with whom I had pleasant literary conversation—the Rev. Mr. Rodwell and Dr. Greenhill. The former is an excellent Oriental scholar, has translated Job and Isaiah from the Hebrew, and given a new version of the Koran, which is his chief work. Like all good thinkers, he interprets Scripture rationally, discarding traditional views if they are repugnant to reason.

I have been reading a new edition or reprint of Archdeacon Hare's sermons on the victory of faith, with preliminary dissertations by Dean Plumptre, F. D. Maurice, and Dean Stanley. Maurice and his followers were in the main traditionalists, not breaking away from the ancient creeds, but holding forth the Incarnation as the pillar and ground of truth. As Churchmen, they adhered to antiquity in ecclesiastical matters, and never attempted the task of reforming the Church by bringing its formularies into accord with the thinking of modern times. It is true that they insisted on the exercise of reason in Biblical matters; but their reason moved in the sphere of tradition, without seriously questioning any current or important doctrine, except, perhaps, the orthodox view of the Atonement on the part of Maurice. The Cambridge Platonists went as far as they in their advocacy of reason in its application to Scripture. In neither case, however, was it Kant's *reine Vernunft*. That Hare remained a sound Church- man is plain from the following language :—

"When the Council of Nicæa declared the consubstan- tiality of the Son with the Father, and when the great Athanasius was called up to proclaim and uphold the true idea of the Trinity, that which had hitherto been the im- plicit faith of the Church was brought out into more distinct enunciation" (p. 94).

Maurice says of him—

"He accepted the words on the subject (of baptism) in the Prayer-Book and Articles without reservation : he pre- ferred them to any that he or anyone else could have sub- stituted for them" (p. lxxxvii).

Outside the sphere of Schleiermacher and his disciples, Hare travelled but a short way, certainly not so far as De Wette. He was a prominent and excellent type of a learned Churchman, whose limitations prevented him from taking any decisive step to free theology from the trammels in which it has been held so long. He was essentially orthodox, as shown by these sermons. Doubtless he was a man of great culture and wide reading, devout, truthful, manly, generous, a Christian gentleman of a high order;

but it is an exaggeration to say, what Dean Stanley says in the last part of this sentence—

"At the time when he first appeared as a scholar, he and his companion Thirlwall were probably the only Englishmen thoroughly well versed in the literature of Germany; and this prominence, even in spite of the ever-increasing knowledge of that country in England, he retained to the last."

His knowledge of German literature was no doubt extensive, and his classical learning great, but he did not keep pace with the critical theology of Germany.

It is common among orthodox writers to go no further back in their defence of religious doctrines than the Nicene Council, ignoring the fact that the doctrine of the Trinity was of gradual development, and unknown to apostolic times. More than two centuries were needed for its establishment in the Christian Church. Instead of Athanasius being praised for his great effort to get it sanctioned by assembled bishops, his argumentation and violent methods of procedure are exploded by the spirit and teaching of Christ, as well as by the theology of Paul himself. The faith delivered to the saints at first is not that embodied in the metaphysical dogmas of the Nicene Creed. In ecclesiastical councils, synods, general assemblies, convocations, congresses, unions, associations, committees—in all gatherings where the majority are clerics —there is neither disposition nor place for the calm settlement of religious questions.

One of Hare's characteristics is worthy of imitation. He spoke out candidly all his mind on theological subjects, nursing no cowardly reserve, and was not afraid of endangering his position by uttering conscientious beliefs. Scorning timid silence on Scripture dogmas, he was honest out and out—a noble thing in a degenerate age. Would that the Church of God had more like him!

12th February.—A curious book has been put into my

hands in this watering-place, with a request for my opinion of it. It is called *The Temperance Bible Commentary*, by Dr. Lees and Dawson Burns, full of learning and ingenuity, but one-sided, and often incorrect in its interpretation of the Hebrew words used for drinks. Where the Bible speaks of wine, it usually implies *fermented* wine. It is impossible to prove that the Scriptures forbid the use of *such* wine or of alcoholic drinks, except they be taken to excess. Their moderate use is inconsistent with no precept or example in the whole Bible. Abstainers should rely on expediency, which is a good argument, and not press the sacred volume into their cause.

I do not think that the editors are fully competent to emend the usual English version, as a few examples taken at random will show. In Isa. xxvii. 2, for "a vineyard of red wine," they have "a vineyard of foaming juice." "Vine-fruit" is often substituted for *wine*. In Nah. i. 10, for "while they are drunken as drunkards" is suggested "as they are soaked with their boiled wine." John ii. 10 has, in our English version, "and when men have well drunk," for which is given here, "and when they are well filled." In 1 Thess. v. 5, for "let us watch and be sober" is given "let us be wakeful and abstain." In 1 Pet. i. 13, "be sober" is emended "being abstinent"; and in the same epistle, iv. 7, "be ye therefore sober and watch unto prayer" is changed into "and be abstinent in order to the prayers." But enough of such revision in the interest of total abstinence from fermented and intoxicating liquors.

23rd February.—In reading the Revised Version of the English Bible, it can hardly surprise any scholar to see passages needing improvement, correction, supplementing. In some cases the absence of a marginal note or rendering excites attention. Examples readily occur, as at Gen. xlix. 10, where the margin has "or having the obedience of the peoples," which is incorrect, because the original means "and (until) to Him shall be the obedience of the nations." At Deut. i. 1, where the word *Suph* is untranslated, the margin has "Some ancient versions have 'the Red Sea,'" as if the sense were doubtful. The word should be so translated without a marginal note. In Isa. liii. 2 this version has rightly, "He grew up before him, etc.," but it lapses immediately into the present tense, "he hath, etc.," which should be in the past to correspond with the context. In Isa. liii. 9 the common translation is retained without any marginal reference to another, which is the right one. It should be "with the godless his tomb." Joseph of Arimathæa cannot be conveniently eliminated by the orthodox from the interpretation of the text. At Ps. xvi. 10 no marginal note alludes to the textual reading, "Thy holy ones," which is probably original. In any case, the sense is not changed, since the Christian interpretation of the singular cannot be sustained.

28th February.—I have been reading Chillingworth's *Religion of Protestants : a Safe Way to Salvation.* The work is essentially polemical, being directed against the Church of Rome, to which he once belonged, though he did not long continue in it. Chillingworth was a rationalist in his day, thinking out for himself such a belief in religious matters as approved itself to his mind. The famous sentence of his so often quoted, "The Bible, I say, the Bible only is the religion of Protestants," is not well expressed, because religion is a subjective thing, and may exist without being based on writings, however sacred. The author's creed is mainly, but not entirely, that contained in the formularies of the Church of England. I regard it as unfair to judge him by the standard of to-day's theology. In advance of the stereotyped orthodoxy of the present, he is far behind the stage at which sound rationalistic views of the Bible have arrived. Still, many

just and liberal sentiments are presented in his writings,
worthy of the man and the Christian. Like most of us,
he had a strong side and a weak. What can be better
than this ?—

"If by reason of the variety of tempers, abilities, educa-
tions, and unavoidable prejudices, whereby men's understandings are variously formed and fashioned, they do
embrace several opinions whereof some must be erroneous;
to say that God will damn them for such errors, who are
lovers of Him and lovers of truth, is to rob man of his comfort and God of His goodness; it is to make man desperate
and God a tyrant." Or this: "To you and your Church we
leave it to separate Christians from the Church, and to pro-
scribe them from heaven upon trivial and trifling causes.
As for ourselves, we conceive a charitable judgment of our
brethren and their errors, though untrue, much more pleasing
to God than a true judgment if it be uncharitable; and
therefore shall always choose (if we do err) to err on the
milder and more merciful part, and rather to retain those in
our communion which deserve to be ejected, than eject those
that deserve to be retained."

On the other hand, the author can write—

"Propose me anything out of this book (the Scriptures)
and require whether I believe it or no, and seem it never so
incomprehensible to human reason, I will subscribe it with
hand and heart, as knowing no demonstration can be stronger
than this; God hath said so, therefore it is true."

The argument against the Romanist opponent is
weighty, though some general statements about the Bible
are inadequate or incorrect. But let Chillingworth be
judged leniently, for he reasoned with a noble independence
unlike acquiescent traditionalism. He assumes that Scripture is the Word of God, an idea long since exploded.
The Word of God *is in* Scripture, but all Scripture is not
the Word of God.

The distinction of things fundamental and not fundamental in the Bible is an unnecessary one, though the

writer has recourse to it in combating his opponent. It is even an impossible one, as he himself admits, acknowledging our inability to give an exact catalogue of the former. Notwithstanding the weak points in the book, it is a powerful defence of the Bible as the divine source from which Protestants discover their duty to God and man without the intervention of an infallible Church. Chillingworth is somewhat of a Bibliolater, for he is disposed to set the Scriptures over against an infallible Church, assuming it to be a divine revelation, and therefore a perfect rule of faith and action. Protestants in denying one infallibility are prone to look for an infallible counteractant. With all his shortcomings, I admire our powerful divine as a defender of the right of private judgment.

3rd March.—Yesterday was at the funeral of my friend Mr. Godwin, formerly Professor of New Testament Exegesis, with Logic and Mental Philosophy, in Highbury, and afterwards in New College. He was an acute and ingenious thinker of a liberal tendency, in consequence of which a *fama clamosa* led to the resignation of his position in the latter seminary. We had many conversations on religious questions; and I shall remember these profitable talks—profitable chiefly because of his candid, ingenious mind, imbued as it was with ardent piety and thorough sincerity. Though Mr. Godwin's liberalism was not far-reaching, it was in the true direction; and whatever his convictions, they were those of one who thought for himself with honest search after truth. His pure heart, full of love to God and man, breathed a spirit like that of Jesus, whom he humbly tried to follow. A hallowed spot in my memory he must ever retain.

12th March.—I have been thinking of the language in which the Deutero-Isaiah speaks of Cyrus (xliv. 28– xlv. 4), which is as eulogistic as any applied by other sacred writers to Semitic kings or to idealised Israel. He is called Jehovah's friend performing all his pleasure; as God's anointed he is upheld by His right hand, called by name; the Almighty goes before him, removing all obstacles from his path, giving him the treasures of Babylon and Sardis; and he is even made a worshipper of Jehovah in Isa. xli. 25. The predicates applied to the heathen monarch show an unusual height of flattering patriotism in the mouth of an inspired prophet; for we know from the annals of Nabunaid that Cyrus did not interfere with the worship of the Babylonian gods, but even restored to their former places deities whom the last king of Babylon had removed from their shrines, and offered daily prayers to Bel and Nebo that they would intercede on his behalf with Merodach the supreme god. How could a sacred prophet call a zealous idolater Jehovah's anointed and shepherd, except by assuming the rôle of a common flatterer? In like manner, a later historian represents the Persian king as acknowledging Jehovah to be the God of heaven, who had given him all the kingdoms of the earth, and charged him to build an house at Jerusalem (Ezra i. 2–4). Such language is Jewish panegyric.

28*th March.*—Since many cuneiform inscriptions have been deciphered, the history and chronology of the Old Testament have had much light thrown upon them. They have been corroborated and corrected, so that commentaries will need revision. As fresh discoveries are made, authoritative exposition will increase. The Book of Daniel, in particular, can be better understood. We now know that Belshazzar was not the last king of Babylon, but Nabunaid; that the latter was defeated on the field of battle; and that his son Belshazzar was only Prince Regent in the lifetime of his father. All that is related of this son as an independent king is legendary. The strong suspicion long ago entertained about Darius the Mede becoming king of Babylon immediately upon the overthrow of its last monarch has been verified. Cyrus the Persian took the city (Belshazzar losing his life at the time), putting an end to the powerful kingdom, so that there was no Median inter-rex between the Babylonian and Persian dynasties. The writer of the Book of Daniel has drawn largely upon his imagination; he has interpreted Jeremiah's seventy years in a curious way, and exalted Daniel excessively, investing him and his companions with grotesque miracles. But his apocalypse served to animate the Maccabean chiefs in their heroic opposition to Antiochus Epiphanes.

30th April.—Do the Creation tablets, as far as they are yet read, show the early existence of a monotheistic religion? Evidence for such an opinion is wanting. The chief deity, as far as we are able to learn from the oldest Babylonian history, was Nabiuv = Nebo, whom both Sumirians and Akkadians worshipped. Among the Assyrians, who adopted the worship of this god from the Babylonians, the grandfather of Tiglath-Pileser (about 1200 B.C.) had a name compounded of Nebo. That was not the adoration of one, but only of the chief god. In the Creation story of the tablets, "gods arose" during the generative processes of chaos, and the creation of men is attributed to the "great gods." The Hebraised Chaldean account in Genesis, proceeding towards monotheism and rising above the early legends of Babylonia, adduces one God as the Creator; but simple monotheism was a late development among the Hebrews, whose writers used the plural Elohim for a long time, and worshipped the deity only as a national god. The prophets were the first who had the monotheistic idea in considerable purity, though some of them were still haunted with faint notions of other divinities, and with anthropomorphic conceptions of Jehovah. We must come down lower than the times of the patriarchs, of Moses, even of David and Solomon,

15

to get at a pure monotheism, when the gods of other nations became nonentities to Jewish thinkers.

3rd May.—Though England is professedly a Christian nation, she continually ignores the teaching of Him who pronounced a blessing on the peacemakers, by her battles and batteries within the last few centuries, in which more blood has been shed by her than by the heathen peoples of the globe in the same period. Her warships, her torpedoes, her soldiers, ever increasing in number, attest a spirit contrary to the genius of Christianity. British interference in Africa, whether in Egypt proper, the Soudan, or among the Zulus, has been unjust and injurious. The slaughter of thousands, simple defenders of their own territories, may be gloried in as "splendid work," but it is inhuman. The annexation of new lands may feed the greed of gain, but it disgraces and demoralises all parties engaged in it.

25th May.—Alas for the loss of friends! Another scholar has departed, adding a fresh sting to the regret I feel when thinking upon the withdrawal of many valued ones with whom I took counsel, and from whose sympathy I received encouragement. Dr. W. Wright, Professor of Arabic in the University of Cambridge, has been removed by death from his studies and friends at the comparatively early age of fifty-nine. An excellent Oriental scholar, he was well known by the works he published—all bearing testimony to extensive and accurate knowledge. He laboured much, tasking severely a constitution not strong. Conscientious, high-minded, devoted to his friends, he was deservedly esteemed by all that knew him. I made my first acquaintance with Cambridge in his house, and we renewed the old personal intercourse which had been interrupted by his transference to a University. While lamenting the loss of a friend whose place cannot be filled, I shall never forget his cheerful presence and instructive talk.

I believe that since the time of Lachmann, critical editors of the Greek Testament have inclined to attach undue importance to the most ancient readings of the texts, depreciating other considerations which should be taken into account. But there are readings which, though well attested by the oldest MSS., must be rejected, because their intrinsic nature and all analogy speak against them. I shall refer to a few.

John i. 18: Here the reading "only-begotten God" is sanctioned by old witnesses, including the Sinaitic and Vatican MSS. It is therefore taken into the text by those who attribute a paramount weight to the two best MSS. as Westcott and Hort do, or by ultra-orthodox persons. As it is without a parallel, Tischendorf properly rejects the innovation. What is the sense of "only-begotten God"?

John xiv. 14: "If ye shall ask of *Me* anything in My name," etc. The pronoun *Me* is so well supported by the oldest authorities that it is adopted by Tischendorf, though Lachmann, Westcott, and Hort have it in brackets. The Revisers follow the Leipzig professor. There is small sense in "if ye shall ask Me anything in My name." It is condemned by context and analogy.

Acts xx. 28: "Feed the Church of God which He purchased with His own blood." This reading is adopted by Westcott and Hort on the authority of the two oldest MSS., and the Revisers follow. But Tischendorf rightly rejects it, and retains the reading, "Church of the Lord." Who can attribute to Paul or to the writer of the Acts "blood of God," which Athanasius himself condemns?

Sometimes a true reading being feebly supported by external evidence is rejected by editors in general, an example of which occurs in Heb. ii. 9, where "apart from" or "without God" should take the place of "by the grace of God," because the latter is inapplicable to Christ and without analogy. Χωρίς for χάριτι has the authority of Origen.

Correct punctuation may also be indicated by analogy along with internal evidence, as in Rom. ix. 4, where the right division is after the Greek word for *flesh*, and is followed by a doxology. "God, who is over all, be blessed for ever." Here Tischendorf's text is correct, that of Westcott and Hort wrong. The Revisers naturally followed the Authorised Version.

At Tit. ii. 13 the Revisers have departed from the right rendering of the Authorised Version. Both ways of interpretation are grammatical; but the Christology of the New Testament clearly indicates what the writer intended. A comma should follow the word *God*. Winer, Winstanley, and De Wette defend the correct meaning.

Jude 4. In this verse editions of the Greek Testament afford no help towards the true interpretation. The words should be rendered, "denying the only Master, God, and our Lord Jesus Christ." Here the Revisers punctuate wrongly. In the matter of dividing and punctuating the text much remains to be done, even after Lachmann's laudable effort to introduce correctness.

Parentheses often assist interpretation, and here the best critical editions are capable of improvement. An example occurs in 1 Thess. ii. 19, where the words "are not ye so?" are rightly put in a parenthesis, or what is equivalent to it, by Westcott and Hort.

Nor should interrogatives be neglected. Thus at Rom. iv. 17, after a stop at "nations," we should read, "Before whom did he believe? Before God," etc.

Even after an ample stock of materials has been collected to obtain an authentic text, conjecture is needed. Some primitive readings which are not found in any MS. version or commentary have still to be brought to light. Thus in Heb. xi. 37, the Greek word translated *were tempted* is awkward in the place it occupies. Probably it should be ἐπρήσθησαν, as Gataker imagined. On this subject, G.

Bowyer, a London printer, published a collection of conjectural emendations in the second volume of his *Greek Testament*, 1763 A.D.; and Dutch scholars like Loman have occupied themselves with the same subject. It is superfluous to say that the exercise of such criticism needs great judgment.

15*th June.*—Finished to-day the reading of the *Books of Kings* in the Hebrew Bible. Their separation into two proceeded from the Septuagint and Jerome. The contents may be divided into three sections: 1. The history of the last years of David, and the life of Solomon, 1 Kings i.–xi. 2. The synchronous history of Judah and Israel, xii.–2 Kings xvii. 3. The history of Judah, 2 Kings xviii.–xxv.

The disagreement of one part with another, as of 1 Kings xix. 15, etc. with 2 Kings viii. 7–15, ix. 1–10, various anachronisms, and the mention of sources by the writer himself, show that he employed documents, though the enumeration of them all is a difficult matter. The character of the history is theocratic and prophetic, the author being less concerned with the political than the religious aspect of events—a fact owing to the prophetic bent of his own mind, as well as to the materials from which he drew his knowledge. A history compiled from a variety of separate documents can scarcely be compact or well digested unless its author be a literary man.

Though the history is authentic on the whole, the mythical and miraculous appear in it, especially in the parts concerning Elijah and Elisha. Solomon's portrait is exaggerated. A writer living long after might naturally invest him with imaginary excellence. The history, however, is very valuable, and should not be judged by a modern standard. The style is stiff, with oft-recurring phrases.

It may be observed that the documents specified by the writer were not official or State records, but separate historical compositions, from which he extracted what seemed suitable to his purpose.

The author of the books cannot be discovered, critics being divided between the Deuteronomist and Jeremiah. The manner and language of both persons are patent. The most Deuteronomistic-like passage is 1 Kings viii. 12–61; the most Jeremiah-like, 2 Kings xxv. 22–30, which is an extract from the Book of Jeremiah (comp. xl. 5, etc., xli. 1, 2, 3, etc.). Objections lie against both opinions. Probably the historian was an exile in Babylon, who took the Deuteronomist and Jeremiah for his models. His standpoint is indicated by an expression in 1 Kings v. 4, which means on the east of the Euphrates. He wrote towards the end of the captivity at Babylon between 562 and 536 B.C.

This is not the place for me to enter on a criticism of Schrader's ingenious analysis of the contents, which is largely conjectural, nor of Graf's weak arguments to show that Jeremiah was the author. In the case of the latter critic, the two leading opinions about authorship coincide, because he holds the identity of the Deuteronomist and Jeremiah. After all the circumstances that have been adduced, it remains doubtful whether either of the two survived till 550 B.C. Schrader finds it necessary to make an appendix of 2 Kings xxv. 22–30, and a gloss of of 1 Kings v. 4, 5.

5th August.—Blessed be God, whose favour has preserved me in safety during my late travels by land and sea to Contrexéville and back to my home. My daughter and I left that familiar place on the 19th of June, returning home on Saturday the 3rd August. We passed through Paris without stopping to see the Exhibition there. Great shows and shops have little attraction for either. The crowds and press are things to be avoided by quiet-loving people.

I feel most grateful to Him who has furthered me and my daughter with His continual help in our frequent journeyings; and pray that all our doings may be begun, continued, and ended with our Heavenly Father's favour.

9th August.—An American friend whose generosity supplies me with papers and magazines has recently sent a number of *The Independent Pulpit*, dated Waco, Texas, February 1889, in which I find strong statements that no thoughtful reader of the Bible can approve. The following examples of naked assertion illustrate my meaning :— Jehovah sanctioned cheating, Ex. iii. 21, 22, xi. 1, 2, xii. 35, 36. Jehovah sanctioned murder, 1 Sam. xv. 3; Ezek. ix. 6; Isa. xii. 16; Hos. xi. 1–16. Jehovah sanctioned slavery, Lev. xxv. 44–46; Ex. xxi. 2–6, 20, 21.

I do not like this way of touching a sacred subject. It is irreverent, coarse, incorrect, having the appearance of proceeding from one who wishes to present the Bible in an odious light. Exalted views of the Supreme Being and monotheism are not usually found in the Hebrew Scriptures till a late period of the history. But Semitic conceptions of the Infinite Being became clearer as civilisation progressed. For a long while Jehovah was regarded as a national god, the presiding deity of the Semites, to whom they attributed much that was human, and in speaking of whom they employed the language of gross anthropomorphism. It was not till the time of the Prophets and after, that more correct ideas were reached of Jehovah as a universal Sovereign, omnipresent, infinitely just and holy. Even Isaiah declares : " I saw the Lord sitting upon a throne high and lifted up, and His train filled the temple," etc. David repeatedly consulted Ahimelech's ephod representing " Jehovah the God of Israel," and received verbal answers. He also delivered up seven of Saul's descendants to the Gibeonites, to be hung up " unto Jehovah " as an expiatory offering. Monotheism did not penetrate the masses, but was limited to a few thinkers. Historical indications are not wanting that the Jews had no special tendency toward monotheism, but attained to it, like other peoples, by the slow process of mental evolution. I do not believe, with Renan, that the Semites were monotheists by nature or instinct. The common rule holds good in their case, namely, that religion begins with fetichism, advances to polytheism, and thence to monotheism, its highest stage. Both Mussulmans and Jews speak of God's dispositions, motives, and purposes with a freedom that seems irreverent to Christians. In other words, their own opinions and injunctions were regarded as revelations verbally communicated to them by God or His angel. That is their way of speaking; and though it be a fiction, we need not blame their simplicity. Superstition or ignorance confounded vague religious impressions with the mind of the deity they worshipped.

Far be it from any rational believer in the Bible to suppose that because certain laws, injunctions, or passions are ascribed to Jehovah by the authors of the Hebrew or Christian Scriptures, the latter were inspired in their utterance of such sentiments. They spoke according to their knowledge—a knowledge imperfect and sometimes erroneous. The evolution of their reason had not reached a pure stage. It is the bibliolatry of the orthodox, who cling to the notion of infallible inspiration, which gives point to such attacks on the Bible as that which suggested these remarks. Nothing shows the fallibility of the sacred authors more clearly than their conceptions of Jehovah's attributes.

10th August.—Many as are the strange assertions made by theologians, and astonishing as most of these are to the reflecting mind, one can scarcely cease to wonder at their repetition by perfunctory men. Conservative writers who have found a position within an orthodox denomination, and whose interest leads them to maintain it, continue to put forth bold statements with pertinacious zeal. Human nature is a curious compound of qualities, and motives are often of a mixed character. In the domain of religious literature let there be perfect freedom of opinion without imputing unworthy motives. I grant that those who call themselves evangelicals may be conscientious, intelligent, and truth-loving students of Scripture; that they have also got a part of the truth; but I hold that their critical faculty is limited, their knowledge of subjects on which they speak dogmatically insufficient. That they do not usually study the topics about which they make strong assertions is patent to every scholar. Good men standing on a narrow strip of scientific knowledge are prone to dogmatise.

These observations were suggested by the perusal of what are called "editorials" in a periodical conducted by a Baptist theologian (Dr. Harper) at New Haven, Conn. The editorials are to some extent apologetic. I extract the following :—

1. "The religion of Israel presents claims that at the very outset differentiate it from all products of natural development. To ignore these claims is an evidence of invincible prejudice."

2. "The record of Israel's career among the nations is not merely inspired history, but the history of inspiration."

3. "The keenest of critical inquiries have failed to discover any difference in the essential elements between the representation of Jesus according to the three first Gospels and that of the fourth." In the latter there is "a record which comes from the personal recollections of the man whose name it bears."

Biblical criticism has already disposed of these antiquated sentiments, and to advance them anew shows the hardihood of ignorance. Is this *inspired history*: " Thus saith the Lord of hosts, Go and smite Amalek, and utterly destroy all that they have, and spare them not; but slay both man and woman, infant and suckling, ox and sheep, camel and ass"? or this: "There are also many things which Jesus did, the which, if they should be written every one, I suppose that even the world itself could not contain the books that should be written"? Is this inspired history: "Moses and Aaron, Nadab and Abihu, and seventy of the elders of Israel saw the God of Israel, and there was under His feet, as it were, a paved work of a sapphire stone: also the nobles of the children of Israel saw God"? Is it inspired history we read where it is said: "The Lord had prepared a great fish to swallow up Jonah"? and again: "the Lord spake unto the fish, and it vomited out Jonah"? Is Jude's statement about Michael disputing with the devil about the body of Moses inspired history? or the assertion made in the Acts of the Apostles (ch. vii.) that the law was given conformably to the arrangement of angels? Are the discrepancies in the Gospel narrative of the resurrection, which Lessing tried in vain to harmonise, inspired history? Who does not know that parts of the Bible are mythical, legendary, traditional? *Inspired history* is a meaningless phrase. History is either true and authentic, or incorrect and supposititious.

11th August.—Religious sects multiply—a bad symptom of the progress of true Christianity in the world, because the bases of them are commonly narrow. One thing sometimes serves for a point of secession from a larger Church, or for a peg to hang a new signal upon. In America a sect called Universalist hardly differs from the Unitarian one; and for its separate existence there is no just reason, since Unitarians as well as Universalists believe that all shall be saved, and reject the tenet of endless torment in hell. As for Universalist literature, it is of no great excellence, being chiefly directed to words bearing upon the doctrine combated, such as everlasting, eternal, sheol, gehenna, abyss, pit, etc. etc. Here a considerable amount of bad interpretation is heaped up to explain away the meaning of Greek words, for no good critic denies that everlasting punishment is sanctioned by the New Testament, and is even involved in language attributed to Jesus Himself. Though reason rightly revolts against the tenet formerly maintained by the orthodox, and holds to the ultimate salvation of all God's rational creatures, yet the plain language of the New Testament should not be twisted in favour of that belief. The right course is to admit that the writers were mistaken in their opinion about the future of the wicked—an opinion which was transferred from the Pharisees. I regard the books and treatises that labour to put the doctrine of universal salvation into the Gospels as examples of perverted exegesis.

22nd August.—The separation of the documents embodied in the books of the Pentateuch is not always easy, though there is little difficulty in apportioning the larger sections or narratives. As an example of differing opinions entertained about the materials composing Genesis, I may take the 49th chapter. According to De Wette, Gramberg, Bleek, and Tuch, the chapter is Elohistic; whereas Hupfeld, Nöldeke, Schrader, Knobel, and Boehmer regard it as Jehovistic, with the exception of vers. 29–33. It is unimportant that some of the latter scholars find a few small exceptions in the Elohistic part, which begins either with the 28th verse, *b*, or ver. 29; but their view of the whole chapter is correct. My lamented friend Dr. Kalisch seems not to have given sufficient attention to the Elohistic and Jehovistic parts of Genesis in his valuable commentary on that book, else he would not have said that xxv. 23 belongs to the Elohist, or that xxviii. 1–9 is Jehovistic.

3rd September.—One of the most touching descriptions, which I have repeatedly read with emotion I myself having passed through more than one similar scene (*quorum pars magna fui*)—is that part of Semler's autobiography in which he tells of the last moments of a beloved daughter, showing that the man who is often called the father of German rationalism had the true religious spirit within him; that, however heterodox, he feared God and led a virtuous life. Even Tholuck, who has given a summary of his literary activity and its far-reaching influence, with a leaning unfavourable to his opinions, does justice to that early religiousness which never left the liberal theologian. It is one of Semler's merits to have apprehended the distinction between religion and theology. Hallowed be the memory of my lamented friend for pages 49, 50 of his *Vermischte Schriften*, zweiter Theil.

4th September.—What crooked reasoning has been used to justify the invasion of Canaan by the Israelites, and their cruelties in trying to exterminate the inhabitants! Not only men but women and children, with the lower animals themselves, were butchered indiscriminately. Fire and sword did what they could to root out the rightful possessors of the country, who seem to have been more civilised than their invaders, and were never altogether subdued. The Bible historians give horrible details of barbarities practised by men who are praised for deeds at which humanity revolts. These cruel actions are attributed to the command of God. It is sickening to read in the Book of Joshua the record of carnage summed up in the repeated statement that the conqueror left none remaining, but utterly destroyed all the souls, crowned with "as the Lord God of Israel commanded." Such was the view of writers belonging to a people who considered themselves the chosen race, and all others outside divine mercy. Overweening self-importance on the part of these Semites urged them on to slaughter, and authors hallowed it with the approval of Heaven. Prophets themselves were not superior to the inhuman sentiments sanctioned in the national histories. Such transference of human likes, dislikes, and doings to an infinitely holy Being is as grossly anthropomorphic as it is unphilosophical. When fanaticism and ignorance take no note of second causes, God Himself becomes the immediate agent of injustice. Should it be said that the Canaanite peoples were idolaters, I reply, the Israelites were the same.

Let it then be well understood that the Israelite invasion of Canaan and the cruel wars waged against the natives were thoroughly unjust; and that the racial patriotism, springing from the assumption that Heaven selected the Israelites to slaughter their fellow-creatures, was unholy.

10th September.—I have lately read again Professor Dozy's book, *The Israelites at Mekka*, and have been specially attracted to his observations on Gilgal, a place suggestive of a difficult subject, "the Passover," which, though described in earlier books than that named after Joshua, was said to have been kept there. The geography of the spot where the Israelites had their first encampment after crossing the Jordan is still unsettled, as far as other places of the same name can be compared with it. Some scholars, as Gesenius, find but one Gilgal in the Bible (Josh. iv. 19, 20), Robinson adds a second, and the number is increased to four by others. On this head all lexicons and Bible dictionaries are disappointing, so that the subject needs fresh examination. The four Gilgals are evidently too many, and must be reduced to one or two. But I do not attempt to clear up the point on the present occasion. The derivation of the name given in Joshua is fictitious; the circumcision of the multitude, including the children that came into Canaan, being a thing all but impossible to Joshua at the time and in the circumstances referred to. 40,000 prepared for war, if multiplied by 4 gives 160,000—and that is a low computation—had the rite performed upon them, a fact altogether improbable. The true derivation of the word yields "a round heap of stones," which was set up in the place as a commemorative monument. The description of crossing the Jordan is a reflex of the passage through the Red Sea, and the writer has decked it out with a miraculous element sufficiently apparent. I consider the stones set up as part of an idolatrous ceremonial, of image-worship borrowed from Egypt and practised in the wilderness, perhaps Baal-worship. It is a gratuitous assumption that "during the wanderings and under the strong rule of Joshua, the idolatry learnt in Egypt was so destroyed as to be afterwards utterly forgotten by the people."

It is further related that Joshua kept the Passover on the fourteenth day of the month (Nisan). The way in which this notice is introduced (v. 10, 11), and the brevity of it, show the writer's acquaintance with an earlier account. The Jehovist copies the Elohist. But the introduction of the feast is too early, indicating a desire to hallow an idolatrous spot, which Gilgal long continued to be, as we learn from Hosea and Amos, though its evil name was partly counteracted by the frequent presence of Samuel and the settlement of prophets there. All that can be allowed is that a ceremony of an idolatrous nature took place at Gilgal under Joshua, commemorating the fortunate crossing of the river, and in honour of a deity to whom they had paid homage before.

The primitive Passover was probably a heathen festival prior to Moses, and of cosmical origin. Whether it was connected with sacrifice is uncertain. But it was of a joyous nature, and its time that of the vernal equinox (Nisan = April), when the sun *passes over* into the sign Aries. The origin of the feast was an astronomical, not an historical, event.

After the Israelites had been settled in Palestine and made some advance in civilisation, being mainly an agricultural people they instituted three festivals connected with the soil, namely, that of the green ears of corn, of the harvest or first fruits, and of ingathering or tabernacles. The first of these was afterwards enlarged and linked to an historical event, which contributed to throw the original purport into the shade. Seven days of unleavened bread were added, and the blood of an animal sprinkled on the two sides and upper post of the doors of every house for a token to Jehovah to pass over and not smite the first-born. Such linking of a later ordinance to the exodus from Egypt was done in a curious fashion, for why should the posts of houses be smeared with blood that the Almighty might distinguish the inmates to be spared? The prescriptions respecting the festival contained in the Book of Exodus, which were intended to fix and perpetuate the memory of a great historical event, overshadowed the agricultural object by importing into it traditional elements. The original, however, was not abolished, but kept in remembrance by the offering of a first-fruits sheaf of barley (Deut. xxvi. 10). The memorial of the vernal equinox, when the sun *passed over* into Aries, had given place to the feast of Abib or green ears ; and the latter was enlarged with the Passover so called, the unleavened cakes, and the sprinkling of blood on houses spared. The time when the Passover proper was instituted cannot be ascertained, any more than that of the agricultural festival which it overshadowed. The origin of it was thrown back to the time of Moses, a procedure not unusual with Jewish writers, who antedated events pretty freely. The first account of it is given in the 12th chapter of Exodus in an Elohistic passage, so that the renovated feast was not later than David's time. But some scholars refer it to Ezra, making Josiah's Passover unhistorical, and assuming the passage

2 Kings xxiii. 21–23 to be interpolated, while they put the Chronicle-writer's mention of the feast under Hezekiah in the same category.   To set aside the Biblical evidence for a tradition mentioned by Clement of Alexandria (*Strom.* i. c. 21), as Dozy does, is too arbitrary.

It is unnecessary to point out the variations in the observance of the Passover which appear in different parts of the Old Testament.   Changes in the description of it are introduced even into parts of the same document. Much of its domestic character disappeared when the animal could be sacrificed only at the common sanctuary (Deut. xvi. 2), not in any place as before ; and it is doubtful if all the prescribed rites were ever observed at one time. In the periods of the kings of Israel and Judah, it was kept imperfectly ; Josiah celebrated it in accordance with the precepts of Deuteronomy ; and in later times, as we learn from Josephus, it was kept agreeably to the collected injunctions of the Pentateuch.   The oldest and strictest regulations were amplified or relaxed as the national life developed, until a backward phase of narrow priestism appeared under Ezra and Nehemiah.

CHAPTER XVII

17th September 1889.—I have often wished that I had taken notes of the conversations I have had with scholars and other thinkers whom I met. But perhaps little that is interesting might have resulted, because few German professors are good talkers, and they have scant humour or vivacity compared with Frenchmen or Irishmen. They are usually grave customers. Tholuck was the most lively professor whom I knew, and not at all destitute of humour. His mind was stored with anecdotes, some of which he introduced even into his lectures. Wolf, the philosopher of Halle, whom Carlyle has described in his *Life of Frederick the Great*, lived in the Leipziger Strasse, where I believe an inserted slab still marks the house he inhabited. During the time of his exile he revisited the town to which he had belonged, looked at the outside of his former dwelling, occupied by a retailer of wine and spirits, exclaiming, " The spirit is there still." So Tholuck told me.

My friend was an indifferent Hebraist, and sometimes betrayed his ignorance unconsciously. Once, in his class, he had been mentioning the plural עָרִים (cities), and on coming downstairs into the professors' room in the University he spoke of its singular as עִיר. That before Gesenius ! The fact was long remembered against him. So Roediger said.

At a pleasant little dinner-party gathered together in my honour at Professor Erdmann's house, where Tholuck

and others were present, I was amused at some of the
little thoughtful preparations which the distinguished host
had made.   He had provided port wine, calling it "wine
of port"; and had put a small German-English dictionary
in his breast-pocket, to look for English words which he
wanted in conversation.   Such was "the last of the
Mohicans," as he called himself—all but the last of German
Hegelians.   It was he who answered me, when I inquired
the reason of so many Halle professors being married twice
or three times (he had but one wife himself), "Oh, we kill
them with kindness."   I was thinking of Guericke.   Years
after, I had an opportunity of showing him and his agreeable lady some little kindness when they came to England
to see the Derby.

The intolerance of Hengstenberg made him justly disliked.   Yet an interview I had with him left a favourable
impression on my mind.   He seemed earnest and sincere.
As a lecturer he was of no account: voice and manner
were bad.   It was not, therefore, to be wondered at that
his class was very small.   All the attempts he made to
defend the authenticity of Daniel and the Mosaic authorship of the Pentateuch, with other orthodox opinions, were
failures.   He approached the Calovius method of interpretation.   Though his knowledge of Hebrew was neither
thorough nor exact, he took every opportunity of depreciating the works and opinions of Gesenius.

In Halle I once witnessed a Fackelzug, *i.e.* a torch
procession of students who wished to do honour to a professor at some particular period of his career: a jubilee
memorial.   It was given to Professor *Leo*, that wonderful
linguist who could read a multitude of languages, though
he could not speak so many as Tholuck did.   When the
procession came opposite the professor's house and stopped,
one of the students read an address to Leo, who stood
at an open window; a suitable reply was made to it; the

torch-bearers marched to the market-place, sang one or more of their stirring songs, threw down their torches in a heap, and departed. Professor Leo was an able man and good lecturer, but he was not popular. He once asked me to accompany him to the University to hear a lecture upon the history of Scotland in the time of Mary, and it showed a full knowledge of the subject on his part. His politics were Tory and despotic—Bismarckian, in fact.

With regard to Fackelzugs, I missed the sight of one which would have pleased me mightily. It was given to Gesenius not long before his death, and his friend De Wette was with him at the time. The pleasant open space in front of his house where he sometimes studied, arched over and ornamented with the green of growing vines, was lighted upon that occasion with small oil-lamps, which were still hanging when I was there. Such was the reception-place where two celebrated scholars welcomed the joyous students. The sight was fitted to exhilarate a phlegmatic spectator ; doubly so a seeker after truth from another land. Alas, when I looked, the little lamps were gone out, the men who lighted up the Hebrew Scriptures had departed, and gloominess hovered o'er the bower.

22nd October.—I observe that Athanasius has been decorated with rhetorical praises by Archdeacon Farrar and Dr. Bright, with their admirer in the *Edinburgh Review*. More judicious and critical is the portrait of him which Gibbon draws. He was a man of great ability and of indomitable zeal for what he believed to be truth, persecuted and persecuting, a sturdy bishop and subtle pleader for Homoousianism, but of a different spirit from that of the meek and lowly Jesus.

The warfare in which the champion of orthodox Trinitarianism was engaged for the greater part of his life is described by his encomiasters as "a phalanx of robust tradition against neologistic speculation." Arianism is called a heresy—"a theory unsatisfactory to reason, repulsive to piety and faith." It is said that the champion was in a struggle "between a rationalistic attempt to graduate the Infinite, and the faith as handed down from age to age, parallel with the spread of Christianity." Such language is opposed to the simple fact that the Apostle Paul was substantially an Arian in his view of Christ's person; and that "robust tradition" in favour of the Athanasian doctrine of the Trinity begins with the Nicene Council. The deification of Jesus was a comparatively slow process. The Alexandrianism of the Epistle to the Hebrews helped it. The conclusion of Matthew's Gospel hastened the result. The translator or interpolator of the Jewish Apocalypse greatly advanced it, as far as the book was accepted as the production of the Apostle John. Indeed, it may be said that the work deifies Him plainly in calling Him Alpha and Omega, in giving one throne to God and the Lamb in the 22nd chapter. The deification did not take place till well on in the second century. Justin was the earliest writer in whom it appears; not, however, in his first apology, but in his dialogue with Trypho, and even there hesitatingly; while the deification of the Spirit as a distinct and third person did not take place till the third century, and that in two writers only, Tertullian and Origen.

In the above remarks I have alluded indirectly to the baptismal formula at the end of the first Gospel, which was undoubtedly used in the second century, but appears nowhere else in the Gospels, and differs from the apostolic formula, which was baptism "in the name of Christ." It is not easy to account for the non-observance of the threefold formula in apostolic times. In any case, it originated earlier than the doctrine of the Trinity. Justin Martyr treats it as common when the deification of Jesus was only beginning, and he wrote half a century before the deification of the Spirit as a distinct person. The great commission, of which baptism is a part, did not belong to the teaching of Christ.

26th October.—I have been reading again the excellent and most instructive biography of that noble-minded Christian, Frederick Robertson of Brighton, the best preacher of this century, who lived but a few years on earth and suffered much. His spirit, tone, and temper were largely in unison with the character of Him whom he loved and adored. In vol. ii., after a conversation with Lady Byron and Mrs. Jamieson, Robertson says that pictures of the Virgin and Child did not appear till the fifth century. This is a mistake. In a cubiculum of the catacombs of St. Priscilla at Rome there is a fine fresco of the Virgin and Child with a star overhead, and a beardless man standing before her, clothed with the pallium, and supposed to be Isaiah. De Rossi assigns the fresco to the earliest time of the Antonines. Nor is this the only representation of the kind prior to the fifth century. A fresco of the Virgin and Child in the cemetery of St. Domitilla belongs to the third century ; and others older than the century mentioned might be cited, but the above examples are sufficient.

28th.—Finished to-day the reading of *Luke's Gospel* in the old Syriac version. It had been interrupted for more than a fortnight by illness. The last clause of the fifty-first verse and the first of the fifty-second (ch. xxiv.), which are later readings, appear in the version, as might have been expected. But Tischendorf has rightly rejected them, though the evidence in their favour includes that of the oldest MSS. Griesbach doubted whether they were sufficiently supported, but Schulz, his editor, approved of their omission.

24th November.—I transcribe a few words from Ben Mordecai (Rev. H. Taylor), which are appropriate now as well as in his time :—

"If the words of Scripture, and what planely and undeniably follows from them, will not unite men in the same sentiments upon any text, we may be well assured that there can be no necessity for union of sentiment upon that text; much less any necessity for murthering one another for disagreeing upon the explanation of it. When Christ preached to the common people, He did not expect them to have clear conceptions on metaphysical subjects, but only on plane practical truth." . . . "It is time to return to the plane doctrine and spirit of the gospel, and to understand it every man for himself, with the best help he can get, as well as he is able; and God will require no more of any man: and so to become one fold under one Shepherd, and bear with one another's errors and infirmities. For the breach of charity is a more heinous offense in the sight of God than a thousand errors upon this (the generation of Jesus) or any other metaphysical subject whatsoever." [1]

I add to these paragraphs a few words from Bishop Butler's second sermon upon love to our neighbour:—

"It is still true, even in the present state of things, bad as it is, that a real good man had rather be deceived than be suspicious: had rather forego his known right than run the venture of doing even a hard thing. This is the general temper of that charity of which the apostle asserts, that if he had it not, *giving his body to be burned would avail him nothing*; and which, he says, *shall never fail.*"

The following is from the dedication of the *Essay on Spirit*, whose reputed author is Bishop Clayton:—

"As to the unthinking herd, whatever was the creed of their father or tutor, that will be theirs, from their infancy to their lives' end; and, accordingly, whatever country you go into, let the religion be what it will, the unthinking part thereof are always the reputed orthodox."

8th December. — Have just finished the reading of *Ezekiel* in Hebrew, with the exception of chs. xl.–xlviii., which are unimportant and uninteresting to the Christian reader. The Book of Ezekiel may be divided into three

---

[1] *An Inquiry into the Opinions of the Learned Christians, both Ancient and Modern, concerning the Generation of Jesus Christ*, p. 116.

parts: chs. i.–xxiv., xxv.–xxxii., xxxiii.–xlviii. The first seems chronologically arranged; the second, which relates to foreign nations, is not so; and the whole probably proceeded from the hand of the prophet in its present state. The first belongs to the time before the siege of Jerusalem; the second falls within that of the siege and after the city's destruction; the third, later.

Ezekiel's manner and style are described by Lowth in his twenty-first lecture on Hebrew poetry with some exaggeration. Though the prophet has characteristic excellences, it is incorrect to say that he equals Isaiah in sublimity, so that Michaelis rightly objects to the bishop's opinion. The poet is vehement, fervid, stern, and grave, but also rugged and prosaic. He abounds in repetitions, and indulges in details which are occasionally followed out too far. Grammatical anomalies, from whatever cause originating, are numerous, such as no accurate or elegant poet could allow. Some of these are noted by Gesenius in his *Geschichte der Hebräischen Sprache und Schrift*, p. 36.

"Wherefore I gave them also statutes that were not good, and judgments whereby they should not live" (xx. 25). These words have been brought into connection with Ex. xiii. 12, 13: "Thou shalt set apart unto the Lord all that openeth the matrix, and every firstling that cometh of a beast which thou hast; the males shall be the Lord's. And every firstling of an ass thou shalt redeem with a lamb; and if thou wilt not redeem it, then thou shalt break his neck: *and all the first-born of man among thy children shalt thou redeem*." It is supposed that the last clause was not in the passage when Ezekiel wrote, so that he could say of Jehovah, "I gave them statutes that were not good." The twelfth verse gives some countenance to the idea, for it seems to mean by the first-born being offered to the Lord, they should be burnt in sacrifice to Him. If it be objected that בָּאֵשׁ (with fire) is wanting after the verb, I answer that it is also absent in Jer. xxxii. 35. It is difficult to find a good reason for the prophet making Jehovah declare, "I gave them statutes that were not good," if the first-born could be redeemed as stated in the last clause; but if the assertion about redemption be an addition of the post-exilians who revised the text, the reason is apparent. Dr. Kalisch's argument against this interpretation violates the plain words by resolving them into, "the statutes did not prove or turn out to be good, since they became occasions for transgression and disobedience." There is no doubt about Ezra and his successors revising the text of the Old Testament and making changes in it, so that the idea of their modifying the 12th and 13th verses of Ex. xiii. by appending the last clause to soften the harshness of a repulsive command is probable enough. No reader of the Old Testament can hesitate to admit that human sacrifices were offered to God by the Jews, from Jephthah to a much later time. The Gibeonite sacrifice to Jehovah, though not made by David himself, was done with his knowledge and consent.

The prophecy against Tyre (chs. xxvi.–xxviii.) which describes its total destruction was not fulfilled, for Nebuchadnezzar, after thirteen years' siege, retired from the place. Doubtless he did it much damage, without, however, leaving it like the top of a rock or a spreading place for fishermen's nets. Alexander the Great destroyed it after seven months' siege. Nebuchadnezzar's failure to take Tyre is afterwards admitted by Ezekiel himself in xxix. 18 in a prophecy against Egypt (588 B.C.), which country he gives to Nebuchadnezzar as if by way of compensation for the monarch's want of success against Tyre. The later prophecy was sixteen years after the earlier. History knows nothing of the Babylonian monarch's conquest of

Egypt. He may indeed have intended it, but his purpose was not carried out. Cambyses subdued it (525 B.C.)— so that this second prophecy was also unfulfilled. Should one point to the present condition of Tyre as fulfilling Ezekiel's prediction, it is sufficient to reply that the seer looked to the immediate future, and to Nebuchadnezzar as the executor of the city's punishment. Prophetic vision did not reach to far-distant and definite events; its horizon was limited to the immediate future.

In like manner, the attack of the confederated princes, under Gog the King of Magog, upon the restored kingdom of Israel, and their defeat, whatever be thought of the country called Magog or its people, is a prophetic description which was not realised in history. Ezekiel idealised, like other prophets. They could not have been poets otherwise (chs. xxxviii., xxxix.).

Ezek. xxi. 10 (Hebrew, 15). This passage has perplexed interpreters and admits of no satisfactory sense. The authorised version of it is unintelligible, and all the expositions proposed by lexicographers or commentators are inadmissible. Without enumerating different opinions, I may say at once that the text is corrupt, and propose the following solution: " It is furbished that there might be to it (the sword) a lightning-flash against the prince of the tribe of my son (Judah), which despises every arrow." Agreeably to this translation, the accent upon מֹרָטָה, the anomalous participle, is neglected; אוֹ is changed into אֵל, which is sanctioned by the LXX. and Syriac; a שׁ is subtracted from מַשֶׂשׂ, and א put in its place; while עֵץ is changed into חֵץ. The proposed interpretation agrees with Gesenius's, except in the last word; and it must be admitted that the meaning he brings out is plausible, " Since the king and people of Judah despise all the wooden rods with which I have hitherto scourged them, therefore I will now bring a sharp sword against them." I allow that חֶרֶב and עֵץ

make a good antithesis, but doubt the meaning of *rod* given to the latter, which is against usage, the nearest approach to it being the plural for "sticks of wood" prepared for fuel or other purposes. The noun does not occur in the sense of a rod of correction. Hence I suggest חץ *arrow*, which is favoured by the interchange of the two words in 1 Sam. xxi. 19 and 1 Chron. xx. 5. The slighter punishment of an arrow is contrasted with the severer one of a sword.

Chs. xl.–xlviii.—These chapters are occupied with a description of the new temple and the new Jerusalem. The future state of the holy land, the reunion of the separated tribes, with their positions, their harmony under one prince, their united worship in one central temple, are sketched in a serious spirit, showing that the prophet believed in their realisation, though he could hardly suppose every detail practicable. The fair-coloured picture of his native land and its inhabitants exhibits imagination, though the minute details are prosaic. Prophetic partialities and peculiarities are alike apparent. Ezekiel ignores a high priest and degrades the Levites. No Messiah presides over the principality: a spiritualised worship is presented under a prince who is not a king. In drawing his picture, the prophet had Solomon's temple for a pattern, but he follows it only in part: and the Kedron, which suggested the holy river, typifies the people's purification. The entire description consists of realistic, symbolical, ideal features, the first-mentioned predominating.

15th December 1889.—Another gloomy anniversary I have been spared to see, and out of the depths I cry to God, who orders all according to His will. Beloved ones are taken; others less useful in the world are left. I meditate day and night on the mysteries of Providence, but find no solution. Hence the ever-felt necessity of living by faith while cheered by hope. I look back on my life, and find the retrospect unpleasing because of neglected opportunities and misspent time. Nothing but God's love can satisfy the soul. It is an abiding comfort to me that she who illumined my earthly path for a while is enjoying a happy life in a higher state; and I wait patiently for my release as the means of our reunion. At my age I can do little work, though I am always occupied with the Word of God, trying to understand the oracles which deeply concern the spiritual interests of mankind and enlighten the noblest powers of our rational nature, lifting them up to the Almighty Father.

16th December.—News of Robert Browning's death has been received, and will naturally create widespread grief. His fame as a poet will endure. I met him once at luncheon in the house of Dr. Leighton, whose daughter has long been one of his enthusiastic admirers, and my recollection of him is a very pleasant one. He was agreeable, polite, a good talker: nothing about him assuming or pretentious. He had all the qualities that make a general favourite. His command of words was so great that he could pour forth good impromptu rhymes on any subject of conversation. In relation to Horace's statement that poets wish either to profit or to please (" Aut prodesse volunt, aut delectare poetæ "), he does not fulfil the pleasing part, though he may profit his readers. His poetry is too rough and obscure to impart delight. Hence, however superior in profundity of thought, he will never be so popular as Pope or Goldsmith.

31st December.—On this last day of the year I have finished the reading of the Book of *Esther.* The work may be called " The Romance of the Purim," its improbabilities being so palpable as to relegate it to the region of fiction. A Jew, after the downfall of the Persian Empire, undertook to describe the origin of a feast, and to recommend it to his countrymen in Palestine—a feast similar to a Persian one, in which he and other coreligionists had doubtless participated. The word *purim* is not of Hebrew but of Persian origin, being apparently derived from the festival of *furdigan*, which was a joyful one dedicated to the memory of the dead. If the Greek text of Esth. ix. 26 be corrected by MSS. reading *phurdaia* (phurim), the resemblance of the words becomes greater. In any case, the etymology of the word in Esther is incorrect, and its real meaning concealed because it might not have recommended the book to the Jews in Palestine. The work is written in degenerate Hebrew mixed with Persian words, and is permeated with an irreligious spirit, not only because the name of God is never mentioned, but because blood-thirsty revenge and a passionate desire of slaughtering heathens fill the minds of Esther and Mordecai. In the post-prophetic time this feeling was not unusual among a race that suffered grievously from foreign nations. The additions in the Septuagint give a somewhat religious character to parts of the story, and so far correct its serious defect. The feast is mentioned as existing about 160 B.C. (2 Macc. xv. 36), from which, and the obscure note at the end of the Septuagint translation, attempts have been made to ascertain the date of the book, which was probably written in the third century before Christ.

1st January 1890.—Blessed be God for the first day of a new year, though it begins in fog and darkness, having a depressing effect on the mind. At such seasons as the present I always feel humbled in looking back at the past year, and seeing how I have advanced so slowly in my spiritual life, and how little good I have done in the world. In some respects I have been little else than a cumberer of the ground; but our Heavenly Father is compassionate and merciful, not rewarding us as we deserve. I look forward to the future with hope and faith—the hope that is unattended with shame, and the faith that rests upon the love of God. May I be prepared for whatever the present year shall bring forth. "The Lord reigneth, let the earth rejoice."

20th January.—So Dr. v. Döllinger has departed to a better world, to the regret of his many friends, but at a ripe age. I well remember the conversation I had with him in his home at Munich. He was a noble-minded man, unsurpassed by any scholar in his knowledge of ecclesiastical history.

I am also sorry to have lost a valuable and kind friend in the Rev. Dr. Littledale, an able theologian and simple-minded Christian, thoroughly versed in ritualistic lore, in whose company I used to spend many pleasant hours, enlivened by humorous stories. But when I think of his constant ill-health and acute sufferings, I am consoled by the idea that he now enjoys happiness without alloy.

Finished to-day the reading of the Book of *Ruth*, a little work which gives an idyllic picture of a pious widow and her two daughters-in-law, skilfully drawn in natural colours. The writer's object, which he carried out in-directly, was a polemic one. Having a more liberal mind than the rigorous Ezra, who required the returned exiles to put away their foreign wives, he recommends another policy by giving the genealogy of David's royal house from a Moabitess; and glorifies that dynasty, whose humble origin led on to greatness; contrary to Deut. xxiii. 3, which excludes a Moabite from the congregation of the Lord, even to the tenth generation. The author probably drew his material from tradition, which may have had a basis of truth; but the history is largely ideal. He throws back the levirate institution to the time of the Judges and earlier, whereas its origin was much later, the first mention of it being in Deut. xxv. 5, etc.; and the description of the fourth chapter scarcely agrees with what Deuteronomy enjoins. There is a difficulty about Naomi's power to sell a property after so long an absence from her native place. What had become of it during the ten years she lived in Moab? The date of the book is after the Babylonian exile, probably in Ezra's time. It was posterior to Deuteronomy: the language has a considerable number of Chaldaisms, and it is among the Hagiographa. The story could not have been acceptable to Ezra and Nehemiah, whose proceedings in the matter of foreign wives were both severe and unjust.

31st January.—Finished to-day the reading of the Fourth Gospel in the Peshito Syriac version. If this translation is to be of use in the textual criticism of the Gospels, MSS. older than any that have been collated must be employed. Do such exist, or where are they?

13th February.—I find that an error which got into one issue of the 1611 edition of the English Bible, commonly called "the authorised," has been perpetuated to the present day in the Bibles issued by the British and Foreign Bible Society. The first printed 1611 Bible reads in Ruth iii. 15, "*he* entered into the city"; the second issue of the same year, "*she* went into the city." The latter, though incorrect, exists in all recent English Bibles. When we look for authority in its favour, the Vulgate appears to be the chief if not the only one. The Septuagint and Luther follow the Hebrew, "*he* went." The American Bible Society copies the mistake of the British one. Why so?

16th February.—I still adhere to what I said in the treatise *On a Fresh Revision of the English Old Testament*, that the Authorised Version was not, strictly speaking, "translated out of the original tongues," as stated on the title-page, but was mainly taken from preceding versions—from the text of the Bishop's Bible in the first instance (1600 A.D., 3rd edition). I have observed, however, that Dr. Scrivener, in his preface to *The New Testament in the Original Greek, according to the Text followed in the Authorised Version*, writes as though the text presumed to underlie the New Testament part of the Authorised Version was that in Beza's last edition (1598). But he confesses that the variations of the authorised (1611) from Beza's are about 190: a tolerably large number, tending to cast doubt on the alleged Greek basis of King James's translation. Which of the two 1611 editions does he take as his standard, for their variations show that they are distinct? The third edition of Stephanus (1550), reprinted by Walton, Mill, Kuster, Birch, and in substance by all Oxford editions since 1707, has almost as good a claim to be the one text which the translators presumably rendered into English. Yet, in fact, they were revisers rather than translators, who based their work on the Bishop's Bible, and compared it with other English versions, especially the Genevan (1560) and the Rhemish New Testament (1582). Nor did they neglect the Septuagint, the Vulgate, and Luther's German translation. It is also highly probable that they consulted several Hebrew and Greek texts in prior editions, without following any one continuously. No fair evidence can be adduced that they translated directly from a single Hebrew or Greek edition.

13th March.—Wishing to read the paper of my friend Sir G. W. Cox, which caused consternation at the Church Congress held in Manchester in October 1888, I got the bulky volume containing a report of the proceedings, and looked over some parts of it. A thoughtful reader need not expect to be profited by the consultations of a clerical assembly, as the history of councils and convocations clearly shows. But it is curious to note the ideas and opinions of men set apart for the promotion of religion. The subjects brought before the Congress were many, as were the readers and speakers ; and earnestness seemed to pervade the sessions.

I could not bring myself to peruse the entire volume, but turned to three parts of the extended programme, namely, "To what extent results of historical and scientific criticism, especially of the Old Testament, should be recognised in sermons and teaching"; "Adaptation of the Prayer-Book to modern needs"; and "Eschatology." One naturally expects to hear a conservative tone running through a Church Congress, and the expectation is seldom wrong. For myself I did not hope to find the assertion of much rational theology, of liberal views, or of wide departure from traditional opinions. A Church having a system hallowed by time and by the adhesion of illustrious names does not readily alter its creeds or formularies.

In the department of historical and scientific criticism, with its results, the fact was emphasised that the Bible must be criticised. Nothing important was said about what such criticism has already effected; but a few perfunctory assertions, such as that the Pentateuch in its present form was not all written by Moses, and that three documents are discoverable in it, were enunciated. The writer of the paper carefully abstained from saying what Moses did write. This caution was also shown in denying that Deuteronomy is the product of Josiah's time, and in attributing 1 Timothy to St. Paul's authorship. A succeeding writer, very orthodox and very confident, but evidently incompetent to judge evidence rightly, asserted the unity of the Book of Isaiah. The same prophet wrote it all. Criticism has therefore done little for the enlightenment of this reverend doctor. Leaving him to his dictum, "If we allow to the language of Scripture its literal force and meaning, we are obliged to concede its divine origin," I pass on to another scholar affirming that "the Church is not officially committed to any definite system of Bible interpretation," and ask: What is the purport of this statement? Is it to show that any mode of interpretation is allowable, *e.g.*, an esoteric or an exoteric, an official or a non-official one? I hold that the Bible should be explained on the same principle as other books. There is but one method of interpretation, the natural common-sense one, all departures from which lead to error; and he who follows another misleads hearers and readers. Individuals are not at liberty to adopt any system but the obvious one, which is to seek the meaning which the author intends to express by the words he employs, and to enunciate it in plain language to such as look up to the expositor.

When another professor of divinity affirms that "to our Lord and His disciples the Old Testament was one organic whole," I am tempted to ask, How do you know that? Existing evidence is against the dictum, because the Old Testament canon was not finally fixed till 90 A.D.

The discussions relating to the adaptation of the Prayer-Book to modern needs elicited no desire for thorough revision of the volume. One cleric maintained that no adaptation of the creeds to modern needs, either in their substance or primitive form, should be allowed. Not a voice was raised for the casting out of the Athanasian Creed, which still disgraces the Prayer-Book. On the contrary, a canon of Lincoln Cathedral said that "it is singularly simple and plain in its statements, so that even children can understand its several propositions." Again, "the creed is no harsher than Holy Scripture." Still farther, "it is my earnest hope that our Church Catechism may be allowed to stand unaltered." The few changes which were suggested affected minor matters and words.

The papers and discussions on Eschatology elicited considerable diversity of opinion. Such topics as universal salvation, conditional immortality, everlasting punishment, the intermediate state, came under partial review; and Canon Farrar naturally led the way with a paper. If, as he says, the Scriptures furnish no certain conclusion about the penalties of the world to come, why does he

17

argue from them at great length as though they favoured universal salvation? Why appeal to Christian consciousness alone as uttering a passionate $\mu\grave{\eta}$ $\gamma\acute{\epsilon}\nu o\iota\tau o$? The plain sense of various passages in the New Testament is that the punishment of hell is everlasting. Both De Wette and Strauss assert this, and they are right. The Canon twists passages and tortures words to favour an opinion consonant with reason and the infinite love of God. His belief is right; the means by which he often supports it are objectionable.

As to immortality being dependent on belief in Christ, the basis is too narrow for the superstructure. I gather both from words of Christ and from the Pauline writings, that the Master and His chief apostle entertained the belief that immortality is an attribute of man's nature. The Pharisees, if not the Sadducees also, held the doctrine, which has much evidence for its truth in reason and Scripture.

The passage in Peter's First Epistle about Christ's descent to Hades was often referred to in the Congress, especially as it is a part of the Apostles' Creed. It stands in the epistle alone, derived from a Jewish notion about the Israelites in Sheol participating in the beneficence of Messiah. The volume contains no allusion to what Christ said to the penitent thief on the cross, which is opposed to the idea that his descent to Hades preceded his ascension. It is far from edifying to hear a congregation, led by the officiating priest, repeat, in the midst of a religious service, their belief in an imaginary event—" He descended into hell." All speculations about an intermediate state, a state of probation between death and the resurrection, are groundless; and I would consign imaginary limbuses to merited oblivion.

The only paper in the volume which touches topics of high importance is that written by Sir G. W. Cox, where the question how far the reporters have given accurately the discourses of Christ, and whether they have not put into His mouth what He never said, was boldly introduced. This is an essential part of the criticism which awaits the New Testament in England, and honour is due to the man who brought it forward in an assembly of clerical brethren. The fallibility of the sacred Scripture will have to be admitted, and with it many errors, which form corner-stones in the traditional building early erected by orthodoxy and still upheld even in an age of progress, shall vanish away.

21st March.—A pleasant neighbour has lately come to reside in this quarter of London, a well-known philosopher of high repute, whose teachings are far superior to those of Carlyle, because they are ethically sounder. Mr. Herbert Spencer has other notions than the Scotchman's might-makes-right doctrine with which he has overwhelmed many commonplace thinkers, clothing it withal in a grotesque style of his own. He tells me that he dictates all his thinkings, and that is easier work for head and hands. I never tried the method, but am sure of its being beyond my power. Goldsmith attempted it and failed. The ways of authors are different, like their mental idiosyncrasies. Dr. Johnson could do with ease what Goldsmith could not. The latter polished, the former poured forth.

26th May.—Finished to-day the reading of the *Acts of the Apostles* in the Peshito. I have observed that in the 20th chapter, 28th verse, the text has "the Church of Christ which," etc. This is undoubtedly spurious. The right reading is τοῦ κυρίου, of the Lord, not τοῦ θεοῦ, with the Sinaitic and Vatican MSS. xxviii. 29 is given in Schaaf and Greenfield's editions, but enclosed in brackets. The version had not the verse at first.

3rd June.—Another friend has departed, Dr. Leonhard Schmitz, leaving a blank which cannot be filled. He was an excellent classical scholar, the author of good and useful books, historical and philological. His life was devoted to the laborious task of teaching, and of writing articles in dictionaries as well as school-books. The public positions he filled were but moderately remunerative. Yet he led a literary life with a cheerful spirit, amid some grievous disappointments. As a man and a friend his worth was great. He was tolerant, upright, conscientious, making no secret of his opinions on religious and other subjects. I shall miss his kindly face and pleasant conversation; but he now rests from suffering, and enjoys the reward of his work. Help, Lord, for the faithful fail from among the children of men.

14th June.—Finished to-day a second reading of *Isaiah*. In doing so I carefully compared " The Holy Bible, etc., edited with various renderings and readings from the best authorities, etc. etc., 1876," and noticed the general excellence attaching to the editorial department, which proceeded from good scholars, and deserves attention. Some corrections, amendments, and supplements are all that I have attempted to make, but many more could be added. The valuable work will be of much use to teachers and students.

2nd August.—Returned from Contrexéville on the 31st July, having left London on the 17th of June. . . . Praised be God for His protection of me and mine during our wandering by land and sea for health's sake. When these wanderings cease at length, we shall arrive in peace at the loved abode of our Heavenly Father.

24th August.—Another very dear friend, Mr. Call, has gone, so that the number of such is fast diminishing. I never consulted him about a difficulty without getting light and support. He was a thinker, a philosopher, a theologian, a man of poetic taste and feeling, conscientious, modest, cheerful, and gifted beyond measure. I shall ever cherish his memory as one belonging to God's nobility.

Mr. Call was educated in Cambridge University and entered upon the ministry of the Church of England, but soon left it from conscientious motives. He wrote regularly in the *Spectator*, under Rintoul's management; afterwards in the *Westminster Review*, where many articles of his are still worthy of perusal. Two volumes of poems appeared at different times, namely, *Golden Histories* and *Reverberations*. His poetry breathes the spirit of progressive humanity and united brotherhood.

I have observed that the Universalists and others who agree with them in holding the doctrine of universal salvation would like to banish certain words from our English Bible, such as *hell, everlasting, damnation*. With this idea we cannot entirely sympathise. In translating γέεννα, what else could be substituted for hell than the retention of the original (Gehenna), which is no rendering; whereas *hell*, a proper English term, denotes that place of Hades where the wicked are punished. Again, αἰώνιος, in cases indicated by the subject, means *everlasting*, or without end; and if translated *eternal*, what difference arises? The Revisers, however, always use the latter. When translating the New Testament I made it a rule to render the adjective by *eternal* when it refers to God, and *everlasting* when to a thing. It is a poor shift to elude the meaning " without end" by denouncing *everlasting* and resorting to *eternal*, as if their sense differed. *Damnation*, when our English version appeared, was tantamount to *condemnation*, a term less offensive to delicate ears, but with the same meaning. Were these three words banished from the English Bible, the true sense would not be in the least invalidated, nor would the cause of the Universalists, who press Greek words to serve them by melting down their force, be the stronger.

5th October.—In Canon Liddon the Church of England lately lost its best and most popular preacher, an earnest and zealous High Churchman, to whom the creeds were precious, and even the so-called Athanasian one so dear that he threatened to withdraw from active service if it were removed from the Prayer-Book. His thinking was thus confined within the limits of an orthodox creed bordering on intolerance. As to his Bampton Lectures, on which some have hastily based his lasting reputation as a divine, they were answered ably and satisfactorily by a clergyman of his own Church in a work which, though boycotted as heretical, has the right side of the question. It is entitled, *An Examination of Canon Liddon's Bampton Lectures*; Trübner 1871. Men will not see that the proper deification of Christ did not take place till well forward in the second century, that it is an undesirable development not sanctioned by the Gospels or Epistles, and a step in the progress of that superstition which went on increasing during the second, third, fourth, and fifth centuries. As far as Canon Liddon's influence reached, it checked the wholesome thinking which will eventually annihilate the ecclesiastical orthodoxy so long domiciled in England.

12th December.—I have glanced through Pfleiderer's new book on the development of philosophy and religion in Germany and England in modern times. The part relating to Germany is excellent, for the professor has ample knowledge of the literature bearing upon the two extensive subjects, and is well able to criticise it. The part that concerns England is less satisfactory, as might have been expected, as the professor did not read all the literature he notices, and his estimates of men are not seldom incorrect. The most patent instance of inaccuracy is his judgment of Edersheim's *Life of Jesus*, a book which reads into the Master's teaching the modern orthodox theology based upon Paulinism and the Fourth Gospel. If this be development, it is of a backward type. His extended notices of Maurice and Kingsley suggest the question, Did these

men advance theology? and the answer must be a negative;
for the former praised and adhered to the creeds of his
Church, and the latter opposed Colenso's views of the
Pentateuch.   But some partialities of Pfleiderer's appear
even in judging the theologians of his own country, as in
depreciatory notices of Keim and Hilgenfeld, where his
excessive attachment to the priority of Mark's Gospel has
interfered with calm judgment.

CHAPTER XVIII

4th January 1891.—I have been ill for weeks, chiefly owing to the intensely cold weather experienced by all, and felt especially by the old. Though far from having recovered in strength and health, I cannot refrain from expressing my thanks to Almighty God, who has spared me to see the beginning of another year. With trembling hand I write these few lines to record my grateful sense of His unmerited goodness to me and mine throughout the past year. I have been a great sinner considering the light I have had; may I live nearer to my Heavenly Father in what remains of my earthly life! May I have more faith and more hope to bear me upward till a better world bursts upon the view.

6th January.—The word *Christian* has been used loosely, vaguely, inadequately, incorrectly. Its primitive sense is a believer that Jesus is the Christ, accompanied with a life corresponding to that belief. He is a Christian who absorbs the spirit, follows the teaching, and walks in the light of Christ's sinless example. The Apostle Paul departed from the simplicity of this sense of the word, elaborating *a system* out of Jewish elements and his own consciousness.

Since writing the above, I see that an American Unitarian of some note has given as his conception of Christianity " the religion of reverence for the infinite worth of man," referring the reader to many assenting scholars and theologians. Christianity appears to me to be the revelation of the Infinite Father's love which Jesus Christ made to men: He being the ideal man, the representative in humanity of the unseen God. In any correct definition of Christianity, Christ should be chief factor.

12th January.—It is said that Calvin published some two hundred sermons and essays on the gospel with never a single text from Christ's sayings, but all from Paul. Most modern theological works follow the same example.

20th January.—The books of the Old Testament have been burdened with comments and deductions, by means of which, rather than by themselves, ecclesiastics have put a yoke on the necks of many, enforcing their own assumptions on persons who could know nothing about them, and that, too, as a condition of fellowship. Such a process is sheer despotism. It is neither to the Word of God nor of Christ that men are now required to subscribe, but to hereditary statements originating with political ecclesiastics. The greatest slavery that existed before Christ came was slavery to mere books that pretended in some way to have come from God. The effect of Christ's teaching was freedom to His true disciples from such bondage.

Like many others in the Established Church, Dr. Stanley did not hesitate about publishing opinions contrary to the Articles, yet he shows some caution in his history of the Jewish Church by occasionally relegating to notes referring to Ewald, heterodox views he disliked the open avowal of. His biography of Arnold is his best work. As to his mediating theology, no scholar cares for it.

25th January.—The usual definition of a miracle is, a violation of natural law; and some think that it may not be a violation of an unknown natural law. But we cannot count on the unknown; we must proceed on the basis of such evidence as comes within the sphere of credible testimony, or upon individual experience. In regard to the miracles of the New Testament, some explain them by believing that Christ received the power of working them from God, which implies their existence as violations of divine law.   This is no proper solution of the problem. These miracles are composites, not simple entities, and therefore they are capable of analysis.   A small fact as the foundation, receives accretions in the progress of time by passing through several minds and mouths.   Old Testament phrases and Messianic ideas are employed.   Words are changed into events, parables become wonders.   Poetic imagination lends its magnifying aid, and the thing comes forth with fair proportions,—striking, wondrous, superhuman, —the small element of fact disappearing from ordinary vision.   The process has had both growth and exaltation.

2nd March.—The religion of Islam as described in the Koran contains some tolerant and just sentiments; for example—

" Surely those who believe, and those who Judaise, and Christians and Sabians, whosoever believeth in God and the last day and doeth that which is right, they shall have their reward with their Lord, there shall come no fear on them, neither shall they be grieved " (ch. ii.).

" Unto every one of you have we given a law and an open path ; and if God had pleased, He had surely made you one people ; but He hath thought to give you different laws, that He might try you in that which He hath given you respectively.   Therefore strive to excel each other in good works ; unto God shall ye all return, and then will He declare unto you that concerning which ye have disagreed " (ch. v.).

Other passages breathe a different spirit, such as—

" Whoever followeth any other religion than Islam, it shall not be accepted of him ; and in the next life he shall be of those who perish " (ch. iii.).

It is vain to interpret this, with Reland, in agreement with the first two.   In practice Islam has been an intolerant religion, and I fear will continue so till it disappears before a better.

21st March.—Finished another reading of *Micah*, to which I was led by the treatise of Mr. Taylor.

I subjoin a translation of the Messianic passage in the 1st verse of the 5th chapter :—

" And thou Bethlehem Ephrath, a little one to be among the families of Judah ; from thee shall come forth to me He that is to be ruler in Israel, and his origin from olden time, from days of antiquity."

The original text is rightly corrected by Hitzig in joining the ה of Ephrata to the following adjective ; but he would omit the next word as having come into the text from its after-occurrence in the verse, which is unnecessary. צָעִיר cannot mean " too little " ; if it could, לִהְיוֹת should be מֵהְיוֹת.

27th March.—Finished the second reading of *Nahum.* The conjectures respecting Huzzah (ii. 7) need not be enumerated. The most probable is that it means the *queen.* This is favoured by the mention of her maids in the immediate context.

I have just lost another old and valued friend, the want of whom I shall feel sorely, J. D. Morell, LL.D., a superior scholar and thinker, liberal in his opinions on all subjects, kind-hearted, generous, free from bigotry or bitter prejudice. The last time I saw him, he gave me his own copy of *The Philosophy of Religion*, a volume to which I attach much value, though he would never reprint or revise it. He appears to most advantage in his works on philosophy, a department in which he excelled. I have met with few men on whose friendship and thorough sincerity I could more confidently rely. He united simplicity of disposition with philosophic insight, gentleness with high reasoning power : combinations seen too seldom. I shall never forget our walks through the woods of Marienbad, our talks about

Kant, whose thoughts on universal peace he was then translating, or other conversations touching Halle and Ulrici. But his last illness had begun even then, gently and insidiously, as appeared afterwards. This true friend has gone before me, I doubt not to a higher state. We may meet again. I warmly cherish the hope.

13*th April.*—Finished the second reading of *Haggai*. In ii. 7 the meaning of the words is, "and the choice of all the nations shall come," etc., *i.e.* the choicest or best of them. Many translate, "the desirable things shall come," which is the Septuagint rendering, but it is much less probable. The Bible published by Eyre & Spottiswoode, with various renderings, gives Ewald among the authorities for the latter. That scholar, however, speaks uncertainly in a note to vol. iv. of his *Geschichte des Volkes Israel*, p. 145, 3rd ed., saying that *if* חֶמְדָּה referred to *treasures* at the time of Haggai, the idea suits the context. But does the Hebrew noun mean "costly things"? That is doubtful. I prefer Ewald's first interpretation, *die ersehensten der Völker*. Had the proposed sense been intended, it is likely that כָּל would have preceded חֶמְדַּת. It is matter for regret that Gesenius omits all reference to the passage, under the noun in question, though he gives no support to the signification "desirable things," standing in the singular number of the Hebrew substantive.

4*th May.*—Finished another reading of *Zachariah*. The third part of the prophecies collected under the name of this writer (chs. xii.–xiv.) is for the most part an imaginary description of the future of Judah and Jerusalem, the partial destruction of the latter, the repentance and purification of the people, the extermination of two parts of the country's inhabitants, the destruction of the nations that fight against Jerusalem, the cessation of the prophetic caste, and the ideal or Messianic state when all worship in the sacred temple, and universal holiness pervades the land. The figurative language has sometimes a gross aspect, as when Jehovah comes with His holy angels and stands on Olivet, which cleaves into two parts, eastward and westward; but the interpreter can readily condone such particulars. The few historical allusions are not definite enough to put the reader in the exact time of the prophet, whose descriptions are vaguely poetic. Even the few passages that refer to facts leave the facts to be guessed. "Him whom they pierced" (xii. 10) may be the prophet Isaiah, whose murderer tradition makes Manasseh; and the man who is called Jehovah's "fellow" is some unknown king (xiii. 7), or Manasseh himself.

Amid sad presentiments of his country's fate the prophet does not lose hope of a bright future for Jerusalem under the rule of its great King, and with the restoration of a pure worship. The ideal Messianic age still floats before him, fostering the patriotic belief.

In ii. 6 (ii. 10, Hebrew) I cannot agree with Hitzig and others in supposing that the perfect is prophetic, meaning "I will spread," but take it to denote the past dispersion of the people into Babylonia and elsewhere. Those who were scattered abroad and did not return are exhorted to flee back to their homes.

6th May.—Finished the reading of the *Epistle to the Ephesians* in the Peshito. I observed that it has the common but erroneous reading in ch. v. 30, "of His flesh and of His bones"; justly rejected by Lachmann and Tischendorf.

8th May.—Finished to-day the reading of *Malachi.*

In iii. 1 the messenger of the covenant is Elijah, not the Lord = Messiah. Elijah comes before the great day of the Lord. The "even" of the English version should be "and." Malachi expected no visible head or king to his ideal theocracy, and never alludes to Messiah.

In iii. 6, instead of "therefore ye sons of Jacob are not

consumed," I translate, " but ye sons of Jacob are not perfect."   This agrees better with the preceding words.

6th October.—This day I finished the revision of my translation of Tischendorf's *Greek Testament* text.   The revision was minute and as accurate as possible.   Grimm's *Lexicon* was of use, though I could not follow that scholar's renderings everywhere.

19th October.—Finished this day the reading of *Amos* in the Hebrew.

Two passages at least demand exposition, namely, iv. 3 and v. 26, both of which are incorrectly rendered in the English version.   The first should be " and ye shall be flung into the tower, saith the Lord."   The Hebrew word may refer to the fortified part of a palace to which the people of Israel should be carried as prisoners or slaves. We change a vowel point in the verb, making it Hophal instead of Hiphil.   The attempts of Ewald and Hitzig to bring out other senses need not be given.   v. 26. These words are best referred to the future, agreeably to the subsequent context, not to the present, as Dahl, Umbreit, and Bunsen suppose ; much less to the past.   " So shall ye take up the stake of your king and the pedestal of your images, the star of your god which ye made," etc. The prophet threatens the people with a hasty flight, as they, terror-stricken, are driven by the Assyrians from their homes into exile, carrying away their idols in pieces.   To take the noun כִּיּן for Saturn, as the Septuagint, followed by the Acts of the Apostles, does, destroys the parallelism. The word is difficult of exposition because it occurs but once.

4th November.—Finished the reading of the Peshito *Epistle to Titus*, which appears to be a better translation than that of the Timothy epistles.

I cannot refrain from saying a few words about Dr. Sadler, my esteemed friend, who exchanged this life for a better in the month of September last, after a long ministry faithfully and successfully performed.   Of the Channing theological type, and therefore more conservative than some of his brethren belonging to the same denomination, his religious services were penetrated with a devotional spirit too seldom exemplified by ministers of the gospel.   I looked upon him as a model preacher, undogmatic, with a large-hearted charity, devoid of intolerance, bitterness, envy, or strife; genial, sympathetic with all good men, whatever their creed might be.   He exemplified the religion of Christ to a degree not often realised.   I listened to his sermons and joined in his prayers with spiritual profit.   What he said was most fitting, neatly and even elegantly expressed, thoughtful, reverent.   My intercourse with him was unconstrained: he expressed his opinions freely, and I did the same.   Alas that so many of my valued friends should leave me in this cold world almost alone.   Dr. Sadler is now a sainted one among the spirits of the just made perfect.   Adieu, faithful brother; only for a time, however.

7th December.—The din of another School Board election is now over, and it may be profitable to take a calm view of the subject.   The scheme was inaugurated by Mr. Forster in 1870; and twenty-one years of its existence afford a fair example of what it has done and is likely to do.   It will be readily granted that it has effected much good by bringing home instruction to thousands of children and young persons who would otherwise have grown up in ignorance, probably in crime also. But besides its inherent need of amendment, serious errors have attended its administration.   Of late it has undergone one change in the instruction being made gratuitous. Free education is a plausible and pleasing phrase, but when looked at closely it loses much of its attractiveness.   The duty of educating children naturally rests upon their parents; and to throw the expense as well as the responsibility of a duty which belongs to one class, upon another, is unjust. This is really what is done. The labouring class, as they are called, who marry early and have large families, are relieved of the care and expense of educating those families, by the classes who are above them in the social scale. Besides, those who pay for what they get, value it most ; what is given for nothing is less esteemed. I doubt whether free schooling will contribute much to the increase of scholars.

What I wish is to see a State provision for secular education alone: no Biblical teaching, no instruction in what is called religion but is not. This should be free only to those who are so poor as to be positively unable to pay for schooling their children. Others should be required to pay. I would have no compulsion to make all come into the schools. All should be invited to come and take advantage of the offered boon, but they should not be forced. If people are so stupid or senseless as to allow their children to grow up in ignorance, they may live to see its evil effects.

The instruction given in these secular schools should be confined to reading, writing, and arithmetic, and not embrace a multitude of things such as drawing, geography, history, music, and the like, which are comprehended in the ambitious School Board programme. Let the parents or guardians of the children provide for religious instruction. If they cannot do it themselves, the accredited ministers of the parish should undertake it, or Scripture readers chosen by them. The inculcation of sound morality ought not to be neglected.

What are the results of all the expensive machinery that has been in operation throughout London for the space of twenty-one years? Has crime lessened perceptibly? Is the language of the young in the crowded streets much improved? Let the daily newspapers answer. I confess

I see not much change for the better—certainly not the improvement that many millions of money might have been expected to show.   A real, true, lasting education comes only from the great spiritual Source of all good; not through man's teaching is it given, but by the divine spirit within, penetrated with the love of God and humanity.

CHAPTER XIX

15th December 1891.—The brief records of these anniversary days approach their end, for I feel the weakness of old age, its discomforts and diseases, more and more. These wear out the body of flesh and blood, which will be exchanged for a different habitation of the emancipated spirit. In a changing, material world like the present, it is my chief consolation to know that a Being of unchanging love presides over all, and that He has provided for the everlasting happiness of His rational creatures. Meanwhile, death has been busy in the world around. The present year has taken away valued friends, the last of them, William Bickham of Manchester, a godly man of a fine and gentle spirit, who stood by me in the days of my calumniation, and remained faithful to the end. At present I am scarcely fit for any work, but can only serve by waiting—serve God by waiting for the realisation of the blessed hope which enters into that within the veil. To-day is one of brooding depression, because it recalls with vivid freshness the image of her who was the centre of my affections. I never expected to survive her about twenty years, yet these have nearly run their course since she fled away.

24th December.—Finished to-day the reading of *Daniel* in the Hebrew Bible, and I now make a few remarks on the book. The Daniel who figures in this work is not the Daniel spoken of in Ezekiel, one who lived in the eighth century B.C., a prophet who predicted the downfall of the Assyrian Empire during his captivity in Nineveh, around whom many traditions and sayings had gathered in the course of centuries. Some of these traditions were adapted to later times, but we are unable to separate what belonged to the old prophet from the later Daniel. A fragment, which is at the same time an evidence of the Assyrian captive, is the mention of the Hiddekel or Tigris (x. 4), called "the great river," an appellation belonging to the Euphrates of Babylon.

The present book was written about 175 B.C., during the reign of Antiochus Epiphanes, not in the sixth century B.C., for the language does not suit the latter, being of a posterior type. The writer was not at home in the use of Hebrew, and therefore he resorts to the Chaldee, with Greek words intermingled, showing that he lived in the time of Grecian predominance. The book is composed of fact and fiction. Some parts are historical, others apocryphal. It presents a varied symbolism, grotesque miracles, and a lofty patriotism foreboding impending destruction to the ruthless enemy of Israel, with the hope of a happy future. It speaks of present things and past as future. Thus Belshazzar is present in vii. 1, and future in vii. 17. The four empires described are the Babylonian, the Median, the Persian, and the Grecian ; the Roman is ignored. It is remarkable that the Median is always separated from the Persian, with a king to itself. Darius the Mede, as far as we know, is an apocryphal king following immediately the last king of Babylon, but there is no room for him before Cyrus. Had the author been accurate, he should have said that the Medo-Persian kingdom under Cyrus followed the Babylonian. Xenophon speaks of Cyaxares as a king of Media, and some identify him with Darius the Mede, but the difficulties against this are strong. It is remarkable that the author does not know the right spelling of Nebuchadrezzar's

name, but calls him Nebuchadnezzar. He is intended as
the type of Antiochus Epiphanes. Belshazzar is called
his *son*, but this is an error. Neither was he the last king
of Babylon, who was Nabonnid or Labynetus, as Herodotus
names him. Between Nebuchadrezzar and Nabonnid were
Evil-Merodak and Neriglosser.

Antiochus Epiphanes, about whose death the writer knew
nothing, simply saying "he shall be broken without hand "
(viii. 25), is represented as dying in Palestine, whereas he
died in Persia (1 Macc. vi. 1–16). The golden age in which
the exaltation and sovereignty of Israel over all nations
should begin with the death of Antiochus is the expectation
of the writer. This shows that he had no knowledge of
the future, but stood on the same platform with the old
prophets. The historical reality was quite different. The
Messiah is not referred to in ch. ix. 24–27. The anointed
one, a prince, in the 25th verse, is Cyrus; in the 26th
verse, the anointed one cut off is Darius III., the high
priest murdered at Antioch; and the prince that should
come is Antiochus Epiphanes. The Persian kingdom is
said to be divided into 120 satrapies, an incredible number,
probably taken from the 20 of Darius Hystaspes, enlarged
into 120 with reference to the 127 governors of provinces
(not satrapies) (Esth. i. 1). The interpretation of this
apocalyptic book requires a knowledge of history, and the
language in some places is difficult to understand. But
it is not my present purpose to enter into explanations of
hard passages. I merely select one because it is badly
explained in the Bible published by Eyre & Spottiswoode,
" with various readings and renderings from the best
authorities." The *best* authorities include some that are
not good. Ch. xi. 39, " And he (Antiochus) procures for
the strongest holds a people of a strange god, whom he
acknowledges he will increase with honour," etc. etc. Here,
as no suitable sense arises from עַם, the vowel point should

be changed; אֲשֶׁר is the accusative, not the nominative, and the preterite הֵפִיר should not be changed with the *kri*, יָפֵיר, but is the true reading. The conduct of the king is illustrated by 1 Macc. iii. 36.

Hebraists of the first rank sometimes err in judgment. So Gesenius takes עָמַד in xii. 13 to mean "arise from the dead," following in this respect a Rabbinical idea. But the verb rejects the sense. Translate, "and thou mayest rest and wait for thy lot at the end of the days" specified in the preceding verse, *i.e.* in the Messianic kingdom. So also Hitzig understands לוֹ אֵין in ix. 26 as equivalent to אֵינֶנּוּ, *i.e.* "be no more," a sense forced upon the phrase, though it had been adopted before by Schmidt and Wieseler. The meaning is "have none," *i.e.* no successor.

1st January 1892.—Blessed be God for the first day of the year 1892, which has dawned auspiciously, bringing vividly before the mind memories of the past, memories tinged with sadness. At the same time, God's unceasing mercies should never be forgotten, and thankfulness to Him should be both felt and expressed. As we know not what a day may bring forth, we cannot tell what is in the bosom of this year; nevertheless, let my trust in the Father of Mercies be stronger and my love to Him more ardent. May His gracious presence be with me, living or dying. None of His rational creatures need lose the hope of a blessed immortality. Let me try to be meeter for the inheritance of the saints in light, whenever it may please Him to call me hence.

9th January.—Encyclopedias, Cyclopedias, Dictionaries of the Bible, Cyclopedias of Biblical Literature, etc., often disappoint the reader who has recourse to them. In a general cyclopedia, such as the *Britannica*, it cannot be expected that biblical or theological subjects should be treated otherwise than perfunctorily, though the editor's judgment may occasionally depart from this rule. But even in dictionaries professedly biblical and theological, an inquiring student will not get the satisfaction he desires; on the contrary, he will meet with inferior or erroneous articles. The causes of this defect are various. Too many writers spoil the unity of the whole work. Some are badly chosen. The editor himself may be incompetent or negligent. In looking cursorily through the volumes of Kitto's *Cyclopedia* and Smith's *Dictionary of the Bible*, works possessing many excellences, because good scholars were concerned with them, I have been astonished to observe evidences not only of injudicious statement, but evasion and error. Both are constructed on conservative or traditionary principles. Both are tinged with a narrow spirit. Both exclude the free breath of a correct and liberal interpretation.

A few specimens will show that implicit dependence on such dictionaries as I have been alluding to cannot be recommended.

Hanes (Isa. xxx. 4). — After a number of useless opinions, the writer in Kitto's *Cyclopedia* comes to the conclusion that the city is identical with Tahpanhes. This is an error. The place is Heracleopolis, Ehnes or Ahnas, a city of Middle Egypt, as is well attested, and accepted by the best scholars, including Gesenius and Hitzig. The city was on an island south of Memphis, and belonged to the Tanite kingdom. The author of the article in Kitto was influenced by the writer of " Hanes " in Smith's *Dictionary*, who is equally in error, absurdly saying that Gesenius has a kind of apology for identifying Hanes with Heracleopolis.

Balaam's ass spoke Hebrew or Aramaean. She had a " spiritual perception," according to the writer of " Balaam " in Smith's *Dictionary*. The corresponding article in Kitto is evasive, giving opinions, but not deciding. The episode about the ass is a myth; so is the entire epic about

Balaam, which was meant to glorify Israel. Neither is real history.

Ages of the antediluvian patriarchs. — A writer in Smith's *Dictionary* argues in favour of these unusually long ages because they are plainly stated in Scripture, which is of divine authority. In Kitto's *Cyclopedia* the same opinion is taken for granted. But Professor Owen has demonstrated, as far as that can be said of the subject, that the thing is impossible. His paper in Fraser's *Magazine* is conclusive. History, properly so called, does not begin in the Book of Genesis till the time of Abraham. All that precedes is legendary and mythical.

"The Pentateuch is the greatest monument of Moses as an author." So it is oracularly stated in Kitto's *Cyclopedia* (vol. iii. p. 222). Dogmatic assertions like this should be at once rejected.

The writer of "Sabaoth, the Lord of," in Smith's *Dictionary* is wrong in interpreting *hosts* of the armies of Israel. It means heavenly hosts, celestial beings surrounding God's throne, chiefly angels. As ignorance is often dogmatic, he says that this, the true sense, is "surely inaccurate," and, "there can be no doubt" that the. *hosts* were the armies of the nation led by Jehovah. Gesenius would have set him right; but perhaps he thought he knew better than the great lexicographer.

Both the cyclopedia and the dictionary argue that the Book of Deuteronomy was written by Moses, in the face of all the internal evidence that it was much later, especially the fact that it has reference to the temple at Jerusalem in chs. xii., xvi. 1–7. What more need be said as a plea for the thorough revision and alteration of the contents of both ?

17th January.—Looking at *Ecclesiastes* again, especially its end, I translated the appendix as follows :—

"But the preacher was not only wise, he also taught the people knowledge ; and examining and searching, he composed many proverbs. The preacher sought to find pleasing words, and they were written uprightly, words of truth. The words of the wise are as goads and as fastened nails, well united, given from one shepherd. And further, by these my son be warned: of making many books there is no end, and much study is a weariness of the flesh. Let us hear the conclusion of the whole matter. Fear God and keep His Commandments, for this is the whole man. For God shall bring every work into judgment upon all that is secret, whether it be good or evil."

Such seems to be a fair translation of this appendix to Coheleth, the book of a sceptical bachelor who wrote, as the best scholars think, in the end of the Persian dominion over Palestine or the beginning of the Grecian supremacy, *i.e.* about 331 B.C. It has struck me as strange that Kamphausen never refers to the probable fact that xii. 9–14 is an addition to the treatise by a later hand, perhaps by one of the great synagogue. It commends the writer, attests one authorship, and by a few final words counteracts the ill repute in which the work was held by some thoughtful Jews, who would have refused it a place in the Canon. The addition facilitated, if it did not cause, the reception of a doubtful book among the sacred writings. There is no reason for supposing, with Kalisch, that various small interpolations were also made throughout the treatise.

The piece has a few obscure expressions, chiefly בַּעֲלֵי אֲסֻפּוֹת, which Gesenius, followed by Fürst, renders " masters of assemblies," but we prefer to make it allude to " the words of the wise," which agrees better with the following clause. Kamphausen's " inhaltsreichen Sätze " is not good, because the allusion is to the proverbs being collected and put together in an excellent way—to their form rather than their value. Ewald's rendering comes nearest to the true one.

The judgment into which all shall be brought by God does not allude to what shall take place in a future world. The doctrine of personal immortality was not believed in among the Jews so early as the Preacher's time, and it does not appear in his book. It is not even in Ecclesiasticus. However, it emerges in the Wisdom of Solomon, which was composed in Alexandria amid the influences of Greek philosophy.

19th January.—Isa. xix. 18 has exercised scholars who had to do with the interpretation of the prophet. The Masoretic reading is הֶרֶס, which means "destruction," "city of destruction." As the context, however, points to a favourable view of the five cities, and of the one specified in particular, a new sense has been found for the phrase, namely, "city of destroyed images," involving the idea that the inhabitants were converts to the true religion. This interpretation, put forth by Delitzsch, is unnatural, because it brings into the words a foreign conception. The simple meaning assuredly is not a city which has ruined its images, but one that is to be destroyed. This reading, though better supported by external evidence than its rival חֶרֶס, and still adopted by Hitzig, is inferior to the latter in the judgment of Gesenius and Ewald, with whom I agree, translating "city of the sun," *i.e.* On or Heliopolis. The versions afford little help towards the original reading. The Chaldee has both. Aquila and Theodotion retain the Masoretic word, but Symmachus favours חֶרֶס. The Septuagint has ἀσεδέκ, "city of righteousness." The Vulgate has "city of the sun"; but the Syriac abides by the common reading. In regard to the signification of the words, some scholars, such as Iken, J. D. Michaelis, and Hitzig, would translate חֶרֶס, after the Arabic, by "lion," and so bring out the lion-city or Leontopolis. This is far-fetched and improbable. Gesenius, who adopts the non-Masoretic reading, has also recourse to the Arabic, and translates "a city preserved." This is unnecessary. I adhere to the usual sense of the word *sun*, "city of the sun," *i.e.* Heliopolis. Though much has been written on the disputed reading and its signification, little has been added to its elucidation since Gesenius published his admirable commentary on Isaiah. The suspicion is not unlikely that the Palestinian Jews changed the original word from their dislike of the temple at On.

26th January.—The criticism of the Old Testament has passed through many phases at different times, and is likely to pass through more. One meets with approval till another pushes it aside. That now in vogue, relating chiefly to the Hexateuch, analyses the books with the view of making their origin as late as possible. Every work is assigned to a more recent time than before, and the innovation becomes popular because of its novelty, till fashion fades. The subject is attended with much difficulty, and scholars disagree widely ; some confident in their opinions, others modest and hesitating. At present it is too early to catch at and plant German or Dutch speculations in English ground. Time is needed for their sifting and settlement. In dealing with the sacred text, Kuenen, Wellhausen, and Reuss are the greatest conjecturers and splitters. I need not describe the proposed analyses of these or other scholars. Vatke's *Einleitung* presents a summary of them, the reading of which suggests the idea that different Jewish hands were busy in supplying glosses, inserting fragments, separating, dividing, composing, supplementing, all along the time of the kings in Judah or Israel during the Babylonian exile, and till after Ezra. The modern dismemberment of these portions, which is greatest in Kuenen and Wellhausen, shows the ingenuity of conjecture, but can scarcely be regarded as sober or probable analysis.

Four writers may be fairly traced in the Pentateuch, namely, the Elohist, the junior Elohist, the Jehovist, and the Deuteronomist. The last mentioned, who wrote before the eighteenth year of Josiah's reign, assumes the existence of

the three first.   Ezra made some insertions in the writings
before him, and he was first redactor of the Pentateuch.
The priestly preceded the prophetic legislation, according
to the natural development of civilisation, and the Elohists
were prior to the Jehovist.   The three intermediate books
of the Pentateuch should not be relegated, or even the
whole of their priestly legislation, to the time or pen of
Ezra.   They belóng to a prior time, not to the east-
Jordanic, which would presuppose their substantially Mosaic
authorship.   The oldest part of all is the ten words of the
Decalogue, which, stripped of their additions, may be from
Moses himself.   Ex. xxi.–xxiv. has been taken by the
Jehovist from some old codex.

28*th January.*—The prevailing fashion of late dating
has not left *the Psalter* untouched or unharmed.   It has
attracted a few scholars who like to show independence of
traditional opinions, and perhaps of the cherished beliefs of
the Churches to which they belong.   The danger of running
from one extreme to another—from popular notions to
sceptical negation—is considerable.   It is not my present
purpose to enter upon one of the most difficult problems
of Old Testament literature.   My design is rather to mark
a commencing current in regard to the Psalms, to show
its error, and to warn against it.   It began to flow over
German sacred literature years ago, without much success,
so that it is not a new thing, and I think it is not likely
to prosper in this country.

Seventy-three psalms are ascribed to David by their
inscriptions, some of the latter stating the historical occasions which gave rise to the hymns.   I am aware that the
inscriptions are not a sure indication of authorship, being
of later origin ; but to pronounce all erroneous is hasty.
In like manner, the contents and language of some are
precarious guides to authorship, though available towards
the ascertainment of age.   I cannot subscribe to the

opinion of Olshausen, von Lengerke, and Vatke, that not a single psalm in the whole collection is David's, but believe Ewald's list, with some alterations, to be pretty correct. It might stand thus: iii. iv. vii. viii. xi. xviii. xxiv. xxix. xxxii. by David. This list is not so large as Hitzig's.

Other psalm-writers belong to the times of David and Solomon, to pre-Exile and Exile times. It would be rash to say that none of the twelve assigned by their inscriptions to Asaph was written by him, or that no prophet had a part in any, since the Septuagint specifies as authors, Jeremiah, Ezekiel, Haggai, and Zachariah. Against the relegation of almost all psalms to the time of the Babylonian exile or later, an opinion which needs no refutation because of its evident erroneousness, we might quote the following examples, which in all probability show their age to be that of the first temple: ii. xvi. xx. xxi. xxiii. xxvi. xxviii. xxxi. xlv. lxi. lxviii. lxxii. The language employed in these and others shows no degeneracy, but rather a purity betokening a flourishing period of national history. Besides, the Book of Jonah, belonging to the latter half of the fifth century B.C., contains a prayer composed out of many existing psalms. All credible evidence shows the vanity of any attempt to bring down the far greater part of the Psalter to a very late date. The division itself of the whole evinces no arbitrary procedure, but one based on history, the oldest odes being in the first.

Maccabean psalms are the favourite topic of innovating critics, and it was Hitzig who first assigned a large number to that time. Von Lengerke followed, pushing the view still further. Some belong to that date, but I can only find these: xliv. lx. lxxiv.–lxxvi. lxxix. lxxx. lxxxix. cx. cxviii. Internal evidence fails to support the assumption that there were more, and external evidence is silent. It was a period of warfare and persecution. To talk of " the Jewish Church " favouring the production of songs and hymns at that time, or of "the Jewish Church" at all, is mere conjecture and unsuitable phraseology. Synagogues existed in different places, but most of them were wasted. Those who have read what Gesenius wrote long ago in the *Ergänzungsblätter* of the *Allgemeine Lehrzeitung*, 1816, No. 81, and know its influence upon Rosenmüller and De Wette, must be slow to believe in the existence of a very large crop of sacred odes having sprung up in the Maccabean period.

Of Messianic psalms, none can be properly called so. Some, indeed, are quoted or applied in the New Testament in that sense, but the fact does not show the purpose of the original writer. In a wide sense such may be called Messianic, as far as they allude to a golden age in the future, or express hopes of blessed times to come to the nation, but a personal Messiah is absent. The 45th is an epithalamium on the marriage of Solomon with a foreign princess; the 72nd expresses in high-flown language the wishes of a poet for the happy reign of a king, perhaps of Solomon.

The wild conjectures of some recent scholars who have undertaken to interpret the Psalter are an unpleasant sign of progress. In the multiplication of Maccabean and the expulsion of Davidic odes, in the throwing of very many into Exile or post-Exile times, which cannot be judiciously put there, haste is too apparent. In expressing ideas which are but the rash fruit of older ones, though they have the appearance of novelty, some are bringing sound criticism into contempt. The problems suggested by the Psalter are hard of solution, because the evidence is so precarious—the path which the scholar takes is slippery; let him therefore exercise judgment and taste.

7th February.—While writing about a commentary on *Isaiah*, my attention was turned to a form in the 53rd chapter, 8th verse; and as my friend Professor Hupfeld avoided an explanation of it, I may be excused from entering upon it, however difficult. לָמוֹ is rightly translated as a plural, *to them*. Some poets, however, employ it as a singular, *to him*, for which Ewald cites, as examples, Ps. xi. 7; Job xxii. 2; Deut. xxxiii. 2, twice; Isa. xliv. 15; (*Ausführliches Lehrbuch der Hebräischen Sprache, achte Ausgabe*, p. 625). On the other hand, Gesenius asserts that wherever it has a singular sense it is collective, giving a number of examples in corroboration, and among them Isa. liii. 8 (*Lehrgebäude der Hebräischen Sprache*, p. 221). It is not easy, however, to see the pertinence of Isa. xliv. 15 as an instance; nor can I get rid of the idea that the form has both senses, as Kimchi formerly thought. The Phenician has been quoted against Gesenius, in which *êm* is both singular and plural, but its evidence in proving Hebrew usage is slight. The word is originally plural, the singular use of it being secondary. Delitzsch says that מ is a *mimation*, but that explains nothing. It seems to me that מ is the essential letter retained from the third person masculine plural הם. When the preposition ל was prefixed, ה was dropped, of course, and ו added.

14th February. — The Hebrew plural Elohim, more generic than the appellative Jehovah, is a remnant of polytheism in its application to God. Originally it means the gods of mythological systems, the deities of peoples other than the Semites (Ex. xii. 12). Hence it is connected with a plural verb or adjective when idolatry is spoken of (Ex. xxxii. 4). Monotheism, retaining the plural but associating with it the idea of *excellence* or *majesty*, to show the superhuman dignity of God, connected it with a singular predicate (Gen. i. 1). This, however, is not done always, as Josh. xxiv. 19 and other places show.

Gesenius regards Elohim as a plural *majestaticus* or *excellentiae*, but Ewald denies this, saying that such usage of the plural is foreign to the Hebrew language; which is a hasty assertion, for Artaxerxes says, in Ezra vii. 24, "*we certify you*," etc.

Does Elohim mean *angels*?　Gesenius denies that it does; but Ewald cites Gen. xxxv. 7 as an example where God and his angels are said to be meant—a very doubtful statement, though Kalisch approves.　I believe that Gesenius is right in maintaining that the plural in question never denotes *angels*, or God attended with or surrounded by them.　The ancient versions, however, are against him, for in Ps. viii. 6, as well as in other passages, the LXX., the Vulgate, Targum, and the Peshito translate *angels*.

25th February.—The force of position in which one is placed is powerful in forming and stereotyping one's belief. The very aspect of surrounding nature influences mental moods.　Parents, teachers, friends mould the views we take of men and things.　How hard it is to divest ourselves of ingrained creeds and traditional opinions I know right well. Taught in my earliest schooldays the Shorter Catechism of the Westminster divines every Saturday, accustomed to look upon their Confession of Faith with a sort of superstitious veneration, trained among orthodox Presbyterians during my youthful years, elected one of their theological Professors in the Belfast Royal Academical Institution, it required time and lengthened meditation to get out of the net in which I had been entangled for years.　Even in the face of evidence I was reluctant to part with most of the dogmas which clung to me with much tenacity.　But the infallibility of the Bible had to be given up, its mistakes and contradictions admitted, the voice of reason had to be listened to, and the duty of interpreting sacred oracles like any other book had to be acknowledged.　If I have now departed far from creed-religion, I believe I have got nearer to truth.　It has been at least my honest endeavour to be so.　After all, a righteous life is a more important part of religion than an orthodox creed.　Intellectual error, when attended with a good conscience, is innocent, but moral error is not so.

2nd March.—The separation of the documents used by the Old Testament writers in composing their books, particularly the Hexateuch, is attended with considerable difficulty, as is exemplified by the divergent views of able critics. The Elohist is easiest seen; the latter two, with the final redactor, are not so evident. Witness the diversities of view respecting the blessing of the dying Jacob in the forty-ninth chapter of Genesis, which was certainly not introduced into the Elohim document from a prior one, as Tuch supposes, but belongs to the Jehovist. I cannot agree with the same scholar that Gen. xlix. 1–28 was of later origin than the blessing of Moses in Deut. xxxiii. Both are assigned to the Jehovist in Schrader's distribution of sources, which cannot be correct. But I need not enumerate the varying opinions of critics touching the source or the succession in time of Gen. xlix., compared with Deut. xxxiii.; enough is suggested to show the uncertainty attaching to cases that come before the scholar. Knobel, Schrader, Hupfeld, and Nöldeke have done good work in this department, not to mention the erudite Vatke; but the task has been made more difficult by Wellhausen, Kuenen, and their followers.

4th March.—I fear that many ministers of religion have not yet reached the rational and liberal view of Whitby the commentator, namely, that sincerity in inquiring, even if one misses the truth, is sufficient to procure the favour of God. The clerical mind moves slowly forward. If it really develops, it is checked by the fear of unpopularity or heresy from proclaiming even correct views in the department of religion. While speaking of Whitby, I cannot refrain from mentioning his masterly work on " the five points," to which Dr. Gill's *Cause of God and Truth* is but a feeble answer.

7th March.—A reverend doctor, formerly student in a class taught by a professor of Biblical criticism, who posed as a very orthodox Presbyterian, was going through his academic course at the time of the Colenso controversy. One day the said professor came into the classroom with a paper containing a list of statements culled from Colenso's books. After reading them before the class, he said, "Gentlemen, how do I answer these? I meet them with a flat negative." That was enough. The answer was complete. The bishop was demolished.

11th March.—Lord Bolingbroke, usually classed among the Deists, dealt severely with the Scriptures. Having never studied them, he speaks rashly, saying of the Jewish books that they have come down to us on the faith of a superstitious people, among whom pious lying remarkably prevailed. There is a grain of truth in this, but we object to the phrase "pious lying" which he employs. Some true history exists in the books, while they have also parts said to have been written by persons long deceased. Yet such conduct sprang from a good motive, namely, to give the authority and prestige of a distinguished name to things said, done, or written. This proceeding should not be judged by modern ideas of right and wrong, because our moral code differs from that of the old Semites. *They* attached no harm to a practice common in their time.

The above observations have been suggested by the perusal of a general survey of the plagues inflicted on Egypt in order to free the Israelites from bondage and oppression. This survey, written by Dr. Kalisch, is based on the alleged fact that a series of miracles was wrought in rapid succession at the command of Moses. A thoughtful reader of Kalisch's five arguments for the miraculous character of the phenomena witnessed, and for the authenticity of the descriptions, will come, in my opinion, to a different conclusion, and will deem the sentence pronounced

19

on Eichhorn unjust. The whole Biblical narrative is skilfully arranged, and has a sort of dramatic form. The number of the plagues is the number of perfection. There is a climax in these punishments of Pharaoh, whose heart becomes harder by degrees. The plagues begin and end at Moses's command. He is a wonder-worker far superior to all the magicians of the land. Every act is calculated to exalt Moses, and to show a demented king persisting in his infatuation. The description is meant to enhance the moral heroism of Moses compared with the impotent stiff-neckedness of Pharaoh. The delineation bears on its face the writer's admirable skill, but the evidence of its authenticity is wanting. It raises up the natural phenomena of Egypt to the miraculous; it introduces God directly hardening Pharaoh's heart (ch. x. 1), and enabling Moses to demonstrate the vanity of idols. Conquered by the last plague, the monarch allows the Israelites to leave their abode, laden with rich *but borrowed* treasure. Here the writer specifies a trait common among his countrymen. Pursued by Pharaoh and his hosts, the favourites of God pass through the Red Sea dry-shod; and all their enemies are drowned. The miraculous element reappears to glorify the Israelites and confound pagans.

Kalisch's survey of the plagues is tentative and conservative, like other parts of his commentary on Exodus, but his treatment of Leviticus shows how he advanced in the free criticism of the Jewish records. No longer with slow steps did he feel his way, but wrote without fear.

CHAPTER XX

Kant on Perpetual Peace

13*th March* 1892.—Notwithstanding Kant's little treatise on perpetual peace, written about a hundred years ago, in which war was shown to be against *Right*, the so-called Christian nations of Europe have not ceased to resort to it, and to keep up the great standing armies which retard the consummation of universal peace. Here is an extract from the tractate, which all politicians as well as moralists should diligently peruse :—

"Reason, from the throne of its high moral tribunal, condemns the very idea that war can be the true mode of establishing Right, and proclaims the condition of peace to be an immediate duty; a duty, however, we well know, which can never be established and secured without a treaty being entered into for that purpose between the nations. Such being the case, nations ought to form amongst themselves a special alliance, which might be termed the alliance of peace, and which would differ from an ordinary treaty of peace inasmuch as it would not merely put an end to *one* war, but would terminate war altogether."[1]

19*th March.*—The Independents of the present day do not adhere to all the views of Watts and Doddridge, the last men of their denomination who have attained to a certain literary eminence with a degree of liberality uncommon in these days, or if existing, hidden from public notice. Dr. Watts was inclined to Arianism, his ideas

[1] From a philosophical treatise on perpetual peace by Immanuel Kant, translated by Dr. Morell, p. 36.

about the Trinity being different from the current orthodox ones. He also held that the State should pay teachers of morality or natural religion, and that the people should be obliged to hear them, except when the plea of conscience is advanced. Dr. Doddridge advocates the principle of a State Church, and favours a scheme of comprehension. He opposed subscription to articles of religion by whomsoever imposed, whether by congregations or ministers of religion. Comparatively few modern Independents think, with Doddridge, that the reason for Dissent has in a great measure ceased, or would confess, with him, that the small congregations in their body, of which there are hundreds, "starve their ministers into a good opinion of Conformity." Like all religious sects outside the Establishment, they are intolerant of avowed departures from their traditional creed, though creed is necessarily a shifting thing.

22nd March.—Bishop Butler's *The Analogy of Religion, Natural and Revealed, to the Constitution and Course of Nature*, is in many respects an admirable work, and justly held in enduring estimation. It appeared at the end of the deistic controversy, having had the advantage of the arguments employed by the writers on both sides; and proceeded from a judicial, calm, and cautious reasoner, whose statements are carefully limited. The design of the treatise, as the bishop himself says, is to show "that the particular parts principally objected against in this whole dispensation (the moral and Christian dispensation) are analogous to what is experienced in the constitution and course of nature, or providence." The book is meant for a defence of Christianity as a divine revelation, though it includes natural religion as well; showing that as the constitution and course of nature, though of divine origin, has difficulties, similar ones may be expected in the Christian dispensation, which has the same Author. I do not think the argument satisfactory or conclusive as regards

Christianity. Of what benefit is a revelation if exposed to objections? Should we not expect it to be clear and simple and unencumbered with difficulties? If analogous difficulties occur in the evidence and contents of revelation and *providence*, why is the former so imperfect as to be encumbered with objections that inhere in the latter? The things assumed as parallel, though both have one Author, are different in their natures. After all, Butler's position is not far removed from the deistic one: the former asserting that "natural religion is the foundation and principal part of Christianity," the latter that it is a sufficient guide. If the one be the foundation of the other, and the latter a republication of it, they are cognate. Butler, however, adds the saving clause, that natural religion is not in any sense the whole of Christianity. Semler said the same thing as Butler had done before him: "The greater part of the Bible is a mere repetition of natural religion, as Paul teaches (Rom. i. 32, ii. 14, 15), but in the Bible it *is adduced with* greater clearness and certainty."

31*st March.*—Messianic hopes did not originate till after King David, in whose reign the nation first awakened to a feeling of its importance and its theocratic privileges. It was he who gave it unity, stability, and strength. When the kingdom was divided, the golden age disappeared, and the hopes of a return to its former flourishing state naturally arose. These, which were merely vague longings for better times, soon attached themselves definitely to the house of David. It was natural that the prophets should think of and expect a descendant of the great king, to whom they looked back with ever-increasing admiration, and whom they painted in glowing colours, to be the restorer of the theocracy to its former state. As such hopes varied with the times and the temperament of the prophets, it is observable that late writers during and after the captivity returned to the first indefinite standpoint. Thus the Deutero-Isaiah makes idealised Israel or Jehovah Himself the mediator and restorer of the theocracy. It is worthy of remark that the name " Messiah " was not a necessary accompaniment of the hopes mentioned, but was of later origin. The ideal king is said to be wonderfully gifted, a pattern of righteousness and justice. Malachi gives him Elijah for forerunner, and Ezekiel supposes Gog to precede ; both fictions.

The Messianic hope was not wholly political : it had a moral and religious element as well. The political aspect Jesus eschewed, and therefore the Jews of· His time rejected Him, looking for a powerful ruler to bring back and extend their former sovereignty. But His teaching has the form and some features of Messianic aspiration.

Josephus is silent respecting the Messianic hopes, probably through fear of the Romans, which influenced him throughout his writings. We might have expected references to them when he speaks of Daniel's prophecies, which he considered important ; but he slides over some of them evasively, saying that though the prophet declared the meaning of the stone cut out of the mountain without hands, he did not think proper to narrate it. The fear of offending the Romans sufficiently accounts for the historian's silence about the overthrow of the eternal city. The prophecy in Gen. xii. 3, xviii. 18 is also noticed vaguely. Yet Messianic hopes had not died out with the downfall of the Jewish state. The stubborn people were ready to rebel against their conquerors, and follow any leader who claimed to be their long-expected Deliverer.

4th April.—John Hales of Eton bade good-night to John Calvin at the Synod of Dort, but all theologians are not so awake to evidence as that memorable man ; or if they be so open to it, they are timid of showing their mood, and look around to see if it would be safe or prudent to avow a change of view. The synod carried out a Calvinistic programme with rigorous logic, and converted the memorable delegate to Arminianism. The Wesleyans have indirectly modified, but not abolished, Calvinism, which still prevails among the Baptists and Congregationalists, though not so much preached as it formerly was. When annual meetings of these bodies take place, no important doctrinal change is introduced for discussion. Minor things engross the talk, including self-glorification and attacks upon the Established Church. But the last has an advantage in that it can embrace both Arminians and Calvinists under the shield of the ambiguous Seventeenth Article, which Archbishop Laurence and Bishop Tomline maintained to be Arminian, while others of their Church asserted that it is Calvinistic. The large disunited body established by law, whether represented in Convocations or in Congresses, is like the Nonconformist sects in one respect, that it never initiates a strong recommendation of any important change in its creeds, but discusses things of little moment. A prevailing feature of most ecclesiastics is contentment with their creeds, or at least abstinence from ostensible disagreement with them because of unpleasant consequences. The theological reformer is sure of getting some opprobrious name fastened to his person, and loses the chance of advancement. Truly does Faust say—

" Those who revealed what they had felt and seen to the multitude, — they, from time immemorial, have been crucified and burned."

I cannot but think that the Churchmen who have left behind the Articles and Creeds which they have subscribed, and yet would subscribe again with a light heart, set a vicious example of conscientiousness. Safe in their position they may be—though they could not well hold the like in most Nonconformist sects—they belie their profession. Their liberality is obtained at a dear rate. Nor is this

conduct confined to Christians. It is exemplified among
Jews, especially the Reformed; notably among the rationalistic Jews of Germany. Fancy a scholar like Geiger, or
the reader in a synagogue where he officiated, bringing out
the Pentateuch roll and prefacing the lesson with "these
are the words that Moses wrote," when he does not believe
that Moses wrote them at all. My lamented friend Kalisch
might well hesitate about accepting an office in which
conscience must have been repeatedly violated.

6th April.—I have been reading of late the little
Talmudic treatise called *Pirke Aboth*, containing sayings
of noted Rabbis who lived about and after the time of
Christ. I used the old edition of *Fagius*, dated 1541.
The epistola nuncupactoria prefixed by the editor gives
the collection a laudatory character, comparing it with the
Proverbs of Solomon, but its value is much lower. These
dicta are moral maxims, chiefly relating to the conduct of
life. It is true that the divine law is recommended and
praised, but they are not usually theological, and faith is
rarely mentioned. They move in a lower plane than one
distinctively religious, having more regard to the present
life than the future. Wisdom and prudence are more
spoken of than love. The practical shrewdness of the
Semitic race is not absent; but many of the noble virtues,
a sense of honour, magnanimity, generosity, liberality,
expansive love, receive scant recognition. The spirit of
ancient prophecy had departed, leaving a bare residuum.
These sentiments and sayings are expressed concisely,
requiring an illustrative paraphase to bring out the sense
clearly. I subjoin a few examples:—

"Rabbi Nechuma son of Hakaman says: Whoever takes
upon him the yoke of the law, they take from him the yoke
of the kingdom and the yoke of seeking a sustenance. But
whoever shakes off the yoke of the law, they put upon him
the yoke of the kingdom and the yoke of getting a living."

"Shammai says: Make your law fixed (*i.e.* have a certain fixed time for studying the law). Speak little and do much, and receive every man with a placid face."

"Rabbi Eliezer says: Let the glory of thy companion be as dear to thee as thine own. And be not prone to anger, and repent one day before your death, and warm yourself at the fire of the wise. In the meantime, beware of their coals, lest you be burned ; for their bite is as the bite of a little fox, and their sting is as the sting of a scorpion and the hissing of a fiery serpent, and all their words like coals of fire."

This last part is directed against offending or irritating the wise, lest they should injure or hate you.

11*th April.*—The difficulty attending the interpretation of the Old Testament is not small. Not only is a good knowledge of the original language necessary, but judgment, acuteness, tact, taste, an acquaintance with the character-istics of each writer's style and with the prevailing manners of his age. Nor must the best lexicographers and grammarians be neglected ; though lexicon and grammar are insufficient to make a good commentator ; for he must also have sympathy with the sacred authors. Cold, intellectual manipulation of their words will not do: the moral nature must move in unison.

I have taken a single verse to demonstrate the per-plexity into which a commentator is sometimes thrown, and his need of modesty in announcing his opinion. In Prov. xxvi. 10 we read in our English version: "The great God, that formed all things, both rewardeth the fool, and rewardeth transgressors."

Ewald translates: "An arrow which wounds everyone, and he who hires fools and street-runners."

Hitzig: "Much procures all ; but he that hires a fool is as he who hires vagrants."

De Wette: "An arrow that wounds all, and he who hires fools and hires passers-by."

Arnheim: "The mighty one makes all tremble, for he hires fools and hires vagrants."

Van Ess: "The great one will procure all ; yea, he has the fools in hire."

Luther: "A good master makes a thing right; but he who hires bunglers, to him it will be destruction."

Bunsen's *Bibelwerk*: "As an arrow which wounds everything, so is he who hires a fool and he who hires vagrants."

Moses Stuart: "An arrow which woundeth everyone is he who hireth a fool and he who hireth vagrants."

The Vulgate and Septuagint are incorrect. Many other translations might be given, but let these suffice.

There is a want of analogy between the first member of the verse and the second, if the first word be translated *arrow*; or if any analogy be found, it is somewhat forced. "As . . . so is he who" must be supplied, and even then the likeness is not patent, but needs filling up. It is better to take the whole verse as referring to a person instead of a thing, and I incline to translate it thus—

"A mighty one (tyrant) makes all tremble; he both hires a fool and hires stragglers" (*i.e.* he makes use of any instruments, however worthless. He is not particular about the nature of his tools).

17th April.—The Holy Spirit is called in the New Testament the spirit of power, of liberty, of truth, of life. From Him is all good; faith, knowledge, love, holiness; all gifts, particularly that of prophesying, all ecclesiastical operations, come from Him, by whom Christians are preserved in union with God and Christ, and are filled with peace and joy.

This Spirit is often mentioned in the New Testament, being called both the Spirit of God and of Christ. He is also said to be one with God (Acts v. 4). The opinion which finds His personality in various passages of the New Testament is incorrect, for nothing more than a personification appears in them. To make Him a person is neither Johannine nor Pauline. The Holy Spirit was thought to be a divine and animating influence diffused through nature—a living, quickening principle proceeding from or identical with God. After the apostolic age this was

deified and definitely distinguished from God. The word
person applied to this principle is not suitable; but it is
difficult to find a better, though it fosters a mistaken belief.

19th April.—Luther, Gesenius, Ewald, De Wette,
Schleiermacher, Hupfeld, Neander, Tholuck, Hengstenberg,
Colenso. Surrounded by the portraits of these famous
scholars and thinkers, whose names will not soon perish,
I have sat, studied, and written for years; and if I have
published aught worth perusal, the sight of these savants has
exerted a stimulating influence upon me. The majority of
them I knew and conversed with in days remembered with
sadness. Though most of the dead lie forgotten, illustrious
reformers and scholars live both literally and figuratively:
they live in happiness, they live in their works. Blest in
their release from toil and malady, they enjoy repose, and
I ere long hope to join the sacred company. If I have
not hid, but used my one talent, I may through divine
mercy be admitted into the society of those whom I
esteemed on earth, and reach a far higher degree of knowledge amid happiness before untasted. I cast upward
glances at the worthies mentioned, as an incentive to work
on while it is day, before the night comes, when work
ceases, and a rest remains for the people of God. But I
can now do little in the service of God or man, for my
strength fails; but God is the strength of my heart and
my portion for ever.

While touching on the subject of notable scholars
around me, I am reminded of others whom I had the
privilege of seeing or knowing, such as Bretschneider, Pott,
Zumpt, Encke, Roediger, Erdmann, Herzog, Nitzsch, Bleek,
Lepsius, Winer, Tischendorf, Lücke, Gieseler, Nöldeke,
Schrader, Kuenen, Pfleiderer, Delagarde, Merx, Knobel,
Boehmer, Bunsen. These scholars I cannot describe ade-
quately; neither would I if I could. Almost all have
passed away. With a few I was on intimate terms, notably

with Hupfeld, Tischendorf, Tholuck, and Ewald. With others I corresponded, as with Gieseler, Bleek, Lücke, Roediger; and my communion with them gave me much pleasure, like Geddes's with Eichhorn, because they readily granted to others the same liberty of conscience and speech which they took themselves. Winer, the veteran scholar *tantum vidi*. Perhaps I owe more to De Wette than to any other German; and I think I resemble him in that he united a speculative intellect with Gefühl, or the seat of religion. All his emotions rose reverently upward. It is sad to dwell on the recollections of conspicuous thinkers now lost to view; but why should we mourn? They did excellent work in their days, and though they may have erred, the innocency of error is a right belief.

22nd April.—Adult baptism by immersion was the primitive Christian form. Converts from heathenism were received in that way into the Christian Church. The baptism of infants was a later thing. This is confirmed by the Church Fathers, who call it an apostolic tradition. Cyprian and some other African bishops, looking upon baptism as a washing away of the sinfulness of human nature, baptized infants; and so *that* Father may be said to have first followed the practice as a principle. The innovation, therefore, is not prior to the close of the third century. As to Tertullian and Origen, they do not speak of the baptism of infants, but of *parvuli*, *i.e.* growing children, perhaps upwards of six years. Neander says that Irenaeus is the first Father who makes any allusion to infant baptism, but the passage he quotes does not support the statement. I cannot say that the Church has been dragged into a wrong path in departing from the apostolic practice, for Christian consciousness should have room for development; but Cyprian was led by a questionable enthusiasm and by a bad interpretation of the Old Testament in making infant baptism correspond to circumcision. The departure from primitive practice, if it be viewed superstitiously or as imparting any virtue, is not to be rejected; neither is sprinkling with water condemnable, though Tertullian's language shows that the original mode of immersion was still observed. Why should we adhere to an unessential thing merely because of its antiquity? We have dropped the kiss of charity: why insist on the original way of performing a symbolical rite, unless the symbolism would be otherwise destroyed? And to found a sect on such a basis appears to me unwise, contributing, as it does, to the disunion of Protestantism. Happily the controversy between Baptists and Paedobaptists has well-nigh ceased. It was little more than a war of words and texts, a theological logomachy.

23rd April.—According to Dr. South, "the Socinians' pedigree runs back from wretch to wretch in a direct line to the devil."

Even the pious Richard Baxter writes in his *Church History*, "our late Socinians are more *perniciously* heretical than Arians."

A controversy, originated by the orthodox in order to discover who were Arians in the General Synod of Ulster, was carried on for years with a bitter spirit, ending in a secession of those inclined to Arian views. The Hudibrastic poem, from which I am about to quote, appeared in the heat of the disgraceful quarrel—

> "All deep-thinking Unitarians,
>   Let them be Deists, Turks, or Arians,
>   Are one in thought, and therefore do
>   Obtain the title, "Thinking Few";
>   And Cain, I need not tell the reader,
>   Was their determined early leader."

I hope that the *odium theologicum* will never raise its head again with such general intensity, though it has since shown its teeth with the same viciousness. Orthodoxy is essentially intolerant in power, and I fear it will be so as long as the dream is cherished that it engrosses all necessary religious truth.   But is not a better spirit gradually springing up with the decay of Calvinism, professing Christians learning at length that the true spirit of religion is love to God, and to man as well?

26th April.—The much-abused Thomas Hobbes, in his great work *The Leviathan*, inserted a remarkable theological part, which it is not my present purpose to describe, but only to call attention to some particulars in which his Biblical criticism is either ahead of or behind the time he lived in.   A good deal of rational theology appears in the chapter.   He denies the eternal punishment of the wicked, as also the personality of the devil; says that Moses did not write the Pentateuch; believes that the Book of Joshua was written long after Joshua's time; and that Judges, Ruth, Samuel, Kings, and Chronicles appeared long after the Captivity.   Reason is pronounced the undoubted word of God, and should be exercised in matters of religion; but he makes faith silence it in regard to the mysteries of religion, which should be accepted blindly, "as a man takes bitter but wholesome pills." This strong language is inconsistent with what he says of reason's function in another part.   No sharp distinction between reason and faith should be drawn, nor should the former be ever blinded by the latter.   Hobbes's explanations of the Trinity and Atonement are unsatisfactory, as is also his resolution of hell into a metaphor.   I am surprised to find him so highly Calvinistic as to believe that God has elected only a small number of the human race, the rest being reprobate.   Still, his insight into theology was remarkable in the case of a layman.   His vigorous mind ranged over many subjects; and while it was often sagacious, it saw some things in a perverted light.   His worst heresy is, that God is corporeal.   Notwithstanding

Hobbes's sketch of an ideal commonwealth, his bump of ideality was small. On the whole, I am unwilling to condemn a scholar who writes that, above all, we should keep the laws of the Infinite, the Eternal, the Incomprehensible, " for this is the greatest worship of all."

29th April.—I still adhere to the opinion expressed in my little book, called the *Doctrine of Last Things*, that the evidence of the New Testament favours the eternity of the future punishment of the wicked, which is indirectly confirmed by the hypothesis of annihilation resorted to by a few in order to evade a repulsive thing. But hypotheses, however welcome, cannot override evidence. The Greek word αἰώνιος and its Hebrew equivalent have been examined by Universalists with the view of showing that they mean a limited, not everlasting, time ; but a good deal of force has been applied to eliminate the natural sense and put another in its place. They cannot answer the able essay on several words relating to future punishment which Moses Stuart wrote, and which was reprinted in the *Edinburgh Biblical Cabinet* for 1842, with a preface. What is of most importance is the fact that the strongest and clearest expression of eternal punishment lies in the words of Christ Himself. This part of the evidence is most perplexing to all who regard never-ending punishment as inconsistent with the nature of God, who is love, and hates nothing He has made. Eternal misery is a disturbing element in the happiness and peace of God's future kingdom, and the existence of a ceaseless hell puts a sort of limit to blissful consummation. What, then, is the solution of the difficulty ? It is a gratuitous supposition that Jesus did not utter the language which the evangelists attribute to Him, neither is it a satisfactory suggestion that His Aramaean words have been badly rendered into Greek. The choice lies between admitting the plain sense of what Jesus said, and confessing inability to reconcile it with the character of God; or, on the other hand, assuming a degree of limitation in Jesus's knowledge of the future. He Himself says that He knew not the day or the hour of His second coming; and in the first chapter of the Acts He speaks of times or seasons which the Father has kept in His own power, implying that the Son did not know them. Besides, He may have learned in His youth from the Pharisees that the bad are eternally punished— a doctrine He did not see fit to contradict, any more than He questioned the current belief in the Mosaic authenticity of the Pentateuch.

3rd May.—How long are we bound with the chains which early education and other training have wound around us? I remember how the rigid Calvinism, instilled into me from early years out of catechism, sermons, and the conversation of all with whom I came into daily contact, developed in strength till it took possession of mind and heart, so that I entertained curious feelings towards those who differed widely from me in creed. The process of divestment was very gradual. Repeated and long-continued thought, aided by books of a certain class, contributed to loosen the fetters till they fell off, and I felt welcome light around and within me. Lengthened study of the original Scriptures was necessary to effect the change.

These remarks have been suggested by reading some sentences in the works of a Lutheran divine who never changed, and with whose opinion on inspiration I once agreed. I cannot blame Abraham Calov's language: " Nullus error vel in leviusculis, nullus memoriae lapsus, nedum mendacium ullum locum habere potest in universa scriptura sacra." Scripture itself contradicts this. But though I deal mildly with a wrong opinion, I am inclined to be severe on a bigoted spirit, and such was Calov's. One who wrote sixteen large volumes on the Bible and had six wives should have exhibited abounding toleration. Alas that intolerance should continue till the present day in those who fancy that they alone have a monopoly of the truth!

9th May.—My ideal of social order is what is commonly called "Christian Socialism," when religion, truth, liberty, individuality, should be universal. At present it is only a tendency, an aim, a conception requiring perhaps centuries to become real; but it is the goal which all thinkers and workers should be anxious to promote. The idealist looks forward to a time when every man shall be a law unto himself, the paraphernalia of government disappear, and the iron hand of rule give place to brotherly association. The methods of nationalism, under whatever form it exists,—imperial, monarchical, republican,—are circuitous, and skilfully adapted to thwart the will of the majority. The few govern, the many are misgoverned. Venality is respectable, selfishness the guiding policy. Jobbery lurks in legislation, and corporations present favourable opportunities to the self-seeker. Wealth resulting from public plunder is abundant. Peculation, waste, extravagance in the public shipyards and dockyards are common. Law is hedged about with such forms, and bristles with so many courts, that the rich alone can obtain justice. The multiplication of idle soldiers proceeds apace. Governments retard moral order, and Christianity is secularised. Associations, syndicates, trusts, commissions, committees, boards, corporations, and the like seek to amass money, instead of the members acting towards one another as true brethren. They are of the earth, earthy. The golden rule, "all things whatsoever ye would that men should do to you, do ye even so to them," is a maxim unheeded by them. Surely there is need of radical reform in the state of society when one thinks of the innumerable evils that inhere in it. Human nature must be changed, the life and mind of Christ be imaged in the entire framework of

20

society, before the ideal, for which all the good long, can become the actual.

15th August.—We read in the English Bible, "The heart is deceitful above all things, and desperately wicked" (Jer. xvii. 9). I have alluded to this passage in my book on the English version of the Old Testament as an example of theological bias in the translators. Unquestionably the language is too strong, not giving a correct rendering of the original. I translated the word אָנֻשׁ "grievously infirm," which is forcible enough, perhaps too much so. The participle means "sick" or "diseased." But though I rightly corrected the current English version, an accusation was launched against me because my rendering lessened the orthodox blackening of human nature; and this by a man totally ignorant of Hebrew. In Bunsen's *Bibelwerk* the word is rendered "a weak thing"; Arnheim and Sachs simply use "sick"; De Wette "corrupt"; and Ewald "morose" or "peevish" (graemlich), which is not happy. No adverb corresponding to *desperately* occurs in the original, nor is it correct to introduce it. In his *Thesaurus* Gesenius gives *aeger, male affectus*; and in his minor Lexicon, when referring to our passage, *de animi indole maligna.* The last word is an incorrect addition to what the *Thesaurus* has, the idea of malignity being absent from the Hebrew adjective.

3rd November.—At the risk of repeating ideas already committed to paper, I return to a subject touched upon before, to make a few additional observations for the last time. After all that has been written on the Pentateuch or Hexateuch, perhaps the different results may be reduced to a few which sober scholars who are not carried away by the wild theories that have been freely indulged in may acknowledge.

1st. It is difficult to discover what the nature of Ezra's revision was, but it is probable that it was not extensive.

2nd. Was Ezra the Elohist, as Delagarde says? Certainly not.

Jewish tradition or legend has not left the memory of Ezra in truthful simplicity, but he has been exalted to the rank of a second Moses, and has been imagined to have been the head of the Great Synagogue. The tradition about him embodied in the Second Book of Esdras is that he restored the law by inspiration, after it had been destroyed by fire when Nebuchadnezzar took Jerusalem. But the book of the law was certainly not burned at that time, though the Christian Fathers of the second and succeeding centuries eagerly took up the legend. It was neither half-burned, as Chrysostom imagined, nor wholly burned; for Ezekiel had it in Babylon, and Ezra, with his helpers, had written documents containing the Pentateuch before him. It is not easy to say whether the tradition be baseless, or whether Ezra introduced many things that were new into the law. The safest judgment is that he revised and re-edited the Pentateuch, not adding a great deal to it, as some critics suppose, but still interpolating some things of importance. What he did to it was in the way of alterations and additions. We are not to suppose, however, that his alterations were so numerous as his additions, or that he proceeded like a modern critic, taking away diversities and contradictions. The Book of Ezekiel is most useful in finding out what he did to the Pentateuch, though internal evidence is of some use for the same purpose. The most probable addition that he made to the Book of Leviticus is an important one, namely, the sixteenth chapter, containing the institution of the great Day of Atonement. That this was an innovation follows from the fact that in Exodus the Day of Atonement is not mentioned among the older festivals. Other insertions or additions may be found by the careful critic, but care should be taken not to put the greater part of Leviticus and Numbers on his shoulders. What he did was rather as editor or reviser.

3rd. Vatke, who gave the first impulse to the criticism of the present day, says of the author of the Books of Kings, who lived in the time of the Babylonian exile, surviving the year 562 B.C., that he was acquainted with the Pentateuch and had a special predilection for Deuteronomy. If so, it matters little whether the Pentateuch was completed by Ezra or by the Deuteronomist.

4th. It is natural to put the Elohist or priestly writer before any other. The Jewish people were early addicted to idolatry, and priests were abundant among them. The prophetic stage marked an advance in civilisation. Hence the Jehovist came after the priestly period; men began to think more rationally of God and to write history in another form than that of priestly annals. Vatke himself puts his two Elohists before the Jehovist.

5th. The priest Manasseh first took the Pentateuch to the people called Samaritans (430 B.C.), who might not willingly have received it because of their dislike to the Jews of Jerusalem—a dislike which had been gradually growing, till it came to a head in the institution of a separate temple. Their rejection of the Book of Joshua shows that, though idolatrous, they made a distinction among sacred books; and the idea of Ezra's extensive interference with the Pentateuch would have increased their unwillingness to accept it.

6th. From the above statement it follows that Graf is incorrect in assigning the Elohist to a post-Exile period. Riehm and Wellhausen properly dissent from his favourite theory of relegating as much priestly legislation as possible to a late time. Yet this writer has had considerable influence upon the views of Kalisch and other scholars.

7th. It must not be thought that the different documents incorporated in the Old Testament books were the only material of which they consist, or that all of them were public documents. Tradition furnished intercalary notices, and even chapters, such as the fourteenth of Genesis. Revisers also drew from their own imagination. In every case what was written was liable to free handling, and formed a part of the national literature.

8th. Readers who are fond of novelties have only to inspect Wellhausen's handling of the two documents called Elohist and Jehovist after they were put together, Reuss's assignment of the present Pentateuch to the time between Nehemiah and Alexander, or Kuenen's treatment of Lev. xvii.–xxvi., and they will be amazed at the facility with which conjectures are made. Workers upon the various parts of the Torah are summoned whenever fancy prompts or the slenderest threads of evidence appear.

The present is not the place for entering further into this question of sources. I can only note conclusions arrived at after long study. If they have a basis, they may be approved by critics who refuse to fall in with the latest conjectures of seekers after new things.

Gen. xxxii. 24–29.—This whole scene is a poetical myth formed to give a divine origin to the name Israel, which means " warrior of God," afterwards interpreted " warrior with God," whence arose " wrestling with God " in the myth. The name Israel was given on the occasion because Jacob prevailed in the struggle. Subordinate features are introduced merely for illustration, the boldest trait being that the divine wrestler was overcome by the human antagonist. In whatever way Jacob got the name Israel, it was not given him by God directly or in this way. The mythical description cannot be taken as literal prose without irrationality.

The thirty-second chapter of Genesis, where the passage occurs, belongs to the junior Elohist with the exception of verses 10–13, which are Jehovistic.

CHAPTER XXI

Final Views

15*th December* 1892.—Twenty years have now passed since my dear wife departed, and I am still left to lament my loss. When her spirit took flight to a higher sphere, I little thought that I should tarry so long upon the earth, to pass through so many trials and troubles. But I linger as yet amid its temptations, and face obstacles in my path which sometimes prove too strong for a weak Christian. During the year which is about to close I have been for a short time in precarious health, but am now comparatively well. The days slip silently by without much show of work done in their fleeting hours. My sight fails fast. Yet the memory of her who died so long ago is not dimmed.

25*th December.*—A committee appointed to discover heresy will generally succeed in doing so. Something, however, depends on its constitution. If the persons composing it be mainly clerics, the conclusion will be all the more easy. It has been said that heresy trials are mere farces, but they are not so to him who is declared heretical ; for the brand is remembered against him, meeting him at every step in all the relations of life. The proper outcome of a heresy trial is the gallows or the stake, but civilisation has discarded these instruments and taken to less violent ones. Unfortunately the old spirit is not dead, however much it is checked. Surely if anything be adverse to true religion, it is an uncharitable disposition towards others because of theological opinions. "Who art thou that judgest another man's servant?" Creedmen continue judging and condemning, to the neglect of the apostle's rebuke. These remarks have been suggested by the heresy trials of two professors belonging to colleges in the United States of America.

28th December.—The Pentateuch does not present throughout a literal history, and to take its wonderful narratives as such is irrational. Let anyone who reflects read the chapters relating to the giving of the Ten Commandments in the Book of Exodus, and then say whether they exhibit a real account of what took place. Moses goes up Mount Sinai twice. On his first ascent he received the tables written "with the finger of God" (Ex. xxxi. 18). "They were the work of God, and the writing was the writing of God graven upon the tables" (xxxii. 18). These stone tablets, though made and written upon by God Himself, Moses cast out of his hands and brake. At his second ascent the tables were renewed and engraved by Moses (Ex. xxxiv. 28). Marvellous as these accounts, with all their details, are, they are nothing else but mythical, like those in xxxiii. 11–23, xxxiv. 29–35. Both here and elsewhere Moses is mythically exalted. The stories contain gross anthropomorphisms: for Jehovah is described as speaking with His servant "face to face, as a man speaketh unto a friend."

Whether the authors believed they were writing literal history or not, one thing is clear: that such mythological descriptions betray an infantine sort of religion.

No authentic memorial of the Mosaic history exists. The Pentateuch or Hexateuch is a legendary document composed of old and heterogeneous elements, traditions, myths, fictions, etc. Its histories partake of the miraculous. Later institutions are attributed in its pages to Moses. It is vain to complain of modern criticism damaging the authority of such an antique aggregate of materials relating to men's fortunes on the earth: it cannot be stopped; it is a part of modern culture. We grant that the miscellaneous mass of matter in the Pentateuch presents a ready field for conjecture's play, but there is conservatism enough to check its wildness; and reason, the final judge, settles all, as far as its grasp reaches.

1st January 1893.—Blessed be God for the light of another year. I could not have thought that I should live to see 1893. But His sparing mercy has been extended to me thus far, and I continue in this state of pilgrimage. For what end? Is it to serve Him here a little longer? All my service is as nothing. Is it to be better prepared for a higher state? Perhaps so. The ways of Heaven are inscrutable. Meantime let me live to please my Creator and Preserver, not myself. Hope bears me upward and onward: the hope of a blessed immortality.

2nd January.—The noblest men in ancient Israel were undoubtedly the prophets, who exerted a saving influence upon people and kings. They were the salt of the kingdoms they served. Having higher views of Jehovah's righteousness and just judgments than those of their contemporaries, standing forth as Jehovah's interpreters and preachers of justice with patriotic aims, they enunciated before the people principles which tended to elevate and purify. Inspired by the spirit of Jehovah, they had visions in an ecstatic state—without loss of consciousness, however. The best of them were also monotheists.

But it is not my present purpose to sketch their character or their doctrines. Their grandest theme was Israel's coming sovereignty over the nations, the future glory of their race in their own land, with peace and plenty even of material things; sometimes having a king of the Davidic dynasty, sometimes without. In descanting on this favourite subject, they gave free play to the imagination, their pictures showing diversity accordingly. Hopes and aspirations allowed ample scope ; and poetry lent images to the portraiture, gilded, as it often is, with showy colours. But it is not all made up of bright hopes or fervid aspirations, for the repeated introductory phrases, " Thus says Jehovah," " Jehovah speaks," with their announcement that theirs is " the word of Jehovah," convey assured confidence. Something stronger and deeper than hopes or fancies filled their vision ; that is, *convictions.* They believed that what they uttered or wrote was the very mind of Jehovah. Speaking of the future, they meant prediction of definite things, not ideal phenomena. And yet their predictions were unfulfilled, because it is not given to man to know future events ; and when he projects himself into that dark region, his anticipations must be fallible. The future glory of Israel in their own land still remains, and ever will be, ideal. It is superfluous to observe that one prophet differs from another in style, that occasionally one copies from a predecessor, and that some are more original than others. The usual variations among writers appear among them likewise. To show that such disagreement is more than superficial, it will only be necessary to compare the twelfth chapter of Daniel with Ezekiel.

In the former the period of freedom from trouble and deliverance from enemies, the reign of happiness and peace, begins with the death of Antiochus Epiphanes, since we read, "and at that time" (xii. 1). The disappearance of the persecuting king, with whom the Grecian dynasty ended, made way at once for the beginning of the golden age. Ezekiel's view is different. He knew nothing of the Grecian subjugation of Palestine. He depicts the state of Israel, who had been delivered from hostile peoples and brought back to their own land ; but their peace and prosperity were interrupted by an attack of Gog from the distant country of Magog, ending disastrously for the enemy. This invasion, peculiar to Ezekiel, has been copied into the Book of Revelation. Thus the prophets viewed the future from the standpoint of their own time. Ardent patriots as they were, they never doubted of their country's being theirs for ever, of the perpetual dominion of their race over all nations, and of the enjoyment of God's unchanging favour.

The assumption that this predicted time is realised in the blessings of Christianity, though favoured by the heading of chapters in English and other Bibles, does violence to the prophetic language. Had the Christian age entered into the conceptions of the writers, they would have described it differently. Palestine and its fruitfulness would have given place to the wide world. The language used would have been more definite. He that interprets the ideal pictures so as to bring out their realisation in Christianity, imports a foreign element into them and perverts their meaning.

3rd January.—Quite unexpectedly I have had an official intimation from Mr. Gladstone that he has put my name on the Civil List for a pension of £100 a year. The initiative in this, as I afterwards learned, was kindly taken by the Rev. Dr. Gloag, formerly of Galashiels. The Premier must know that our religious beliefs are widely different, so that his kindness is all the more creditable to him.

2nd February.

> "But I know that my Vindicator lives,
>   And that He shall arise at last upon the earth ;
>   And after they shall have destroyed my skin this shall be.
>   Yea without my flesh shall I see God,
>   Whom I shall see for myself, and mine eyes shall behold
>   and not as a stranger.
>   My reins are consumed within me."

Such appears to me the best translation of a difficult passage in *Job* xix. 25–27, the text of which has been suspected corrupt, perhaps because of its difficulty and abruptness. The confidence expressed by the speaker in relation to his future is remarkable. The words have been interpreted as if Job avowed his belief in a future resurrection-state. Such was the idea of Jerome as well as of Luther; it has passed into creeds and confessions, forms part of the Church of England's "order for the burial of the dead," and is still approved by many. The original words may certainly bear the sense in question; but the analogy of the whole book is against it, showing that the author had no belief in a future state, except the shadowy existence in Sheol current among his countrymen, which can hardly be called an existence. The knowledge of a future state which the gospel reveals remains a mystery to the writer, who is unable to anticipate the Christian doctrine of rewards and punishments. Had he believed in the resurrection, it is highly improbable that the statement of it would have been confined to a solitary and obscure passage. The key to the solution of the problem he wrestles with was too important to be treated in this way had he known of it. The entire argument of the poem proves the author's ignorance of the doctrine of immortality.

I take the expected vision of God literally, consistently with other passages in the Old Testament descriptive of men so favoured. Accordingly, Job is represented as seeing the Lord (xlii. 5), and the wished-for vindication of his character resolves itself into absolute submission to the Almighty's will; and he receives ample compensation for his worldly losses, without the least hint being given of any spiritual reward in another life. His recompense is in this world, agreeably to the Jewish economy. He submits, repents, and is rewarded. Such is his deliverance from all calamities; it corresponds to his expectation, and even exceeds it.

19*th March.—Ps.* xxii. 17. This is what is commonly called a vexed passage. There are three forms of the essential word in the passage, כארי, כארו, כרו; but the last two being properly one, the choice is between the first two. According to the Masoretic text, which good critics are loth to leave without necessity, the meaning of the word is "like the lion," giving a good sense, notwithstanding the objections raised against it.   The passage then runs—

> "For dogs have compassed me about;
> The crowd of evil-doers have inclosed me
> Like the lion, my hands and my feet (all my limbs)."

Such meaning of the Hebrew word agrees with the same where it occurs in Isa. xxxviii. 13. But some ancient versions—the Septuagint, Vulgate, and Syriac—render the word in question "they pierced," following the second reading, and harmonising with the idea of the 22nd Psalm being Messianic, especially as a certain parallelism exists between the case of Christ when He gave up His life on the cross in founding the kingdom of God on the earth; but the parallel is interrupted by many diversities that disagree with it. Though the idea of a suffering Messiah is foreign to the Old Testament, Christ is assumed to be the direct speaker; and surely such language as "I am a worm, and no man," the sufferer's enemies being called bulls, dogs, buffaloes, lions, is wholly unsuitable in His mouth. Besides, the sufferer is not yet in the power of his enemies: they only threaten him.

The Psalm is not Messianic; nor does the speaker in it transfer himself into the person of Christ. It is historical, not prophetic. Neither is the speaker a typical man. He describes his treatment by enemies ready to tear him in pieces.

Still the rendering "they pierced" is advocated by some, agreeably to an alteration or manipulation of the Masoretic reading required by that sense, and in accordance with the few MSS. that have a verb in the perfect tense, presumably from Christian hands. But why leave the Masoretic text, supported as it is by the vastly preponderating authority of MSS.? Is it necessary to resort to unknown verbs or verbs that have another sense than *pierce*, or to uncommon grammatical forms, or to different vowel points? The figure of a roaring lion gaping upon the sufferer occurs in the foregoing context, and it is pertinent here also. I therefore believe the rendering "they pierced," and the readings on which it depends, to be incorrect. It is also disapproved by the best scholars: by Gesenius, Hupfeld, De Wette, and others.

21st March.—A good deal of writing has been lately spent on the question, Is Christianity played out? and the tendency of the letters has been towards an affirmative answer. But the writers in the *Daily Chronicle* were mostly journalists, a class not conspicuous for their exact knowledge of the subject, nor for conscientious following of the precepts presented by the religion in question. At least their notions about what constitutes its essence were vague. My own opinion is that Christianity has not been played out, and is not even yet fully played in, and that the religion in question, adapted as it is by its very nature to regenerate universal humanity, has been hampered by the soil in which it should grow: in other words, by the worse side of man's nature, which does not imbibe its essence. It is treated with neglect by those whom it ought to raise and purify. The ideal it presents is admittedly a high one; but the aim to reach it is salutary and saving. What other religion can equal it for excellence? Can Judaism, with its limited capabilities and legal enactments? Can Buddhism, with its Nirvana? As long as nominal Christians live as though they never heard of Christ and His teaching, as long as nations despotic, monarchical, republican do unjust actions against others weaker than themselves, as long as assemblies are under the influence of filthy lucre, how can the true spirit of Christianity spread? Perhaps England is the most Christian country in the world; but look at its metropolis, that huge city where many millions congregate. Is it as wicked as Babylon of old? So thought Mark Pattison; but I hesitate to believe so, though its immorality is great. The amount of false swearing in its law courts is fearful. The frauds of companies, syndicates, and committees sadden the newspaper reader every morning. The proceedings of the House of Commons show love of party and lack of principle. The great number of lawyers is a bad symptom. Numerous divorces or judicial separations manifest a deteriorated state of the married life. Brutal assaults upon women and children are frequent. Drunkenness abounds, and resistance to the lessening of drink shops is active not only among the class that frequents them, but among the wealthy brewers. All this is opposed to the progress of a religion which condemns the love of money and the indulgence of unholy passions. It is true that faithful ministers of the gospel labour to counteract influences and actions adverse to religion and morality,—they are the salt of the earth,—but their voice is well-nigh lost amid the tumult of a people hurrying after gain, and elbowing out of their way all hindrances. It seems to me that great cities foster every form of vice. Roughs and criminals crowd into them with the idea that they can more easily escape detection there. The wholesomeness of the country is preferable to the dangers of the city, where wits are sharpened and frauds favoured. Scripture tells us truly that the world lies in wickedness; and because of that fact, aided by a moral obliquity early developed in man, Christianity is robbed of its natural effect. It will not be so always. A better future awaits it, when God shall be universally worshipped in spirit and in truth.

2nd April. — In translating a book from another language into English, especially in the case of the Bible, one should show taste. By successive English versions which appeared, from Tyndale's Testaments in 1525 A.D. down to our authorised English Bible of 1611, the latter acquired wonderful rhythm and fluency with choice words of Saxon origin which please the reader's ear. Hence it is admirably adapted to be the Bible of the people rather than that of the scholar; and in any revision to which it is subjected, the changes should be as few as possible consistently with faithfulness to the original.

These remarks have been suggested by a late version of the 90th Psalm in which the translation appears, " before the mountains *were born*," etc. Surely this is a violation of good taste, because *born* applied to inanimate things is unusual in the English language. It is true that the tropical original allows the German *geboren* as a rendering of the Hebrew word, and it is used by Ewald, Hupfeld, Delitzsch, De Wette, and Kamphausen ; but what may be consistent with German taste is not necessarily so with good English taste. To leave the common version in this case makes the adopted one grate on the ear. Neither is there any good reason, I may remark, for changing the vowels of the Hebrew verb, translated *thou hadst formed*, in order to make it a Pual form with a passive signification, though good scholars adopt the alteration.

17th September 1893.—The Home Rule Bill for Ireland which has passed the House of Commons after meeting with obstinate and shameful obstruction from Tories and Unionists, though it is a most important measure deserving the thanks of all reformers to the one prominent statesman at the head of Her Majesty's councils, is not in a complete or final state, being rather an instal-ment, and in part a compromise. Its checks and limitations are too many, fettering the Irish Parliament with unneces-sary restrictions. Irishmen should have control of the police and taxation of their own country without let or hindrance at once. The office of Lord Lieutenant, and with it the Irish Secretaryship, should be abolished; a second chamber is not needed; neither should representatives be sent to the House of Commons in England. The Irish Protestants who wish to keep the iron heel of England on the subject country are no patriots. The sooner Ireland gets her independence of England the better. But, alas, many are so mean-spirited as to love the yoke. Seven hundred years of hard bondage have extinguished all their manly spirit.

No doubt Mr. Gladstone did what he could to make his Bill acceptable to all, especially to the noisy Ulster Unionists; but he conceded too much, leaving to future politicians difficulties which prejudices will make it a hard task to solve; for the feeling is deep-rooted in the minds of the English people that the Irish are an inferior race, unfit to manage their own affairs—a notion contradicted by history, but still stupidly cherished.

16*th October.*—I lost an esteemed friend on the 8th of this month, whose memory I must ever cherish. An excellent scholar and liberal thinker, a cultivated theologian and thoughtful preacher, Professor Jowett occupied a prominent place in the University of Oxford. He took great interest in young students of promising ability, assisting them both with private instruction and money. Many such will remember with grateful feelings the kind-hearted scholar who helped them to attain to future eminence. But he had little enthusiasm or sympathy in his nature. His was not the character of the martyr who hugs the stake he is bound to. No man attached less weight to doctrinal opinions, therefore he could subscribe the Church's Creed and Articles without compunction. Not so was the Rev. H. B. Wilson, who told me he could not sign the Articles again. The latter felt more deeply, was a much wider scholar and a better thinker, less solicitous about style or language.   Jowett would wrap the most heterodox sentiments in an elegant and enticing dress. Both were men of mark, whom it was a privilege to know —men whose influence was far-reaching and ever in the direction of freedom, charity, and benevolence.   Jowett's position was much more favourable to an extended power for good, and he used that power for the welfare of humanity.   There was an element of nobility in his nature. I urged him more than once to reprint his two volumes of commentaries on some of Paul's epistles, but he hesitated and never did it, probably disgusted with the reception he had met with in the field of theology, and annoyed by the fact that some Churchmen were promoted to high places merely for writing against *Essays and Reviews*.   But he might even have enjoyed a pleasure in seeing rewards in the Church dispensed to clerical brethren, as Gibbon did in procuring a royal pension for Mr. Davies, and collating Dr. Apthorp to an archiepiscopal living.

But though the professor's influence was wide, it was lacking in spiritual depth.   His religious profession bordered too much on the world to manifest a self-sacrificing type of piety.   We must, however, remember that natural temperament affects the feelings even of a true Christian.

30*th November.*—The English are a domineering race. Wherever they go to colonise or to take possession of territory, they act as if the earth were made for them. Their civilising processes are rough and cruel.   The empire has often been extended by methods unjust, high-handed, and deceitful.   I have read enough, and am still reading, of the doings of the South African Chartered Company towards the Matabele to see that they are both cruel and disgraceful.   The treatment of that uncivilised race by a set of freebooters and filibusters is sufficient to excite the indignation of every man who has a heart to feel.   Greed of gold and of land is at the bottom of all their proceed-

21

ings, and for it they shoot down and massacre the poor savages as though they were big game. Such is English conduct. Strange to say, it is approved by commissioners, governors, dukes, etc., and, what is still more shameful, by men called Christians, as if Christianity were not utterly opposed to all kinds of inhumanity. I need scarcely say that the treatment of these uncivilised people is a national disgrace. It is a disgrace to the Liberal Government now in power, who might and ought to have stopped the unequal war at its commencement: a war of extermination against an unoffending people. Liberals in office are much the same as their Tory opponents. In the present state of the case, King Lobengula is being hunted like a wild beast, and Maxim guns are ready to thin his followers till they be all destroyed. Who can blame him for not trusting himself to the hands of the whites? Our empire is extending and civilising other races by guns, but as sure as there exists an overruling Providence, the empire is preparing for its downfall. Robbers of land and murderers of fellow-men cannot escape the consequences of wicked deeds for ever. All that I, a humble individual, can do at present is to record my protest against the barbarous and wholesale murder of a people by a nation (for the nation is responsible) which boasts of its civilisation and of its Christian missions. I cannot finish without commending Mr. H. Labouchere, M.P., and the *Daily Chronicle* for their just and righteous exposure of a company whose nefarious doings deserve the execration of all honourable men.

20th December.—At the risk of repetition, I reiterate my belief that purely intellectual error is innocent. In other words, intellectual speculation, when followed with earnestness, is not to be condemned, even if it leads to erroneous conclusions. A man may be conscientious in error at one stage of life, but may see more correctly at a later period. An honest inquirer ought, however, to be very certain that his investigations do not infringe on conscience. Chillingworth, who was a true rationalist, says, "To ask pardon of simple and involuntary errors is tacitly to imply that God is angry with us for them, and that were to impute to Him this strange tyranny of requiring brick where He gives no straw: of expecting to gather where He strewed not: of being offended with us for not doing what He knows we cannot do." In *De Wette* we have a prominent example of a man who, though highly speculative, had a strong feeling of religion which dominated all his actions. Dugald Stewart's division of the powers of the mind into active and intellectual leaves room enough to throw religion chiefly on the moral powers.

I have a great regard for the memory of *Dr. Daniel Whitby*, who was among the best commentators on all the New Testament—he did good service to theology—he was honest, upright, and sincere; he, too, admits involuntary error to be innocent. According to him, "Sincerity in inquiry, even if a man misses the truth, is sufficient to procure the favour of God"; so too: "Heresy is a work of the flesh, and therefore no good man, whatever be his errors, can be a heretic." Similarly Kettlewell and Chillingworth, the latter of whom says that God will not impute errors to those who have done their best to discover the truth. With respect to error—since no definite line can be drawn between the moral and the intellectual powers, we must rely on the mercy of God for forgiveness.

December 1893.—The sands of life are running out fast, and the time of my rejoining the loved ones that have gone before approaches. All God's ways are right, characterised by perfect wisdom and love. I linger on here and wait till my Heavenly Father calls me away, I hope and believe to be reunited to her whom I loved, and to the happy children taken early out of a wicked world. I can only rest in God, look up with increasing faith, brighter hope, and stronger love, while I think of her who journeyed with me through thirty-six weary years until a merciful Father translated her. I can do no more work—my strength is nearly gone, and my eyesight much failed. Weary of theologies with their bitter jarrings, of creed-controversies and their attendant jealousies, I am satisfied with the simple religion which Jesus taught,—a religion of feeling and fact, —resting upon it as a safe anchor to the soul. . . . May these lengthening years make me more meet for the inheritance of the saints in light.

May I be enabled with God's help to walk more by faith and less by sight while I am on this earth, till faith give place to fruition, and the glorified spirit realises that God is love.

The diary was continued in my father's own hand till May 1894—a subsequent entry, in September of that year, consisting only of the words, "The night is far spent ; the day is at hand." Afterwards it was carried on by dictation until a few weeks before his death, and dealt for the most part with critical questions. *December* 15 is, however, invariably commemorated by some expression of hope or faith, and January 1, 1895, has the following reference to the death of a friend : "A good man and true, whose intellect was superior and his heart warm, has passed away in Dr. David Thomas." It was not until the last fortnight of his life that my father was entirely confined to bed, a period of extreme prostration and painful exhaustion then setting in, during which his only intelligible words were those of the Lord's Prayer, often repeated. He died on 1st April 1898, and is buried in Hampstead Cemetery.—ED.

CHAPTER XXII

Confession of Faith

Written in 1876

My creed may be summed up in the following statements:—

1. I cannot but disapprove of the attempts that are made to apprehend all nature and external phenomena without an intelligent First Cause, or to identify the universe with God as infinite substance. Such speculations are injurious to religion. The different kinds of pantheism—Ionic, Stoic, Spinozistic, Fichtian, Schellingian, Hegelian—*amount to* atheism. If the world be regarded as the self-revelation or evolution of God, He ceases to be enthroned above the world as its governor, and is far removed from the Christian idea of a loving Father in whom the soul reposes with trusting affection. If God be conceived as infinite substance, then is immortality a dream, because the soul is but one of the phenomena or accidences of that substance: a wave of the great ocean, into which it sinks back again; its eternal existence is *in* God, not *from* Him; it is a part of His essence not really distinct, so that the feeling of freedom is lost. Yet I should hesitate to say plumply, with Jacobi, that Spinozism *is* atheism, though it issues in and cannot be separated from atheism. Its direct tendency is atheistical. It is certainly *fatalism*. Human will and moral freedom are annihilated by it. I allow that there is a higher form of pantheism akin to right conceptions of the Omnipresent and Omniscient One, believing that He is the immanent substance in the stream

of phenomena which are but accidences, so that a pious man surrendering his own will attains to the consciousness of his oneness with God, but a *personal* God is excluded by pantheism proper. Personality consists in the unity of self-consciousness, and every being that has the consciousness of identity is a person. When I ascribe consciousness to God, His personality follows as an unquestionable truth. I do not see that the idea of personality implies *limitation*, unless language, which is necessarily imperfect in relation to such a being, be argumentatively pressed. I must therefore assume an intelligence distinct from the world and above it. If this be not true, whence comes it that the daemon, or good genius of man as the ancients called it, the conscience, inner sense, reason or logos, witnesses to an unknown Spirit apart from itself?

2. I believe in one God, the Infinite and Unknown, and in Jesus Christ His Son, the highest, purest likeness of God in humanity. I believe in the Holy Ghost, the divine influence diffused through creation, which is specially the uniting Spirit that dwells in all believers, sustaining and pervading their life. This inhabitation of the Spirit is an important element in redemption. The Bible presents the union of the Divine Being with the nature of man in such form. The Holy Spirit was afterwards hypostatised, and became the Third Person in the Trinity. It is the immanent God—immanent in nature, immanent in man's spirit. It proceeds from and is the omnipresent God. It proceeds from the Son as far as He reflects and manifests the Infinite. Both Son and Spirit are manifestations of God in the world and of His agency in the purification of humanity. They express God's relations to the world as man apprehends and distinguishes them. We think of God either as He is in Self-independence as the highest object of reason, *i.e.* Father ; or as that by which He is declared to the world, *i.e.* Son— or as that which penetrates and fills nature, the principle of

life and light, *i.e.* Spirit. The distinction betweed *person* and *substance* is meaningless; or if it refer to the so-called *opera ad intra*, the *actus personales*, it lies beyond human apprehension. As far as we know, no *essential* distinctions exist in the divine nature behind the *manifested* ones.

The ecclesiastical doctrine of the Trinity cannot be reconciled with reason or philosophy. The philosophical form, which conceives God not only as He is in His independent existence, but as He is *to the world and nature*, seems the only correct one. God's relations to the objective, *i.e.* His *opera ad extra* as apprehended by the human mind, are the only knowable distinctions. Such a view of the Deity comes home to the yearning heart with conscious nearness, while abstract monotheism leaves it empty and cold. Though it be in a sense ideal and aesthetic, idealism enters largely into the element of religion, giving it warmth and fulness. Doctrines unacceptable to *the understanding* may have a value to *faith and feeling* which it were a loss to forego.

3. Man is imperfect and sinful. His original state was one of low intelligence, little above the brute creation, out of which he has been developing very slowly. His educational process is of long duration. Through how many ages has it passed already? They cannot be computed. And he is still most imperfect, only half civilised even in countries nominally Christian.

The degeneration theory of man's state cannot be maintained on good grounds. The progression theory is the true one. The earliest religion, if such it can be called, was fetichism. It was succeeded by polytheism, out of which monotheism was developed. The monotheistic idea we owe to the Semitic race. The arguments by which Hume strengthens his opinion that idolatry or polytheism must have been the most ancient religion of mankind are entirely convincing.

4. The religious sentiment in man is more easily realised

by the contemplation of an objective model,—a pattern of perfection with which sympathetic converse is practicable, a near image of perfect holiness, such as the Gospels present ; in dim outline it is true, but so that the divine effulgence is seen in human form.   The example of Jesus Christ is the most effectual means of regeneration.   The more one is changed into His likeness, the more spiritual he becomes. The steady contemplation of Jesus, resulting in transformation into His image, is the instrument of renovation.   As religion lies in the emotions, its moving power being love to God and man, our concern is the ethical and practical— the being good and doing good.   *To be* good is to follow the intuitions of our nature, the inborn instincts which the thoughtful themselves heed but little ; while they lie, an unconscious embryo, within the millions that people the earth. When we are good and do good we are *justified*.   For what is justification ?   It is man's altered relation to God ; in other words, his reception into living communion with Christ through faith.   When the heart is brought into harmony with the will of God, there is a consciousness of the divine approval, a firm trust in God's love.   Faith is the means of bringing man into this new relation—faith working by love.   The *objective* aspect of justification has been considered, to the neglect of the *subjective*.   It speaks of a *forensic act*.   This is too anthropomorphic.   Whatever judicial process there be, it is in the conscience.   The new disposition includes a measure of satisfaction.   Faith and works are inseparable.   The two together *declare and make* a man just.

Our spiritual consciousness finds aliment and attachment in the words and works of Jesus, which strengthen and stimulate it outwards.   But it is exceedingly difficult to discover His words, because they are obscure, perverted or invented, in the Gospels, while the works have also been distorted.   Yet His summing up of the law and the prophets is an authentic saying, and no higher rule than that can be imagined. I do not think that there will be a fuller manifestation of God to humanity than what has been in Christ Jesus, or that the divine image in man will have a purer development than in Him who was the Son pre-eminently. " The Light of the World " will ever be a beacon to direct the worn and weary soul to the Unseen. God's revelation in Jesus, attested as it is by man's consciousness apart from writings, touches the faint chords of the revelation within, attuning them to the harmony of the divine will. Hence faith in Jesus promotes true life. It lifts us out of time: we feel we are eternal because we *are such.*

Aberrations of intellect are harmless. Error is innocent. Aberration of the moral nature is not innocent. The development of our religious consciousness is a sacred trust; the right direction of the emotions a duty of high moment.

5. Of the future after death little is known. Heaven and hell are states rather than places. The punishment of the wicked will be internal: remorse, remembrance of past sins, a low development at the outset, issuing slowly in purification. When the spirit leaves the body, it will probably have some sort of material covering—what, it is impossible to say. The standard of moral attainment here is the measure of the stage at which we start again. Life is continued in new relations. Our present experiences will be enlarged, our capacity for more knowledge and power will be satisfied. We shall be nearer and nearer to God, the infinite source of perfection. Advancement will be freer, larger, happier. The love of personal conscious life is the best proof that it will be continued and perfected. At present everything is prospective. We look onward, upward. The yearning for higher gifts of knowledge, for wider scope to the faculties, for the full exercise of reason, memory, imagination, and hope is the surest ground for believing that there is a future for the adequate nurture of

these mental states. We aspire to a spiritual reality which is immortal, and through that we are immortal. Hence death is not a curse, but a benefit, as Schiller said. Its universality proclaims it such. According to an inexorable law, his leaden footfall comes to all, but his power is only over matter. The soul is immortal. At the close of life the mind should therefore brighten with the thought that true immortality is but beginning. Though our name and memory pass from the recollection of the busy generations of men, what is good and true will endure, because it is from God who blesses it.

In the low state of moral and intellectual development where real life has scarcely begun, the attainment of perfection hereafter will necessarily require a long period. Slowness is an element in the remedial punishment of the wicked. All will be finally saved.

6. The general judgment of mankind conducted by Christ reappearing in person is founded on Paul's teaching, and this again on Jewish ideas and formulas. The solemn process of a future tribunal cannot be accepted. It is eminently Pauline. The apostle and the early Christians generally believed that this coming to judgment was at hand: that they themselves should even live to see it. In this expectation they were disappointed. The Fourth Gospel has another view, more philosophical and rational. According to it, the judging process takes place here. Christ came into the world to set forth a higher salvation by placing before everyone the choice of determining his own lot: in loving darkness or light. Thus man judges himself by his own feelings and acts. He pronounces his own sentence by the life he leads. He is self-judged; acquitted or condemned at the bar of conscience, saved or destroyed through his own will. In other words, the absence of Christ's spirit condemns; its presence is life eternal. A visible return of Jesus disappears from the Fourth Gospel

if certain passages, such as chaps. v. 28, 29, vi. 39*b*, 40*b*, 44*b*, xii. 48*b*, be of later origin, inserted by the hand that wrote xxi. 22, 23. They are too Jewish-Christian to harmonise with the general teaching of the Gospel. It is possible, however, that the evangelist's view of the resurrection and final judgment was fluctuating. He may have wavered between abstract and sensuous conceptions of them. If such be the case, the passages in question cannot be attributed to another hand. Whatever be thought of this evangelist's teaching, we must suppose that the resurrection is a spiritual process—an awakening from death to life which believers experience here. They may also be said to awake at death, so far as they spring into freer life. In this view the phrase "resurrection of the dead" is permissible. "The resurrection of the body" is an objectionable expression, involving an idea contrary to reason.

7. Religion consists in *feeling*: a sort of prophetic faculty with its spiritual presaging, its reaching after something beyond itself, its longing after the Infinite. Such is the element and atmosphere of religion. It is intuitional, God's image in man, a holy twilight in which the finite and the Infinite mysteriously meet—the portal of eternity. Its manifestations are partly directed by *the understanding*, which gives strength and definiteness to them, though it be still subordinate. The feeling is diviner and deeper, because it mirrors the infinite, dimly on account of the finite conditions to which it is subject. *Feeling* as the essence of religion is expressed in various ways. It is Milton's "reason intuitive, the being of the soul." It is the God-consciousness, the religious sense, a sentiment or instinct, an intuition. The supremacy of it is the ideal of humanity—the consummation which the noblest of the race aspire to. The world will not be regenerated by the supremacy of intellect or of science, but by the best possible development of such feeling manifested as love,

reverence, awe, gratitude, hope. The acts of this *feeling* constitute what is called *natural religion*. Here is a divine revelation, *immanent* or *immediate*, the Infinite operating on the finite. Being conditioned by the nature of the individual mind, it appears with different degrees. The imperfect medium through which the Deity is manifested obscures and enfeebles the manifestation. *Positive* or *revealed* religion enlarges the former, showing its connection with the advancement of mankind. The historical religion which exhibits the most additions to natural religion is not necessarily the best, but that which offers the smallest limitation and widest scope to the wholesome operation of natural religion. Christianity is the only religion that answers the conditions in which the essential elements of natural religion are greatly extended. It enforces *the latter*. Exciting and developing the God-consciousness, it makes it a more active and living principle. But it imparts no truth perfectly new ; for nothing absolutely new can be communicated to man externally—nothing that was not *potentially* in the universal reason. An historical religion is only an *illustration* of stages in the intuitional consciousness.

These observations explain the relation between reason and revelation. It is wrong to assume their antagonism or the superiority of the one to the other : they should be harmonised. The one progresses with the other. Their stages coincide *essentially*, both being parts of one process viewed in different aspects : from above and from beneath. Revelation is merely the continuous advancing God-consciousness of humanity developing and perfecting itself, not an extraordinary phenomenon attested by signs and wonders. No book coming with an external divine authority can present an objective limit to the intuitional feeling : the book itself is the product of that very faculty—in other words, of the spiritual elevation of mankind at a certain time. The Bible is divine inasmuch as it is the outcome of the inner sense, which is God's light in man; but it is a human book withal. Religion existed before the Bible; it would still exist if the Bible were destroyed. Belief in the books composing the Bible—in their inspiration, authenticity, authority—is not religion. Bibliolatry has usurped the name and place of religion in the opinion of many. Religion consists in an attitude of the soul. The Bible is *a record*; not a *revelation*, but the expression of different phases of the religious consciousness. An objective revelation, consisting of infallible records, is a misconception. How can records full of imperfections, contradictions, and inconsistencies, which represent God as cruel and vindictive, interfering in the petty affairs of His creatures, selecting one people from among all others as the object of His peculiar favour (and that people stubborn, rebellious, wicked), punishing the innocent for the guilty, approving of impure motives and unjust acts—how can such records be a revelation of the divine mind? The inconsistencies of the documents alone are sufficient to show that they are the production of fallible men. Intuition is God's revelation, which the Bible illuminates by the precepts and examples that touch its sympathetic chords. The immortal legends, miracles, mysteries, and prophecies of the Bible, judged by the ordinary principles of evidence founded on general experience, and that is our only criterion, could not have directly proceeded from the Diving Being.

8. *The inspiration* of the Scriptures is an incorrect expression. Inspiration belongs to *men*, not *books*. It has degrees; in other words, men have different measures of light and knowledge. The conceptions of the writers were often incompatible. They had various degrees of inspiration, like the good and gifted of the present day. Their idiosyncrasies moulded their conceptions into different forms; and their apprehension of the relations between God and man, of divine justice and man's future, varied

accordingly. To some extent they reflected the views of their age: a necessity inherent in humanity. The original apostles and St. Paul differed widely in their views of the law and works. No two Biblical writers possessed the same measure of inspiration. I believe, therefore, that it is an influence of the Divine Spirit on the hearts of men, quickening and strengthening their perception; and belongs to all who have developed their moral powers to a certain extent—to all who have developed their emotional nature. The notion of its being an *extraordinary* influence peculiar to a few cannot be sustained. Prophets and apostles had it pre-eminently, as compared with their contemporaries; but it is still the prerogative of the true Church, possessed in proportion to her faithfulness.

9. Jesus propounded no dogma, and therefore a complete theology is not derivable from His sayings. He purified whatever was important in Judaism, especially its monotheism, into which He infused life by bringing out its moral bearings in the domain of faith. The fundamental principle of His religion was the idea of God as a Father.

The teaching of Jesus must be distinguished from the conception of it by apostles and evangelists. There are also characteristic differences in the doctrines taught by apostles themselves and the New Testament writings. Two types are apparent, Jewish and Hellenistic Christianity; the latter again being subdivided into Pauline and Alexandrine Christianity. The New Testament books do not exhibit these types perfectly free from the commingling elements of one another, but they may be classified according to their prevailing features. The Book of Revelation is the most Jewish: the Johannine writings, which breathe an Alexandrine spirit, the most Hellenistic. The Acts and First Epistle of Peter, though Pauline in the main, are less so than the four leading letters universally attributed to the Apostle Paul.

10. The propositions and dogmas formulated in the second, third, and fourth centuries displaced to a great extent the genuine doctrine of Jesus, introducing metaphysical subtleties and distinctions unknown to the Founder of the new religion. The dogmatics of Paul overshadowed the simple ethics of Jesus. Elements of Jewish origin, such as expiation, were incorporated with primitive Christian ideas. When a Jew embraced the belief that Jesus was the Messiah though He suffered and died, when he saw the end of the expiations provided for by the Levitical code and his consciousness of sin became uneasy, it was natural to attach a propitiatory virtue to the sufferings of Jesus, especially as the idea appeared to have the sanction of the Old Testament. Isa. lii. 13–liii. 12 presented a ready basis for it. On the ground of that prophecy, the death of Jesus was held to be a propitiation for the sins of the world, though such application of the language to a single person is contrary to its original sense. This idea of the atoning death of Jesus, received by Paul from the early disciples, became the basis of his doctrinal system, and as such runs through his epistles. There is but one way in which that death may be regarded as a vicarious atonement, though it is very different from Paul's, as well as from the current ecclesiastical view. His death is *a symbol* of reconciliation to God. It is true that every death brought about by self-consecration and self-sacrifice may be considered a like symbol; but His is *the unique symbol*, because of the greatness of His person and the sinlessness of His life. As such, it becomes a pattern. No other sacrificial death has the same significance, because no sufferer is perfectly innocent like Him. Nor can any other death be compared with His, except so far as it takes place *in* and *by* ideal communion with Him. *Feeling* appropriates His death as the highest example of self-sacrifice, and acts accordingly upon the springs of our nature with peculiar power. Kindling a flame within, it

burns up selfishness, calls forth repentance, and induces obedience to the divine will. For feeling and faith, the value of Christ's sacrifice as the most effectual instrument in bringing man into union with God, is incalculable.

The doctrine of vicarious atonement by the death of Jesus, which He Himself never taught, was introduced by Paul along with others of similar origin, such as that of predestination, or God's absolute decree respecting certain individuals of the human race, derived from Jewish particularism. Human nature was also pronounced corrupt in consequence of Adam's sin; and man was said to become righteous through the merit of another's righteousness imputed to him. Paulinism is profoundly *doctrinal* and harmonises with phases of the human soul, but differs from the pure *ethics* of Jesus. Psychological and logical, complex and comprehensive, bearing the strong impress of personal idiosyncrasy, it is inferior to the panoramic ideal presented in Jesus's teaching: a kingdom of God on earth, in which men, united in love, delivered from the bonds of sin, penetrated by the spirit of truth, should live in communion with God, the peculiar objects of His love, and doing His will. None of the apostles could reach the freedom and purity of Jesus's spiritual consciousness, for earthliness entered more or less into their views. Ideas of the *understanding* mingled with their intuitions. Knowledge gradually acquired by experience blurred the living spirit within.

After the death of the apostles, and when the *Catholic Church* was being founded, men believed that they should maintain Christian truth as an external and positive thing in and by *the Church* episcopally governed, and by *the tradition* which bishops transmitted. The consequence was the suppression of religious independence, and the revival of a priestly order at variance with the genius of Christianity.

11. Eighteen hundred years of light emanating from Judea have brightened the world but partially. Growth and civilisation are retarded by various causes; by none more than the conduct of Christian professors, who act out badly the principles of the Founder and the greatest of His apostles. Imitation of Christ, baptism with His spirit, self-sacrificing love, the moral transformation wrought by a sympathetic view of His character, are the sanctifying instruments of the race: how poorly exhibited, the world's history tells. One of the saddest spectacles of this sad history is the tendency of religious teachers to encourage and applaud murderous wars. Instead of systematically condemning wholesale butchery, undertaken on frivolous grounds or none at all; instead of denouncing the wickedness of shedding innocent blood, the clergy have often blessed the work of destruction. The passion for war, fostered as it is by standing armies, is diabolical: directly opposed to the genius of the gospel. Yet Christian men favour it, notwithstanding the terrible crimes that follow in its train. Here the Old Testament history has been faithfully copied, in which inhuman wars are often said to be commanded or approved by the Almighty. The intensely narrow patriotism of the writers attributes its unhallowed passion, its hatred of others, to Jehovah Himself!

Whether the Christian religion is destined to be universal is doubtful. Whether it be susceptible of improvement and perfection in the hands of succeeding generations is also doubtful. If its initial stage has given place to others less pure, if corruption has marked its course hitherto, no higher consummation seems probable in the future. Perhaps the original state was the best. Simplest it certainly was, breathing a childlike innocence coloured by the locality of Judea, and though ideal, capable of application to other circumstances. We are not, indeed, required to believe what the first Christians believed, because their faith was

22

Jewish to a considerable extent. They had communist and millennarian notions. Time falsified many of their views. They did not apprehend the full scope or spirituality of Jesus's teaching. But the strength and fire of their faith are things for permanent imitation. Nobly did they bear the reproach of the Cross; they withstood tyranny manfully. They were brave warriors in their Master's service. A faith more logical in its nature, but unable to remove mountains, is less valuable.

12. Another cause of the little progress which Christianity has made in the world is the intolerance shown by its professors. The clergy, in particular, have evinced an amount of bigotry that reflects upon them nothing but dishonour. They have hated and persecuted men differing from themselves in opinion. As long as they exhibit such temper, their advocacy of truth, *i.e.* of their own apprehension of truth, will not make it a power for good in the world. Were it not for the progress of civilisation outside Christianity, and the restraining power of civil rulers, persecution in some form would still be practised. Can we wonder that Christianity proper has spread so slowly, and has so little influence upon the conduct of men? The doctrine of toleration is learned with difficulty by the majority of professing Christians.

13. The sectarian spirit that prevails so widely is another impediment to religion. It is difficult to see how this spirit can be removed without abolishing the sects themselves. These organised bodies, setting up as they do small points of doctrine or practice, sometimes even negations, as badges of association, nurture a narrow spirit, and hold out temptations to trifle with conscience in the matter of subscription to dogmas. All stand in the way of free thought, dwarfing the mind with petty particulars. Sectarianism has largely blighted the prospects of genuine Christianity in Great Britain and Ireland. Mutual jeal-

ousies and antagonisms hinder cordial union, proselytes are sought that their souls may be saved from hell, and men are hereticated for expressing ideas foreign to traditional orthodoxy. Such are the fruits of the sects, especially of those not established by law. The breaking up of these organisations would purify the atmosphere and inaugurate a better state, putting an end to the social excommunications resulting from thought outside them. Do not prejudice and passion often usurp the place of reason in these self-constituted societies? Is not their devotion tinged with self-satisfaction? Bigotry based on superstition and ignorance appears in them. An external religiosity with a large infusion of worldliness, a spirit akin to intolerance, a comfortable adherence to notions that do not interfere with the conveniences or conventionalities of life: these are the manifestations of ecclesiasticism, the outcome of sect, the product of organised Christianity.

14. The compact systems of doctrine made by man—Calvinism, Romanism, Arminianism, etc.—are equally unedifying and injurious. Constructed as they are out of discordant materials,—the Old Testament and the New, the Pauline Epistles and the post-Pauline, out of Jewish-Christian documents and half-Jewish ones,—they present varieties of belief peculiar to early Christian times as a standard for the perpetual regulation of faith. None of the apostles or their immediate followers thought of propounding sentiments perpetually binding. They had the spirit of God in different degrees and spoke according to their light, and no proof is needed to show that their ideas are sometimes incorrect.

These systems are the basis of Churches and sects. All rest on the false principle that the Bible is *one book*, true in all its parts. But when religion is made into dogma, spirit into letter; when the emotions give place to the understanding and creeds become badges of discipleship—devotion departs, leaving sects to their logic and disputes, their

idols and illiberalities.   Many are the victims of those who
moulded religious doctrines into rounded systems.   It
cannot be too strenuously insisted on that dogma is a
limitation of piety.   The Church lapsed early into dogma ;
she must rise into spirit and life.   Christianity has been
stiffened, straitened, stunted by creed-religion.   Nor will
it ever revive till creeds cease to have supremacy.   Only
by reverting to the teaching of Christ will it cast off the
grave-clothes wrapped round it by hands unholy, put on
the armour of light, and bring back the image of God to
degenerate humanity.   Thus may it yet return to a world
in which the ideals of Jesus's teaching lie far beyond the
vision of the many,—a world where selfishness, hollow conventionalities, commercial rivalry, bear baneful sway.   The
spirit of Jesus, the spirit of love, reverence, faith, and hope,
is as mighty as ever, and baptism with it would be followed
by a wave of salvation.   But it must be carefully nourished,
and the bosom be open to receive it.   Then will it expand,
bearing the fruits of righteousness, and making the wilderness blossom as the rose.

15. The persistent reluctance of the Churches to reform
their creeds is an unhealthy symptom.   If philosophy,
science, and thought have got beyond them, if biblical
criticism has outrun them, why should they not be brought
into accordance with the best results of inquiry, by abridgment or otherwise?   They contain tenets from which some
who subscribe the documents depart, which is a bad example
to the world, demoralising those who exhibit it ; for trifling
with conscience is a serious matter.   A Church which pro-
fesses to hold articles of faith, requiring subscription to them
from all teachers, yet allowing or conniving at their dis-
belief, is an unedifying spectacle.   The interests of morality
demand that subscription should represent belief in the
things subscribed.   It is notorious, however, that independent
thinkers disbelieve, or attach no intelligible meaning to, the

metaphysical distinctions expressed. These creeds are mostly traditional, their dogmas having been formed at an early age, and that not the purest of the Church. But it is not uncommon to idealise the early Church, and to transfer its beliefs to the present time, as though they were infallibly correct.

16. I think that it is best, considering the present state of education in Great Britain, to have a national Church as comprehensive as possible, with a very short creed. The clergy belonging to it should be supported by the Government, as instructors in the principles of righteousness, morality, and virtue. They should be regarded as *the religious educators of the people.* The evils inherent in the Voluntary system are greater than those connected with an established Church. Hume's reflections, though tinged with undue severity towards the race of clerics, have much weight.

17. The ultimate object of all religious associations is the realisation of a state in which everyone shall be his own priest, addressing the Deity directly; when the intelligence of Christians shall dispense with organisations; when all shall be sufficiently taught to see that the priestly office, tending as it does to make religion a matter of proxy, retards individual enlightenment. Meantime ministers of the gospel are teachers educating the people for a state of mental independence. In doing their work they would be more successful if they were less of a caste, less fettered by antiquated creeds or traditional beliefs. As a pure and holy life is the best preparation for the world to come, the principles which directly maintain that life should be inculcated, apart from the propositions of a dead orthodoxy. The simple ethics of Jesus are the true basis of the education of the race; and when the race is educated, God will be worshipped without human mediators. At present, the ghostly power of priests and presbyters hinders the growth of the many, who indolently lean upon the opinions of others instead of thinking for themselves.

18. In view of the prevailing Church creeds, this confession of faith may seem to present the character of
doubt. But there is more faith in honest doubt than in
half the creeds. It may appear *negative*; but a negation
of the current theology is a negation of darkness, and
leads to day. It leaves the positive lying beneath, the
intuitions of the soul which reveal God. It leaves the
doctrine of a blessed immortality, the light and hope of
man amid the misery of the world. And the idea of the
soul's immortality is a firm basis for the elevation of the
spirit above all lower aims : above the changes and chances
of the present life. It teaches us to live in eternity; to
think and act in a way worthy of it. Perhaps it is impossible to avoid some curious prying into the future, or
to repress conjectures about what we may expect hereafter.
But such peering is unprofitable. Idle forecasting of an
ample compensation in the future for the misery of the
present must be checked. While keeping death constantly
in view, and looking at it calmly as a necessary arrangement of Providence, we should realise the eternal even
here : finding it in our own breast, in the higher dignity
of our spiritual life. Surrounded with mystery and groping
after light, we repose in the Eternal, walking by faith not
by sight. Life secluded from the world, but rich in the
feeling of immortality, is my highest enjoyment.

LONDON, *December* 1876.

HAMPSTEAD, 8*th June* 1889.

The following addition to the confession sets some
statements in a clearer light, and expands ideas which were
merely suggested. It may be taken as a supplement.

Religion is a feeling, a sentiment, an intuition, the
consciousness of dependence on an Infinite Being. It is
not morality, not action, but an immediate, living consciousness of an Infinite Intelligence ; and has to be sought

neither in books nor traditions, but in the human heart. Dogmas indicate only the conventional expressions in which certain sentiments are clothed. The religious consciousness which everyone carries within him has various aspects, and is no part of the intellectual life.

Theology is based on religion, and is therefore posterior to it. In other words, the spontaneous life precedes the reflective. Without the impulse of religious intuition there would have been no desire to create theological science.

Man has an inherited propensity to evil, existing prior to the sin of the individual. Sin is not the consequence of an incomprehensible event called *the Fall*, the author of which was Satan; but it is the fault of each person. Original sin, in the sense of the creeds, is a misnomer; the history of Adam's fall being a symbolical representation of every temptation, not the history of a single one. Man is not originally unable to develop the religious consciousness within him; aided by grace, this innate principle grows, strengthens, expands, till the antagonism of the flesh is overpowered and the dualism of human nature becomes an unequal balance. Ego is free to act; but if undeveloped, the flesh rules and misery ensues. Science is no more than a secondary element in man's moral development.

Jesus Christ is the perfect realisation of the idea of humanity in the highest sphere. He should not be called God-man or man-God, because the absolute opposition between the Infinite and the finite being does not admit of a union of the two attributes, the divine and human, in a single person without involving the annihilation of both. Though He was the ideal type of humanity, and His personality unique, there was development in His religious consciousness, and this without His ever being affected by sin or error. Being thus subject to the law of human development, He partook in some measure of the national character belonging to His countrymen.[1]

The divinity of Christianity resolves itself into the person, work, and teaching of Jesus. Whatever is essentially connected with His consciousness of the divine is normative in the sphere of religion. The divinity of Christianity does not depend on the authenticity of early canonical books ; neither is dogma its centre, but faith in Christ. In relation to His redemptive work, the juridical idea of a vicarious death should give place to a moral one. He did not suffer what humanity should have suffered ; nor had He any feeling of a divine law offended, or of condemnation because of it. He suffered as a martyr all the evil that could be inflicted on Him by the hatred of sinful men. What He did and suffered was at once a manifestation of God's love to man and His hatred of sin. The theory of substitutionary satisfaction on Christ's part, or the imputation of His merits, is exposed to insuperable objections. Paying a ransom for mankind either to God or the devil contravenes the Father's essential nature, which is love. Spiritual development, nourished by the Redeemer's life and death, is owing to assimilation of His righteousness and its determining influence over the will : by appropriation of His self-sacrificing love, so that His redemptive work resolves itself into a sanctifying energy upon the whole man. Love to God, inspired by the view of His beloved Son, who, though Himself sinless, suffered from the sins of others, enables the believer to put away selfishness and put on the image of the Crucified. The presentation of a unique example facilitates the Christian's deliverance from the domination of his lower powers.

Miracles and prophecy are the external works of religion, both insufficient evidences of Christianity because

---

[1] *Publishers' Note.*—Dr. Davidson's favourite quotations, as recorded on page 360, will probably satisfy his friends of earlier days.

the laws of God are inviolable ; and projection of himself
into the future so far as to predict definite events is not
given to man.   Though the spiritual consciousness of prophets was well advanced, and their prospecting of the
future often sagacious, they were fallible men.   Amid
their weighty and solemn proclamations of Jehovah's mind
as they could divine it, human limitations were still seen.

The internal evidence of Christianity is the only valid
test of its nature, showing it to be a religion suited to
the spiritual needs of man in developing his intuitional
emotions.

The canonical books are normative only to a certain
extent.   No fixed line can be drawn between them and
the non-canonical, which are also normal, but in a less
degree.

CHAPTER XXIII

REMINISCENCES BY FRIENDS

I. DR. SIMON

ONE of the things in your father that used greatly to amuse us students, whilst it also endeared him to us, was the curious form which his occasional visits to our studies took. Some time during the evening a knock would be heard. Thinking it was a fellow-student, one shouted, somewhat roughly, " Come in," or " Who's there ? " The door was gently opened, and the Doctor pushed his way in far enough to stand between the edge of the door and the wall, with his hand on the handle. Out of this position it was impossible to coax him. To offers of a chair, or requests to walk in and sit down, he would smilingly nod and reply " No—o." As long as he stood thus he seemed to think he was only just taking a peep in—spending neither our time nor his own ; yet there he would stand, occasionally half an hour or more, talking about books and Germany, and answering all sorts of questions that were put to him. These interviews, queer as they were in form, had a high value for some of us. To me personally they were most stimulating ; indeed, I am not sure that they did not constitute the best part of the learned Doctor's instructions.

On one occasion, at least, a visit of this sort was made under conditions that must have caused him as much amusement as us embarrassment. It was during the

Christmas holidays, when some of us had stayed in the college. Three or four were together, making the absurd noises in which even students sometimes indulge, when a knock at the door made itself heard—evidently after being several times repeated. One of the number, not of course knowing who was there, shouted to the knocker something that was more vigorous than respectful. Then came a still louder knock; and beginning to suspect who it was, we made a frantic effort to hide ourselves under a table. The door opened: in walked Dr. Davidson, and looking under the table, drily observed, "There are more legs there than belong to one man." Thereupon, of course, we revealed ourselves, and the end was a long and interesting talk about books and theology. We felt then, and for myself, after nearly thirty years of experience in positions similar to that held by your father, I *know* now, that he was a wise man who could deal with students in this way. The effect of such treatment was that we loved the Professor even though we were at times not slow—as what student, endowed as they all are with unerring sagacity, ever is?—to criticise him.

As to your father in the classroom—his lectures were undoubtedly always solid, clear, packed with learning, and we could not but feel a profound respect for the lecturer; but as a teacher of *the elements* of Hebrew he was not a success. He was, in fact, far too innocent for the task. He knew his subject himself, but he did not appreciate our ignorance or our need of drill. But one of the weaknesses of the college system was setting a man of learning to teach the very elements of grammar. Some may be able to play the scholar and philosopher and yet coach beginners, but, to say the least, it is a rare combination.

My own personal indebtedness to your father seems to have lain far more in what I got from his conversations about books, Biblical Theology, Germany, and the like,

than from his regular lectures.   I should never have dreamt
of going to Germany to continue my studies there but for
the information and encouragement he gave.   And I owe
both your father and mother a great debt for their kindness to me when I reached Halle, where they were then
spending their summer holidays.   Besides introducing me
to professors like Tholuck, Hupfeld, and others, they made
me as free of their *Wohnung* and their table as if I had
been a child of their own.

I will conclude with a reference to your father's conduct of the college family worship, when it was his week.
There were few students who did not enjoy both his reading
of Scripture and his prayers.   Of the rhetorical mouthing
which frequently passes for good reading there was no
trace.   But the reading and particularly the prayers were
marked by a simplicity, sense of reality, directness, inward-
ness, that I have never found excelled, even if equalled.
His words were like well-made glass—they were a transparent medium through which one saw the soul behind.
The same quality characterised his sermons and more
public ministrations, and they were accordingly most edifying and quickening for people who hungered and thirsted
for spiritual food and drink.

D. W. Simon.

The United College, Bradford,
    8th July 1898.

2. DR. GLOAG

In the year 1886 my acquaintance with Dr. Davidson
commenced in a most incidental manner. . . . I met him
at dinner in the house of a mutual friend.   He was then
approaching his eightieth year.   I have no notes of our
conversation at that time, but was greatly impressed with
the force of his remarks.   I remember that the subject

of our discussion was the genuineness of the Ignatian
Epistles. The great work of Bishop Lightfoot had just
been published, and was the subject of much discussion
among critics.   Dr. Davidson called in question their
genuineness, on the ground that episcopacy could not at
so early a period have been so far advanced as these
epistles indicated; whilst I defended their general authenticity, admitting that there might be in them interpolated
passages, from the numerous undesigned coincidences which
were found in them, and considered that Bishop Lightfoot
had proved his case.

This acquaintance, so unexpectedly commenced, was
carried on by a regular and unbroken correspondence.
The first letter which I received from him bears the date of
March 1886, a few days after we had met; the last letter
from his own hand is dated 13th April 1894.   From this
time his increased infirmities—a want of steadiness of
hand and failing eyesight—made writing impossible to
him; but the correspondence was still carried on until the
close of his life through the medium of his daughter.
The letters of Dr. Davidson are written with all the freedom
of friendly correspondence, and are in general concerned
with the theological writings of the present day, his stric-
tures on men and books, especially on the writings of living
German theologians,—the works of Holtzmann, Zahn, Weiss,
and Pfleiderer,—and his opinions on various controversial
questions.   They are written in a clear style and are well
worthy of perusal, especially in these days when Biblical
criticism has made such great progress, and when all traditional opinions are subjected to a test of unwonted
severity.

It is superfluous to mention the vast learning of Dr.
Davidson; for this is universally acknowledged.   However
much theologians may differ from him, and however
strongly they may dissent from his opinions, and however

keenly they may attack his statements as in their view
subversive of the truth, his learning cannot be called in
question.   He has fully demonstrated by his writings his
minute and accurate acquaintance with the Scriptures of
the Old and New Testaments.   His linguistic acquire-
ments, his knowledge of the Greek, Hebrew, and Syriac
languages is evident.   The extent of his acquaintance with
the works of the Fathers and with theological writings, both
in ancient and modern times, is obvious to everyone in the
least degree acquainted with his works.   His intimate knowledge of the text and languages of the books of the Old and
New Testaments is seen in the lists given of peculiar and
characteristic words and phrases when discussing the style
and language of each scriptural book.   He was a complete
master of German theology relevant to his subject : many
will think that he was too much imbued with it—too
deferential to the opinions of the great German critics, and
inclined to place too much weight upon them.   He
visited many of the German universities : according to
Dr. Schaff, he enjoyed the friendship of Tholuck, Hupfeld, Roediger, Erdmann, Bleek, Lücke, Gieseler, Neander,
Ewald, Tischendorf, and other distinguished German
theologians.

Dr. Davidson belonged to the rationalistic school of
theology.   In the views which he adopted in the latter half
of his life concerning the genuineness and integrity of the
books of the New Testament, he approached the most
advanced school of German critics.   It would be going
too far to assert that he belonged to the Tübingen school
in their views of the contest between Pauline and Petrine
Christianity, and of the *tendency* character of the books of
the New Testament, but many passages in his writings
might be adduced to show such a direction.   At the same
time, there is no arrogance nor prevailing dogmatism in his
assertions.   " After all," he observes in his first letter to

myself, "our ignorance is great: we can only grope at conclusions; but this ignorance will be done away in that future state toward which we now hasten, and for which all the good long." And in another letter: "We wait for another world, in which I trust we shall see clearly what we are now in the dark about." And again: "After all, we are but fallible creatures, who have but a small part of the truth; but if we are conscientious in seeking and acting, we shall be rewarded at last."

It is well known that in the early part of his career Dr. Davidson was decidedly more orthodox and positive in his views; indeed, some of the best defences of the traditional views are still derived from his early works, especially from his *Introduction to the New Testament*, in three volumes, published in 1848. Evidently a great alteration had come over his critical opinions; but when this alteration arose, and what was the occasion of it, I am ignorant. It was evidently of gradual growth—a growth which may be traced in his writings. If I may venture a conjecture. I think it was fostered by his exaggerated estimate of the writings of the great German theologians of the negative school, as Baur, Pfleiderer, and others; whether he had a personal acquaintance with Baur I cannot tell, but he was intimately acquainted with Pfleiderer. I think, also, that Dr. Davidson, in judging the genuineness of the books of Scripture, placed too much stress on subjective considerations, to the depreciation of the external evidence; whereas to me the external arguments always appear stronger, as you have something tangible to go upon, whereas subjective arguments are dependent on one's own feelings. But although my views are very different from those of Dr. Davidson,—even antagonistic: he belonging to the negative, and I to the positive school of Biblical criticism,—yet his great scholarship has commanded my respect and admiration, whilst his urbanity, geniality, and reverence have attracted my esteem.

One of the most learned of Dr. Davidson's works is his *Treatise on Biblical Criticism*. In 1839 he published a series of lectures on that subject, being his first publication. These were superseded by his *Treatise on Biblical Criticism*, which followed in 1852. This work is in two volumes, one volume being devoted to the Old and the other to the New Testament. It is a complete storehouse of information concerning the manuscripts and versions of Scripture, especially in that volume which refers to the New Testament. And although Biblical criticism has made great progress since then, especially by the writings of the late Dr. Scrivener, and by Dr. Hort in the introduction to Westcott and Hort's Greek Testament, yet Dr. Davidson's work is still frequently referred to for the readings of the different manuscripts on disputed passages. At the time it was written it was a masterpiece and the result of enormous labour and erudition. It was then without a rival in English theology.

The most valuable of Dr. Davidson's works are the two Introductions to the New Testament: the one entitled the *Introduction to the New Testament*, in three volumes, published in 1848–51 ; and the other, the *Introduction to the Study of the New Testament*, in two volumes, published in 1868. This last reached a second edition in 1882, and a third edition in 1894. These two Introductions proceed on very different lines ; so much so that if it were not for the unity of style, the sameness of many of the critical references, the lists of words and phrases, and the frequent common line of argument, one would think that they were by different authors. The first proceeds on orthodox or traditional lines ; the second is advanced, almost approaching to the views of the Tübingen school. The first defends the genuineness of all the books of the New

Testament; the second only acknowledges some of the
Pauline Epistles, namely, Romans, 1 and 2 Corinthians,
Galatians, Philippians, 1 Thessalonians and Philemon, and
the Apocalypse, and even the Apocalypse is rejected in the
last edition. Both works are exceedingly valuable, full of
learning, and affording a store from which theological critics
can draw. Dr. Davidson himself naturally wishes that
quotations and references to his works should be taken
from the last edition of his later Introduction. Thus referring to my quoting from his first Introduction, he writes:
" The only work of mine which I wish to be quoted on the
books of the New Testament is the last edition of my
Introduction, dated 1882 (the third edition, that of 1894,
was not published when this letter was written), which is a
considerable advance on that of 1868. As to the three-
volume one of 1848, it is entirely superseded and out of
print. It represents views no longer mine." In his second
Introduction he completely ignores his first, and, so far as
I can find, never refers to it ; nor does he make any statement as to the alteration in his views. But notwithstanding
this declaration, I must still hold that the first Introduction
is most valuable ; and though it ceased to represent Dr.
Davidson's own views, it contains arguments and statements
which in my opinion have not been refuted ; and I am free
to confess that in my critical studies there is no English
work from which I have derived greater assistance than
from Dr. Davidson's (first) *Introduction to the New Testament.* Indeed, this work still occupies a high place in
modern defences of the genuineness of the books of the
New Testament. To use the language of Dr. Watkins in
his Bampton Lectures : " The book had no equal in the
English language at the time ; it has in some respects no
equal now."

The third edition of Dr. Davidson's *Introduction to the
Study of the New Testament,* published in 1894, was a

23

wonderful literary feat.   Dr. Davidson was then in his eighty-seventh year, and yet this edition of his Introduction is not a mere reprint or reproduction of a former edition, or even a careful revision, but much of it has evidently been rewritten and altered.   Very important changes have been made, and large additions annexed.   And yet there are hardly to be discerned in it any marks of old age.   The same minuteness of criticism, the same accurate knowledge of New Testament Greek, the same careful research into the patristic references to the scriptural writings, and even the same severity of judgment so conspicuous in his other writings are seen in this.   Notwithstanding his advanced age, far exceeding that of most writers, his mental strength shows in it no signs of abatement.

Dr. Davidson was a diligent student throughout life, and as he advanced in years his diligence in study, especially of the Scriptures, showed no signs of abatement.   Thus toward the close of his life he writes: " I read every day a certain portion of the Hebrew Bible and the old Syriac translation of the New Testament, so that I do not lose my knowledge of these two languages at least.   I believe that I have read already both the Old Testament and the New in these tongues, and am now engaged in a second perusal. Sometimes I jot down a few notes relating to words, passages, or whole books."

The modern school of Biblical criticism has in certain quarters gone to an extreme, one might almost say an extravagant, length.   The opinions of Dr. Davidson, at one time considered so extreme, are now surpassed by those who belong to the so-called higher criticism.   In the last edition of his Introduction he opposes those Dutch and German critics who called in question the genuineness of Paul's four great epistles.   " The arguments," he writes, " adduced against Paul's leading epistles are for the most part arbitrary and extravagant, showing inability to estimate the true nature and value of evidence. As this wave of hypercriticism is rejected by the best critics of Germany, and will soon pass away, if indeed it has not already done so, it is needless to describe it, or to show its futility. Whatever permanence it may have is in the minds of ingenious seekers after novelty, but it is devoid of interest for English theologians. The Pauline authorship cannot be shaken by shadowy or conjectural evidence." So also, in one of his letters, he expresses his disapprobation of the extent to which destructive criticism is carried on with regard to the books of the Old Testament. " Not long ago I wrote paragraphs in it (his Autobiography) bearing directly on the two books by Driver and Cheyne with which I altogether disagree. The fashion of dating all writings of the Old Testament as late as possible has taken possession of these scholars; but, like fashions in dress, I believe it will pass away."

My acquaintance with Dr. Davidson was almost entirely formed from correspondence. Living at a distance, we seldom met; so far as I recollect, I only saw him thrice, and that for short intervals. And as his letters are chiefly on critical subjects, they afford little insight into his character or peculiar theological views. I have no doubt of the perfect honesty of his convictions; and although the alteration of his views is great, yet it arose from the conscientiousness of his nature. For him the truth, or what he believed to be the truth, was everything. He proved his honesty by the sacrifices which he made. He suffered for his opinions, by the loss of office and emolument, and the desertion of friends. Dr. Davidson was of a reverent and religious spirit. This I infer not so much from my few and short conversations with him, as from the general tone of his correspondence. I think that it may not be out of place to give a few extracts from letters received by me, as

they throw light upon his religious character. "Your friend
. . . sorrows too much for his departed wife. Many have
lost their partners as well as he, and have bowed the head
in submission to the will of God, hoping for reunion in a
better world. It is this blessed hope that bears the spirit
up and cherishes the longing for a happier existence." "I
have not been well of late, and cannot get out for a little
walk often enough because of the changing weather. My
eyesight is very dim, and even spectacles do little to improve it. But I must not complain. God has been very
good to me, and I thank Him daily for the merciful preservation of His humble servant. May the blessing of
God abide with you amid your works of faith and labours
of love." And in the last letter written by his own hand
he, as all earnest-minded men in general, deplores the im-
perfection of his life, that it comes so far short of the ideal.
" My present health is precarious. My right hand is apt
to shake, which makes writing difficult ; and my sight is so
bad that it is irksome for me to read. But I must bear
patiently those ills which are common to old age. My
work, such as it was, is ended. How imperfect it has been
none knows better than myself." And he concludes with
his benediction, " May the peace of God be ever with you
is the prayer of your sincere friend, Samuel Davidson."

PATON J. GLOAG.

EDINBURGH, 1898.

3. MR. URWICK

It is now nearly fifty years since I became a student
under *Dr. Samuel Davidson*, at the Lancashire Independent
College. He was then (1848) about forty years of age,
of middle height, bald-headed, wearing a badly-fitting wig
which was soon discarded, and revealed a thoughtful and
intellectual forehead. He was unassuming in manner, slow

of speech, absent-minded sometimes to awkwardness, but affable and kind-hearted; moreover, a pattern student, a non-smoker, calm and slow in study or in class; always at his desk, seated almost immovably on a stool without back, pen in hand, and his books, like tools, about him. In those days I never saw him in an easy-chair; and when he came to our studies, it was not to lounge nor to find fault, but to encourage and help in our work, as he stood with his hand upon the door. For three years I attended his Hebrew class. In his lectures on the *Old* and the *New Testament*, he taught us what the Germans call *Einleitung*, *Introduction*, explaining the occasion, object, date, authorship, genuineness, contents, of each book; and these lectures on the New Testament were embodied in the three large volumes of his *Introduction to the New Testament*, published 1848–51. He and Mrs. Davidson were most kind, often inviting us to their house. Dr. Davidson took part in my ordination at *Hatherlow* in Cheshire, on 19th June 1851, and gave a very able *Introductory Discourse*, embodying what he more fully developed in his *Congregational Lecture*.

When the unfortunate differences arose upon the publication in 1856 of his book *On the Text of the Old Testament*, the students rallied round their wounded tutor, wounded in the house of his friends. Those still resident, and those also who had left the college, with few exceptions, held meetings and presented addresses of warmest sympathy and firmest loyalty. Friends also, connected with the college, flocked round him, among them some of the most eminent men in Lancashire, and raised for him a substantial testimonial.[1] They also assisted him in opening a school at Bank House, Hatherlow, and intrusted their sons to his care. Thus during my ministry, for the space of four years, I had the advantage of his friendship, counsel, and assistance in Hebrew. He and

---

[1] £1500, raised to £3000.

his boys attended my ministry, and he would occasionally preach for me. To me and mine he and his family were valuable and loyal friends. On one important occasion he took a kindly and courageous part in defending the pastor when attacked by certain disaffected persons. Unswerving loyalty to those who had befriended him was a striking feature of Dr. Davidson's character. His sermons were simple in outline and free from any allusion to critical questions. At the Jubilee of the *Hatherlow Sunday School* in 1867, he preached in the afternoon from Jer. vi. 16, *Ask for the old paths*; and in the evening from Rev. xiv. 13, *Blessed are the dead which die in the Lord*: two very impressive and comforting sermons.

Removing to London, his beloved wife became a confirmed invalid, and his tenderness and solicitude for her were most touching. She died in December 1872, and I officiated by his side at her funeral in the dreary Rusholme Road Cemetery, where their children lie. She was a true helpmeet to her husband, beloved by all who knew her, and he deeply felt the bereavement. Our close friendship was renewed on my coming to the Chair of Hebrew in New College, London; and in 1880 he became again a near neighbour in Hampstead. From that date onwards he was almost my daily companion in walks over the Heath, and in frequent social evenings at home. Intercourse with him and with his family has been one of the greatest pleasures of my life. The contrast was striking between the boldness and sometimes harshness of his criticisms with the pen, and the tolerance, the gentleness and childlike piety, blended with a certain playfulness and humour, that permeated his conversation. He never referred to past unkindnesses, nor cherished revengeful feelings. His soul was gentle as a lamb, and his family prayers were full of the love of God. He had a wonderfully accurate memory, and a thorough knowledge of foreign theological literature. In politics he was a warm admirer of Mr. Gladstone, and a firm adherent of his policy of Home Rule for Ireland. He was three years Gladstone's senior, and it was a pleasant reflection that the pension from the *Civil Fund* was granted by Gladstone in recognition of his contributions to Bible Exegesis. He used often to speak of the sufferings of the *United Irishmen* in 1798, and in particular of the Presbyterian ministers who sided with the people, one of whom was hanged by the Government troops in front of his own chapel. Davidson was also a staunch adherent of the *Peace Society*, and spoke at its meetings. He knew Cobden and Bright personally.

In his later years, when between seventy and eighty, he still read his Hebrew Bible morning by morning, studying a few verses critically, and discussing the meaning of more important words. He also read daily a portion of the New Testament in the Peshito or Syriac version. Thus he went through the Old Testament books from Genesis onwards, and the New Testament throughout. Our talks would often be upon some text in his morning's reading.

Calling on 21st December 1894, when he was in his eighty-ninth year, I found him seeking the origin of the modern term *Agnostic*. "It is," he said, "synonymous with *Atheist*—softer, but involving the denial of our possible knowledge of the spiritual, and of everything beyond phenomena." He spoke of *evolution* as denoting the same scepticism. "In my day," he added, "we read Reid, Dugald Stewart, and Brown: they are right." Then passing to higher things, "I do not believe," he said, "in an intermediate sleep: the spirit enters at once into the presence of the Lord"; and he repeated a Scotch paraphrase "which," said he, "I learnt in childhood"—

> "We walk by faith and not by sight,
> Till we shall see the Lord."

When strength for walking failed, and his days were spent on the sofa, the mind was still active and the heart tender. He frequently shed tears during the last illness of my wife, whom he had known from a child. I used to read the Scriptures and pray with him every week and oftener, to the very end. He was particularly fond of hymns, especially Watts's, whom he often called a true poet ; and his favourites were the 90th Psalm, beginning—

> " Our God, our help in ages past,
>   Our hope for years to come,
>   Our shelter from the stormy blast,
>   And our eternal home."

and Dr. Horatio Bonar's hymn—

> " I heard the voice of Jesus say,
>   ' Come unto Me and rest ;
>   Lay down, thou weary one, lay down
>   Thy head upon My breast.'
>   I looked to Jesus, and I found
>   In Him my star, my sun ;
>   And in that light of life I'll walk,
>   Till travelling days are done."

On 4th February of the present year, 1898, returning from a visit to lay snowdrops on my beloved wife's grave at the cemetery, I found my old tutor as clear in intellect as ever. Quoting the text, " To depart and to be with Christ, which is far better," he responded, " Far better ! " " Do you desire to depart ? " I asked. " Yes," he replied. I read a few verses of John xiv., and prayed. He responded earnestly to the Lord's Prayer. Our parting seemed like a last farewell, though I saw him frequently to the end. During those closing months he was still tended lovingly by his daughter and Miss Kirkpatrick, his wife's sister, together with a faithful attendant who never left him at night. His only surviving son, Samuel James Davidson, residing at Clapham, was also a constant visitor.

After a hard struggle for breath, he expired on Friday, 1st April 1898, and was buried, according to his desire, in the Hampstead New Cemetery, close to my wife's grave, on the following Tuesday, 5th April. I conducted the service in the presence of his son, his nephews William K. Murphy, M.D., and the Rev. John H. Murphy, of Cork; also the Rev. R. Gwynne, and a few other friends.

W. URWICK.

HAMPSTEAD,
LONDON, 16th *July* 1898.

WORKS BY DR. SAMUEL DAVIDSON

1. Lectures on Biblical Criticism. Edinburgh, 1839.
2. Sacred Hermeneutics, 1843.
3. Gieseler's Compendium of Ecclesiastical History, translated from the German, 1846–47, 2 vols.
4. Ecclesiastical Polity of the New Testament. London, 1848 ; 2nd ed., 1854.
5. Introduction to the New Testament, 1848, 1849, 1851, 3 vols. Bagster.
6. A Treatise on Biblical Criticism (superseding No. 1). Bagster, 1852. 2 vols. New edition, London, 1855.
7. The Hebrew Text of the Old Testament revised from Critical Sources. London, 1855.
8. The Text of the Old Testament considered ; with a Treatise on Sacred Interpretation, and a brief Introduction to the Old Testament Books and the Apocrypha (forming vol. ii. of the tenth edition of Horne's Introduction to the Scriptures), 1856, London ; 2nd ed., 1859.
9. Facts, Statements, and Explanations connected with the publication of the above (No. 8). Longman, 1857.
10. An Introduction to the Old Testament, Critical, Historical, and Theological, 1862–63, 3 vols. Williams & Norgate.
11. Fürst's Hebrew and Chaldee Lexicon, translated from the German, 1865 ; 4th ed., 1871. Preface to this Translation, 1867.
12. An Introduction to the New Testament (superseding No. 5), 1868, 2 vols. ; 2nd ed., 1882.
13. On a Fresh Revision of the English Old Testament, 1873.
14. The New Testament, translated from the Critical Text of Von Tischendorf, with an Introduction on the Criticism, Translation, and Interpretation of the Book, 1875 ; 2nd ed., 1876.
15. The Canon of the Bible, 1877, 3rd ed., 1880.
16. The Doctrine of Last Things contained in the New Testament, compared with the Notions of the Jews and the Statements of Church Creeds, 1882. 12mo.

Articles in Kitto's Cyclopedia.
Articles in Smith's Dictionary of Biography and Mythology.
Articles in ninth edition of Encyclopædia Britannica.
Articles in the Theological Review, 1869, 1870, On the
  Jewish Messiah.
An Essay on Alford's Greek Testament.

Began to write *in Athenæum* in 1862 ; first article being
  a review of Forster's book on the Sinaitic Inscriptions.
  Reviewed also *in Athenæum*—
      Tischendorf's Greek Testament, vol. i., last edition.
      Tregelles' Greek Testament.
      Successive volumes of the Speaker's Commentary.
      Stanley's Jewish Church, vol. iii.
      Reuss's Les Prophètes, etc. etc.

Notices of Books on *Philosophy and Theology*, under
  "Contemporary Literature," in *Westminster Review*,
  1871, 1872, and part of 1873.

INDEX I

NAMES OF PERSONS AND PLACES

ABERDEEN, 14.
Adams, Ed. L., 71.
Albula Pass, 116.
Alexandria, 158, 281.
Amalfi, 120.
Amari, Prof., 107.
Ambrosian Library, 110.
Amiens, 132.
Amsteg, 112.
Andermatt, 112.
Apthorp, Dr., 321.
Aquila, 281.
Armitage, Sir E., 62.
Arnheim, 297, 306.
Arnold, Dr., 265.
Arnold, Matthew, 122.
Ashton, R. S., 62, 67.
Athanasius, 219, 227, 243.
Atkin, Rev. T., 61, 65.
Avernus, Lake, 110, 120.

BABYLON, 225, 230.
Bacoli, 110.
Baiæ, 120.
Ballymena, 7, 9, 10, 146.
Barker, J. T., 72.
Barrow, Isaac, 98.
Basel, 115.
Baur, F. C., 38, 150.
Bavarian Tyrol, 124.
Baxter, Richard, 86, 93, 128, 301.
Bayle, P., 119.
Belfast, 11, 15, 198.
Benson, J. W., 71.
Berlin, 21, 84, 180, 214.
Bevan, R., 62.
Beyschlag, Prof., 171.
Bickham, Wm., 274.
Biddle, John, 119.
Birch, A., 255.
Bismarck, Prince, 214.
Blakely, Mr., 9.
Bleek, Prof. F., 22, 78, 235, 299, 300.

Boehmer. Prof., 235, 299.
Böttcher, Fr., 164.
Bolingbroke, Lord, 289.
Bologna, 116.
Bonn, 22.
Bowyer, G., 229.
Bretschneider, Prof., 22, 299.
Bright, Dr., 243.
Bright, John, 64.
British Museum, 111.
Brown, Rev. W., 17.
Browne, Simon, 200.
Browning, Robert, 251.
Bruce, Dr. Balmain, 182.
Bruce, Robert, 71.
Bruce, Prof. W., 11.
Bruno Giordano, 118.
Bubier, Rev. G. B., 61, 62, 63.
Bunsen, Baron, 32, 38, 70, 75, 76, 134, 157, 164, 165, 172, 208, 270, 298, 299, 306.
Bunyan, John, 48.
Burinah, 154, 158.
Burns, Dawson, 220.
Burns, Robert, 146.
Burrows, Wm., 72.
Butler, Bishop, 78, 98, 191, 246, 292, 293.
Buxtorf, J., 115.
Byron, Lady, 245.

CADENABBIA, 116.
Call, W. M. W., 85, 215, 260.
Calov, Abraham, 242, 304.
Calvin, John, 80, 113, 114, 265, 294.
Cambridge, 226.
Cameron, Jas., 71.
Candlish, Dr., 58.
Capo Miseno, 110, 120.
Capri, 110, 120.
Carlsruhe, 125.
Carlyle, Thos., 241, 259.
Carriere, M., 95.

Carrington, S. R., 62.
Casaubon, the younger, 141.
Caspari, G., 174.
Catiline, 118.
Ceriani, Dr. Antonio, 110.
Chalmers, Dr. Thos., 88, 91, 92.
Chandler, S., 209.
Chillingworth, W., 130, 221, 222, 223, 323.
Chur, 112.
Cicero, 118.
Clapham, G. W., 71.
Clark, Absalom, 71.
Clarke, Francis, 72.
Clarke, Dr. S., 98.
Clayton, Bishop, 204, 246.
Clement of Alexandria, 240.
Cobden, Richard, 30.
Colenso, Bishop, 81, 82, 83, 191, 193, 194, 195, 263, 289, 299.
Collier, Jeremy, 141.
Coltart, G. A., 72.
Como, Lake, 116.
Constance, 125.
Contrexéville, 132, 150, 157, 158, 180, 230, 260.
Conybeare, Rev. W. J., 90.
Cox, Sir G. W., 210, 255, 258.
Creighton, James, 11.
Cromwell, Oliver, 135.
Crux, G., 62.
Cudworth, Ralph, 130.
Cureton, Canon, 102, 134.
Cyprian, 300.

Dahl, 270.
Darmstadt, 126.
Darragh, James, 9.
Davidson, Abraham, 8.
Davidson, Margaret, 8.
Davidson, Samuel James, 360.
Davies, H. E., 321.
Davies, Rev. R. M., 47, 61, 65, 67.
Delagarde, Prof., 107, 299, 307.
Delitzsch, Prof., 160, 185, 186, 217, 281, 286, 319.
De Rossi, 32, 245.
De Wette, 115, 126, 132, 165, 184, 185, 194, 197, 218, 228, 235, 243, 258, 285, 297, 299, 300, 306, 317, 319, 323.
Dijon, 181.
Dillmann, Prof., 160.
Disraeli, 197.
Doddridge, Philip, 93, 291, 292.
Döllinger, Dr. von, 106, 253.
Dort, 114, 294.
Dozy, Prof., 237, 240.
Dracup, J., 62.
Dresden, 120.
Dyson, Simeon, 71.

Edersheim, Prof., 262.
Eger, 124.
Egypt, 153.
Eichhorn, J. G., 290, 300.
Einsiedeln, 112.
Encke, Prof., 21, 299.
Erasmus, 115.
Erdmann, Prof., 31, 241, 299.
Euphrates River, 230.
Evans, E. K., 72.
Ewald, Prof. Heinrich, 81, 83, 84, 88, 160, 164, 167, 185, 196, 216, 217, 265, 268, 270, 280, 281, 284, 286, 287, 297, 299, 300, 306, 319.
Eyre & Spottiswoode, 268.

Farrar, Archdeacon, 243.
Firth, John, 71.
Florence, 116, 120.
Ford, Rev. D. E., 41, 42, 43, 45, 53, 60, 61.
Forster, J. F., 271.
Fox, W. J., 30.
Fuerst, Julius, 92, 188, 217, 280.

Galileo, 118.
Gasquoine, T., 62, 72.
Gataker, T., 141.
Geddes, Alex., 300.
Geiger, 164, 296.
Geneva, 119.
Gerardmer, 158.
Gesenius, 22, 126, 160, 164, 165, 173, 184, 216, 237, 241, 243, 249, 268, 277, 278, 279, 280, 281, 282, 285, 286, 287, 299, 306, 317.
Gibbon, Edw., 118, 119, 243, 321.
Gieseler, Prof., 22, 23, 31, 299, 300.
Giessen, 214.
Gill, Dr. John, 288.
Gladstone, W. E., 135, 154, 197, 314, 320.
Glasgow, 15, 91.
Gloag, Rev. Paton J., 314.
Godwin, Rev. J. H., 85, 223.
Goldsmith, Oliver, 251, 259.
Göschenen, 112.
Göttingen, 31, 84.
Gotha, 22.
Graf, Prof., 151, 230, 308.
Gramberg, K. P. W., 235.
Grant, Dr., 107.
Graves, Rich., 141.
Greenfield, W., 183, 189, 190, 191, 196, 259.
Greenhill, Dr., 217.
Griesbach, J. J., 245.
Griffiths, W. F., 72.
Grimm, J., 197.
Guericke, Prof., 28, 242.
Gutbier, Aeg., 171.

Gwynne, Rev. R., 361.
Gwyther, Rev. James, 47, 61.
Gwyther, J. H., 72.

HAGENBACH, PROF., 115.
Hague, The, 140.
Hales, John, 114, 294.
Haley, Joseph, 71.
Hall, Prof. T. D., 61.
Halle, 22, 26, 27, 28, 31, 84, 242, 268.
Halley, Rev. Dr., 47, 53, 61.
Hammond, Henry, 165.
Hampton, T. F., 62.
Hankinson, Josiah, 71.
Hare, Archdeacon, 26, 217, 218, 219.
Harker, John, 72.
Harnack, Prof., 214.
Harper, Dr., 233.
Harrison, Thos. J., 71, 74.
Hartley, R. G., 72.
Hassencamp, Prof., 132.
Hastings, 104, 213, 217.
Hatherlow, 80.
Haug, Martin, 116.
Haworth, C., 72.
Heard, Mr., 97.
Heidelberg, 32, 112.
Heliopolis, 281.
Henderson, Dr. E., 15, 29.
Hengstenberg, Prof., 113, 126, 216,
    242, 299.
Herculaneum, 110.
Herzog, Prof., 31, 299.
Hilgenfeld, Prof., 171, 172, 263.
Hincks, Rev. Dr. T. D., 14, 16.
Hirzel, L., 160.
Hitzig, Prof., 157, 164, 166, 173, 174,
    184, 185, 196, 216, 217, 269, 270,
    277, 278, 281, 284, 297.
Hobbes, Thomas, 302, 303.
Hodgson, John, 71.
Holmes, O. W., 200.
Holtzmann, Prof., 170, 177.
Homburg, 114, 115.
Hooker, Ri., 98, 128.
Hooper, Stephen, 71.
Horace, 117.
Horne, Rev. T. H., 36, 41, 57, 59.
Hort, Dr., 153, 156, 227, 228.
Hug, Prof., 108.
Hume, Joseph, 327, 341.
Hupfeld, Prof. Hermann, 22, 27, 31,
    33, 84, 92, 184, 185, 186, 187,
    188, 193, 196, 217, 235, 285,
    288, 299, 300, 317, 319.
Hurry, Nicholas, 71.
Huss, John, 119, 125.

IKEN, KONR., 281.
Irenaeus, 95, 142.
Italy, 106.

JACKSON, THOS. H., 72.
Jacobi, Prof., 325.
Jameson, Mrs. Anna, 245.
Jennings and Lowe, 186, 188.
Jerome, 229, 315.
Johns, Ed. W., 71.
Johnson, Rev. G. B., 61.
Johnson, Dr. Samuel, 259.
Jones, J., 93.
Josephus, 294.
Jowett, Prof. Benjamin, 85, 101, 211,
    320, 321.
Justin Martyr, 142, 244.

KALISCH, Dr. M., 150, 166, 193, 235,
    248, 280, 287, 289, 290, 296,
    308.
Kamphausen, Prof. A., 81, 88, 186,
    280, 319.
Kant, Imm., 218, 268, 291.
Kautzsch, Prof., 115.
Kay, Dr., 93, 186, 188.
Keim, Prof., 263.
Kellswater, 7, 146.
Kelly, Rev. John, 45, 46, 47, 54, 55,
    56, 60, 61, 62, 65, 66, 67.
Kendall, Henry, 72.
Kennard, Mr., 214.
Kennicott, Benj., 32.
Kettlewell, John, 323.
Kidder, Bp., 165.
Kimchi, 286.
Kingsley, Chas., 262.
Kirkpatrick, Rev. W. B., 6.
Kirkpatrick, A. J., 14.
Kirkpatrick, Miss, 362.
Kirkus, Wm., 51, 71.
Knobel, Prof., 70, 77, 235, 288, 299.
Knott, J., 62.
Koester, Prof., 155, 161.
Kuenen, Prof., 164, 172, 173, 282, 288,
    299, 309.
Kuster, L., 255.

LABOUCHERE, H., M.P., 322.
Lachmann, C., 227, 269.
Lambert, Father, 107.
Lane. Ind. Col., 18, 35, 202.
Lardner, N., 93.
Lassen, Ch., 174.
Laurence, Archbishop, 295.
Lawson, Thomas, 72.
Lee, Dr. Samuel, 27.
Lees, Dr., 220.
Leibnitz, 119.
Leighton, Dr., 251.
Leipzig, 84, 105.
Lengerke, Von, 184, 216, 281.
Leo, Prof., 242, 243.
Leontopolis, 281.
Lepsius, K. R., 84, 180, 299.

Liddon, Canon, 261, 262.
Lightfoot, Bishop, 142, 146, 180.
Lignana, Prof., 107.
Littledale, Rev. Dr., 85, 253.
Liverpool, 11, 16, 20.
Locke, John, 119.
Loman, 229.
London, 24, 81.
Londonderry, 11.
Long, Rd. England, 72.
Longman, 36.
Lowe, *see* Jennings.
Lowth, Bishop, 247.
Lucerne, 112.
Lücke, Prof., 31, 299, 300.
Lünemann, Prof., 102.
Luther, 298, 299, 315.
Lymington, 42.
Lynch, T. T., 95.

M'ALL, ROBERT W., 71, 73.
Magee, Bishop, 180, 181.
Maloya Pass, 116.
Manchester, 16, 18, 20, 105, 139, 202.
Marburg, 214.
Marcus Antoninus, 127.
Marcus Aurelius, 141.
Marienbad, 120, 124, 140.
Marischal Coll., Aberdeen, 14.
Martineau, Dr. James, 85, 212.
Mason, Hugh, 62.
Maurice, F. D., 126, 217, 218, 262.
Maybole, 15.
Mayo, 198.
Mede, Joseph, 165.
Merx, Prof., 172, 299.
Michaelis, J. D., 247, 281.
Middleton, Conyers, 200.
Milan, 110, 116.
Mill, J., 255.
Milman, Dean, 127.
Milton, 113, 331.
Minerva Library, 120.
Mittenwald, 124.
Montgomery, Rev. A., 18.
Morell, J. D., 85, 267, 291.
Mozley, Dr., 182.
Müller, Prof., 187.
Müller, Julius, 22.
Müller, Max, 201.
Mullooly, Father, 119.
Munich, 106, 124.
Murphy, Rev. Dr. J. G., 6.
Murphy, Rev. John H., 361.
Murphy, W. K., M.D., 361.

NAPLES, 110, 120.
Napoleon, 108.
Neander, Prof. Aug., 21, 22, 25, 126,
    299, 300.
Nelson, Rev. Isaac, 198.

Nero, 110.
Newcome, W., 165.
Newman, Cardinal, 46.
Newth, Rev. A., 61.
Nichol, Prof., 15.
Nicholas Thomas, 71, 85.
Nitzsch, K. Im., 299.
Nöldeke, Prof., 106, 235, 288, 299.
Nuremberg, 140.

OBERALP, THE, 112.
Oberammergau, 124.
Œcolampadius, 115.
O'Hagan, Mr., 10.
O'Hanlon, W. M., 11.
Olshausen, Justus, 180, 184, 284.
On, 281.
Orelli, 115.
Origen, 215, 244, 300.
Overbeck, Prof., 115.
Owen, Prof., 279.

PALMERSTON, LORD, 42.
Parkes, William, 71.
Partenkirchen, 124.
Pattison, Mark, 318.
Pearce, Rev. A. E., 61.
Perowne, J. J. S., 186, 187, 188.
Perrin, A., 80.
Petermann, Prof., 84, 180.
Pfleiderer, Prof., 150, 171, 262, 263,
    299.
Philo, 191, 215.
Picton, J. Allanson, 34, 35, 71, 74.
Pio Nono, 107.
Plumptre, Dean, 217.
Polycarp, 95.
Pompeii, 110, 120.
Pontresina, 116.
Pope, Alex., 251.
Pott, Prof., 111, 179, 299.
Potter, C., 62.
Pozzuoli, 110.
Preston, William C., 72.
Priestley, Dr., 93.
Pugsley, Rev. N. K., 61.
Pusey, Dr., 93, 216.
Pye Smith, Dr., 15, 93.

RAFFLES, REV. DR., 61.
Ragatz, 112, 116.
Rapperschwyl, 112.
Reichenau, 112.
Renan, E., 232.
Reuss, Prof., 106, 282, 309.
Riehm, Prof., 308.
Rigi, The, 112.
Roaf, Rev. W., 61.
Robbins, George, 71.
Robertson, F. W., 245.
Robertson, Prof., 187.

Robinson, Dr., 197, 216, 217, 237.
Robinson, Pastor, 49, 50.
Rodwell, Rev. Mr., 160, 217.
Roediger, Prof., 22, 31, 32, **84**, 111, **179**, 180, 241, 299, 300.
Rogers, Rev. J. G., 61.
Rome, 107, 108, 117, 120.
Rosenmüller, Prof., 174, 285.
Rotterdam, 140.
Rowland, Mr., 11.
Ryle, Bishop, **210**.

SACHS, 306.
Sadler, Dr. Thomas, 271.
Salerno, 120.
Salkeld, Richard, 71.
Sallust, 118.
Samaden, 116.
San Clemente, 119.
Saxon Switzerland, 120.
Schaaf, Ch., 171, 183, 190, 191, 196, 259.
Schelling, Prof., 21, 116.
Schiller, 330.
Schlangenbad, 112.
Schleiermacher, Prof., 38, 218, 299.
Schlottmann, K., 160.
Schmidt, Prof., 277.
Schmitz, Dr. Leonhard, 85, 259.
Schopenhauer, 140.
Schrader, Prof., 152, 168, 174, 230, 235, 288, 299.
Schulz, D., 245.
Schwalbach, 112.
Scott, Thomas, 58.
Scrivener, Dr. F. H., 254.
Selbie, R. W., 71.
Semler, Prof., 22, 236, 293.
Sens, 181.
Servetus, 80, 117.
Shaftesbury, Lord, 210.
Shaw, Samuel, 71.
Sidebottom, James, 62, 66.
Simon, David W., 71, 346.
Smith, Dr., 107, 117, 119.
Smith, George C., 72.
Soper, R. G., 71.
Soudan, The, 226.
South, Dr. R., 301.
Southworth, T., 62.
Spencer, Herbert, 259.
Spinoza, 117, 140.
Spottiswoode, 268.
Spurgeon, Rev. Charles, 63.
St. Calixtus, 119.
St. Moritz, 116.
Stade, B., 164, 167.
Stanley, Dean, 217, 219, 265.
Stewart, Alexander, 71, 150.
Stewart, Dugald, 323.
Stewart, Rev. Dr., 11.

Stillingfleet, Edw., Bp., 98.
Stitt, J., 62.
Stonor, Monsignor, 107, 117.
Stowe, Prof. C. E., 19.
Straker, Edward, **71**.
Strasburg, 106.
Stratford, Lord, 105.
Strauss, 38, 113, 115, 126, **258**.
Stroyan, Abraham, 71.
Stroyan, John, 71.
Stuart, Moses, 298, **303**.
Sunderland, W., 62.
Sykes, G. F. H., 71.
Sykes, William, 72.
Symmachus, 281.

TAYLER, PROF. J. J., 85.
Taylor, Rev. Henry, 204, 205, 245.
Taylor, Jeremy, 93, 130.
Taylor, Peter, M.P., 204.
Tertullian, 142, 144, 244, 300, 301.
Thayer, Dr., 270.
Theodotion, 281.
Thirlwall, Bishop, 26, 219.
Tholuck, F. A. G., 22, 27, 28, 31, 126, 236, 241, 242, 299, 300.
Thomas, Dr. David, 324.
Thompson, James, 62.
Thompson, Joseph, 61, 66.
Thompson, Thomas, 62.
Thomson, Prof., 15.
Thomson, Rev. P., 47, 61.
Thorburn, Rev. W. R., 47, 61.
Thusis, 112.
Tindal, Matthew, 200.
Tischendorf, A. F. C., 84, 104, 105, 106, 107, 108, 111, 121, 156, 196, 227, 228, 245, 269, 270, 299, 300.
Toland, John, 96, 113, 119.
Tomline, Bishop, 295.
Tregelles, Dr. S. P., 37, 41, 42, 59, 216.
Trinity College, Dublin, 10, 18.
Tuch, F., 235, 288.
Tyndale, William, 319.

UFNAU, 112.
Ullmann, Prof., 125, 126.
Ulrich von Hutten, 112, 115.
Ulrici, Prof., 268.
Umbreit, Prof., 270.
Urwick, Rev. William, 71, 80, 85, 358.
Ussher, Archibald, 98.

VAIHINGER, J. G., 174.
Van Ess, K., 279.
Varese, 116.
Vatican Library, 107, 120.
Vatke, J. K. W., 164, 168, 172, 193, 282, 284, 288, 308.
Vaughan, Dr. R., 61, 65, 69.

Vesuvius, Mt., 110.
Via Mala, 112.
Victoria, Queen, 179.
Virgil, 110, 117.
Vorarlberg, The, 125.

Walker, John, 150.
Wallenstein, 124.
Walton, Brian, 255.
Waterland, Dan., 98.
Watts, Dr. Isaac, 93, 291, 361.
Watts, Sir James, 62, 80.
Weber, Prof., 84.
Wegscheider, Prof., 27, 126.
Weiss, Prof., 171.
Wellhausen, Prof., 151, 208, 282, 288, 308, 309.
Wesley, John, 127.
Westcott, Rev. Dr. B. F., 101, 156, 227, 228.
Wetstein, J. J., 115.

Whiston, William, 165.
Whitby, Dr. Daniel, 288, 323.
Widmanstad, Albert, 171.
Wieseler, K., 277.
Wilkins, Prof. A. S., 69.
Williams, Rev. Rowland, 83.
Willis, Dr. Robert, 82, 116.
Wilson, Rev. H. B., 85, 100, 101, 203, 214, 215, 320.
Winer, G. B., 228, 299, 300.
Winstanley, 228.
Wislicenus, 28.
Wolf, Ch. v., 126, 241.
Wood, George, 62.
Wright, Prof. W., 85, 226.

Zeller, Prof. E., 150.
Zürich, 112.
Zumpt, 21, 299.
Zwingli, Ulrich, 112.

INDEX II

TEXTS REFERRED TO

	PAGE		PAGE
Gen. i. 1	286	Josh. iv. 19, 20	237
xii. 3	294	v. 10, 11	238
xviii. 18	294	xiii. 22	191
xxv. 23	235	xxiv. 19	286
xxviii. 1–9	235	Ruth iii. 15	254
xxxii. 24–29	309	1 Sam. i.–viii.	207
xxxv. 7	287	ix. 1–x. 16, etc.	206
xlix. 10	220	xv. 3	231
xlix. 1–28	288	xvi.	207
xlix. 29–33	235	xvii.	208
Ex. iii. 21, 22	231	xvii. 55, etc.	207
x. 1	290	xix. 9–24	207
xi. 1, 2	231	xx. 1	207
xii.	239	xxi. 19	250
xii. 12	286	2 Sam. xii. 31	208
xii. 35, 36	231	xxi.–xxiv.	207
xiii. 12, 13	247, 248	xxi. 8	152
xx.	194, 195	xxi. 19	208
xxi. 2–6, 20, 21	231	xxii. 18	187
xxi.–xxiv.	283	1 Kings i.–xi.	229
xxxi. 18	311	v. 4, 5	230
xxxii. 4	286	viii. 12–61	230
xxxii. 18	311	xii.–2 Kings xvii.	229
xxxiii. 11–23	311	xix. 15, etc.	229
xxxiv. 28	311	2 Kings viii. 7–15	229
xxxiv. 29–35	311	ix. 1–10	229
Lev. vi. 3	187	xviii.–xxv.	229
xvii.–xxvi.	309	xxiii. 21–23	240
xxv. 44–46	231	xxv. 22–30	230
xxvi. 42	187	1 Chron. xx. 2	209
Num. xxii. 2–xxiv. 25	192	xx. 5	208
xxii. 22–35	192, 193	Ezra i. 2–4	224
xxiv. 20–24	193	vii. 24	287
xxxi. 16	191	Esther i. 1	276
Deut. i. 1	221	ix. 26	252
xii.	279	Job xix. 25–27	314
xvi. 1–7	279	xxii. 2	286
xvi. 2	240	xlii. 5	315
xxiii. 3	253	Ps. ii. 12	188
xxv. 5, etc.	253	viii. 6	287
xxvi. 10	239	xi. 7	286
xxxiii.	288	xvi. 10	187, 221
xxxiii. 2	286	xxii. 17	315

	PAGE		PAGE
Ps. xlv. 7	186	Hos. xiii. 9	164
xlvii. 5	173	xiv. 3	164
li.	196	Joel ii. 8	172
li. 4	188	ii. 23	172
lx.	196	iv. 20	172
lxviii.	196	Amos iv. 3	270
lxxxi. 7	187	v. 26	270
xc.	319, 361	v. 27	173
cxxxvii. 9	188	vi. 8	173
cxlix. 2	188	vii. 11, 17	173
Prov. i. 7-ix.	157	viii. 7	173
x.-xxii. 16	157	ix. 14	173
xxvi. 10	297	Obad. 1-7	174
Eccles. iv. 8-12	156	12-14	174
xii. 9-14	156, 280	20	174
Isa. i. 1	162	Micah ii. 12, 13	167
xi. 9	152	iii. 12	167
xii. 16	231	iv. 10	167
xix. 18	281	v. 1	267
xxvii. 2	220	v. 5, 6	167
xxx. 4	278	Nahum i. 8	168
xxxviii. 13	316	i. 10	220
xli. 25	224	ii. 7	267
xliv. 15	286	Hab. ii. 3-iii. 13	168
xliv. 28-xlv. 4	223	Zeph. ii. 13	170
lii. 15	152	Hag. ii. 7	268
liii. 2	221	Zach. ii. 6	269
liii. 8	285, 286	iii. 5	164
liii. 9	221	xii. 10	269
Jer. vi. 16	359	xiii. 7	269
xvii. 9	306	Mal. i. 8	165
xxxii. 35	248	ii. 15	165
xl. 5, etc.	230	iii. 1	269
xli. 1, 2, 3, etc.	230	iii. 6	269
Ezek. ix. 6	231		
xviii. 7	187	1 Macc. iii. 36	277
xx. 25	247	vi. 1-16	276
xxi. 10	249	2 Macc. xv. 36	252
xxvi.-xxviii.	248		
xxix. 18	248	Matt. vi. 13	126
xl.-xlviii.	246, 250	xi. 5	217
Dan. vii. 1	275	Luke xxiv. 42, 51, 52, 53	156, 245
vii. 17	275	John i. 18	227
viii. 25	276	ii. 10	220
ix. 24-27	276, 277	xiv. 14	227
x. 4	275	Acts i.	304
xi. 39	276	v. 4	298
xii. 1	313	vii. 51 *et seq.*	53
xii. 13	277	viii. 39	171
Hos. v. 2	163	xx. 28	227, 259
vii. 16	163	xxviii. 29	259
viii. 13	163	xxviii. 37	171
ix. 3-6	163	Rom. ii. 14, 15	128
ix. 8	163	iv. 17	228
x. 10	163	ix. 4	228
x. 12	163	x. 12, 13	196, 197
xi. 1-16	231	xvi. 24	175
xi. 5	163	1 Cor. i. 2	196
xii. 4	163	2 Cor. xii. 8	193, 196
xiii. 2	163	Gal. ii. 14	52

				PAGE						PAGE
Eph. v. 30			.	269	Heb. vii. 12	.		.	.	190
Philip. ii. 6–8			.	178	x. 38	.	.	.	.	190
ii. 13	.		.	178	xi. 37	.	.	.	.	228
1 Thess. v. 5			.	220	xii. 1	.	.	.	.	190
ii. 19	.		.	228	1 Pet. i. 13	.	.	.	.	220
1 Tim. iii. 16			.	183	ii. 8	.	.	.	.	55
2 Tim. ii. 15			.	183	iv. 7	.	.	.	.	220
iii. 16	.		.	183	2 Pet. ii. 12, 13	.		.	.	191
iv. 13	.		.	183	1 John iii. 1	.	.	.	.	196
Titus ii. 13		183,	228	v. 7	.	.	.	.	196
Heb. ii. 9	.		.	227	Jude 4	.	.	.	.	228
vi. 1	.		.	190	Rev. xiv. 13	.	.	.	.	359
vii. 3	.		.	190	xxii.	.	.	.	.	244

PRINTED BY MORRISON AND GIBB LIMITED, EDINBURGH

WORKS BY PATON J. GLOAG, D.D.

Introduction to the Synoptic Gospels. By Rev. PATON J. GLOAG, D.D., Edinburgh. In demy 8vo, price 7s. 6d.

'Dr. Gloag has kept his mind open to the light, and has produced a volume which the student of theology will find most helpful to him in his professional work.'—*Scotsman.*

'A volume of sterling value; learned, clear, candid, cautious, thoroughly well considered; it should be a welcome addition to the library of the biblical student.'—*London Quarterly Review.*

Introduction to the Catholic Epistles. In demy 8vo, price 10s. 6d.

'Dr. Gloag, whilst courteous to men of erudition who differ from him, is firm and fearless in his criticism, and meets the erudition of others with an equal erudition of his own. He has displayed all the attributes of a singularly accomplished divine in this volume, which ought to be eagerly welcomed as a solid contribution to theological literature; it is a work of masterly strength and uncommon merit.'—*Evangelical Magazine.*

'We have here a great mass of facts and arguments relevant in the strictest sense to the subject, presented with skill and sound judgment, and calculated to be of very great service to the student.'—*Literary Churchman.*

Exegetical Studies. In crown 8vo, price 5s.

'Careful and valuable pieces of work.'—*Spectator.*

'Dr. Gloag handles his subjects very ably, displaying everywhere accurate and extensive scholarship, and a fine appreciation of the lines of thought in those passages with which he deals.'—*Baptist.*

The Messianic Prophecies (one of the Baird Lectures). In crown 8vo, price 7s. 6d.

'It has seldom fallen to our lot to read a book which we think is entitled to such unqualified praise as the one now before us. Dr. Gloag has displayed consummate ability.'—*London Quarterly Review.*

'We regard Dr. Gloag's work as a valuable contribution to theological literature. We have not space to give the extended notice which its intrinsic excellence demands, and must content ourselves with cordially recommending it to our readers.'—*Spectator.*

The Primeval World: A Treatise on the Relations of Geology to Theology. Crown 8vo, 3s.

Contemporary Theology and Theism. By Professor R. M. WENLEY, M.A., D.Phil., D.Sc., University of Michigan. Crown 8vo, price 4s. 6d.

'Is worthy of a disciple of Caird, and will repay the perusal of anyone who wishes to have an intelligent grasp of the bearings of recent theological speculation.'—*Scotsman.*

The Right of Systematic Theology. By Professor B. B. WARFIELD, D.D., Princeton University. With an Introduction by Professor J. ORR, D.D., Edinburgh. Crown 8vo, price 2s.

'A powerful blow directed against the attempt to abolish doctrine and creeds and reduce Christianity to mere sentiment. The protest made in this strong essay is most timely. We join Dr. Orr and other Scottish divines in earnestly commending it to the notice of theological readers.'—*Methodist Times.*

GRIMM'S LEXICON.

Greek-English Lexicon of the New Testament, being Grimm's Wilke's Clavis Novi Testamenti. Translated, Revised, and Enlarged by JOSEPH HENRY THAYER, D.D., Bussey Professor of New Testament Criticism and Interpretation in the Divinity School of Harvard University. Fourth Edition, demy 4to, price 36s.

'The best New Testament Greek Lexicon. . . . It is a treasury of the results of exact scholarship.'—Bishop WESTCOTT.

'I regard it as a work of the greatest importance. . . . It seems to me a work showing the most patient diligence, and the most carefully arranged collection of useful and helpful references.'—THE BISHOP OF GLOUCESTER AND BRISTOL.

'An excellent book, the value of which for English students will, I feel sure, be best appreciated by those who use it most carefully.'—Professor F. J. A. HORT, D.D.

'This work has been eagerly looked for. . . . The result is an excellent book, which I do not doubt will be the best in the field for many years to come.'—Professor W. SANDAY, D.D., in *The Academy.*

'Undoubtedly the best of its kind. Beautifully printed and well translated, . . . it will be prized by students of the Christian Scriptures.'—*Athenæum.*

CREMER'S LEXICON.

Biblico - Theological Lexicon of New Testament Greek. By HERMANN CREMER, D.D., Professor of Theology in the University of Greifswald. Translated from the German of the Second Edition by WILLIAM URWICK, M.A. In demy 4to, Fourth Edition, with SUPPLEMENT, price 38s.

This Lexicon deals with words whose meaning in the Classics is modified or changed in Scripture, words which have become the bases and watchwords of Christian theology, tracing their history in their transference from the Classics into the LXX., and from the LXX. into the New Testament, and the gradual deepening and elevation of their meaning till they reach the fulness of New Testament thought.

'Dr. Cremer's work is highly and deservedly esteemed in Germany. It gives with care and thoroughness a complete history, as far as it goes, of each word and phrase that it deals with. . . . Dr. Cremer's explanations are most lucidly set out.'—*Guardian.*

'It is hardly possible to exaggerate the value of this work to the student of the Greek Testament. . . . The translation is accurate and idiomatic, and the additions to the later edition are considerable and important.'—*Church Bells.*

'We cannot find an important word in our Greek New Testament which is not discussed with a fulness and discrimination which leaves nothing to be desired.'—*Nonconformist.*

A Treatise on the Grammar of New Testament Greek, regarded as a Sure Basis for New Testament Exegesis. Translated from the German of Dr. G. B. WINER. Edited by Rev. W. F. MOULTON, D.D. With large additions and full Indices. In One large 8vo Volume, Ninth English Edition, price 15s.

'We need not say it is *the* Grammar of the New Testament. It is not only superior to all others, but *so* superior as to be by common consent the one work of reference on the subject. No other could be mentioned with it.'—*Literary Churchman.*

Greek and English Lexicon of the New Testament. By Professor EDWARD ROBINSON, D.D. In demy 8vo, price 9s.

'Excellent.'—Principal CAVE, D.D., Hackney College.

BEYSCHLAG'S NEW TESTAMENT THEOLOGY.

New Testament Theology; or, Historical Account of the Teaching of Jesus and of Primitive Christianity according to the New Testament Sources. By Dr. WILLIBALD BEYSCHLAG, Professor of Theology at Halle. Translated by Rev. NEIL BUCHANAN. In Two Volumes, demy 8vo, Second Edition, price 18s. net.

'It is not only very able, but it is a truly valuable contribution to its subject, and no one who takes upon himself to expound the deep things of God as set forth by the New Testament writers should neglect to make an earnest study of it, and thus enrich his ministration of the word.'—Professor A. S. PEAKE, M.A.

'Dr. Beyschlag has achieved so large a measure of success as to have furnished one of the best guides to an understanding of the New Testament. . . . These pages teem with suggestions. . . . In the belief that it will stimulate thought and prove of much service to ministers and all students of the sacred text it expounds, we heartily commend it to our readers.'—*Methodist Recorder.*

'A book of much interest and importance, independent in conception and treatment; happy in seizing and characterising the courses of thought with which he has to deal; ingenious in combination, and acute in criticism; expressing the results which he reaches, often with terseness and point, almost always with clearness and vigour. . . . The work well merits translation into English.'—Professor W. P. DICKSON, D.D., in *The Critical Review.*

WENDT'S TEACHING OF JESUS.

The Teaching of Jesus. By Professor HANS HINRICH WENDT, D.D., Jena. Translated by Rev. JOHN WILSON, M.A., Montreux. In Two Volumes, 8vo, price 21s.

'Dr. Wendt's work is of the utmost importance for the study of the Gospels, both with regard to the origin of them and to their doctrinal contents. It is a work of distinguished learning, of great originality, and of profound thought. The second part [now translated into English], which sets forth the contents of the doctrine of Jesus, is the most important contribution yet made to biblical theology, and the method and results of Dr. Wendt deserve the closest attention. . . . No greater contribution to the study of biblical theology has been made in our time. A brilliant and satisfactory exposition of the teaching of Christ.'—Professor J. IVERACH, D.D., in *The Expositor.*

'Dr. Wendt has produced a remarkably fresh and suggestive work, deserving to be ranked among the most important contributions to biblical theology. . . . There is hardly a page which is not suggestive; and, apart from the general value of its conclusions, there are numerous specimens of ingenious exegesis thrown out with more or less confidence as to particular passages.'—*The Critical Review.*

Dr. R. F. HORTON refers to Beyschlag's 'New Testament Theology' and Wendt's 'Teaching of Jesus' as 'two invaluable books.'

Messianic Prophecy: Its Origin, Historical Growth, and Relation to New Testament Fulfilment. By Dr. EDWARD RIEHM. New Edition, Translated by Rev. L. A. MUIRHEAD, B.D. With an Introduction by Prof. A. B. DAVIDSON, D.D. In post 8vo, price 7s. 6d.

'No work of the same compass could be named that contains so much that is instructive on the nature of prophecy in general, and particularly on the branch of it specially treated in the book.'—Professor A. B. DAVIDSON, D.D.

'I would venture to recommend Riehm's "Messianic Prophecy" as a summary account of prophecy both reverent and critical.'—Canon GORE in *Lux Mundi.*

BY PRINCIPAL A. CAVE, D.D.

An Introduction to Theology: Its Principles, Its Branches, Its Results, and Its Literature. By ALFRED CAVE, B.A., D.D., Principal of Hackney College, London. Second Edition, largely rewritten, and the Bibliographical Lists carefully revised to date. In demy 8vo, price 12s.

'The best original work on the subject in the English language.'—PHILIP SCHAFF, D.D., LL.D.

'Its arrangement is perfect, its learning accurate and extensive, and its practical hints invaluable.'—*Christian World.*

'A marvel of industry, and simply invaluable to theologians.'—*Clergyman's Magazine.*

The Scriptural Doctrine of Sacrifice and Atonement. In demy 8vo, New Edition, Revised throughout, price 10s. 6d.

'Every page in this edition has been carefully revised in the light of the latest relative researches. The literary references have also been brought down to date. . . . More than half of the New Testament portion has been rewritten.'—*Extract from the Preface.*

'Let readers judge—is this not now the best systematic study of the Atonement in the English language?'—*Expository Times.*

BY PRINCIPAL D. W. SIMON, D.D.

Reconciliation by Incarnation: The Reconciliation of God and Man by the Incarnation of the Divine Word. By the Rev. D. W. SIMON, D.D., Principal of the United College, Bradford. In post 8vo, price 7s. 6d.

'A treatise of great value, for its broad philosophical grasp, its subtle spiritual insight, and its apt illustrations. It is a fresh, timely, and independent study of a subject which must ever be to the fore.'—*Baptist Magazine.*

The Redemption of Man: Discussions Bearing on the Atonement. In demy 8vo, price 10s. 6d.

Principal FAIRBAIRN, Mansfield College, writes: 'I wish to say how stimulating and helpful I have found your book. Its criticism is constructive as well as incisive, while its point of view is elevated and commanding. It made me feel quite vividly how superficial most of the recent discussions on the Atonement have been.'

'Its learning, ample although that be, is its least merit: it has the far higher and rarer qualities of freshness of view and deep ethical insight. I hope it will find the general and cordial reception it so well deserves.'—Professor R. FLINT, D.D.

The Bible an Outgrowth of Theocratic Life. In crown 8vo, price 4s. 6d.

Dr. JOHN BROWN, of Bedford, writes: 'I feel sure that such of your readers as may make acquaintance with it, will be as grateful for its valuable help as I have been myself.'

Delivery and Development of Christian Doctrine. By ROBERT RAINY, D.D., Principal, and Professor of Divinity and Church History, New College, Edinburgh. Price 10s. 6d.

'We gladly acknowledge the high excellence and the extensive learning which these lectures display. They are able to the last degree, and the author has, in an unusual measure, the power of acute and brilliant generalisation.'—*Literary Churchman.*

BY THE REV. J. B. HEARD, M.A.

Alexandrian and Carthaginian Theology Contrasted. (Hulsean Lectures.) By the Rev. J. B. HEARD, M.A. In crown 8vo, price 6s.

'We can heartily recommend these lectures as pursuing a most interesting branch of inquiry in a thoroughly able, scholarly, and instructive way.'—*Scotsman.*

'Mr. Heard is a vigorous writer and a bold, not to say headstrong, thinker. No one is likely to go asleep over his page . . . he advocates his hypothesis with no small power.'—*Literary World.*

Old and New Theology: A Constructive Critique. In crown 8vo, price 6s.

'We can promise all real students of Holy Scripture who have found their way out of some of the worst of the scholastic bye-lanes and ruts, and are striving to reach the broad and firm high road that leads to the Eternal City, a real treat from the perusal of these pages. Progressive theologians, who desire to find "the old in the new, and the new in the old," will be deeply grateful to Mr. Heard for this courageous and able work.'—*Christian World.*

The Tripartite Nature of Man: Spirit, Soul, and Body. Applied to illustrate and explain the Doctrines of Original Sin, the New Birth, the Disembodied State, and the Spiritual Body. In crown 8vo, Fifth Edition, price 6s.

'The author has got a striking and consistent theory. Whether agreeing or disagreeing with that theory, it is a book which any student of the Bible may read with pleasure.'—*Guardian.*

'An elaborate, ingenious, and very able book.'—*London Quarterly Review.*

The Servant of Jehovah. A Commentary, Grammatical and Critical, upon Isaiah lii. 13—liii. 12. With Dissertations upon the Authorship of Isaiah xl.—lxvi., etc. By WILLIAM URWICK, M.A., Tutor in Hebrew, New College, London. Demy 8vo, price 3s.

'A work of great and permanent value.'—*Weekly Review.*

The Text of Jeremiah; or, A Critical Investigation of the Greek and Hebrew, with the Variations in the LXX. retranslated into the Original and Explained. By Professor G. C. WORKMAN, M.A. With an Introduction by Prof. F. DELITZSCH, D.D. Post 8vo, 9s.

'The most painstaking and elaborate illustration of the application of his principles to this end that has yet been given to the world. . . . Scholars will hail it with gratitude, and peruse it with interest.'—*Guardian.*

The Kingdom of God: A Plan of Study. By F. HERBERT STEAD, M.A. (In the Series of *Bible-Class Primers.*) In Three Parts, paper covers, 6d. each; or, in cloth covers, 8d. each.

The Three Parts may also be had in One Volume, cloth, price 1s. 6d.

'It is a plan well worth a trial from every Bible-class teacher.'—*Expository Times.*